A War of Flowers

By the same author:

The Winter Garden
Black Roses
The Weighing of the Heart
Patrimony
The Shell House

A War of Flowers

JANE THYNNE

**SIMON &
SCHUSTER**

London · New York · Sydney · Toronto · New Delhi

A CBS COMPANY

First published in Great Britain by Simon & Schuster UK Ltd, 2014
A CBS COMPANY

Copyright © Thynker Ltd 2014

1 3 5 7 9 10 8 6 4 2

Simon & Schuster UK Ltd
1st Floor
222 Gray's Inn Road
London WC1X 8HB

www.simonandschuster.co.uk

Simon & Schuster Australia, Sydney
Simon & Schuster India, New Delhi

A CIP catalogue record for this book
is available from the British Library

HB ISBN: 978-1-47113-188-2
TPB ISBN: 978-1-47113-189-9
EBOOK ISBN: 978-1-47113-191-2

Typeset in Bembo by M Rules
Printed and bound by CPI Group (UK) Ltd, Croydon, CR0 4YY

For Charlie

'How horrible, fantastic, incredible it is that we should be digging trenches and trying on gas masks here because of a quarrel in a faraway country between people of whom we know nothing.'

Neville Chamberlain, September 1938

'Our displacement of women from public life occurs solely to restore their essential dignity to them.'

Joseph Goebbels

'In my state, the Mother is the most important citizen.'

Adolf Hitler

Prologue

Another fine, summer's day and the MS *Wilhelm Gustloff* cruise liner was making its leisurely way across the Atlantic Ocean. The 25,000 ton ship rose like a sheer white cliff from the water, eight storeys high, gracefully transporting a cargo of more than a thousand citizens of the German Reich. The sun was already dazzling, bouncing back from a sea of hammered cobalt as the liner's prow carved a confident line past the spectacular coastline of Madeira. The island, with its black volcanic sand, its coves fringed with laurel trees and red-roofed houses clambering up the mountain slopes, glittered in the sapphire morning light. Birds with iridescent necks and little dashes of blood at their throats fluttered through the wooded mountains, which were swathed at their peaks with a light garland of cloud. A fine spray, thick with the tang of salt, pearled the faces of the people watching from the deck, many of whom had never set foot outside the Reich and had mostly never seen the sea. The liner was the first tailor-made ship of the National Socialist Strength Through Joy movement, the Kraft durch Freude, organized by the German Labour Front, and it was the only way an ordinary German was able to leave the country now. The fact that they were getting a glimpse of the world that lay beyond the borders of the Reich – for now at any rate – and they were seeing it on a two-week cruise costing less than a fortnight's wages, was yet another reason to be grateful for the Führer's reforms.

Ada Freitag had never seen the sea before either, but that didn't mean she wanted to hang over the deck, waving a swastika flag at it. Smearing a little more Elizabeth Arden suncream on her freckles and over the skin on her shoulders, already turning a rich caramel, she anchored her bag more firmly beneath one arm, lay back in her deckchair and tried unsuccessfully to relax.

Relaxing was not, Ada had quickly realized, a priority on a Strength Through Joy holiday. Even when at sea, any citizen enjoying a KdF tour had a packed schedule of daily activity, requiring daunting levels of enthusiasm and stamina. The day began in the main dining room with a ceremony of dedication to the Führer (compulsory), presided over by a portrait of the man himself, regulation scowl in place, tar-black hair slicing diagonally across his brow. The ship had originally been named the *Adolf Hitler*, until the assassination of Gustloff, Party leader in Switzerland, by a Jewish upstart provided a Nazi martyr tailor-made for the bow of a ship. But even without his name on the side, Hitler's image was still everywhere; in the cocktail lounge, above the swimming pool, even glowering out at passengers when they took a bath. There was no such thing as a holiday from the Führer.

The morning's dedication ceremony was followed by a strenuous series of PE workouts on deck, gym sessions, fencing, table tennis, dancing lessons, piano recitals, swimming galas and bridge parties, all of which were not so much obligatory as strongly recommended by the ship's holiday reps who didn't leave you alone until you gave in.

Just walking round the ship was a major expedition. There was the Führer suite on B deck, kept for VIPs, the walnut-panelled Folk Costume lounge, and the Winter Garden. The German hall, the Music salon, the Ballroom and seven different bars. There was an indoor swimming pool, bouncing with echoes from excited Bund Deutscher Mädel girls bathed in dazzling, refracted light. And then there were meals, meals and more meals that you had to dress up for and were served with napkins folded into swastika shapes, beneath banners sewn with the KdF slogan '*Enjoy Your Lives!*'. The coffee tables had ashtrays with pictures of the ship on their plastic bases, and matchbooks, with *Wilhelm Gustloff* printed in gold lettering alongside them. Someone had put the Hitler Jugend in charge of the ship radio, which meant that in between the dance music and regular broadcasts from Joseph Goebbels, random exhortations were bellowed over the Tannoy, mostly concerning military excitements. The most recent one had come when the *Wilhelm Gustloff* passed a couple of German warships idling off the coast of France, and passengers were urged to 'think of the man who had given the German people their reputation and their position of power in the world: our Führer'. The HJ boys had also instituted a daily quiz – sample question 'What is Adolf Hitler's favourite flower?' – to which the passengers roared the answers in unison.

In her deckchair on the sun deck, a silk scarf round her head, Ada kept her eyes shut and sighed. Looking at the sea made her feel sick, what with the glare of the sun off its writhing currents and the smell of fish. The vast expanse of water only reminded her how far from home she was, and the proximity of so many others made her feel nervous. Far better to lie back and pretend to be asleep, even if there was no chance of relaxing.

Yesterday, to break the tedium, she had taken a trip ashore, but even on dry land the pace did not relent. It was an outing to Funchal to view the flora. The group wended their way past jacarandas thrusting fiery purple blossom in their faces, giant ferns and dragon trees, yellow frangipani and tremulous orchids. Above them the mountain slopes were tumbling with verdant growth and in the market old women in shawls attempted to sell them lace, wicker baskets and painted gourds. One woman had a fruit Ada had never seen, pomegranate it was called, a fruit like a cup full of jewels, but as she stretched out her hand, the tour guide leapt forward and advised her not to touch it on account of disease. The guides were exactly like schoolteachers. While everyone was marvelling at the banana trees and the birds of paradise and flamingo flowers, the tour guide kept pointing out the poverty of the local inhabitants, their ramshackle homes and gutters flowing with waste, saying it proved how other cultures were inferior to the Germans. It was lucky the locals didn't understand. The peasant women kept on smiling their toothless smiles while the group ignored them and hurried on. Bringing up the rear were a couple of SS surveillance staff, employed to prevent the women striking up holiday romances with foreign men. The guards were a burly pair, who saw everything and wouldn't hesitate to rough up any locals who tried as much as a friendly greeting.

Avoiding men had become a full time occupation for Ada. She couldn't help having good legs, a nice dress and a suntan, but the ship was full of lads who had qualified for their tickets in groups from the factories where they worked and were delighted to find any unattached women, let alone a pretty twenty-three-year-old with a voluptuous figure, a snub nose, full lips and eyes of bright Aryan blue. Ada's creamy blonde plaits framed a face as delicate as a porcelain doll and her red and yellow halter-neck sundress emphasized her generous curves. They hung around her like wasps, offering to buy her a beer and asking for a dance. Even when she picked up one of her stack of film magazines they didn't let up, making idiotic comments about movie stars or suggesting, predictably, she should be on screen herself.

But Ada had not the slightest interest in men just then, or Madeira and its flowers. She was far too nervous for that. Her entire attention was fixed on the ship's next stop, Lisbon, where the *Wilhelm Gustloff* would dock and she would complete the business she had come for. Then there would be plenty of time to enjoy herself and she might even take one of the young men up on his offer. In the meantime, to stop being bothered, she had come up with a pretty good deterrent.

At first, when the teenager from the neighbouring cabin had begun stealing glances at her, she sighed inwardly. He couldn't have been more than fifteen, with a wiry boy's frame just beginning to fill out and the faintest dusting of hair on his upper lip. Actually his lean, dark-eyed face reminded Ada of her little brother. The lad was on holiday with his grandmother, who had qualified for the tickets through her job at Berlin's Charité hospital, and they had been assigned to Ada's table at breakfast. As she tried to eat her eggs, Ada found herself machine-gunned with questions. Where did she come from? Berlin? Them too! Weren't they lucky to have tickets on the best ship of the fleet? And only its second cruise. How had she qualified for hers? Then the boy noticed the film magazines and an album of movie star cards she had – the kind you sent off for with coupons from your cigarette packet – and he became even more excited. Did she know his own godmother was a film actress? Her name was Clara Vine and she featured on a cigarette card herself. Perhaps Ada had her picture?

Enboldened at this shared enthusiasm, the boy had skipped his post-breakfast gym session and offered to carry Ada's coffee up to the sun deck. She groaned inwardly, until she suddenly realized the boy might actually be an advantage. His name was Erich Schmidt, and he wanted to tell her all about his plans to join the Luftwaffe. That was fine by Ada. She closed her eyes and instructed Erich to keep talking.

The fact was, it wasn't just the factory workers who had set Ada's nerves on edge. Yesterday, she had been lying in the same spot on her lounger when she caught a brief snatch of scent that made her sit up in alarm. She couldn't understand why she had reacted the way she did. It was inexplicable. But there was some

prickle of danger in that harsh, citrus-edged cologne, some quality in its musky base notes that left an ominous imprint on the air.
It was the kind of perfume that hung on a person, like garlic on
the breath. For a second the perfume formed itself into something
mistily substantial – a wraith with an arrogant face, eyes black as
olive pits and a smile sharp as a knife – but the image was gone as
soon as it had come, like a puff of breath misting a mirror, wiped
away to reveal nothing. Ada tried to conceal her alarm, yet she
must have looked worried because a girl in a deckchair near to
hers, with pasty skin, lank braids and thick spectacles, noticed her
distraction.

'Is anything the matter?'

Ada was tempted to ask whether the girl herself had seen
anyone, but realized instinctively that this was a matter she needed
to keep to herself, so she turned a dismissive, suntanned shoulder
and said rudely,

'No. Why should it be?'

That morning, after Erich had gone off to fetch the coffee, Ada
caught a trace of the cologne again. There was definitely a
memory floating there, amid the mix of lemon, amber and moss.
Though the day was perfectly warm, a chill crept over her and she
clutched her cardigan to her and sat up, her filmy scarf snapping
in the breeze. She looked around at the women, wedged in their
deckchairs with their copies of *Stern* and *Die Dame,* and their husbands with their trousers rolled up, but she could see nothing to
account for it. Yet like an animal hearing a note much higher than
human ears can hear, Ada detected in that perfume a note of
danger, a high, ringing register of alarm with a bass undertone of
fear. Attempting to rationalize the feeling, she reminded herself
how many different thousands of people used the same scent.
Kölnwasser, Eau de Cologne, for instance, Germany's oldest scent,
was used by millions. It was said to be the Führer's favourite. There
was no reason why this one particular scent should mean anything
at all. It reminded her of something though, and it was something

that made her afraid. It was a male scent, so it must be a man she was reminded of, but which man?

Was it someone back home? She frowned and chewed her lip as she tried to place it, but all she knew was that the scent made her heart race and the hairs rise on the back of her neck. She needed to know where that perfume came from, if only for her peace of mind.

Thank goodness for the boy, who was just coming back at that moment, balancing two cups on a tray and two pastries which he must have bought with his own cash.

'What a darling you are, Erich! Now I have to go somewhere, just for a minute. Could you look after my things? Make sure you keep an eye on them. And don't let anyone take this deckchair.'

The boy looked dismayed at having his coffee spurned and she felt a pang of guilt, but there was nothing for it.

Decisively Ada put down her magazine, rose from the deckchair and strode off.

Erich waited an hour watching Ada's coffee grow cold and ate both pastries himself, before he realized that she did not have an important appointment at all. She had just been trying to get rid of him. A humiliated flush spread across his cheeks as he imagined all the fat women – friends of his grandmother's sitting around in their deckchairs – secretly laughing at him while they pretended to read their magazines. They must assume he had an adolescent crush. He felt a twist of anger. He had never wanted to take a summer holiday with his grandmother, what boy would? Oma kept going on about what a privilege it was to go on a KdF trip and how the ship would be luxurious beyond their wildest dreams. There was even a library on board. But what boy in his right mind wanted a library on holiday?

A little after four o'clock that afternoon a squall blew in from the east, pitting the watered silk of the sea and driving everyone from the sun decks inside to play Skat or table tennis and watch the spray lashing the portholes from the warmth of the recreation areas. Only one hardy passenger, shivering in the spitting rain, remained on deck to witness what followed.

The first thing she noticed was a commotion at the port side of the ship, where a gaggle of sailors were shouting and hauling an object onto the rain-lashed deck. She thought at first it was a fish, a shark perhaps, or a porpoise, but looking closer she saw it was a young woman's body, beached like a delicate, exotic mermaid from some child's fairy story. The dead girl lay on her back, curly hair plastered across her face like seaweed and skin as white as a fish, her flesh already turning to ice. Water gushed from her mouth and nostrils and ran in rivulets down her face, pooling around her body as it lay defencelessly still. For a second the sailors stood staring at her until the youngest of them, the one who had first glimpsed the white shape rolling on the waves and raised the alarm, felt sick and grabbed a tarpaulin to wrap her up. So the woman watching caught only a glimpse of the girl's face, just enough to see that it was extraordinarily pretty in the conventional Germanic model, with high, arched eyebrows and blue eyes now fixed and empty, as if their colour had already been washed out by the sea. She wore a halter-necked sundress that clung to every voluptuous curve, leaving nothing to the imagination except, perhaps, the method of her death. For on the back of her head was a great bloody mess of hair and bone, the kind of wound that might have been sustained by hitting the side of the ship as she fell, or even, perhaps, a blow from a heavy instrument, if such a thing were possible.

The horrified passenger was moved swiftly away from the scene and later that day received a personal visit in her cabin from Heinrich Bertram, the ship's captain, who was most solicitous about her shock. He suggested that she try to forget it as much as possible and enjoy the rest of her holiday. It would be wrong to allow a tragedy like this to mar such a special voyage, let alone spoil the enjoyment of others by talking about it. Going further,

Captain Bertram had to warn the gnädiges Fräulein that any mention of the incident anywhere else at all would have serious repercussions for her, both at home and in the workplace, and put at risk the chance of any future trips she or her family might hope to make with the KdF.

Chapter One

Paris

Paris in late August, 1938, was a city living on its nerves.

Rumours swarmed like rats around the streets, refugees from every corner of Europe brushed shoulders on the boulevards, and the cafés were a babel of foreign languages, Spanish, Italian, Czech and, of course, German, rising and falling in anxious disputation. In the city centre the clatter of cream-topped buses, the blare of taxi horns and the shouts of traffic gendarmes were overlaid with the distant sound of reservists, in hastily assembled khaki, marching along the Champs Elysées. German, Austrian, Polish and Hungarian Jews congregated in the Marais quarter in anxious exile, scraping a living by day, and drinking it by night. Morsels of foreign news were picked up and ravenously chewed on, then discarded as propaganda or lies. Refugees choked the railway stations. Native Parisians were packing up and moving their families to the country. Others spent longer than usual in the churches. A dry summer wind blew around the city, chivvying along the gutters a vortex of leaves and litter and small scraps of newspaper alarm. Hitler was claiming that the German-speaking population of Czechoslovakia's Sudetenland, just south of the German border, desired reunion with the Reich. If the Czech government did not agree then he would march in and take it. France and England seemed certain to reject Germany's demands. Hitler had set the date of 1st October for military action. The threat of war hung like a distant thunderstorm on a sunny day.

Clara Vine threw open the tall shutters, leaned over the narrow balcony, and gazed down at the Boulevard de Sébastopol below. She only had three days in Paris and the last two had been spent shooting scenes for her latest film, an adaptation of Maupassant's *Bel Ami,* but the third, today, was entirely free. A whole day ahead of her and only an engagement that evening before catching a train at the Gare du Nord early the next morning and heading back home to Berlin. She could visit the Louvre, go shopping, see a concert, or maybe just sit in a square beneath the dusty trees and drink a café crème. An entire day to herself in Paris. No lines to learn, no character to assume. No takes or retakes, no director's tiff or costume fittings. No delays or disputes. After filming almost non-stop for months, a day off in a foreign location felt like a fantasy. And despite the mood of the city, Clara was determined to make the most of it.

The Bellevue, where the cast were staying, was not everyone's idea of Parisian chic. Its forty rooms were squeezed into a narrow, five-storey building and Clara's bedroom on the top floor was sweltering. The paint on the wrought-iron balconies was flaking, the plaster decayed and the entire building was imbued with the reek of drains. But who cared about that when there was all of Paris to look at?

The city seemed impossibly beautiful, the elegant precision of its buildings and the classical uniformity of its blocks and streets complemented by a golden light that seemed to saturate the pale stone. Even now, in high summer, when most Parisians were on their August vacation, the pavements were thronged with people. Immediately below Clara's window, between the patchy trunks of the plane trees, a cart of flowers bulged with red, yellow and pink blooms, like a bright shout of colour in the morning air. Vans making deliveries and a porter hauling a crate of baguettes almost collided with a man bearing a box of oranges on his head. In the fishmonger's window a chorus line of doomed lobsters waved their limbs helplessly on a tray. Young women with crimson lips and kohl-lined eyes clipped past wearing Breton-necked tops with wide scarves slung diagonally across them, in keeping with the latest fashion, and little felt hats studded with flowers or feathers. Some wore printed summer dresses in ice-cream colours and they even managed to make their heavy wooden-soled shoes look stylish. Men in open-necked shirts and berets swaggered past. Despite the undercurrent of nerves that ran through the city, the citizens on the Boulevard de Sébastopol were doing their best impression of elegant nonchalance.

What a contrast with Berlin. In Clara's home city the daily round-up of Jews and the sporadic Gestapo cruelties had worsened throughout the year. That spring Hitler had marched into Austria and found himself greeted not with hostilities but with a carpet of roses; *Blumenkrieg*, he called it, a war of flowers. The lack of international outcry over the Anschluss had only emboldened him. Hitler was, everyone realized, more confident than ever.

Unlike Clara herself.

As an Anglo-German actress, who had grown up in England, Clara Vine had made a successful career for herself since arriving in Berlin five years earlier. She had seven films to her name, and by sheer chance had forged connections with many people in Berlin's high society. Yet despite her acquaintance with the wives of several politicians, Joseph Goebbels, the Minister for Propaganda and Public Enlightenment, had become increasingly suspicious of Clara's motives. The previous year he had even had her arrested briefly, and interrogated. For Clara, merely thinking of that day in the Gestapo headquarters, and of the tightrope she trod daily in Berlin, brought a chill to the morning's warmth and a familiar sick twist of nerves. It was as though Goebbels was determined to prove what he suspected – that even though Clara's father was a

British aristocrat and Nazi sympathizer, and she herself was working full-time in the Babelsberg film studios, Clara was an agent of British Intelligence. That she was passing snippets of information and gossip to her contacts in the British Embassy. That she purposefully mingled in Nazi society to observe the private life of the Third Reich.

It would have been absurd, if it hadn't also been true.

What made Clara's position more perilous was her discovery, when she arrived in Germany, that her own grandmother was a Jew. The document of Aryan heritage Clara carried everywhere was as much a fabrication as the russet highlights in her hair, but infinitely more significant.

Every day she asked herself why she stayed in Berlin. Every day she came up with the same answer. She would stay in Berlin as long as she could because it meant seeing her godson Erich. He was the only man in her life right now, and for his sake most of all she prayed that war could somehow be averted.

A passing barrow boy aimed an admiring whistle up at her balcony, forcing Clara's mind back to the present. Paris had always been one of those big, statement places, like a famous perfume that everyone knows, burdened with the weight of expectation. The Parisian air was a complex fragrance of baking and drains, a whisper of flowers, undercut with something acrid and rotten. The leavings of vegetables from the market stalls mingled with the enticing aroma of garlic and coffee. Berlin's own air, by contrast, carried the grey, metallic edge of wet stone and steel offset by the tang of pine from the Grunewald.

Much as she relished the prospect of a day in Paris, Clara wished she had someone to share it with. Most of the time she liked her solitude; at the age of thirty-one it was part of her identity almost, her self-sufficiency a toughened carapace against the barbs of loneliness, and safer too. But solitude seemed wrong in the city of romance. This was Paris after all, whose streets murmured with the promises of lovers through the ages, and she was alone. Leaning back against the casement, a whirlwind of memories assailed her, like leaves thrown around in a breeze.

She had not seen Ralph Sommers, the man she had met in Berlin the previous year, since the day he left for London. Since then, his work as a British agent had been exposed and now it was too dangerous for him to return to Germany. He had sent Clara a message saying that so long as she stayed there, she must do her best to forget him. It hurt, but she was trying her hardest.

Then there was Leo Quinn. Leo, who had returned to England after she turned down his proposal of marriage. In her darkest moments Clara questioned if there was something within her that destroyed her deepest relationships. Did she shy away from intimacy or deliberately reject it? Did she emit some invisible signal that said, 'Leave me alone'?

The previous evening the director, Willi Forst, had hosted a dinner at Maxim's for the cast. Maxim's, just off the Place de la Concorde, was the restaurant of choice for German visitors to Paris and Willi Forst thought its Art Nouveau opulence perfectly suited to celebrating Maupassant's story. The group had the best table in the house, the one usually reserved for the Aga Khan, spread with snowy linen tablecloths and silver cutlery, and they were served platters of oysters with vinegar and shallots, *quenelles de brochet* floating in a rich cream sauce, and *crème brûlée* to finish. Ice buckets holding bottles of vintage Krug rested to one side, furred with frost. Even though they had had an early start, the actors indulged themselves loudly, jokes and stories flowing, impressions performed, anecdotes related. The sheer relief of being away from Berlin inspired a feverish jollity, a holiday atmosphere that had already prompted a couple of romantic liaisons amongst members of the cast and promised more nights of passion ahead. But none of the male actors had propositioned Clara. It was as though they divined something in her which told them their approaches would be rebuffed. As they revelled in the unaccustomed fine food and called loudly for more wine, Clara felt the

restaurant's other clientele eyeing the Germans, in their expensive
suits and scented furs, with wariness and resentment.

'To my magnificent cast!'

Willi Forst raised a glass and beamed. Sitting there, Clara thought
back to the newspaper pictures in March, when Hitler entered
Vienna in his six-wheeled bulletproof Mercedes, striking his familiar pose, upright, holding on to the windscreen with his left hand
while raising the other in the Nazi salute. The crowd erupting in
a volcano of feeling and the flowers raining down on him like ash.
Would these Paris streets too be overtaken by tramping boots and
thumping drums? Might France go the way of Austria? Austria
wasn't even Austria any more, it was part of Greater Germany. It
seemed countries could end, just as much as relationships.

A knock at her door made her turn. It was the bellboy, wearing
a little navy cap and holding out a manila envelope.

'Pour vous, mademoiselle.'

'Merci.' She fished for a coin and opened the envelope curiously. Inside was a cream notecard, heavy and good quality, with
a logo of Big Ben and a company name at the top. Beneath was
spiky, academic handwriting.

Dear Miss Vine,

*Please forgive me for approaching you directly, but I noticed
from an article in Paris-Soir that you were in Paris and felt
compelled to get in touch. We would be very interested in
discussing a proposal with you. Would you be free to meet at the
café Chez André in the Rue Marbeuf at 12 p.m. today? If you
are able to come I shall be looking out for you,*

Sincerely, Guy Hamilton,
Representative, London Films

London Films? Clara frowned. She had heard of it. From what
she remembered it had been started by the Hungarian émigré

Alexander Korda. It was based at Denham in Buckinghamshire and had hired Winston Churchill as a screenwriter. Hadn't they made *The Private Life of Henry VIII* and *Things To Come* and last year's *Fire Over England*, with Laurence Olivier and Vivien Leigh? Clara had taken a special interest in that one because a director had once casually referred to her as 'the German Vivien Leigh', so she had attended the first night at the Ufa Palast and sat in the cinema, closely studying the actress's classic, porcelain beauty, before concluding that the director, unfortunately, was exaggerating. Clara might have the same heart-shaped face, clear brow and dark eyebrows, but her cheeks were fuller, her skin more olive and her mouth had a rebellious purse to it which gave her looks a distinctive, less classic edge.

She checked her watch. It was already 11 a.m. She was suddenly, unaccountably excited. This proposal would almost certainly be the offer of a part – she was gradually becoming better known, and as many of the German Jewish actors and directors who had been forced to leave Berlin had now relocated to England, it was likely that one of them had mentioned her name. Evidently someone was looking out for her. And maybe, if this company was offering her a job, she should take it. What might it be like returning to London, picking up the threads of a life she had left five years ago and doing an ordinary job without risk or subterfuge? Seeing her father, sister and brother and other people who had been consigned firmly to the past?

Clanging the shutters to, she grabbed a short jacket to slip over her dress. Peering in the mirror she applied a thin layer of Elizabeth Arden's Velvet Red – always her first weapon of concealment – and gave her reflection an encouraging smile. Dabbing a trace of powder over the freckles that the sun had brought out, she pulled a brush through her hair and pinned it loosely at the nape of her neck with a diamanté clip. Then she donned her sunglasses. Evidently the idea of a day without business was just a fantasy after all.

Chapter Two

The bistro Chez André was a twenty-minute walk away, situated on the other side of the Champs Elysées. Past the Rue de Rivoli, Clara entered the Tuileries Garden, enjoying the perfect mathematical precision of its gravel and greenery. She had always loved patterns. Her father had noticed, when he still noticed his children, that Clara possessed an unusually retentive memory and he had done his best to develop it with memory techniques and card games and mathematical exercises. For a short while Clara, the cleverest of the Vine children, had been an experiment for him, a project almost, to be developed and tested and trialled before, as abruptly as he began, he lost interest. Yet for Clara puzzles remained a lasting passion. She loved word games and riddles of any kind. She learned how to memorize a deck of cards using images of their old home in Surrey. She liked to work out crosswords in her head, with a stock of the esoteric words – triptych, orris, eidetic – that compilers tended to favour. Her mind organized the world into patterns quite unconsciously; the number of tiles on a floor, biscuits in a box, the repetition of trees or flags or lampposts, or, as here, the perfectly mirror-like symmetry of the flowerbeds and paths. By the same token, she noticed anomalies too. Even without knowing she was doing it her brain sought out anything that was wrong, any asymmetry or deviation from the norm. Difference leapt out at her. The knots in a piece of wood, the fleck in the glass, the flaw in a Turkish carpet that spoiled the line.

But that morning everything was normal, or as normal as a city could be, perched on the edge of war.

The Champs Elysées was planted with geraniums and begonias, the flowers pushing up in the beds, and bees, like a hundred seamstresses, were nipping and dipping their way through the blooms. Clara threaded her way through elegant women pulling along children in smocked dresses and dogs on plaited leather leashes. Parisians always made other nationalities feel worse-dressed, she concluded, even though her own dress flattered her, with its delicate leaf-green cotton cinched at the waist and setting off the colour of her eyes.

From its scarlet awning to its basket-weave chairs and pavement tables, Chez André in the Rue Marbeuf conformed in every respect to an idealized vision of a Parisian café. Inside, nicotine-stained walls enclosed globe lamps and vinyl banquettes. A poster warned customers to beware of pickpockets. Potted palms and a glass partition separated the smarter part of the restaurant from the café area, and at the zinc counter the patron was polishing glasses while a waitress in white collar and apron deposited cups of coffee on a table.

As she was early, Clara decided to walk to the end of the street and dawdle, loitering in front of the shops, making the most of the shopping trip she had been obliged to forego. She lingered outside a chocolaterie whose window was decked with jewel-coloured jellied fruits, sugar almonds, rich dark chocolate, and cakes with labels that made them sound like perfect, individual works of art – *soleil levant, opéra, charlotte aux fruits exotiques, religieuse*. Her mouth watered and her stomach clenched as the dark waft of chocolate emerged from the shop.

As she gazed in the window Clara noticed something curious

reflected behind her. On the other side of the road, a man was slouched with a wide flat cap rammed onto his head, customary cigarette perched to one side of his mouth, and his hands thrust into his pockets. The archetypal Parisian flâneur. He was leaning against the peeling green paint of an advertisement column, apparently loitering the day away; yet suddenly, this air of profound relaxation was interrupted by a swift, instinctive look from right to left down the road, before he slumped back into his previous position. Clara was instantly alert. Even in the hazy grain of a shop window's reflection, she recognized that look. It was not the glance of a casual bystander, dawdling the day away. Something was wrong about this situation. The man was a watcher. A tail.

Alarm and astonishment rose in her. Was she really being followed, here in Paris? Could she not manage a brief respite from the all-encompassing surveillance of the Gestapo? Being in France had encouraged her to relax and let her guard down, yet she had forgotten that foreigners, and Germans in particular, were conspicuous just now.

If the shadow was looking down the road, he must be waiting for someone, probably a colleague, which meant there were two people on her tail. A team. A swift glance confirmed that she was right. A second man, with dark, brilliantined hair, a copy of *Paris-Soir* under his arm and a smart, velvet-napped felt hat tipped over his face, was strolling in her direction. Unlike his accomplice, something about this man was adamantly not French. For one thing he was wearing a trench coat, even in the height of summer, over a well-cut suit, and for another, his bearing, the determined nature of his strut and the touch of arrogance in the tilt of his head, told her in a single glance that he was German.

Even as she registered this information, Clara's brain began to formulate a plan. Operating on a sharp, inbuilt reflex, and despite her urge to vanish, she remained rooted to the spot while she worked out her next move. Watching her own ghost in the window, apparently choosing chocolates, she decided her best

option would be to enter the shop and spend a long time delib-
erating between Montélimar and Noisettes, before slipping out
and, instead of returning to her hotel, heading back to the
Boulevard Haussmann for one of the large department stores,
Galeries Lafayette or Printemps, and giving her followers the slip
from the ladies' changing rooms. Either that, or disappear into the
nearest Métro station and lead them a dance round the whole of
Paris. She had done it before. It was a part she played well.

In the few seconds it took for these thoughts to form in Clara's
mind, the man in the felt hat passed her, and she saw the flâneur
swivel and follow suit. Glancing to her right she realized in a flash
that she had made a mistake. The watchers had no interest in her
at all. Instead, their attention was fixed on a middle-aged man in
horn-rimmed spectacles and a herringbone suit, who had entered
Chez André and was making his way to a seat at the back. The
flâneur took up residence in a doorway opposite and the felt hat
man kept walking. The pair were shadows, but Clara was not the
target of their surveillance. That target was, quite evidently, the
person she had come to meet. She lingered a few moments more
in front of the shop, before entering Chez André and heading for
the bar.

The man Clara assumed to be Guy Hamilton was sitting on a
red vinyl banquette, extracting a pen from his inside pocket and
applying himself to a postcard of the Eiffel Tower with a glass of
beer beside him. He was in his mid-forties and above average
height, with tightly cropped sandy hair, a tawny moustache and a
face as mild and forgettable as an English summer's day. If she were
forced to memorize him, Clara would have focused on the dusting of freckles across his sallow complexion or the receding
hairline which gave him a faintly donnish air. As it was, there was
no time for analysis because she needed to alert him, as soon as she
could, without compromising herself.

Crossing the café, she walked straight past him, letting her handbag dangle from her arm so that it swung across, knocking the big

sugar shaker on its side and unleashing a sticky white tide over the tabletop.

'Oh, I'm so sorry. How clumsy of me.'

Hearing an English voice, he looked up immediately, recognition dawning in his eyes.

Clara bent over the table, her back to the window.

'Here. Let me.'

The sugar coated the table like sand. With one finger, Clara quickly wrote in the granular tide, 'NO'. She waited until Hamilton had blinked through his horn-rims and nodded before grabbing a napkin and quickly wiping the spillage away.

'Awfully silly of me.'

'Not at all.'

Nonchalantly Hamilton rose to his feet as a waitress armed with a napkin bore down on them and brushed a few specks of sugar from his jacket with a fastidious flick. 'I hope you don't mind me guessing, but I'd say you're a visitor here. Have you ever seen Paris from the top of Notre-Dame?'

'Afraid not.'

'You should, you know. It's quite a sight. Gives you the big picture of the place. The best time to go is in the afternoon, while the crowds are still having lunch.' He rolled his newspaper and tapped it in her direction like a lecturer's baton. 'Around two o'clock is ideal. I recommend it.'

'Well, thank you. I might try it.'

'I hope you do.'

Tipping his hat, Hamilton strolled across to the bar, paid the patron, and left. Glancing through the window Clara saw the flâneur rouse himself, thrust his cigarette butt away and carry languidly on down the street in his wake.

She found herself a table at the back and made herself linger for a further thirty minutes, which was not much of a hardship as it involved ordering an *omelette aux champignons*, as light as a pale yellow cloud and sizzling with butter and herbs. She ate slowly, savouring every last scrap. Eggs were in short supply in Berlin, and it was rare to find any butter that was not rancid or bad. She followed it with a café crème that was deep and mellow, with none of the chicory or hazelnut coffee substitute one found in Germany. She passed the time riffling through *The Times*, trying and failing to concentrate on news that Len Hutton had scored a triple century in the fifth Test Match against Australia, the government was leading an allotment drive called Keep Calm And Dig, and the Queen was heading a new charity for disabled ex-servicemen. Occasionally she glanced outside, her mind working furiously.

What species of film producer had a surveillance team on his tail? Was Guy Hamilton really a representative of London Films, and if so, what kind of role was he proposing for Clara? However much she might project the picture of a relaxed tourist enjoying a day in Paris, Clara had never felt more cautious, or more alone. Surely it was madness to involve herself with a man who was being tailed by German agents. Briefly she contemplated forgetting Guy Hamilton and whatever proposal he had for her, but even as she considered it, she knew perfectly well that curiosity would overcome her.

Chapter Three

The brooding gargoyles on the parapet of Notre-Dame Cathedral looked over Paris like stony invaders from some Gothic land intent on the city's conquest. From the tower, tourists who were prepared to climb the four hundred-odd steps up the spiral staircase could gaze far across the russet rooftops to the bone-white byzantine domes of Sacré-Coeur on the heights of Montmartre. Beyond the crenellations of Notre-Dame, the skyline, pierced by the Eiffel Tower and the gold-leaved dome of Les Invalides, wavered in the heat. Far below, people the size of insects crossed the square and bateaux mouches ploughed the thick green stripe of the Seine.

At two o'clock, in the heat of the day, the place was almost deserted. Ranks of pigeons clustered in the shade, shuffling mutilated feet, like war-wounded soldiers. A pair of priests in long dark coats flapped past, and at the far western corner of the parapet Guy Hamilton, in his well-cut herringbone suit and brown felt hat, leant his elbows on the stone, looking down at the scene below. Her heart thudding with exertion, prickling with sweat and trying not to appear out of breath, Clara approached, keeping her sunglasses on. She disliked heights, and tried not to look down.

Hamilton removed his hat and gave a little bow.

'I'm told Herr Hitler detests Gothic architecture. He thinks it's strange and unnatural and fosters Christian mysticism.' He made a little gesture, like a tour guide. 'All these grotesque gargoyles.'

'Some might say he has a taste for the grotesque.'

'Indeed. Perhaps he recognizes himself. At any rate, let's hope he never makes a visit.' He nodded. 'Thank you for your warning, Miss Vine, and forgive my choice of venue. I couldn't resist mixing business with pleasure.'

Hamilton's manner was pleasantly self-effacing in a way which suggested a talent for anonymity. He seemed more like a civil servant than a film producer. He might have been one of thousands of men who streamed across London Bridge every morning, clutching an umbrella and a briefcase. Perhaps with a weekend hobby for church architecture, judging by the way he was assessing the construction of the flying buttresses.

'Is this the pleasure then?'

'Absolutely. I've always wanted to see the view from up here. And I must admit, it's worth it. Takes the breath away, doesn't it?'

It certainly did for Clara. She felt an instant rush of vertigo as she looked down and the continuous dim rush of the city, punctured by car horns, rose up towards them.

'That's assuming you've managed to get your breath back to begin with. But I'm sure you didn't invite me here to discuss the view.'

'Of course.' He swivelled towards her, smiled smoothly and extended a hand. His grasp was surprisingly firm and Clara detected a wiry strength beneath the mild-mannered exterior.

'I should have introduced myself properly. I'm afraid I neglected my courtesies when I met you this morning.'

'It rather looked like someone wanted to meet *you*.'

'Indeed. I discovered last night I had company but I thought I'd shaken them off. Unfortunately it means I'll have to leave Paris very shortly and I'm afraid my wife will have to miss out on her face cream. Anything French Diana likes, but there's no time now. I daresay it can wait.' He smiled cheerfully. 'What's that motto? *Good manners and a fine disposition are the best beauty treatments.*'

'Not one I know.'

'It's a Latin tag. Ovid, I think.'

For a second Clara thought she had misheard him, or that the wind had lifted and twisted his words. Her throat tightened.

'Ovid, did you say?'

The name rang through her like a depth charge, but it was not the Latin poet whose face rose to the surface of her mind, nor an enthusiasm for the classics that made her catch her breath. She was thinking of her former lover, the man who had first persuaded her to pass information to British Intelligence. Leo Quinn translated Ovid in his spare time, as a way of relieving the escalating pressures of work in a British consulate besieged by German Jews desperate to emigrate. The image of Leo, reading aloud the *Metamorphoses* in bed, was a memory Clara cherished, yet here was another Englishman standing in front of her making a casual reference to the same poet.

'Are you very familiar with Ovid?'

He laughed. 'Heavens no! Don't ask me to quote any more. I can't imagine how that line stuck in my mind. The remnants of a classical education, I suppose.'

With supreme effort Clara stopped herself probing further. If Guy Hamilton did know Leo, she would only want to ask if he was settled or married, or still in England, and Hamilton wouldn't tell her. And what difference would it make to know? The past was a foreign country you revisited at your peril.

Nonetheless the quote decided her. She was going to trust Guy Hamilton.

'I take it you're not a film producer?'

He blinked. 'But of course. I've seen a lot of your work. I'm an admirer.'

'Thank you.'

'You're right though. It's not film making I wanted to discuss. Not exactly.' He hesitated and looked about him. They were entirely alone on the windswept parapet. 'Ever heard of Colonel Claude Dansey?'

Clara shook her head.

'Dansey was, until recently, the British chief of station in Rome. Codename Z. He's spent his life in the intelligence service. He's a good fellow, a little irascible, but he inspires tremendous loyalty. Unfortunately Dansey has become disillusioned over the state of our intelligence network in Europe. He thinks it is badly compromised, and it could collapse entirely, which I don't need to tell you would leave us in a parlous position. His view is that one mistake could leave us without any proper contacts in the case of war.'

'The entire European network?'

'Precisely. As a result of which, he's established a shadow intelligence network. They call it Z, after him. It runs parallel to the existing European operation. Its operatives are businessmen mostly. People helping out for the principle of it. There's over two hundred of them now.'

He paused. 'Care for a smoke?'

Freeing a cigarette packet from his jacket pocket, he lit one for her, then himself, and turned his back, leaning against the parapet to prevent the curls of smoke being blown back into their faces.

'Anyhow, that's where I come in. Let me explain.'

Alexander Korda's London Films, Hamilton said, was all above board and a thriving enterprise, but it had a second, more secret endeavour. In the course of establishing a Europe-wide network of offices, Korda and his employees were undertaking espionage and reconnaissance.

'Reconnaissance?'

'Their cover is Foreign Sales, or Talent Scout or Location Search, but the job is to check out locations, photograph coastlines, make connections. What better excuse could there be for having a camera to hand than hunting out locations for your forthcoming travel movie? When the inevitable comes, we'll need to be prepared. But I don't need to tell you this, Miss Vine.'

He didn't. It seemed half the world was making preparations for war and the other half resolving to ignore them. The copy of

The Times Clara had just bought featured a front page photograph of men digging trenches in Hyde Park. Two long trenches had been gouged into the ground, with four shorter ones at right angles to them, like a ladder descending into the bowels of the earth. On a bench in the foreground a man in a bowler hat sat quite unconcerned, as if the great gaping hole behind him simply did not exist. A lot of people in Britain preferred to think that way.

'Not everyone assumes war's inevitable.'

'That's true. Prime Minister Daladier here has no illusions, nor do men like Churchill and Vansittart at home, but Halifax and Chamberlain seem to be far more sanguine about Herr Hitler's intentions. An awful lot of people seem hellbent on appeasing him.'

Fastidiously he removed a strand of tobacco from his mouth.

'Our Prime Minister thinks all Herr Hitler wants is a little territorial readjustment for the benefit of the German minority in the Sudetenland. Whereas it's clear to us that he wants to wipe the whole of Czechoslovakia off the map. If not Poland and Romania. We run the risk of everything we won in the war being thrown away because Chamberlain misreads Hitler's intentions.'

'You sound entirely pessimistic.'

'Not entirely. Though time's getting tight. It's not an exaggeration to say that the future of the continent hinges on events of the next month. We're hearing that Hitler intends to enter Czechoslovakia in October. France is Czechoslovakia's ally and will be duty bound to respond. They've already mobilized a million men. War could be just weeks away. But there's still a chance to avert it.'

Clara shrugged. 'You mean if Chamberlain and the others agree to stand by while Hitler goes ahead and takes what he wants?'

'No. That's not what I meant. But if the British stand firm, and Daladier comes in alongside them and denounces any incursion into Czechoslovakia, that will enable certain highly placed people in Berlin to paint Hitler as a warmonger who is about to drag his unwilling people into another European conflict.'

'I appreciate that. But why are you telling me this?'

Hamilton lowered his voice as if there were any possibility of being heard on those windblown ramparts, high above Paris. A breeze lifted his sparse hair and buffeted his jacket.

'It's Dansey's view that it will help our side very much if we can gain an insight into Hitler's thinking. His mood that could make the difference between peace and immediate war. The fellow is immensely mercurial. It's incredible how enormous actions can turn on the whim of a single man.'

He waited until a family with two children had passed out of earshot, and said, 'That, Miss Vine, is where you come in.'

Startled, Clara took off her sunglasses. 'Me?'

'Indeed. If you're willing. You know who I mean by Eva Braun?'

Clara gave a cautious frown. 'The Führer's girlfriend? Only because Magda Goebbels told me about her. The rest of Germany has no idea who she is.'

'And it's likely to stay that way, particularly if . . .' He paused.

'If what?'

'If someone decides to remove her. Apparently the top brass – Goebbels and Goering, and to an extent Hess – are concerned at Miss Braun's hysterical moods. She's attempted suicide twice. The one thing worse than people knowing Hitler has a relationship with a little blonde secretary, would be knowing that he makes her so unhappy she's tried to do herself in. As it is, she remains Germany's best-kept secret. It's easier to breach the operational security of the Wehrmacht than discover anything about Miss Eva Braun.'

'I'm sorry, but I can't see what Eva Braun or her happiness has to do with me.'

'Ah.' He stubbed out his cigarette, tossed it into the air and watched as it was snatched away by the Parisian breeze. 'There's the thing. The fact is, we'd rather like you to get to know her.'

Clara gasped. 'Eva Braun? If she's Germany's best-kept secret, how on earth would I go about even meeting her?'

'She admires your work, doesn't she?'

Clara paused, remembering a postcard with a scrap of neat, curly handwriting on it that had arrived at the Babelsberg studios the previous year. '*Just wanted to tell you how much I enjoyed Black Roses.*'

'You're talking about that fan letter.'

'Exactly.'

'She sends plenty of actors fan letters. She sees all our films, several times over. None of us know who she is, of course. She doesn't mention the fact that she's seen our films sitting next to Hitler at the Berghof. Anyhow, how on earth did you hear about it? I didn't exactly pin that postcard up in my dressing room.'

He shrugged. 'All her mail is monitored. They keep a very close eye on her, as you can imagine. So I'm sure your letter was genuine. She adores Ufa movies, as you say. Appears to be somewhat fanatical about the cinema. She's going to the Venice Film Festival next year.'

Clara looked out at the city beneath her, but in her mind's eye she had already travelled far beyond it, across Europe to the distant Alps of Bavaria, towards the slight, blonde figure of the Führer's girlfriend watching movie after movie in the Great Hall of Hitler's impregnable mountain retreat.

'I don't see how . . . just because she sent me a letter . . . I mean, Hitler keeps her out of sight, doesn't he? Magda Goebbels says Eva Braun wasn't even allowed to meet the Duke of Windsor when he was in Berlin last year. Hitler made her hide in her room. Not even the top brass are supposed to know Eva Braun's exact status. She can have anything she wants, except to be known as Hitler's girlfriend.'

'And one of the things she wants is to meet some famous actors. Celebrities, you know. Perhaps have a look around a film set. You could offer to show her round.'

Despite herself, Clara laughed out loud. 'I think you're rather overestimating my powers of persuasion. How on earth would I do that?'

'We've thought of that. There's a film being shot in Munich. *Good King George*, it's called. About the Hanoverian monarch, I hasten to add, rather than our present king. All entirely above board. It's directed by a chap called Mr Fritz Gutmann, who we understand would like to make his career in England very soon. He'll be getting in touch with you about an audition for the role of Sophia, the unfaithful wife. She falls in love with a Swedish count, but their affair is destined to be unrequited.' He squinted pensively. 'It goes without saying we're hoping you get the part.'

Clara looked across the rooftops and a wave of vertigo hit her in a panicky rush, making her stomach heave and her head swirl. Guy Hamilton's proposition seemed an equally dizzying prospect.

'Why would you expect this of me? I mean . . . to go to another city and attempt something that is almost certainly going to be entirely unfeasible. It's an impossible task.'

He looked at her, puzzled. 'It's what you do, isn't it?'

Clara had a sudden vision of a great web of people, strung out across Europe, all assembled by this man Colonel Dansey and responding to his requests. All like her, carrying on with their ordinary lives, and living an entirely different life in the shadows. Holding their secrets and their loyalties close. Waking each day not knowing what it might bring. Despite herself she was already knitting her fingers, already calculating the task in hand.

'If I do . . . manage to meet her . . . what would you want to know?'

'Any little details you think might be relevant. Pillow talk, I think they call it. We believe Miss Braun could be the chink in Hitler's armour. We're hoping she will provide that crucial "back door" into the Führer's thinking.'

'I can't imagine he would confide military detail in her.'

'Who knows what he would confide? The man's an enigma.

He's very careful with his top people. Plays them off against each other. Miss Braun may be the only person he's completely straight with.'

'If I find anything, what then? How do I let you know?'

'Put a classified advertisement in the Situations Wanted column of one of the British newspapers.' He reflected a moment. 'Include the word "Latin". That should stand out. We'll set up a meeting at the Siegessäule in the Tiergarten, the Thursday after the message appears. Let us know the time and so on. We'll keep a look-out.'

'What if it's urgent?'

'There's always a DLB we have in Berlin. It's checked regularly.'

'A DLB?'

'A dead letter box.'

'Oh, of course.'

That was one of the things that Leo Quinn had tried to teach her, along with other espionage terms. It belonged to the world of 'brush contacts' and 'switches' and 'box surveillance'. A world where people passed messages rolled up inside cigarettes or secreted inside tubes of toothpaste. A world with which Clara still felt somewhat unfamiliar.

'You'd have to go back to Berlin. Do you know the Volkspark in Friedrichshain?' continued Hamilton. 'There's a fountain there. The fairy-tale fountain, I think it's called.'

'The Märchenbrunnen.'

It was an elaborate fountain surrounded by sculptures of fairy-tale characters which had been created for the children of Berlin in the nineteenth century. Cinderella, Hansel and Gretel and the Frog Prince were all there; but despite the theme, the serried ranks of stone figures with their frozen limbs and vacant eyes had very little magic about them.

'I know it well.'

'Excellent. Look for the stone bench on the left-hand side closest to the pillar. There's a cavity on the underside.'

'That's a little public, isn't it?'

'It needs to be somewhere people congregate so one doesn't arouse suspicion. But time, as I said, is of the essence.'

A rabble of voices rose from the entrance to the stairwell behind her and Hamilton looked over her shoulder. A party of schoolboys had emerged and were making their way along the walkway, giggling and play-fighting, pretending to throw each other off the side.

'It's getting a little crowded up here. Shall we go down?'

They descended the stairway into the chilly, flickering gloom of the Cathedral itself and Clara pulled on her jacket. The place felt like the sanctuary it once was, resounding with hushed murmuring, heavy with the odour of incense, its glimmering shadows pierced by great shafts of light. Hamilton went over to light a candle at one of the side chapels, dropped to his knees and gazed fixedly at the countenance of the Madonna in an attitude of pious contemplation. Clara knelt beside him. Now that her vertigo had disappeared, the sense of panic had ebbed too, allowing her to fix her mind on the task in hand.

'About those men this morning,' she murmured. 'They were Germans, weren't they? I thought at first they were following me.'

'Has that happened recently?'

'Not here, as far as I know.'

'Yes. I apologise. I changed hotels and I thought I'd thrown them off. I was warned about it last night by a chap we have working for us here, a fellow called Steinbrecher. Steinbrecher says the Gestapo's pretty well entrenched in Paris now. Heydrich has an extensive network of informers in place and Steinbrecher thinks they've been watching me for a couple of days. I'm glad you've been free of them, but if I were you, Miss Vine, I'd be very careful all the same. Check your hotel room for bugs. All the usual things. Watch out for any gifts. I'm sure there's nothing I need tell you.'

He rose, brushed the knees of his trousers and gave a warm smile.

'Have a pleasant journey. And very good luck. Forgive me if I don't shake hands.'

He strode off into the dim interior, transforming instantly into the amateur enthusiast, guidebook in pocket, contemplating the splintered ruby and violet majesty of the famous south rose window.

Clara walked slowly back through the winding, cobbled streets of the Ile de la Cité, onto the Ile St Louis. She watched the fishermen down at the water's edge throwing out their lines, fracturing the Seine into a thousand choppy diamonds. The meeting with Hamilton had unsettled her profoundly. Partly because his mild, unassuming Englishness had provoked a sharp nostalgia for her homeland, yet also because his request was daunting. The mention of the mysterious Dansey reminded her that there was an entire realm of people in England whom she had never met, yet who knew of her existence. Uniformed men in Whitehall, perhaps even well-known politicians like Winston Churchill and Sir Robert Vansittart, and others sitting behind desks in shabby, anonymous London offices, posing as civil servants or accountants or film producers, while they ran shadowy intelligence networks. People who were aware of her activities, and whose confidence in her was seemingly far greater than her own.

She thought of the task they were asking of her now. Getting close to Eva Braun, and in the space of a month? How was she possibly going to manage that? She didn't even know what Eva Braun looked like. Emmy Goering had once said she looked like the film star Lilian Harvey only stupider, but that wasn't much to go on. And even if Clara was to meet the girl and manage to talk to her, what were the chances that she would be willing to confide private details about Hitler's state of mind? Clara would need to employ all her persuasive skills. She had become well versed in asking ingenuous questions under the guise of female curiosity – the paranoid, isolated existences of most Nazi wives meant they

tended to open up gratefully to an apparently sympathetic listener – so all she could hope was that Hitler's girlfriend felt the
same. Yet even if she did manage to talk to Eva Braun, and to
extract information, what good would that do? Could it really be
the case that the fate of nations rested on the whim of one man,
or that a Munich shop girl could do anything to affect it?

The thought of Leo Quinn rose once again to her mind. The
man who had met her and trained her in this new and dangerous
life, and then proposed to take her away from it. The more she
thought, the more she realized that Guy Hamilton's mention of
Ovid had been exactly what it appeared – a coincidence – simply
proof that Leo was never far from her mind. After all, she reasoned, Leo had never wanted her to put herself at risk. He'd made
it a condition of his marriage proposal that she abandon her secret
work and return to England out of harm's way, so he was hardly
likely to encourage her to undertake an even more risky enterprise
now. When she had refused to give up her work, Leo had abruptly
left Berlin himself, taking her quite by surprise. She had never
really believed that he was serious in his ultimatum. Maybe she
thought she could persuade him otherwise, but before she knew
it, it was too late.

Still, there was no point dwelling on the past. It was the present that required all her attention now. Before she returned to
Berlin she had another intriguing errand to run. On her last
evening in Paris she was to visit the salon of Coco Chanel. French
cosmetics were hard to come by in Germany now, even for VIPs,
and Clara's mission was to collect some perfume for the
Propaganda Chief's wife, Magda Goebbels herself.

Chapter Four

The Place Vendôme had, in mediaeval times, been a cloister for Capuchin nuns, but now the exclusive octagonal arena at the heart of the Right Bank was the shrine to another form of female devotions. The spectacular adornments of Van Cleef & Arpels, Chaumet and Cartier were showcased in opulent shop fronts clustered around the chief attraction of the Place, the Ritz Hotel. And the star occupant of the Ritz was Coco Chanel, who had been given the use of an entire third-floor suite and decided to make it her home. The couturier had redesigned every aspect of the suite to reflect her personal style and now the room seemed to float with colour and light, a mirrored cocoon of cream, black and gold. Around the lavish sitting room with its white satin armchairs, lacquered, Ming dynasty Coromandel screens were grouped, whose silver cranes and dragons glinted beneath crystal chandeliers. Banks of sofas were piled with velvet cushions and heavy gold drapes framed the long windows. Long, smoky Venetian mirrors turned the guests into Mondrians and oriental tables were clustered with silver vermeil boxes, bronze animals and a gold-plated frog. The guests at Chanel's salons – international socialites, playwrights, poets, politicians and artists, members of the *haut monde* – were just as gilded. Jean Cocteau was a regular. Salvador Dali came frequently. Winston Churchill was known to call in.

Clara caught sight of her elongated image and thought how easy it was to change a perspective. Being here, in this looking-glass world, had a transformative effect on the guests. Just like certain actresses who, on the street, seemed as unremarkable as any waitress or shop assistant, yet were transformed into astonishing beauties once they stepped in front of the camera, so these elegant people might have existed in a different universe from the anxious crowd outside. They even smelt different. Most of the people you passed on the street, or pressed up close against on the Métro, smelt of old clothes, sweat-stained at worst, mothballed at best, but patched and mended and made good. Here there was a mingled aroma of fur, cigars, champagne and perfume, a haze of opulence dominated by the complex undertow of Chanel's own No.5, which the hostess liked to spritz on the coals in the fireplace.

'*Good manners and a fine disposition are the best beauty treatments.*' It might have seemed that way to Ovid, but that view wouldn't pass muster here. The women, long and lean in sumptuous confections of lace and tulle, with hair as sleek and polished as the pelts of the animals they wore, were made up to the nines. They held flutes of sparkling champagne and their antique Russian necklaces, star medallions and enamel cuffs were studded with glass stones according to Chanel's own fashion for costume jewellery, which mixed real gems with glass and paste, so that one didn't know what was real and what was fake. As far as the guests' clothes went however they were all genuine. Every dress was by Chanel; no one would have dared to wear a Schiaparelli suit or a dress by Patou, Lanvin or Mainbocher. The only fake in the room was Clara herself, who had always admired the sleek dresses and narrow jersey tailored suits that made Chanel's name, but would never be able to afford her prices. That evening she was wearing a green silk dress with a matching short jacket with pearl buttons made by her friend Steffi Schaeffer, a Berlin dressmaker who tailored costumes for the Ufa studios and ran up clothes for Clara at bargain rates.

Her hair was fastened at the back and fell to her shoulders in loose curls.

Sipping her champagne, she wondered if there was any way Chanel would be able to detect that Clara's lipstick was by her arch rival Elizabeth Arden. The manager of the Elizabeth Arden salon on the Kurfürstendamm, Sabine Friedmann, was another friend and often gave Clara samples of lipstick, mascara and the fabulous Eight Hour Cream. Indeed Sabine had sent a couple of messages recently asking her to call in. She hoped it was for something nice.

Across the room the mellifluous flow of French conversation was intercut with the jagged, polysyllabic growl of German. There was no need for Nazi uniforms here; the men in their impeccable Hugo Boss suits and mandatory swastika pins were identifiably Nazi government officials, but in Chanel's salon they were spared the looks of hostility or trepidation they met elsewhere in Paris. That must account for their boisterous good humour. The leader of the group was a handsome man with sandy hair swept off a high brow whom Clara recognized as Chanel's lover, Baron Hans Günther von Dincklage, better known as Spatz.

Though Chanel was famous for loving black and white, her love life was a distinctly grey area. Most of her relationships were with married men, including a long running affair with the Duke of Westminster, but the scandal which had recently leaked into the Paris newspapers concerned her liaison with Spatz, the special attaché at the German Embassy in Paris. Sections of the French press had waged war on Spatz, accusing him of building up a spy network throughout Paris reporting directly to the Gestapo, monitoring German exiles in Paris and passing on their addresses to Reinhard Heydrich. Watching Spatz now, possessed of the loud, confident demeanour of a German abroad, Clara could understand, just, what Chanel must see in him. She was known for liking winners, and Spatz, with his suave, playboy's manners, blond hair and distinguished looks, fitted precisely that template, not to mention the fact that he was more than a decade younger than her.

The man Spatz was talking to was his equal in good looks, with a broad, intelligent forehead and neatly parted tawny hair above eyes set widely apart. In his well-cut grey flannel suit he looked vaguely familiar and Clara racked her brains to place him. Was he a studio executive? A politician perhaps? She hoped very much that she would not be obliged to talk to him.

A waiter approached with a bottle of champagne and, unthinkingly, Clara held out her glass. The conversation that afternoon, and Guy Hamilton's request, had set her nerves on edge. It was not only the thought of what she was being asked to do, but the timescale involved – just weeks perhaps – that alarmed her. She took a sip of crisp bubbles and tuned into the conversation of the women beside her, who were arguing about the secret of Chanel's success.

'It's all down to tailoring,' said an exquisite blonde, wearing the gold lamé evening dress and short jacket that Chanel had showed for that year's collections. 'Chanel can make a woman look like a princess just through tailoring.'

'Except when she's a real princess,' said another.

There was general laughter. Everyone knew this was a reference to Elizabeth, the frumpy new queen of England, elevated as a result of Edward VIII's liaison with Wallis Simpson.

'In London Wallis and Elizabeth both used the Elizabeth Arden salon in Bond Street,' murmured another woman. 'The staff had a terrific job trying to keep them apart. Sometimes they had to pretend they were closed for redecoration when there was a clash. Anything rather than have that pair end up side by side.'

'Wallis can be most awfully amusing,' said a petite figure with a bob as sleek and black as a bird's wing sweeping across her cheekbones. 'When she was asked what Queen Elizabeth could do to boost British fashion, she said, "She could stay at home!"'

'The Duchess of Windsor is a loyal customer,' came an imperious voice. 'I won't tolerate gossip about her.'

Coco Chanel had materialized among the women as silently as

a cat, accompanied by a gust of Camel cigarettes. She had a hard face and taut neck, from which several ropes of pearls were hanging. Her skinny legs were bowed like a grasshopper and her intelligent, feline glance travelled across Clara's moss-green dress as though calculating to the last pfennig its provenance and likely cost.

'Good evening, Mademoiselle Vine,' she said softly, resting a silken claw briefly on Clara's arm. Then more loudly she addressed the women around her.

'I have always been a great admirer of the Duchess. When the Duke was courting Wallis, Winston Churchill came to dine here with me at the Ritz and begged me to exert my influence. He wanted me to persuade the King of England not to marry an American divorcée.' She gave a laugh, like the snort of an aggressive little bull. 'Winston burst into tears and said, "A king should never abdicate!" David should do his duty. Could I not persuade him to think again? I said, "Winston, are you asking me to stand in the path of true love?"'

'What would you have done, Mademoiselle Vine?' She switched to English, with a glance of cool scrutiny. 'Do you believe anyone should stand in the way of true love?'

'I think love has its place, but Churchill's right. There are times when duty is more important.'

'Ah, a realist then! I think you, Mademoiselle Vine, are like me. Passion fades. Only work remains. You need to be a realist when your work is peddling dreams. Because that's what we both do, isn't it? We peddle dreams. We put romance in people's lives, even when there's none in our own.'

'I suppose that's true.'

Chanel's feline smile was shot through with spite. 'I'm sorry I don't know your work. Perhaps you think me rude, but since my time in Hollywood I never go to the movies. I find them insufferably dull.'

Though Chanel had made the trek to America, her hopes of a

new life designing for Hollywood had fallen flat and she had returned to France with a lasting grudge against a film industry too philistine and shallow to appreciate her talents.

'As it happens, my new film is based on a novel. And a French novel at that. *Bel Ami.*'

'Ha! Well I approve of that, certainly. I like to think in my salon we are all of us, French, German and English, meilleurs amis. Like Herr Brandt here.'

Clara looked round to see a man watching her. She had noticed him earlier, in the thicket of guests, because he stood out from the polished and manicured crowd. Though as smartly dressed as the other men, in perfectly cut dark blue suit and tie, his powerful build and glowing tan made her think of the countryside and vigorous exercise, rather than the refined air of this couturier's perfumed parlour. He must have been in his late forties, with golden brown eyes, hair that was greying around the temples, a deeply cleft chin and little arrows of laughter crinkling his eyes.

He advanced and held out a hand.

'Max Brandt.'

'Clara Vine.'

'Herr Brandt is a cultural attaché at the German Embassy.'

'How interesting,' said Clara politely. 'I imagine that means an awful lot of opera.'

He chuckled and swept a lock of hair from his brow. 'Indeed. But we must all perform our duty for the Fatherland, no matter how arduous. Besides, sometimes only opera can make our German language sound as lovely as French.'

Clara, who often thought that sounds had their own colours, imagined Brandt's voice as a rich, chocolate brown. He had the languid, easy demeanour of a man secure in his own attractiveness and well used to the company of women. His expression had a subtle sparkle to it, as though he knew already who she was. Perhaps he had seen one of her films, Clara thought. Detecting her schoolgirl French, he switched to German and raised his voice against the dance music that had started up in the background.

'Can I ask what brings you here?'

'I'm making a film. With Willi Forst. It's called *Bel Ami*.'

'Maupassant, eh? Do you have official clearance for that? It's hard to imagine our Propaganda Minister favouring a film whose hero is a lying cheating womanizer.'

Laughter danced in his eyes but Clara dipped her head. Jokes about the notoriously womanizing minister were dangerous.

'Perhaps Doktor Goebbels hasn't read the script.'

'Don't all scripts have to gain his approval? Besides, I thought nothing escaped his eyes.'

'Maybe he admires Maupassant.'

'Possible,' he nodded, pretending to consider this. 'And of course, romance is a keen interest of his.'

'I'm sorry?'

'Romanticism. His doctoral thesis was on the German Romantics, I recall.'

Brandt smiled, and Chanel chose the moment to intervene sinuously. 'Mademoiselle Vine is here this evening on the recommendation of Madame Goebbels.'

A frisson of surprise passed across Max Brandt's face at this information. He had just made fun of Goebbels' womanizing, only to discover that the woman in front of him was on friendly terms with the Propaganda Minister's wife.

Chanel, however, seemed to delight in his faux pas.

'Magda has entrusted Mademoiselle Vine to collect a special package of my perfume. If you wait here, I'll go and fetch it.'

Brandt took a deep drag of his cigarette and smiled.

'So our Culture Minister's wife prefers a French scent? I thought the Minister was most strict about a perfume's provenance?'

That much was true. Goebbels was frequently delivering radio diatribes about how buying foreign cosmetics meant robbing the German Volk. He himself was generally preceded by a blast of

Scherk's Tarr pomade, a citrussy blend made by one of Berlin's biggest perfumiers, whose smell always provoked in Clara a Pavlovian shudder.

Clara surveyed Max Brandt warily.

'I would have thought perfume, of all things, was free of nationality.'

'You're right, of course. It's a holy thing. Comes from the Latin actually, *per fumus*, by means of smoke.' He exhaled, as if to illustrate his point. 'Perfume once meant the sacred incense in temples but it's rather more debased now, I fear. Did you know they make civet out of the musk of a wild cat? It's pretty disgusting, isn't it? Strange how something so rank can be transformed into something so alluring.'

Clara focused on his swastika tiepin. 'But then people do sometimes find the most repugnant things appealing.'

'I suppose you're right. And perfume's power has nothing to do with sweetness. Apparently, it works on the brain in the most extraordinary way – it stimulates olfactory memory. That's the part which lies in the deepest part of the brain and connects with our primal drives. So you see, perfume unleashes our most primitive desires.'

'How funny. Perfume always seems so sophisticated to me. I love the words they use. Ambergris, attar, wormwood. Wormwood, especially.'

'Yes! I've always thought that too. But those words don't work so well in German – you have to say them in French. Like your own perfume. *Soir de Paris.*'

Clara regarded him, astonished.

'You can tell?'

'But of course.'

Then he laughed. 'Don't look like that. I can't really tell a thing. The only reason I recognized *Soir de Paris* is that someone I know used to wear it. It's sweet. It suits you. And it's somewhat appropriate, in the circumstances.'

Responding to the gramophone music, some of the couples had cleared a space on the parquet floor and begun an impromptu dance. Brandt looked round.

'I wonder, would you permit me?'

Without waiting for an answer, he reached for her waist and drew her towards him. The imprint of his hand, firm against the flimsy silk of her dress, was suddenly at the centre of her consciousness. The music was hypnotic and her body fitted perfectly into the rhythm of his own, the more easily because he was a natural dancer. As she moved beside him, Clara felt the champagne spreading like a warm tide through all the veins of her body, relaxing her and softening the edges of the world. Normally she refrained from drinking; it only let down her guard, and in most situations it was far too dangerous to lower her defences. But the mere fact of being in Paris had induced a certain recklessness and she had already downed two glasses of Chanel's Pol Roger. She pressed closer to Max Brandt. His hand rested on her back in a way that would have seemed erotically possessive, if it wasn't merely customary. Not for the first time, Clara wondered how dancing ever came to be seen as an empty convention of polite society, rather than the tantalizing, sensuous experience it was.

'Perhaps I spoke a little hastily earlier,' he murmured. 'About our Culture Minister.'

'Don't worry. If you can't relax at a party . . .'

'Quite so. And our hostess is good at getting people to relax. She likes us to shed our defences so we render up better gossip. She sees it as a challenge. Whenever I come here I go away wondering what indiscretions I've committed.'

'A few glasses of Pol Roger must help that.'

'It's true. Perfume's not the only expensive substance Chanel understands. She's an expert practitioner in the use of champagne. She has a saying, "I drink champagne on only two occasions; when I'm in love, and when I'm not."'

Clara laughed. 'I wonder which it is tonight?'

Brandt nodded his head in the direction of Spatz, whose head was bent close to Chanel's, in intimate conversation.

'Can't you guess?'

'Your fellow attaché, I presume.'

'We both work at the Embassy but our paths don't often cross. I'm not sure Spatz shares my tastes.'

'Your tastes?'

'In opera and so on.'

'Who's that other man he was talking to?'

Clara nodded at the man in the grey pinstripe, who had seemed vaguely familiar.

'That's Schellenberg. SS Hauptsturmführer Walter Schellenberg, to be precise. Ever heard of him?'

Clara shook her head.

'That's good. You don't want to have heard of him.'

'Why's that?'

He smiled. 'It doesn't matter. I'd rather talk about you. So you're a friend of Frau Doktor Goebbels'?'

Clara sensed him trying to place her, to gauge her status in the Nazis' social hierarchy. It was unusual for actresses to befriend the Propaganda Minister's wife. Usually they were too busy trying to escape the clutches of her husband.

'More of an acquaintance. I modelled for her Fashion Bureau when I first came to Germany from London. My father's English, you see, and I grew up there.'

'You're English?'

Surprise hardened his voice. His eyes held a flicker of suspicion at discovering she was not what he thought.

'Half English, half German,' she clarified. 'My mother was born in Hamburg but she left for England at the age of twenty-two. She was a concert pianist. My father went to Germany on holiday and fell in love with her when he saw her playing Brahms.'

'What a romantic story.'

'I suppose so,' she replied. It wasn't in fact. Though it had started well, her parents' marriage had been far from happy ever after. Rows and silences had punctuated their relationship for years as her father's need to control clashed like a harsh bow against her mother's highly strung nature.

'What about you, Herr Brandt? Is your wife here?'

She sensed him stiffen.

'A less romantic story, I'm afraid. My wife is no longer with me.'

'I'm sorry.'

'You needn't be. She's certainly not. Gisela found the appeal of an instructor at the Grunewald Riding School an infinitely more exciting prospect than travelling the capitals of Europe as the wife of a cultural attaché.'

He shrugged and smiled down at her, moving lightly, and swaying closely to the music. Clasped in his arms, Clara felt at once soothed, and at the same time intensely alive.

'But you, Miss Clara Vine, agree with Chanel.' His voice was a teasing murmur in her ear. 'You're a realist, like her. You think we should all put love firmly on one side when duty calls.'

Clara laughed. 'That's hardly what I said!'

'Don't be ashamed, it's an admirable thought. In these difficult times, duty must drive us. Though as Paris is the city of lovers, I don't think you'd find it a popular sentiment here.'

'What I said was, there were times when duty is more important than love.'

He moved her round the floor with the lightest of touches. Was he aware that with every movement of his body, a current of heat ran through her, making the blood rush to her face? That he was provoking in her the most unseemly tide of excitement? Clara guessed that he was and she looked away, hoping he didn't see the blush suffuse her cheeks.

'And,' he whispered, 'is this one of those times?'

Hamilton's comment ran through her mind. *War could be just weeks away.*

'I suppose it is.'

'Some might say people must seize their pleasures where they find them. *Carpe diem.*'

She looked up at him and tried to keep herself from smiling.

'Some might. But at the moment my duty is to catch a train tomorrow for Berlin.'

'Are you leaving Paris?' He seemed dismayed. 'Surely not. Stay a while, won't you? There's so much to see.'

'I'd like to, but I can't.'

'It would be a crime to leave Paris without seeing the Louvre. You have to walk in the Left Bank and take coffee at the Dôme. Visit Fouquet's on the Champs Elysées. See the zoo at the Jardin des Plantes. There's an ape there who can make a charcoal drawing as well as a human. Surely you couldn't leave without seeing him?'

'I'm sure I'll come back sometime.'

The music finished and the couples began picking up their glasses and lighting cigarettes, but Brandt's hand remained on the small of her back. Clara felt the pulse of his body against her and could tell the dance had stirred him too.

'I wonder . . .' he began.

Clara glanced across the room to see Chanel watching them fixedly, a trace of irritation creasing her brow. She was holding a black and white package with intertwined double C, tied with a lavish amount of black ribbon.

Swiftly, Clara detached herself.

'Actually, I should leave now.'

'So soon?'

'I'm sorry. It's been a long day and I've a bit of a headache.'

'Where are you staying?'

'The Hotel Bellevue. It's not far.'

'Perhaps I could walk with you then?'

'No. Really, thank you, Herr Brandt, but I'm quite all right. The fresh air will clear my head.'

He kept hold of her hand for a moment, as if unwilling to let her go, or unable to believe she was leaving, and she had to give a little tug before he freed her fingers from his grasp.

Chanel proffered the package with a little smile.

'Tell Madame Goebbels this comes with my compliments. I'm flattered that she wants to try my No. 5. Please let her know that my perfume always tells a personal story, as well as a public one, so although my perfume is popular, for every woman it is unique.'

Accepting the package, Clara clattered down the stairs and nodded as the reception manager in his long cut-away coat bowed solemnly to her, as she passed through the Ritz's gilded doors.

She walked swiftly to the north of the Place Vendôme, making her way westwards through the streets towards the fourth arrondissement. The mingled fragrance of garlic and roasting meat blew across her path, and the cobbles beneath her feet, wet from a brief shower, were sequinned with light as she peered into court-yards behind high wrought-iron gates, past tall doors illuminated with iron lanterns with elaborate stone scrolling above them.

The poignant refrain of *J'Attendrai*, the hit song of the moment, snaked up from a basement bar.

'*J'attendrai, le jour et la nuit, j'attendrai toujours ton retour.*'

I will wait, every day and night, for your return. How perfectly Jean Sablon's melancholy lilt suited the mood of the time, Clara thought. Waiting was what everyone was doing now. There was a sense of time suspended and breath bated as Europe's leaders, like invisible chess players, bided their next move.

In the deserted marketplace of Les Halles the cleaners were sweep-ing the vestiges of cabbage leaves and rotten fruit left over from the day's trading and hosing down the floor. Clara loved this louche aspect to Paris, the blast of petrol and urine from the Métro entrance and the slick of oil on the pavement that reminded you how closely earthiness and glamour co-existed here. Huge wheels of cheese were being rolled onto a cart, the last traders were stack-ing boxes and a litter of dead chrysanthemums withered in a heap.

As she picked her way through the remnants of vegetation, a flock of starlings whirred balletically up into the glass and iron vault, and, turning to watch them, she noticed out of the corner of her eye the figure of Max Brandt rounding the corner about two hundred yards behind her, his shadow under the streetlamp stalking boldly ahead of him. At once, a bubble of laughter rose in her throat. Brandt was actually in pursuit of her! He was evidently a man who couldn't take no for an answer. He couldn't possibly have known that he was following a woman expertly versed in the arts of evasion. She could lose him in an instant if she wanted. But did she want to?

Quickening her step, Clara wove through the streets, doubling back on herself, choosing side streets and alleys. A current of exhilaration spurred her on, as she walked away up the Rue Quincampoix, and ducked into a tiny cul de sac containing a couple of shops and the back door of a bar. Easing herself into a doorway, she saw Brandt stride past, heard him hesitate, grunting with frustration as he looked from right to left, wondering how she could have disappeared. The heat made her skin prickle with sweat and she shifted a little in the darkness, stifling a laugh.

Suddenly, behind her, a door swung open and a ribbon of noise billowed out. A man was emerging from the bar backwards, manoeuvring a crate of empty bottles towards her. A blade of light, as sharp as any Gestapo lamp, sliced across Clara's face and at that moment Brandt glanced down the alley and saw her.

He smiled, and she couldn't help smiling too.

'Fräulein Vine.' He came slowly towards her, ambling now that he had his prey in his sights. 'When you wanted to clear your head, I hadn't imagined you intended to walk halfway around the city.'

'I enjoy a long walk.'

'It is refreshing, isn't it?'

He smiled and leant a hand on the wall beside her head, imprisoning her in the circle of his arms. Clara felt a familiar giddiness rise within her.

'In fact, I have an even more refreshing idea. Why don't you and
I go for a cognac at my apartment?'

'You forget. I need an early night.'

'Of course. What if I promise not to detain you too long?'

His hand brushed lightly along her arm. An electric thrill ran
the length of her body and her pulse quickened. Brandt was right;
she did find him attractive and he knew it. Perhaps a man like him
assumed that women would fall at his feet. Or maybe he thought
that an actress on her own in a foreign city for a single evening
would be an easy target. He was not to know that Clara would not
dream of succumbing to the approaches of a Nazi bureaucrat. If
indeed a bureaucrat was what he was. She thought again of
Hamilton's comment. *Steinbrecher says the Gestapo's pretty well
entrenched in Paris now. Heydrich has an extensive network of informers
in place.*

'I don't think my boyfriend would like that very much.'

Brandt recoiled visibly and straightened up.

'A boyfriend? You didn't mention him. Is he here, or back in
Berlin?'

'He's in Berlin.'

'Of course. Is he an actor too? Perhaps I know him. Can I ask
his name?'

Clara's mind went blank. The only two men she had ever cared
for – Ralph Sommers and Leo Quinn – were both English. In the
heat of the moment, she conjured the first name that entered her
head and gave him a rank for good measure.

'He's not an actor. His name is Sturmbannführer Steinbrecher.'

It worked. The seductive nonchalance of Brandt's face vanished
and he placed his hands in his pockets. He lit a cigarette and
inhaled, continuing to scrutinize her all the while.

'Is that so? Well, if you won't come to bed with me, Clara Vine,
perhaps you'll come to dinner?'

Clara wanted to. She had an urge so deep it surprised her. It had
been a year since she had had a dinner date with a man. There

were always actors, of course, at the studios, who would meet up at one of the popular restaurants in town, the Einstein Café or Borchardt's or Lutter und Wegner's, but a dinner date, with a single man, who did not want to dissect his own film career or fret about his future in the Reich Chamber of Culture, was a rarity. Yet now was not the time and besides . . . there was something about Brandt that felt not quite right. Clara had a sixth sense that there was more to him than met the eye. Chanel's salon was full of Nazi agents and she feared a trap.

'I'd like to, Herr Brandt. Believe me, I would. But I leave at six in the morning and I don't want to miss my train.'

'It wouldn't do to be stuck here in Paris, you mean?'

'I mean I do genuinely need to get some sleep.'

'Perhaps we'll meet again in Berlin then.'

'Maybe.'

'Could I not tempt you to stay? Just a day? We could see the Mona Lisa, the only woman in Paris more inscrutable than you.'

She smiled.

'The Tour d'Eiffel? Montmartre?'

She shook her head. 'Maybe another time.'

'What about the artistic ape in the zoo? The one who makes beautiful drawings?'

'I'm sorry.'

'Auf wiedersehen, then.'

Taking her hand, he raised it to his lips and kissed each knuckle in turn. The gesture caused a soft, melting sensation deep inside her, so that for a moment she longed to raise her own lips to his mouth in response, but instead she steeled herself to keep her face down as Brandt lifted his hat to her and turned away.

Clara took the long way back to the Hotel Bellevue, almost losing track of time as she wandered the streets, deep in thought. Partly, she wanted to savour the last vestiges of her time in Paris and partly, after the encounter with Max Brandt, she was too full of nervous energy to sleep. The moon hung over Paris like one of Chanel's own pearls, its soft brilliance blackening the sky around it. As she walked, Chanel's remark sounded in her mind. *I think you, Mademoiselle Vine, are like me.* Was Chanel suggesting that Clara, like her, was cynical and accustomed to using men for her own advantage? If so, then the accusation resonated uncomfortably. She had rejected an offer from the only man she had ever considered marrying, Leo Quinn, in order to commit herself to her life as an agent in Berlin. The last man she felt anything for had advised her to forget him. Was she destined to become one of those single women who rattled from affair to affair, finding nothing profound or lasting, searching for love the way an ageing actress searches for parts, sleeping with whichever handsome Nazi diplomat came her way? Or did Chanel think a 'realist' meant forgetting your country and your loyalties and siding with whoever might be a winner?

And yet, she thought, perhaps you should take pleasure wherever you found it, in case it never came again. Sometimes you passed love like a blossoming tree, without properly noticing it, hurrying on to a future where you imagined that it would be in endless supply, not realizing that you had already bypassed your entire chance of happiness.

Clara stopped, and gave herself a mental shake. Chanel was right about one thing. She was growing cynical about her chances of finding enduring love. But that didn't mean she was not prepared to defend everything else that she held dear.

When she got back there was a bouquet waiting for her at the reception desk. It was a lavish bunch of roses, papery white petals with a soft blush at their hearts. Clara closed the door of her room behind her and removed the note that was tucked in the tissue paper.

Dinner in Berlin.

That was all. She rested the petals for a moment against her cheek and inhaled their sharp fragrance. It was intense and delicate, with an edge of dew-drenched gardens and freshly cut grass. Then she took the flowers over to the basin and stripped the petals methodically one by one, until a heap of bruised shapes littered the porcelain beneath. But there was no listening device inside. Nothing suspicious at all. Just roses.

Chapter Five

Berlin

'He fixes the horoscopes, you know.'

Steffi Schaeffer nodded towards Clara's copy of the *Berliner Tageblatt* and gave a sniff more robust than seemed possible for a woman of such refined appearance, in her pale grey linen skirt and jacket, with a silk flower in her lapel.

'Who does?' asked Clara.

'Goebbels,' said Steffi, scornfully. 'He tailors them. He likes people to think that everything's going well. He orders them to print lines like *A successful and happy day. Germany is a land of smiles!* Ha! Has he looked at the faces in the streets recently? You don't notice many smiles there.'

Clara glanced out of the window at the street below. She was back in Berlin all right, and just as Steffi said, a single glance at the citizens was better than any horoscope at predicting the general mood. The sultry heat had not broken and worry whipped the streets like a dry summer wind. Most people darted along in a hurried way, as if on urgent business, heads down, trying not to attract attention. Most likely the people in the street below were heading home because they were Jews served with a curfew and must perform all necessary tasks within daylight hours or risk arrest.

The two women were in a small studio with a scruffy, pock-

marked façade, north of the Hackescher Markt in the Scheunenviertel. This quarter had been the centre of Jewish life in Berlin
for centuries. Its narrow streets were the first port of call for
Ostjuden refugees fleeing from the east and it was now the hub
of Berlin's textile trade. Shafts of light from the high windows
illuminated a room dominated by a large wooden table, crowded
with rolled bolts of vivid cloth, scissors, pins and kaleidoscopic
spools of cotton. Tailors' dummies stood around like ghostly
guests in half-finished finery, and hat stands bore toques, turbans,
pillboxes and tip-brimmed hats in felt, flowers, feathers and pastel
braided straw. It was a place of disguise and concealment, which
was fitting considering that Steffi Schaeffer's other role was as part
of a resistance network helping Jews to leave Germany. Clara had
never discussed this aspect of Steffi's secret life with her, but her
friend Bruno Weiss, the painter, had secured a false passport and
travel documents to Switzerland courtesy of this elegant and popular woman.

Outside, a passage led off from the street to a dingy courtyard
containing a patchwork of workspaces and storage areas occupied
by tailors and cloth sellers. Stalls on the pavement sold ribbons and
buttons and the shops were largely selling clothing, stockings and
shoes. On the street side many of the shop fronts were painted
with a white J, as well as obscene cartoons, six-pointed stars and
pictures of Jews being hanged, a decoration for which they had
roving bands of stormtroopers to thank, or sometimes brigades of
Hitler Youth sent out on Saturday mornings with paint pots and
brushes.

Clara turned back to Steffi, who was at that moment darting
around her dress with a mouthful of pins, adjusting the hem.

'I thought Goebbels took horoscopes really seriously,' she said.
'He and Hitler often consult the horoscope of the Third Reich
when they're planning policy.'

'He does,' said Steffi. 'He even loves Nostradamus. He says that
Nostradamus predicted German troops would march to the Rhine

and occupy Vienna and now he's saying that Nostradamus predicts Hitler will triumph in the Sudetenland too. The destiny of the Third Reich is written in the stars, though that doesn't stop Goebbels from giving it a helping hand.'

She pursed her mouth and jabbed the pins into the cushion on the table. 'But then I suppose none of us knows what's coming so it may as well be Goebbels as anyone else.'

A tough life and the loss of her husband five years ago, not to mention nights of sleepless anxiety since, had etched hard lines on Steffi's face, yet she was still a beautiful woman in her mid-thirties, petite, with dark blonde hair, sharp, elegant cheekbones and eyes of violet blue. Her talents as a dressmaker had won her steady work from the costume department of the Ufa studios, until the Aryanization measures introduced by Goebbels outlawed Jews from working there. As a Jew on her mother's side, Steffi was barred from working in any part of the Reich Chamber of Culture and now the commissions she had from society women were drying up too.

She stretched the cornflower-blue cotton for Clara's dress between thumb and forefinger.

'It's hard enough to get the material with this textile shortage, so I can't think why you want to spoil it by making it look like a dirndl,' she said, curling her lip at the square, low-cut neckline. 'It's not your style at all. You always prefer something elegant.'

'It's not a dirndl. It's just a little lace at the neck. Besides, I'm going to be working in Munich. They like things a little more traditional down there.'

'Well, I've done my best to give this dress a Marlene Dietrich twist.'

Steffi made the final stitch on the hem and began to fold the dress up.

'Thank you, Steffi. And for the lovely green silk dress. You'll never guess – I meant to tell you – I wore it to the salon of Coco Chanel.'

Steffi Schaeffer widened her eyes and laughed, displaying even, white teeth. 'Coco Chanel saw my work! I can't believe it! I would have loved to have been there. Perhaps she could give me some commissions!'

'I assume things are getting worse?'

Steffi shrugged. 'Of course. Most of my regular customers are going elsewhere now. On the other hand, in the past few weeks I've found a new income stream.'

Clara tilted an inquisitive head and Steffi hesitated, obeying a deep, instinctive caution, until their eyes met and she confessed, 'It's a new type of tailoring I'm doing. Since the latest announcement.'

'Which one is that?'

Since the introduction of the Nuremberg laws three years ago, the lives of Jews in Germany had grown ever more circumscribed. They were no longer allowed to marry gentiles, or even call themselves citizens. In recent months, however, the daily stream of restrictions had gathered pace. Almost every day there would be a fresh encroachment on Jewish freedom announced in the upper right-hand side of the newspaper front pages. Jews could no longer practise medicine or law. They could not hold bank accounts. Their cars were issued with Jewish licence plates and all too often Jews with cars were called to report to the police station and when they were released, their cars remained in custody. Just that week Jews had been told they would all be photographed and fingerprinted and issued with new ID cards.

The escalation in tension was visible everywhere. In June shops with Jewish owners had been freshly plastered with smears of 'Jew' all over the walls and doors, shop fronts smashed and shopkeepers forced to pick up the glass of their smashed windows with their own bleeding hands. Restaurants known to admit Jews were raided and their customers taken away in Gestapo trucks.

'This month all non-Aryans had letters ordering them to give up their jewellery to the state. They have to take everything to the nearest police station and hand it over. Can you believe it? The thieves! My friend asked for a receipt and the cop said, "What do you want a receipt for? You won't be seeing these again in your lifetime".'

'So what's this new tailoring you're doing?'

'Simple.' Steffi walked across to a tailor's dummy on which hung a coat of checked tweed and drew it back to reveal the lining.

'You know how we sometimes put pfennigs in the lining? So it hangs properly? Well, this time it's not pfennigs. It's a little more valuable.'

She ran her neat, painted fingernails down the navy satin and found an edge which had been left unsewn. Tucking her fingers inside, she withdrew a pearl necklace and from the lined flaps of the pockets, she picked out a pair of ruby and diamond earrings.

'If you need to leave the country, you're going to need to take your coat. Or your jacket, or your suit. This way, you can take your jewellery too.'

Clara shook her head in admiration.

'But it has to be done by a professional so the seams lie flat. See? It's no good botching the job, the Gestapo aren't stupid. I do hats too.' Steffi gestured at a hat stand on the table. 'They're even better because, look—' She ran her fingers along the intricate folds, where the raffia was stitched into rivulets. 'They're stiffer. They have more detail. They're harder to unpick.'

She pulled over a creation of plum velvet, with a scrap of veiling, and removed a rosette from the crown. In the cavity beneath glistened a gold ring.

'Everyone who leaves gets searched. The guards on the trains take the soles out of shoes and they even squeeze tubes of toothpaste looking for valuables, so it pays to be very careful if you're going to conceal something.'

'It's so cleverly done.'

Steffi shrugged.

'Women don't mind leaving everything else, but they won't

leave their jewellery. It's not just the value. It makes them feel beautiful. We all need that now.'

'I'm glad you've found some business.'

Steffi crossed her arms and frowned. 'Business? I'm not sure I'd call it that. Sometimes they pay me with a bit of butter or a few eggs. Sometimes, I do it for nothing. What's the point of money if it's going to be taken away from you?'

'I'm sorry. That was thoughtless of me. I didn't mean . . .'

'Don't worry.' She smiled. 'Besides, I'm not the only one with extra work. A friend of mine, Herr Feinmann, is a paper manufacturer and he says the demand for blackout cardboard has soared. He can't keep up with it. You know what that means.'

Clara did. Bomb shelters and blackout materials were on everyone's mind. Troops were visible on the street in ever greater numbers. Public buildings were being transformed into barracks.

Steffi looked at Clara intently. Though she knew no detail of Clara's real life, their four-year friendship meant they trusted each other implicitly.

'Last month they told us we have to change our names. Did you hear that? All Jewish passports will be stamped with a J and Jewish people who have names of "non-Jewish" origin have to add Israel or Sara to their given names. Gentiles will be banned from giving their children Jewish names.'

'What? Like Joseph, you mean?'

They laughed, despite themselves, at the monstrous absurdity of Goebbels.

'Joseph is exempted. It's been declared an honorary Aryan name.'

Steffi's brave smile died and her voice hushed, even though there was no chance of them being overheard.

'It's dreadful, Clara. Every day people are being fetched from their homes and taken to Oranienburg or Buchenwald. They take away their belts and ties and shoelaces, and when they get there, they make them stand in the square all night with spotlights on them. A lot of the men round here spend the day dodging the

Gestapo. They stay with friends and their wives pretend that they're travelling. Everyone's leaving. Why wouldn't they? It's that or stay here and take poison. A woman I know killed herself just the other day, up in the West End. Everyone I know is trying to get to Palestine, or South Africa, or Italy. We're being forced to creep away from our homes like criminals.'

Clara had the impression that Steffi was only just holding herself together. That every day the knocks and the fear carved the lines a little deeper in her face.

'First the Nazis want you to leave, then they make it impossible for you to get out. People spend all day going to different embassies and all they do is learn the word "no" in twenty different languages. People turn up at the embassies with hundred-mark notes folded into their passports. They send baskets of fruit and flowers. But it never does any good. That's why I'm trying to help.'

'What can you do?'

Though Clara's voice was hushed, it still sounded unnaturally loud in the quiet of the workshop.

'I do what I can. There are several of us.' She bit her lip, and frowned at Clara. 'You must know.'

Clara did. They were called U-boats, the escapees, because of the sudden descent they made into the vast Berlin underground.

'There are houses all over Berlin, and further out. Some people are going into hiding, you know, sleeping in friends' basements, or moving from house to house. We all contribute what we can. Look here.'

She walked across to a wardrobe built into the wall and pushed at the back. The wooden panel gave way to reveal a further, narrow space, in which a series of uniforms hung.

'I have a friend – not a Jew – who owns a clothing company that is now obliged to work for the Wehrmacht. He knows how the uniforms are made, and how to make them up. They check everything, you know. The way the cloth is cut, the precise location of the buttonholes. They leave nothing to chance.'

'What about you, Steffi? Are you trying to leave?'

'I can't.' Steffi folded her arms and looked at Clara resolutely. 'There's my mother to think of. I couldn't leave her.'

Clara had met Steffi's mother once, a smiley woman with snow-white hair and eyes clouded by cataracts, confined to a chair by a bout of polio.

'Even if I could go, what would happen to Mutti? There's no one to look after her. Except my brother of course and he's hopeless. He says, "We Jews made it through the Red Sea. We'll make it through the Brown shit." Mutti can't even feed herself so I'm staying put. But it's Nina I'm worried about.'

'How old is she now?' Clara recalled Steffi's only child, an anaemic-looking girl with narrow shoulders whom she had met when collecting a dress from Steffi's home. Like her mother, Nina was dressed beautifully in neatly pressed, hand-stitched blouse and handmade skirt, but unlike her blonde mother, Nina was dark, with her father's sallow skin and golden brown eyes. It was those eyes Clara remembered most, taking in every detail of her face and clothes, hesitating before eating the cake that Clara had brought. Nina reminded Clara of herself at that age, observing the world without intruding on it, creating an elaborate interior universe behind a self-effacing façade.

'She's ten. And she's different from other children. It's probably because she's an only child. Or she lost her Vati. In some ways she's really advanced for her age, but in other ways she's ... I don't know. Too naïve. Or rebellious.' Steffi gave a quick, instinctive glance around her.

'The other day she got in trouble. She defaced a cabinet of *Der Stürmer* on her way home from school. They put the stands deliberately right outside the schools so the children see them and have to walk past them every day, but Nina decided to kick an entire cabinet down.'

Despite herself, Clara gasped. *Der Stürmer* was the Jew-hating Nazi newspaper whose pages were dominated with stories of how criminal and defective the Jews were, and editorials on how to resolve the Jewish question. The idea of any child – let alone a Jewish child – defacing one of its Stürmerstands was alarming.

'Thankfully, one of the kinder teachers saw, and the matter hasn't gone any further. But when I talk to Nina about it, she just looks at me and I can't tell what's going on behind those eyes. She's unfathomable, even to me. In fact, most of all to me. What I would really like is to send her away, but lone children are not allowed to leave Germany unaccompanied. And that's not all . . .'

Steffi took Clara's hands in her own and lifted her face. Her normally calm hands were shaking, and her eyes glistened with unshed tears.

'I'm nervous, Clara. I think they're planning something round here. We've had bands of stormtroopers walking around the streets for months, painting on the walls and kicking in the windows, but there's a man – one of the Blockwarts here – who said something bad was coming. He has contacts in the Gestapo and he took me aside the other morning and said, "They have something planned for the Jews. They're drawing up lists of names and properties. No one will be able to help you." He was doing me a favour by advising me to go as soon as I could.'

'Something planned?'

'That's what he said. Why does nobody do anything? Sometimes, I think to myself, when all of us Jews have gone, what will the Nazis do? What will they do with their hatred then?'

Steffi turned away to busy herself parcelling up Clara's new summer dress and Clara realized that she simply couldn't talk any more.

'I'd better be off. I'm meeting my godson at the Lehrter Bahnhof.'

There was no way she was going to tell Steffi that her godson had been on a KdF cruise. The idea of some Germans heading off on sunny foreign jaunts while others did everything in their power to leave the country only to be obstructed by bureaucracy at every level was simply too grotesque.

She touched Steffi lightly on the arm. It was hard to show the sympathy she felt, or the gratitude that Steffi had trusted her enough to confide her dangerous secret.

'I'm sure that Blockwart was scaremongering. About something happening. It'll be OK.'

But secretly she thought that was about as credible as the horoscopes in the *Berliner Tageblatt*.

She was late, of course. At the Lehrter Bahnhof the train from Hamburg had already arrived and the clatter of disembarking passengers rose high into the crisscrossed steel arches of the vaulted roof. Clara searched frantically for the two figures in the crowd.

Physically brown as a nut and bursting with health, Erich looked just how Clara expected him to look after two weeks in the sole company of his grandmother. Mutinous, grumpy, bordering on truculent. The interests of a widow in her seventies had little in common with those of a teenage boy and old Frau Schmidt's desire to see her grandson avoid the kind of tragedy that had befallen his late mother tended to express itself in a perpetual low-level nagging. The nagging was born of love, of course, but that didn't make it any easier for Erich, and Clara knew that both of them would be longing to escape each other's company for a while. The pair of them lived in Neukölln, in an apartment at the end of a long corridor stinking of cabbage stew and drying nappies.

'Here, let me take that, Frau Schmidt.' Clara heaved a couple of bags from the old lady and looked around for a porter. Frau Schmidt was stout, with swollen ankles and knuckles like walnuts. Whenever she looked at those hands Clara remembered Helga talking of her mother returning from the hospital where she worked as a nurse each night, her apron dark with blood and her hands raw with scrubbing.

'Why don't I take Erich off for a meal and let you get back home?'

Her face lit up. 'That would be kind, Fräulein Vine.' Though she had known Clara since the death of her daughter five years ago, and accepted a monthly payment to help with Erich's costs, old Frau Schmidt still found it difficult to address Clara informally. 'It will give me a chance to unpack and Erich can tell you all about our excitements.'

Clara saw the old lady into a taxi and, turning brightly to Erich, took the smaller of his bags from him and headed for the tram.

'What would you say to tea at the Konditorei Schilling?'

The Konditorei Schilling on the corner of Koch Strasse and Friedrichstrasse was their new favourite place, largely because of its famous selection of excellent cakes, which were irresistible to Erich's sweet tooth. A long counter displaying baked goods and pastries led to a series of tables and chairs at the back. Erich would devote several minutes of serious scrutiny to the trays of cinnamon-speckled Apfeltorte, syrupy honey cakes and towering chocolate cake layered with cream before making his choice. They were not as delicious as they used to be – sugar was in short supply and the chocolate cakes were layered with a peculiar artificial cream that tasted like petrol – but they still looked splendid, and it was a pleasure for Clara to have Erich to herself.

They established themselves with a hot chocolate and Butterkuchen for Erich and a glass of tea and Apfelkuchen for Clara, but Erich kept his eyes lowered and fiddled with his spoon, tapping it annoyingly on the side of his cup.

'So tell me everything,' said Clara, partly to stop the tapping.

'Not much to tell,' he shrugged, continuing to tap his spoon.

Clara tried to contain her irritation and focus on the pleasure of being with her godson. 'Tell me anyhow. I want to hear everything. You don't look like someone who's just had the holiday of a lifetime.'

'It was all right.'

'Just all right?'

'OK. It wasn't then.'

Erich frowned and squinted up at her. When she had first become involved in Erich's life, as a promise she made to his dead mother, Clara had seen Helga in him all the time. But now it was just the occasional flash of his sceptical, dark eyes that reminded her of his mother and when that happened Clara felt a pang of sorrow at what Helga had missed and a renewed resolve to look after Erich as well as his mother would have wanted. They talked about Helga less and less now, and Clara found herself hesitating to mention her name, in case Erich should be upset.

Erich paused, as if assessing whether to confide in her, then frowned.

'There was this woman – lady. She was very friendly. She had the cabin next to mine. We got talking because of you actually.'

'Me?'

'She was interested in film. She had this collection of cigarette cards, like the one I have, only much better.'

Cigarette cards were a craze that crossed all age groups. All the tobacco companies did them, with subjects ranging from cars and aeroplanes, to flowers or film actors. The idea was to acquire a complete set, and in the process to smoke a lot of cigarettes. One brand, Reemtsma, had recently produced a series of Ufa actors and Clara's own photo had been included.

'She had the one you did for *The Pilot's Wife* and I told her you were my godmother.'

Clara smiled.

'Sounds nice. What was her name?'

'Ada Freitag. But that's not the point.' Erich traced the pattern on the table's linoleum surface, as if the path of its shiny tessellations might help him comprehend the sequence of events. 'The thing is . . . she disappeared.'

'Disappeared?' Clara cocked her head curiously. A lot of people were disappearing right now. But not from cruise ships in the middle of the Atlantic Ocean.

'Where was the ship docked at the time? Do you think she just wandered off and didn't get back in time?'

Tightly, he said, 'It wasn't in port. It was at sea. I think she fell overboard.'

'Oh, Erich, that's terrible.' Clara reached a hand across to him. 'That can't be true. Are you sure?'

Erich shifted his arm slightly to detach Clara's hand.

'I don't know. One moment she was there talking to me, the next she said she had something to do and could I look after her things. But she never came back.'

Clara's mind leapt to the obvious conclusion. The girl had formed a romantic attachment with another passenger and spent the remainder of the voyage in his bunk. It was a holiday, after all, though Erich might be too innocent to understand the concept of a holiday romance.

'I think,' she said tentatively, 'that perhaps Ada might have met a friend, and decided to spend the rest of the cruise with them. Maybe a boyfriend.'

'I'm not a baby, Clara. I thought that too. Of course I did. But she never came back to her cabin. And all her belongings in her cabin disappeared too.'

'Perhaps she moved into another cabin.'

'I wondered that. So I thought I'd go to the captain and ask him.'

'Goodness.' Clara quailed at the thought of her godson interrogating the ship's captain. It was entirely in character. Though small for his age, Erich was assertive, and possessed a stubborn inclination to stand up to authority. He had inherited it from his mother and in her case it had proved fatal.

'Are you sure you should have bothered the captain?'

'Of course. He's in charge of the ship, isn't he? He ought to be worried if one of his passengers just vanishes. Anyway, he was

happy to help. He told me she had disembarked at Funchal. He
even showed me this ship's log, with all the names and dates on it,
and I could see that it was written there: Fräulein Ada Freitag.
Disembarked Funchal, 23rd August.'

'So that's the explanation.'

'No.' Erich frowned, impatient for Clara to keep up. 'Because
I know that wasn't true. I talked to Ada after we left Madeira.'

'Are you sure?'

He gave her a brief, withering look.

'I asked Oma about it, but she said the ship's captain knew best.
And after I'd asked a couple of times, she got cross and refused to
talk about it any more. So I decided on a plan.'

'Which is?'

'It involves you. Do you think, Clara, you could ask someone?'

'Me! Who could I ask?'

'I don't know. Journalists. You meet them. They interview you.
There must be someone.'

Clara wanted to ask Erich why the fate of a chance acquaintance, even if it was a pretty young woman, should matter so much
to him, but the answer was staring her in the face. Or rather it was
sitting before her, a bundle of tempestuous adolescent emotion, his
boyish features becoming sharper, and his body growing so swiftly
that the HJ uniform she had so recently invested in would all too
soon need to be replaced.

'I'll see what I can do.'

His face softened in relief. 'Thank you, Clara. I knew I could
count on you. Especially as she was so interested in you. I think
she was a fan.'

Clara saw Erich onto the U-Bahn back to his grandmother's apartment in Neukölln, and then headed down Friedrichstrasse,
puzzling over his story. The fact that the woman's departure was
noted in the ship's log seemed pretty conclusive, but it was not like
Erich to make a mistake like that. He had an excellent memory

and a sharp mind for figures. Above all, Clara was sorry that the mix-up should have spoiled his first foreign trip. There was no telling when he would get another chance to travel abroad, and God forbid it should be in the cabin of a Luftwaffe plane. Erich never stopped talking about his ambition to begin pilot training the moment he reached seventeen.

Sunk in thought, she received a sharp blow in the ribs as she collided with a man and apologized instinctively, or at least the English half of her did, even though it was she who had been jostled.

'I'm sorry.'

The man had a handsome face with a thin moustache. His lips twitched upwards in a ghost of a smile.

'You want to watch yourself, Fräulein.'

Clara frowned.

Why did no one have any manners these days? But then, perhaps it was absurd to mind about Berliners losing their manners when you considered everything else they were losing.

Chapter Six

There was always a small crowd of sightseers outside the Reich Chancellery in Wilhelmstrasse. Mostly they were tourists from out of town, hoping to catch the glimpse of the Führer that would form the highlight of their trip to Berlin. Hitler knew this, and when he was in Berlin he would often make an impromptu appearance on a first-floor balcony that had been added onto the building for precisely this purpose. He would emerge like a god on Mount Olympus, albeit a putty-faced god in brown uniform with a swastika armband, accepting the salutes of the crowd before ducking away again as the disembodied white gloves of SS guards, like stage magicians, closed the curtains behind him. That day, as the sky pressed down like a hard blue lid and a blast of heat rose from the pavement, the crowd was there as usual, but they looked clammy and less excitable. The sentries, rigid in their steel helmets and massive black boots, sweated through the seams of their uniforms as they stood outside the newly refurbished bronze double doors. The Chancellery was in the process of being extensively rebuilt by Hitler's favourite architect, Albert Speer, and this week it had gained another, unexpected decoration. Like all the other public buildings in this city, the roof had been fitted with slender anti-aircraft guns pointing menacingly up at the sky and, as if in response, a squadron of silver Luftwaffe planes flew directly overhead. Along with the bunkers and the bomb shelters now being dug, the belligerently billowing swastika flags and the detachments of soldiers marching along Unter den Linden in their high boots, everything suggested a city preparing for war.

Clara clicked along the road, saw the crowd and crossed to the eastern side of the Wilhelmstrasse, where the buildings cast welcome blocks of shade. The windows of the Propaganda Ministry, known to everyone as the Promi, had been opened and the faint clatter of typewriters could be heard, compiling the daily stream of orders and directives which reminded the nation's newspapers about the atrocities of the Czechs or reprimanded them for printing unhappy horoscopes. It was an oppressive, airless day. Not a whisper of breeze flickered the leaves on the linden trees. It was the kind of day to be in Berlin's great park, the Tiergarten, or farther out, walking by the Grunewald lakes or sunbathing on the silver sand of the Strandbad Wannsee, but sunbathing was the last thing on Clara's mind as she made her way back towards her apartment, a few streets beyond Nollendorfplatz. She had more important things to contemplate.

The more Clara pondered Eva Braun, the more she realized how little she knew about her. No more than a handful of facts. Eva came from Munich, where Hitler had first encountered her working in the shop of Heinrich Hoffmann, his official photographer. She was much younger than him, no more than twenty-six, Clara thought, but still the Führer considered her a pleasant enough companion for the opera and excursions to the Berghof, his retreat in the Obersalzberg mountains. Eva Braun came to Berlin sometimes, but Clara had never even glimpsed her. Magda Goebbels had dismissed her as silly, ill-educated and provincial and Emmy Goering said she liked cheap jewellery and perfume. To Clara, the more astonishing question was what such a young, and apparently ordinary, girl could have in common with a man like Hitler. How she could bear to be brushed from the public record, because Hitler had proclaimed himself married to the nation? And now Clara had been asked to get close to her. She had no idea how she would even meet the girl, let alone get to know her. It was a mission which seemed as fraught and difficult as scaling the cliffs of the Obersalzberg itself.

Turning into Winterfeldtstrasse, Clara quickly scanned the street. This kind of automatic scrutiny came as second nature to her now, one of a number of little habits like memorizing the numberplates of cars parked outside her apartment or counting the pedestrians she passed. Her impulse was to note anything unfamiliar, but today the long, leafy street of residential blocks, including her own ochre-painted nineteenth-century building with its heavy wooden front door, looked the same as ever. The only changes she detected were an advertisement for Leni Riefenstahl's latest film *Festival of Beauty*, featuring three young women in swimming costumes, that had been erected on a hoarding at the end of the road next to a poster in which Berlin's top illusionist Alois Kassner posed menacingly over a nubile brunette with the slogan *Kassner makes a girl vanish!* And there was a brand new swastika flag hanging on the pole outside the apartment door.

Nothing out of the ordinary.

Entering the dim hallway, and noting as always the single missing tile in the chipped chequerboard floor, Clara heard the familiar greeting from the cubicle of Rudi, the Blockwart.

'Heil Hitler! Fräulein Vine!'

Rudi, a fanatical old Nazi with a leathery complexion and a clutch of brown teeth, was in charge of the maintenance and caretaking of the apartment. His spine was severely bent from scoliosis, but he was still able to dart swiftly from his cubicle like some barnacled sea creature scuttling from its hole. Despite his inauspicious appearance, Rudi was a perfect example of the way that the Nazis managed to keep Berlin's four million residents under control while they were behind closed doors. The old man maintained a relentless scrutiny of the residents of the block, and reported the slightest deviation from proper behaviour to the authorities. Even

activities not in themselves illegal could still suggest potential crim-
inality to Rudi's luridly suspicious mind. Excessive typewriting
might imply the production of resistance pamphlets, and tantalizing cooking smells could mean the resident had been benefiting
from black market food. Recently, Clara suspected that the arrest
of Herr Kaufmann, the shy bachelor who worked as a fiction
reader at Ullstein publishers and occupied the apartment adjoin-
ing hers, had been prompted by a denunciation from Rudi about
his visits from young men. The vast majority of arrests for homosexuality came from local informers. Herr Kaufmann might no
longer be there, but the suspicion of his homosexuality lingered
like a stain and the other residents grew more cautious of Rudi's
all-encompassing gaze.

Though Clara was rarely able to avoid Rudi, she always ensured
that she was carrying something in both hands so she didn't have
to return the *Führergruss*. That day she had a rolled-up magazine
in one hand and her handbag in the other.

'Is that mail for me?'

She might just as well have asked what was in it too, given that
Rudi had almost certainly had a look. If ever her letters escaped
the attentions of the censors, which was unlikely, they faced a
second censor in the person of Rudi. Clara knew he would not
hesitate to steam her post open if he thought it contained anything
incriminating.

'By the way, we have a new resident in the block. A Herr Engel.
A very pleasant gentleman. He has the apartment next to yours.'

'So Herr Kaufmann's not expected back?'

Rudi gave her a look which signalled that Herr Kaufmann
would be as welcome as a case of typhoid if and when he ever
made it out of the camp. Accepting her letters, Clara ascended in
the rickety elevator to the top floor, closed the door of her apartment behind her and felt her whole body relax.

This apartment was her refuge, the place where she tried to
instil a sense of security that was so lacking in the city outside. She

had laid thick rugs on the floor and painted the walls a soothing pale grey. Even in the heat of a stifling summer, it was cool. The narrow hall opened into a wide space, lined on one side with bookcases and on the other a large mirror reflected back the light from the window which looked over the crooked roofs towards Nollendorfplatz. There was a desk with a wobbly leg, a gramophone and a red velvet armchair, with a new English novel that her sister had sent her, *Rebecca*, lying invitingly open beside a pile of scripts. On the mantelpiece a signed photograph of the entire cast of *Es leuchten die Sterne,* Clara's most recent film, stood beside a picture of her late mother, and one of Erich aged six. At the times when she felt almost resigned to being alone, this place was her solace, as familiar to her as the face of an old friend. Even the air in the apartment was distilled with the fragrances that spelt comfort; from the row of herbs on the kitchen windowsill to the bowl of apples on the table and the tang of the tar melting on the asphalt outside.

Putting on the kettle and sitting at the kitchen table, she took out of her bag the identity cards she carried at all times. The grey, standard identity document certifying that she was Clara Vine, born 1907, with her fingerprint and photograph and the purple stamp of the Ministry of the Interior. The other was a red cardboard document with an eagle on the cover and inside an Aryan certificate, the *Ariernachweis,* confirming that Fräulein Clara Vine was a member of the Aryan race, possessing birth and baptismal records of her parents and grandparents and a genealogy table in which the Jewish ancestry of her mother and grandmother was replaced with Christian blood. It was a forgery, produced not by the government race office but by an underground printer in a basement in Wedding equipped with a variety of inks and papers, a knife and a set of stamps intricately carved from champagne corks. By day this man printed musical manuscripts and by night he risked execution working for British Intelligence. This document, which Clara carried with her everywhere, was the last communication she had received from Leo Quinn. It was tattered now, and dog-eared, but still essential. Her entire life in Germany, and her whole film career, depended on it. No one with Jewish blood could work in any part of the Reich Chamber of Culture, be it film, radio, theatre or newspapers. Every time she handled that document she thought of Leo. His presence still lingered in her life, the image of him always at the edge of her thoughts. The document, like the pale blue book of Rilke's poems he had left her, was yet another way that he had made her who she was.

But Leo was gone now, resettled in England, no doubt with a pretty wife in tow. And Ralph Sommers, the man she had met the previous year, wanted her to forget him. '*Your work matters more than personal happiness, Clara. It matters more than ever.*' By work, he didn't mean acting. Clara felt a sudden, painful shaft of longing and, sifting through her wallet, extracted a couple of photographs, one of her brother Kenneth in school uniform – grey shorts, blazer and cap – eyes squinting into the sun, grubby legs almost visibly twitching with an eagerness to escape, and the other of herself with Angela, three years older than Clara and far more beautiful. Where had it come from, the distance between them? They hadn't always been adversaries. As a child Clara had adored her, and Angela took her responsibilities in shepherding her younger sister seriously. She had taught her the piano and coaxed her at chess, giving up hastily when Clara started to beat her. Angela directed Kenneth and Clara in the plays they staged for their parents, and it was Angela who taught her always to carry a handkerchief stuffed in her left knicker leg, instructed her on applying foundation and eye shadow long before Clara was old enough to wear it, and who explained, albeit enigmatically, what happened on a girl's wedding night. Her description, though vague and couched in terms of Kenneth's dogs, provided Clara with a lot more information than any of her friends had at the time.

She sighed and turned at last to the thick, vanilla-coloured envelope, franked with the Big Ben logo of London Films which had come with her mail. Her fingers trembled slightly as she opened it. The immensity of the task ahead of her was still daunting.

Inside was a card with a perfectly bland instruction.

Dear Fellow Member of the Reich Chamber of Film,
    You are invited to audition with Herr Fritz Gutmann for the role of Sophia in Good King George, *to be made at the Bavaria Film studios at Geiselgasteig, Munich. Initial meetings will be held at the Artists' House on Lenbachplatz in Munich, 8th September. Please report to reception at 3 pm.*
    Heil Hitler!

Two days away! Clara's heart sank. She had never expected it would be so soon.

She flicked quickly through the rest of the mail. There was a postcard from Vienna with a photograph of Ringstrasse and the suggestion of a drink the following day. The card carried no signature but Clara instantly recognized the handwriting of Rupert Allingham, a British journalist who always dropped her postcards on his travels and never signed them. The other letter was a reminder from her friend Sabine, manager of the Elizabeth Arden salon on the Ku'damm, to pay a visit. Across the bottom of the card she had scrawled:

'*Please come soon, Fräulein Vine, it's important.*'

What on earth could be important about a session at the beauty parlour? People in the world of fashion and beauty seemed incapable of getting their priorities right. As if the whole business of creams and potions was anything other than utterly trivial at a time like this.

On the other hand, if she was attending an audition, it might be a good idea to arrive looking her best. And, as Clara never forgot, sexual allure was an essential weapon in her secret work. Lipstick, mascara and perfume were all important items in the toolkit of a female spy, and her favourite lipstick, Elizabeth Arden's Velvet Red, in its prettily engraved gold tube, was right down to a stub. However much the Führer might hate cosmetics, the female citizens of the Reich liked them even more at a time when new clothes were hard to come by. Yet lipstick, like coffee and butter and oranges, was getting scarcer and fresh supplies were difficult to find. On reflection, Clara resolved to visit the salon that afternoon.

Chapter Seven

Rosa Winter flinched and tried valiantly to shut her ears to the shrieking children in the adjacent room as she carried on with her typing. Secretarial duties were dull enough without children being brought into the office to disrupt everything. When their mother had arrived that morning for her interview, hands clamped on the shoulders of her offspring – two boys of around eight and ten years old – she had shrugged apologetically and Rosa had smiled and nodded towards the empty office next door. The boys had brought a board game with them, the mother explained, which would keep them quiet for at least twenty minutes. Instead it was having the opposite effect. The game was the current craze, *Juden Raus* and it looked fairly normal – in that it involved a dice and playing pieces in the shape of large pointed hats, with 'Jewish' faces on them – but in terms of the aggression it aroused it was more like a boxing match than a board game and every few moments the boys punctuated the air with cries of victory and howls of dismay. Rosa was developing a splitting headache. It would be distracting at any time, let alone at ten o' clock in the morning.

She sighed. She liked children, indeed she often identified with them, but she had no intention of having any of her own. Not yet, at any rate, or for a good long time. That was something she had never told anyone. It was not the sort of thing a twenty-five-year-old woman confessed in Germany in 1938, not out loud, not to friends, not even to her own parents. Not now, when children were the chief justification of a woman's existence and having more than four of them – being 'kinderreich' – was every woman's ambition. Not when being voluntarily childless was deemed 'deliberately harmful to the German nation', which sounded an awful lot like treason if you thought about it. And most of all, not if your workplace, this drab office packed with filing cabinets and smelling of carbolic and unwashed clothes, happened to be the very epicentre of the family in Germany, a veritable shrine to the place of women as housewives and mothers – the headquarters of the National Socialist Women's League, the NS Frauenschaft. Whose leader, installed within close barking distance in the office next to Rosa's, was Gertrud Scholtz-Klink, universally known as the Führerin, the most important woman in the entire Reich.

With six children of her own and ten million German women at her polish-free fingertips, the female Führer was described by Hitler as 'the perfect Nazi woman'. She wore her hair snaked round her head in braids, a field-grey uniform shirt buttoned to the neck and an expression like thunder, exacerbated by the fact that she was currently going through a divorce, because she deemed her country doctor husband insufficiently Nazified. Rosa sometimes wondered if Hitler himself was frightened of the Führerin, given that everyone else was. Rosa had met the Führer once. He had paid a visit to the office and talked about his mother and the importance of women to the future of the Fatherland. He was much less intimidating than the Führerin herself. He had a pudgy, pale face and strangely penetrating eyes that looked at you as though they were looking through you. He was so different from the shrieking figure on the platform she had seen on the newsreel, rattling away like a machine gun, that she could almost understand those women who were said to turn up at the Reich Chancellery offering to carry his baby. But not quite.

The only person who was certainly not scared of the Führerin was the SS-Reichsführer Himmler, who had responsibility for coordinating the activities of the Woman's Bureau at ministerial level because no women were allowed in Hitler's cabinet. Rosa had picked up the telephone once to Himmler and the sound of his soft, menacing rasp almost caused her to drop the receiver. The idea that he too might pop in for a courtesy visit was frankly terrifying. She couldn't help imagining Himmler with his moon face and receding chin standing over the desk, peering at her like an owl eyeing its prey, interrogating her about why she, Rosa Winter, was risking treason and actively weakening her nation by refusing to become kinderreich.

What Rosa did want, and had always wanted, was to become a journalist. She had no intention of following her elder sister Susi into marriage and downtrodden motherhood, especially not to a thuggish civil servant who was not averse to the occasional bout of wife-beating. After leaving school Rosa had taken a typing course in preparation, quickly became a skilled and fluent typist, and readied herself for an exciting career. Growing up in Berlin there had been a hundred newspapers – it was a city that loved journalism and Germany, her father often reminded her, had more newspapers than Britain, France and Italy put together. But after Hitler came to power in 1933, closing opposition papers and dragging the journalists off to concentration camps, the press grew cautious. The number of newspapers halved, and government directives on saving meat or mending socks had far more chance of getting into the news pages than murders or burglaries. To Rosa's dismay, getting a break as a journalist turned out to be next to impossible. She traipsed around the newspaper district for months but whenever she applied for jobs, the editor, either apologetic or dismissive, would explain that male employees must now take priority. Each time she returned disheartened to the apartment she still shared with her parents, her mother would say, *'Never mind. No one in our family has ever been a journalist . . .'* But it didn't mean Rosa's typing skills need go to waste. There were always secretarial positions to be filled. Journalism could wait. *But I don't want to be a secretary!* Rosa screamed inside. Yet sure enough, eight years after leaving school, here she was in front of a type-writer, with a stack of letters on one side and a dictation pad on the other. The Führerin had taken one look at the skinny girl, mousy hair parted dead down the middle, bitten nails and grey, blinking eyes behind wire-rimmed glasses, and hired Fräulein Winter on the spot. The fact was, she looked infinitely more con-vincing as secretary than a journalist.

Even then, despite her role, the first time Rosa had sat behind this typewriter her fingers had flitted over it with a visceral thrill, as though perhaps on this machine she might still get the chance to type dispatches, personal reports, maybe a newsletter for her new employers. That was until she had received her first letter to type – a report on the marriage allowance scheme to the Interior Ministry – and she felt the excitement in her fingers drain away. Instead she had taken to feeding her passion by keeping a note-book of what she called her 'Observations' – articles based on the kind of essays she used to read in the newspapers by famous writ-ers like Joseph Roth, made up of eyewitness observations of Berlin. Not earth-shattering events, but little things about life in the city; people she noticed, small incidents in the streets. She liked to watch people and work out what she could tell about them from the trivial details they gave away. The fact that Rosa herself was shy and self-effacing by nature meant no one gave her a second look. Who took any notice of a drab young woman in a headscarf, peering at them through meek, secretarial spectacles? Rosa wrote up her Observations at night, letting her imagination run wild. Writing was where her soul revealed itself.

The boys let out another volley of shouts and Rosa shot a quick glance at the closed door, behind which the Führerin was inter-viewing their mother. Perhaps it was punishment for her unnatural desire to forego children that she should now get to spend her days with a portrait of the flaxen-haired Goebbels family staring down at her desk. It was the standard, Party-issue photograph and whenever she looked up from her typewriter, or ate her sandwiches during busy lunch hours, or paused to wonder whether she might actually spend her entire life here, the Goebbels family would return her gaze. Being the model family, they had produced an entire marching squad of children for the Führer, little girls in pigtails and the boy in Lederhosen, flanked by their mother, Magda, with a jaw clenched like an industrial vice, and the minister himself, with a smile as sharp as a broken bottle.

Rosa squinted across to the opposite wall, to a map of Germany complete with flags bearing tiny swastikas, each one signalling the presence of an office of the NS Frauenschaft in that vicinity. It looked like something a general might use, charting the progress of Panzer divisions across hostile terrain. The hostile terrain in this case being anyone who attempted to frustrate the aim of providing ever bigger families for the Reich. Occasionally the Führerin would enter the office and stab a fresh flag in the map, proving that the doctrine of increasing the birth rate was being carried to the farthest corners of the Reich.

The door opened and the job candidate walked dejectedly past Rosa's desk to retrieve her children, yanking both boys up by their arms in a practised gesture that provoked howls of protest. As Rosa understood it, the woman's husband had recently been killed in Spain and she was keen to return to work, but Rosa didn't fancy her chances here. Rosa's predecessor had been obliged to leave when she got engaged. It wouldn't do for the head of the entire Nazi women's service to contravene all Party doctrine by employing a married woman, let alone one with children.

Rosa, on the other hand, gave no impression of having a boyfriend at all, which obviously suited the Führerin very well. After all, she had just given Rosa the trip of a lifetime – two weeks in the sun, with negligible duties and no typing at all. The Kraft durch Freude organization was organizing a Congress of Physical

Fitness next month which would welcome delegations from thirty-two countries, and top guests, including Heinrich Himmler himself, were to be accommodated on the KdF flagship vessel, the *Wilhelm Gustloff*. Therefore it had been deemed useful for Rosa to undertake a little reconnaissance. She was briefed to sample the ship's amenities and provide a report to the Führerin which would avert any potential embarrassments and ensure that nothing would compromise the smooth running of the event. Rosa's colleagues had been jealous, especially when she put a framed photograph of herself on the desk, standing in front of the ship with hair blown in her face, wearing a new peach-coloured sundress and straw hat and a most unlikely tan on her skin. Smiling, as much as Rosa ever smiled, with her lip bitten in one corner and an elusive look in her eye. All the girls at work stopped at her desk and marvelled. She must have had the time of her life, they cooed.

Instead, Rosa Winter bitterly wished that she had never gone.

Chapter Eight

The Goebbels family had a new address. Only technically though; they still lived in the same imposing villa on the corner of Behrenstrasse and Hermann Goering Strasse that they had occupied for the past five years, but having undergone a three-and-a-half-million-mark refurbishment the residence was now officially designated a palace. The grounds running down to the Tiergarten were clipped and pruned, the lawns laid with gravelled paths and statuary, and the interior had been entirely updated. The parquet floors and ornate ceilings were still there, but in keeping with the house's elevated status carpets had been imported from Berlin's Art History Museum to match the National Gallery Old Masters on the walls, and marquetry tables and Louis XIV furniture had been acquired from a villa of a Jewish banker in return for his passage out of the country. In front of a glass display case of antique china, recently liberated from the Schloss Charlottenburg, a vase of lilies and roses scented the air. But it was going to take more than flowers, plush furniture and rich tapestries to warm the frigid atmosphere of the Goebbels family home.

Magda Goebbels didn't seem especially grateful to receive her gift of Chanel No. 5. She unravelled the packaging listlessly, drawing aside the black ribbons as though unwrapping a parcel of socks sent in for the Winterhilfswerk rather than a hundred marks' worth of perfume. After a quick glance at the opulent glass bottle reeking of wealth and luxury, she gave it a brief squirt, and put it aside.

'Thank you for fetching this. It's kind of you to spare the time,' she said with a martyred sigh. 'I suppose I'll be buying all my own perfume from now on.'

'It's a good choice,' replied Clara politely, choosing not to point out that the perfume had cost Frau Doktor Goebbels precisely nothing.

'Yes. It's a new one for me, and at least it's not Drachenfutter.'

Clara grimaced despite herself. *Drachenfutter*, dragon fodder, was slang for presents given by men to pacify their wives. From what she had heard of relations between the Propaganda Minister and his wife over the past summer, Magda must have received Drachenfutter by the kilo, but it was having little effect. Clara took a sip of the tea she had been offered and hunted for some small talk.

'Madame Chanel was flattered you'd chosen her perfume.'

Magda shrugged. 'Was she? I thought it would make a change. We all have to embrace change sometimes, don't we? At least, that's what I'm told. And I understand this perfume is very popular in certain quarters.'

That seemed like a strange thing to say about the world's most famous perfume, but Clara had grown used to Magda's gnomic utterances, with their peculiar, bitter subtext, in the years that she had known the Propaganda Minister's wife. Back in 1933, Magda's request that Clara model for the Reich Fashion Bureau had given her unrivalled access to the gossip and feuds of the senior Nazi wives, not to mention an insight into the tortured relationship between Magda and her relentlessly unfaithful husband. Now, Clara guessed, Magda was ruminating on a new low in the relationship, wrought by Goebbels' fraught love affair with the Czech actress Lída Baarová.

Magda aside, there were enough comic aspects to the affair to keep everyone else amused. It was on the set of the aptly named movie *Hour of Temptation* that the pair met and Goebbels immediately succumbed. Unfortunately, Lída Baarová was living with another Ufa heartthrob, Gustav Fröhlich, at the time, in a house just a few doors down from the Goebbels' country villa in Schwanenwerder. On finding the lovers together, Fröhlich had punched the Propaganda Minister in the face, blackening his eye and forcing him to pretend he had injured himself in a car accident, but Fröhlich's resistance proved futile. The delicate brunette with high, Slavic cheekbones was referred to everywhere, with a liberal dose of Berliner humour, as Goebbels' 'Czech conquest' and her latest film, *A Prussian Love Story*, provoked yet more laughter. While the Nazi hierarchy were plotting their entry to Czechoslovakia, Goebbels was fighting to keep hold of both his wife and his Czech mistress, and according to recent rumours, it was a battle he was losing.

'I meant to say, congratulations, Frau Doktor, on your new daughter!'

'Thank you. She's sweet. She's four months already.'

'So you have five children now!'

'Six,' Magda replied tersely, as if correcting the asperities of an especially forward maid. 'You forget the son of my first marriage, Harald.'

Unlike other wives of the leading Nazis, Magda Goebbels had always been surrounded by a miasma of nerves, but now her complexion was cracked with anxiety, like paint, and there was a grim set to her mouth. She was beautifully dressed in a cobalt-blue dress by Hilda Romatzki, one of Berlin's leading designers, but her eyes were hollow from lack of sleep and the latest baby had left another layer of flesh around her waist.

She stared at Clara without speaking, then suddenly she looked away.

'There's no point pretending, Fräulein Vine. I've confided in you before, after all. Things are very bad here.'

'I'm sorry to hear that, Frau Doktor.'

'Oh, I know people think it's always bad, but they have no idea. First, my husband insisted on building an annexe at Schwanenwerder where he could take his actresses "to play records to them". That was awkward enough but I didn't object. I know a man in his position, under a lot of pressure, sometimes falls victim to predatory women and imagines himself infatuated. I thought the best thing I could do was try to contain it until it wore itself out. Keep them away from the children, but otherwise try to put up with it. That was until his latest request.' She cast Clara a savage glance. 'You've heard about this woman, I'm sure. I daresay it's the talk of the studios.'

It was, of course. Clara guessed the best response was to remain impassive.

'He takes her everywhere, out on his yacht, on little trips in his car. He has no shame, but his latest proposition really astonished me. He asked me to have her over for a meeting where we would all agree to live in a ménage à trois. He's a heartless devil. Can you believe such a thing?'

Clara could, but she was not about to say so. She confined herself to a sympathetic frown of assent.

'I was so miserable I said yes, and he came back with this big diamond ring for me. What a fool I was. The moment she moved in, I discovered he'd given her one too. Exactly the same! He loves her more than any woman he has ever met.'

'I'm sure, Frau Doktor, that . . .'

'Oh yes he does! I read it in his infernal diary. It's that diary he loves most of all, actually. He shuts himself away every night, noting down his thoughts and he has them preserved on photographic plates to be stored in the vaults of the Reichsbank. I never hear the end of that diary. It's his testament for posterity. Well, posterity's welcome to it.' She stopped and gave a sniff. Like many women unburdening marital unhappiness, her misery, once unleashed, became a torrent that showed no sign of slacking.

'Anyway, the ménage à trois was intolerable. I couldn't stop crying – I even thought of killing myself and the children. I did, honestly. When we accompanied the Führer to Bayreuth in July, I sobbed all the way through *Tristan und Isolde*.' Red patches had formed on the bands of her neck, as always when she was over-wrought. 'Then do you know what I did?'

Clara dreaded to think.

'I got up the courage to go down to Berchtesgaden and ask the Führer for permission to divorce.'

'Divorce?' echoed Clara, instinctively wishing Magda would speak more softly. Even if all this was true, she doubted that the Propaganda Minister wanted his love life discussed in detail with casual callers, and everything she knew about Goebbels convinced her he was paranoid enough to bug his own home.

'Exactly. And the Führer listened to me so kindly and was quite horrified to hear everything Joseph had done, but it was no good. He was furious of course, with my husband. He summoned Joseph and banged his desk so hard all the pencils jumped in the air.' At the idea of this, Magda's voice hushed and she seemed to pale. Even if you were the favourite of the senior wives, even if he called you the First Lady of the Reich, there was no doubt that an interview with an enraged Führer would be traumatic.

'But he wouldn't hear of a divorce. He adamantly instructed us to reconcile. He said it would never do for the first family in the Reich to separate – in fact, quite the opposite. Joseph must increase the press focus on the importance of the family and run more photographs in the newspapers of our children. And the newspapers must be made to print articles about the home life of the Goebbels. Ha! We're a model family, after all. The whole of the Reich looks up to us.'

Bitterly she dragged a moist handkerchief from her sleeve.

'Joseph is to institute more cultural emphasis on large families and the importance of child-bearing.'

'I thought that was SS Reichsführer Himmler's domain?'

'It is. But the Führer wants Joseph to find ways of encouraging women who have yet to have children. Addresses on film and radio and so on. What do I care? It's of no concern to me.'

She stalked over to the mirror and pretended to adjust a lock of hair that had escaped from the stiff ranks of curls on her forehead.

'Joseph's livid with me, of course.' She frowned at her reflection. 'He hates me for blackening his name to the Führer. He actually cried. He said Hitler will only speak to him on official business and will only receive him in an outer room. He's in deep disgrace. He sits there every night confiding his misery to his wretched diary and now he's planning some eye-catching event to rehabilitate himself in Hitler's eyes.'

'You mean like a parade?'

A contemptuous shrug. 'God knows what he'll dream up. He's been plotting it with his police chief friend, von Helldorf.'

'Count von Helldorf?'

The chief of the Berlin police was a notable gambler and anti-Semite, who hosted sex parties on his yacht involving brigades of HJ boys.

'Yes. He said it would make headlines but that doesn't bother me. Anyhow,' she turned to Clara defiantly, 'some good did come out of it. The Führer barred that marriage-wrecker from appearing in any films or plays or attending any social functions. Her current effort is to be her last. She's to be completely blacklisted. So that's something at least!'

She smiled, grimly, at this triumph.

'I'm so sorry, Frau Doktor . . .'

'Oh, don't imagine I'm looking for your sympathy, Fräulein,' Magda snapped, her eyes flashing and her misery transformed to frank hostility. 'I'm telling you all this for a reason. I want you to let all your little actress friends at Ufa know that the Führer has commanded my husband to remain faithful. If I'm to stay with him, they can keep that in their silly heads. If they're tempted to stray they will be disobeying the orders of Adolf Hitler. It probably counts as treason. I will make sure the Führer knows their names and the punishment will be a camp, at the very least. Can you manage that?'

In the background a car door slammed, and then there was the sound of the front door closing and steps proceeding along the narrow hallway. It was a tread so distinctive that everyone recognized it, one foot firm, the other slightly dragging. The steps hesitated outside the drawing room, then suddenly, the door was thrown open and the diminutive figure of Joseph Goebbels stared into the room.

As always, when she encountered the Reich's most vicious baiter of the Jews, an involuntary shudder ran through Clara and she had to work hard to control the tremble of her hands and paste a polite smile on her face. This was the man who had had her ordered in for questioning only the previous year, suspecting her motives and her allegiances. When their paths first crossed, Goebbels had thought Clara might be useful to him; he had summoned her to his ministry and asked her to keep a confidential eye on his wife. But all that was long ago. Now Joseph Goebbels no longer treated her with anything but suspicious distance. He had put his agents on her tail in the past and would do so again in an instant. He was probably as familiar with the contents of Clara's underclothes drawer as she was herself.

Yet now his appearance shocked her. As a senior cabinet minister of a country on the precipice of war, one might expect Joseph Goebbels to look preoccupied, but beyond his natty white double-breasted suit and beige fedora, there was a wild air about him. His cadaverous face was deathly pale, his eyes red–rimmed and his crippled foot seemed more than usually pronounced. He was clearly in torment but whether it was over the hostilities in the Sudetenland or those in his private life, Clara couldn't say.

She smiled a greeting but Goebbels didn't bother to return it. Indeed he barely acknowledged her. He stood frozen in the doorway, a clutch of manila files under one arm, surveying the room with a frantic gleam in his eye, as though it must contain more than just Clara and his wife.

For a second, Clara was bewildered and a glance at Magda's face puzzled her yet further. Magda's expression was pure, malicious satisfaction.

'Are you looking for someone, Joseph? It's just myself and Fräulein Vine here, I'm afraid. Did you expect anyone else?'

Clearly Goebbels had assumed someone else was there, but why would he think that? There was no other voice but hers and Magda's, and no car on the drive outside. What did Goebbels imagine was going on?

Suddenly her eye fell on the golden gleam of Chanel No.5 on the table beside Magda, and she realized why. It must be Lída's perfume. Presumably Goebbels scented its distinctive rose-laden trail and hoped, against all hope, that his lover was present. Following her glance, he saw his mistake.

'Fräulein Vine has brought me a delightful gift!' said Magda with hideous brightness.

Goebbels glowered. 'So I see,' he said tightly. 'That's an interesting choice of perfume.'

'We all have to make choices,' said Magda, newly miserable now that her ploy had succeeded. 'Isn't that what you said? And I seem to recall this perfume is one of your favourites.'

Goebbels gave his wife a savage glance and Clara cursed silently, hoping that the Minister did not suspect her of a deliberate provocation. She couldn't afford to get on his wrong side, but nor could she point out Magda's machinations in this marital firefight.

'Actually, Herr Doktor, it was a gift from Coco Chanel. I happened to see her in Paris.'

'So you've been filming there?'

He knew already, she could tell that from the flatness of his eyes. Every movie schedule in the Ufa studios had to be submitted to his office before filming began.

'Yes, I'm just back. I'm about to leave again for an audition in Munich.'

That did take him by surprise. Goebbels liked to think he knew everything that went on in the cultural life of the Reich and that included the movements of actresses.

'Are you? What's the film?'

'It's called *Good King George.*'

Goebbels raised an eyebrow, so Clara elaborated.

'Not the current King of England, of course. George 1st. The Hanoverian who took the English throne.'

If England was ever to be represented in German film, Goebbels preferred a historical setting. He especially liked films about Britain which featured people in wigs. It was all part of his campaign to present England as old-fashioned and class-ridden beside a modern, dynamic Germany. With its setting of seventeenth-century Hanover coupled with the theme of a German succeeding to the English throne, *Good King George* might have been engineered specifically to appeal to the Propaganda Minister. Indeed it probably was.

'It's being directed by Fritz Gutmann. At the Bavaria Film studios at Geiselgasteig.'

'Interesting. Sounds like an improvement on Gutmann's usual sub-Expressionist tripe. What's your role?'

'I'm auditioning to play Sophia.'

'The unfaithful wife. She dies, doesn't she, at the end?'

'I think so.'

'Fitting,' he remarked briefly, but already his mind was on other things. A calculating flicker ran across his face.

'Report to me, would you, when you get back. I have a task for you.'

'A task, Herr Doktor?'

'It's to do with a new documentary I'm planning. Fräulein Riefenstahl's *Triumph of the Will* has provoked a raging appetite around the world for German documentary – the Americans have been particularly complimentary. Our relationship with Hollywood is of great importance to the Reich, so it's very gratifying that they love our documentaries. These Hollywood producers are so much more impressive than their rather poor British counterparts.'

Clara did not allow her smile to waver.

'Anyhow, I've decided our next international effort will focus on the place of German families. There's a new decoration for kinderreich mothers to be awarded by the National Socialist Frauenschaft – it's a fresh initiative of Reich domestic policy I'm announcing this week – and that would be a good place to start. I sense a global excitement about our plans for German womanhood, and this documentary will satisfy that hunger. I think you would be ideal to narrate it.'

'I'm flattered.'

'Don't be. I need an English speaker for the American version and there aren't many of those around. I'll be in touch.'

Without another glance at the kinderreich mother of his own children, who was staring stonily out of the window, he left the room.

Chapter Nine

Rupert Allingham, Berlin bureau chief of the *Daily Chronicle*, downed his Eiercognac as reverently as communion wine and signalled for another. These days his thirst seemed to increase in inverse proportion to the quality of the stuff on offer. And this cognac was unusually rough.

To all outward appearances, the Café Kottler on the leafy Motz Strasse in Schöneberg was a model restaurant of the Reich. Beneath the old-fashioned brass lamps its panelled oak walls and generous chairs glowed with a sense of comfort and security. It purveyed Swabian cuisine, the starchy food of southern Germany beloved of the Nazi top brass, and like many cafés it took the opportunity of a captive audience to hand out some worthy advice about smoking, for example, or not wasting food. That month the proprietor had hung a sign over the bar reminding customers of the importance of the Führer salute.

Der deutsche grüsst 'Heil Hitler!'

The sign was, however, a disguise, as was the photograph of Hitler surrounded by flower girls that sat next to the liquor stand on an adjacent wall. These outward manifestations of Nazi zeal only masked an establishment where the opponents of the Party felt unusually safe. Everything about the Café Kottler, from the layout of tables in discreet alcoves to the dim lighting and the enthusiasm of the zither player whose music drowned out conversations, made it the perfect place to congregate without fear of being overheard. The restaurant owner was a jokey, swaggering character, who was known to be sympathetic to anti-Nazis, or at the very least unlikely to bug their conversations and forward the tapes to the Gestapo.

What's more, Rupert actually liked the food. Although, like all restaurants in Berlin, the menu had more lines through it than a Mozart manuscript, he positively relished hard-boiled potatoes and overdone cabbage. He enjoyed fried onions, rubbery, substantial noodles and heavy cakes soaked in rough alcohol. It was the German version of English comfort food, though he did wish the bread didn't taste quite so convincingly of plaster of Paris. For a moment his mind travelled to the warm golden rolls nestling in a linen napkin baked by his mother's cook in Belgrave Square. Lady Allingham disapproved of foreign food almost as much as she did of her only son's decision to become a hack writer instead of running the family estate. Her entire demeanour since Rupert took his job as Berlin bureau chief of the *Chronicle* had been one of pained displeasure. What would Mother have made of this black rye bread that crumbled into sawdust as you raised it to your lips?

He looked out of the window to see Clara Vine approaching, head down, glossy, dark hair falling to her shoulders in loose curls. There was a kind of chameleon quality to her. You could pass her on the street without noticing her, yet when she spoke you saw at once why the camera loved her. She had a way of holding herself that suggested some inner reserve of calm, or so he liked to think. She reminded him of a girl in a Flemish painting – one that hung in the Allingham family castle in Northumbria, in fact – with her look of resolute serenity concealing a sharp and lively mind. The high, squarish forehead and those eyes, at once cool and calculating, which made it impossible to guess what she was thinking. He had loved that portrait since he was a boy, marvelling at the woman's grace and composure, the subtle beauty of her freckled skin and pursed, preoccupied lips, so unlike the milky, bovine women the Nazis loved.

Clara was a loner, he supposed, like himself. He remembered how much Leo Quinn, his oldest friend, had been in love with her. Indeed Rupert himself had been responsible for introducing them. If he hadn't met Clara at that party in London five years ago and suggested casually that she come and try out for the Ufa studios, she would no doubt be buried in Knightsbridge or Kensington by now, volunteering for the FANY or trying on gas masks in Chelsea town hall, like every other woman he knew back home. She would not have come to Berlin, or met Leo, or broken his heart. For that reason, Rupert's feelings about Clara were conflicted, even though he knew pretty much what kept her here. She had never mentioned her intelligence work, nor would he have asked, but he was able to put two and two together and he respected it. He also kept in touch out of an obscure duty to Leo – one of the few friends of his that Mother really liked, even though she referred to him as 'that polite young man', *polite* being a way of signifying that Leo belonged to a lower class than themselves. Leo never asked after Clara, but Rupert wanted the answers in case he ever did, so he had resolved to keep in contact with Clara for Leo's sake, and what had started out as duty had soon become a pleasure.

The door clanged open and Clara slid into the seat next to him with a grimace of amused disgust at his meal – two boiled weisse Wurst coiled around a swamp of congealing vegetables, a dish of cabbage and a jar of brown sauce.

'I don't know how you can eat that.'

'It's a Proustian madeleine to me. Reminds me of boarding school. Especially the sawdust in the sausages.'

Clara smiled affectionately at Rupert. Even now, when he was almost perpetually drunk, in a battered tweed suit that had seen better days and two days' growth of stubble, there was no disguising his aristocratic good looks. The chiselled, blue-blooded features were blurred by drink, like a decayed seraph, but there was a sceptical intelligence behind those sleepy eyes and the rhetorical flourishes were undercut by the ironic slant of his smile. When she had first met him, at a grand London party given by a friend of her sister, she had taken Rupert for exactly what he resembled – a well-born, Oxford-educated, cultural dilettante with absolutely no need to earn a living. The only son of Lady Allingham, heir to a thousand acres of Northumbria and destined from birth to occupy the most comfortable of berths in the English establishment. Instead of which, Rupert had emerged as a passionate journalistic opponent of the Nazi regime who came regularly close to being ejected from Germany. It was a difficult balancing act. Every bit of copy he filed had to get by a series of Nazi censors, so often he had to rely on a deep English sense of irony to convey the opposite of what his Nazi minders would read. He was an embodiment of upper-class charm which simultaneously baffled his Nazi minders and pleased his interviewees.

Yet that same upper-class charm acted like an impenetrable barrier to his private self. Though she had known Rupert for five years, and he took a lively interest in her romantic life, Clara still had no real idea of his own. She rarely saw him with a woman in tow and his evenings were resolutely male – not the Herrenabends that German men went in for, but endless sessions at the bar of the Adlon, trading stories with the VIPs of the foreign press, Quentin Reynolds from Hearst, the mild-mannered, pipe-smoking Bill Shirer, Ed Murrow and the *Daily Telegraph*'s Hugh Carleton Greene. Herbert Melcher of the Associated Press and Chuck Lewis of the *Chicago Herald*. And drinking, of course, which appeared to be Rupert's principal recreation these days.

She leant over and flicked some crumbs from his jacket.

'Had you ever thought of getting this cleaned?'

'No point. My laundry's run out of soap. They say it's harder to get soap than tobacco now.'

He took another bite of his sausage and chewed it.

'I'll manage fine so long as Kottler's never run out of sausage. This Wurst may be an acquired taste, but once one has acquired it one can't get enough.'

'I suppose you have to eat it to soak up the alcohol.'

Rupert assumed a hangdog expression.

'It was a rough night,' he conceded. 'But you should eat something too, Clara. You're getting thin. Those Nazis like their film stars with a bit of meat on them.'

'I'm not a star. I don't even want to be. And I already ate with my godson Erich. I'll just have a drink.'

Rupert called the waiter for some coffee then turned back to her.

'How is that lad of yours?'

'He's just got back from a KdF cruise.'

'A National Socialist holiday?' He swallowed the remainder of his food. 'I always think that sounds like a contradiction in terms.'

'It was rather. Not because Erich objects to the Nazis, of course. He's all in favour. He was upset because a woman fell overboard.'

'I can understand wanting to get off one of those godawful cruises, but that's a bit drastic.'

'Don't joke. It was a young woman. I think Erich had taken a shine to her.'

She thought of Erich's face as he told her about it. He was growing so fast. His familiar round features, which she had known and loved since he was ten, were now sharpened with incipient adulthood. The light in his eyes was becoming guarded – that was when he didn't avoid her gaze altogether. Clara didn't blame him. She remembered how secretive adolescence was. A time when excruciating self-consciousness made contact with other people intense, like rubbing on raw skin. The fact that Erich was an orphan, with only an elderly grandmother to fight his corner, had made the naturally shy boy even more defensive.

'It's a strange story, from what I could get out of him. He was pretty awkward about telling me.'

She recalled the nervous glances he shot at her as he imparted little bits of information, leaving Clara to fill in the gaps.

'They were on the *Wilhelm Gustloff.*'

Rupert's eyes widened. 'The pride of the fleet. Last word in luxury, apparently. How did they get the tickets?'

'His grandmother's a nurse at the Charité hospital and she qualified for them through work. From what I could gather, Erich became friendly with this woman who had the cabin next to his. Her name was Ada and he got in the habit of fetching coffee for her each morning. One day she asked him to look after her bag and she never came back. Erich seems to believe she fell overboard.'

'Sounds like a bit of a story. Is he the imaginative kind? You don't think he made it up, do you?'

That thought had occurred to her. It seemed so unlikely. Erich had a solid, scientific kind of mind, with a liking for facts and figures. He loved quoting to Clara the number of planes in the Luftwaffe, or the different specifications of every single model of Mercedes-Benz going back to the 1920s. He enjoyed hearing stories, certainly, but he'd never been one for making them up, and besides, why would he fabricate a tale like that?

'Why do you ask?'

Rupert shrugged. 'Simply because I've not heard anything about a woman being lost overboard on a KdF cruise. An accident like that would generally make the papers and I do read the German papers, as you know, courtesy of the Propaganda Ministry. They ensure that the Foreign Press Club is lavishly provided with Berlin's finest and they like us correspondents to read them all. Which now that they've gone down so much in size doesn't take long.'

'The thing is, Erich was so anxious about it, I told him I'd find out about this woman. He seems to feel an obscure loyalty to her and—' Clara felt a surge of love at the thought of his face, a mix of bewilderment and hurt pride, 'I'm determined to look into it.'

'Clara . . .'

'I have to. Poor boy. It was his first foreign holiday too.' She took a sip of the coffee the waiter had brought and put it quickly down again. It tasted of acorns, or what she imagined acorns must taste like, a bitter mix of wood chippings and grit, with the consistency of sand scraped from the bottom of the Spree.

'Anyhow, I said I'd ask you.'

'Me?' Rupert paused mid-fork and frowned.

'No not you specifically, of course, but a responsible journalist I happened to know through my work. You are that, aren't you?'

'I suppose.'

'So as a favour to me would you ask around, see if you can find anything about a woman called Ada Freitag, lost on a cruise? You know policemen, don't you? You must have contacts.'

He raised his eyebrows. 'I don't know if you've noticed, but there's a rather different kind of foreign travel at the top of the news list right now. Herr Hitler's packing his bags for Prague by the look of it.'

Clara leant her arms across the table and plucked at his sleeve. 'I do understand you're busy with far more important things, Rupert. I know this is fairly trivial, but it broke my heart to see Erich so upset. I don't think he's ever had a crush on a girl before. You remember what it's like to be that age, don't you?'

'Every day.'

At fifteen Rupert was immured in Winchester, spending his evenings taking sherry with a German master who liked to read Goethe to the more intelligent and appealing of his pupils. It was a time of intense adolescent ferment but crushes on girls had not been part of the picture.

'Erich feels it's his duty to find out, and if he hadn't told me, he would be pursuing it with the local police, which would lead to all sorts of attention he could do without. So I have to get him some answers one way or another.'

For some reason, tears glimmered in her eyes. Clara was certainly attached to this lad, Rupert thought. God knows what
would happen when war broke out and she had to leave him here.
He smiled and mimed a little courtly bow, then reached for the
notebook in his top pocket and scribbled a note.

'I'll do what I can. Perhaps it's understandable it got hushed up.
I suppose a tragedy like that's not exactly great publicity for the
Reich. Can't compete with this, for example.'

He gestured at the *Berliner Tageblatt* on the table beside him.
From an inside page the face of little Hedda, the latest Goebbels
daughter, stared out under the headline, *Baby joy for the Reich
Minister's family*. Evidently, Goebbels was fully obeying his master's
order to produce more copy about the home life of the Reich's
model family.

Clara squinted at it. 'Magda told me he's determined to increase
coverage of German families. In fact he's asked me to present a
documentary about the work of the Deutsche Frauenschaft.'

'I never quite understand what that involves. Is it like the
Women's Institute, but without jam and Jerusalem?'

'More like the WI run along military lines. It oversees everything to do with women in the Reich. It's headed by Gertrud
Scholtz-Klink.'

'That horror? I don't know why they don't put her in charge of
the Wehrmacht. She's enough to scare any enemy.'

'Apparently there's a new initiative for women that Goebbels wants
publicized. Something to do with honouring German families.'

'He is keen on family news at the moment, isn't he?' Rupert
gestured to the facing page. '*In the Sudetenland, Women and Children
mown down by Czech armoured cars.*' He looked from one headline
to the other with bemusement. 'It's hard to know what to believe.
Goebbels invents these atrocities to arouse fury. All these riots and
shootings by Czech bandits or Bolsheviks in the Sudetenland. Half
of them never happened, or if they did, they were staged by
German agents themselves.'

'Is Prague next, do you think?'

'I think Hitler's caught between two sides. Goering and Goebbels urge caution, but von Ribbentrop wants him to act aggressively. Ribbentrop seems to be consumed by the desire for war. The more I meet that man, the more I'm convinced that he has very little between his ears. He loathes the British in particular. He told Churchill that if Germany was allowed a free hand to take Lebensraum in the East, then he could guarantee Britain's security.'

'What did Churchill say?'

'He said the Royal Navy had been guaranteeing Britain's security for several centuries and didn't need Hitler's help, thank you.'

Clara smiled.

'It's a shame Hitler never really sees what the British think of him.'

Rupert gave a delighted laugh. 'That, my dear Clara, is where you're wrong. He does, and it drives him crazy! Von Ribbentrop held a special meeting with Lord Halifax this summer to complain about the *Evening Standard* cartoonist, Low. He said if Germany ever went to war with England, Low is one of the first people Hitler wants shot.'

'He probably means it too.'

'Undoubtedly. Von Ribbentrop doesn't understand humour. Goebbels does, though, and he even took me aside. It was after one of the morning briefings; he came over all confidential and made a play for sympathy. He said, "Low makes the most offensive and lying cartoons which I am obliged to show the Führer and each time I do he blows up. It absolutely spoils his day."'

'So that's something.'

'That's what I thought. Nice to think the British press can provide a useful service. I only wish my articles had the same effect.' His face darkened and Clara sensed that she had touched on some underlying trouble.

'Has something happened?'

Rupert drained another glass. An alcoholic flush was beginning to develop on his face and the laughter drained from his eyes.

'You could say that. There's a new editor at the *Chronicle*. Reginald Winstanley. He couldn't be more different from the previous chap. He hates anything critical of the regime here. Believes Herr Hitler is much misunderstood. Britain's place is on the sidelines, etcetera.'

'Surely he must see what you write?'

'If so, he seems determined to ensure that no one else does. He thinks I should be more conciliatory to the regime. He says, "Ward Price of the *Daily Mail* gets to visit Herr Hitler at the Berghof. Why are you never invited?"'

'To the Berghof? I can't think of anything worse.'

'I've heard the view is spectacular.'

'Oh, Rupert. What are you going to do?'

He wiped his mouth and cast the napkin carelessly aside.

'God knows. On top of it all my office assistant quit. She got married and says the place of a German wife is in the home. Apparently keeping my office in order is incompatible with keeping her husband in hot meals. The place is a frightful mess.'

'I'm surprised you can tell.'

'Now then. I may never have maintained Nazi levels of order, but it's come to something when you need to mount a search and rescue operation for the telephone every time your editor rings.'

He drained his drink and added, 'Winstanley's a good friend of your father's, as it happens.'

Clara looked swiftly away. She hated any mention of her father. Sir Ronald Vine, a former Conservative MP, had formed a group of aristocrats and senior politicians active in the cause of Anglo-German friendship. But in recent years, their cause had gone beyond friendship to appeasement of Hitler, and their powerful, covert coterie did everything it could to advocate the National Socialist cause to the English government.

'I saw them together, actually, last time I went back. Winstanley

was giving a talk to the Anglo-German alliance at the Grosvenor House Hotel.'

'So you want me to intercede with my father?'

'If the occasion arises.'

'If that's what you'd like.'

He caught the wistfulness in her eyes. 'Do you miss England?'

Spending time with Rupert, speaking English, always awoke a stab of yearning for her birthplace. London in all its sooty glory, the museums, the National Gallery, Hyde Park, the Thames. The stucco terraces, cracked like brittle icing on a cake, the crowds on the Underground. English gardens with their blowsy pink roses and tidy lawns. The BBC, her old theatrical friends, even her family. Though Clara was only half English, that Englishness was profound – the Vines had come over with the Conqueror and they had been based in the West Country for hundreds of years – yet still, England felt forbidden to her. Was it because she had insisted to her family that she loved life in Berlin? Or was it because England contained a piece of her past that she could never revisit?

'A little.'

'Nothing stopping you making a short trip.'

There was nothing. But there was also everything. The thought of her mission in Munich rose vividly to her mind.

'I think we have company.'

They had been talking in English and Clara noticed that a party of men at the table next to them had dropped their voices and were eavesdropping. Rupert gave a quick, redundant dab of his mouth with his napkin and stood up.

'If I really can't tempt you to sample this delicious food, perhaps we should take a walk.'

They strolled west along the street towards Viktoria-Luise-Platz where a fountain provided a cooling mist in the sultry heat. It was a popular place for an evening drink and the pavement was crowded with café customers, but these were no relaxed, late

summer evening meetings, full of laughter and beer. Instead, a subdued mood prevailed. People seemed jittery, exchanging information and whispers.

'You won't forget, will you, to ask about that girl on the cruise?'

'Sure. I'll ask, of course.' Already Rupert could envisage the moment at the daily press conference when he interrupted Doktor Goebbels' daily drone about Jewish affairs with a query about something extraordinary, a girl falling into the sea. On a KdF cruise, too.

'You didn't tell me about Paris. It's a while since I've been there. Is it lovely as ever? Did you enjoy yourself? Meet anyone nice?'

The image of Max Brandt came into her mind. The saturnine face growing slightly fleshy about the jaw, the smudge of grey beneath the eyes. The receding hair and the air of impatient physicality about him, like a wild animal confined by convention and society. His unconcealed astonishment when she said she needed to leave, and his slow, seductive smile when he cornered her in the alley. The extraordinary presumption of his remark.

If you won't come to bed with me, perhaps you'll come to dinner.

Did people really behave like that? Did the urgency of the times mean traditional conventions could be overlooked? Something about Max Brandt provoked images she had never thought about before, forbidden images of hotel beds with rumpled sheets and glasses of champagne on the bedside tables, and clothes cast carelessly on the floor.

Rupert observed the flicker of thought that passed across her eyes and laughed.

'You did enjoy yourself! Tell me everything. Was it a seductive Frenchman? You want to watch out for those.'

Clara pushed him away playfully. 'It wasn't anyone, Rupert. It was work.'

'I'm not sure I believe you, but if so, what a waste. Never mind. You'll have to make do with me. There's a party coming up for the foreign press. Perhaps you'd like to accompany me.'

It was risky for her to be seen with an English journalist, so she said,

'I may still be in Munich. I'm off the day after tomorrow. '

'Munich?'

Even though Rupert must have some idea of her double life, Clara was careful never to share any more information than she needed to. Generally, he understood this and refrained from asking any questions, but he was a journalist all the same, and he had curiosity in his veins where other people had blood.

'I'm up for a part in a film at the Bavarian Film studios. It's called *Good King George*. It's a historical picture about the Hanoverian dynasty taking over the throne of England.'

He gave a dry laugh. 'Let's hope it's historical. These days the idea of Germans seizing the throne of England might count as current affairs.'

Chapter Ten

For a government department dedicated to the domestic arts, the headquarters of the National Socialist Frauenschaft in Derfflinger Strasse, Tiergarten district, bore few signs of homeliness. The entrance opened to a parquet hall painted institutional green and scented with carbolic bleach and the faint tang of infant vomit. Famous faces of the regime – all men – hung along a corridor interspersed with cork boards fluttering with instructions on infant care, hygiene, nursing the sick at home, children's education, cooking and sewing. Glass-panelled doors led off to a series of offices and conference rooms and at the far end was the library, which was more like a vast collection of filing cabinets than a conventional library, containing every letter, pronouncement and pamphlet ever issued concerning the NS Frauenschaft, sparsely leavened with volumes on maternal health and childcare and a few government-sanctioned children's books. Needless to say, no one went in the library looking for light entertainment.

Next to the library was the domestic science room, where a couple of aproned women were that morning completing a demonstration of nutritious national recipes – pig cheek's broth and pickled herring rolled in breadcrumbs – whose unappetizing smells snaked out into the surrounding corridor, and into the conference room, where an instructor from the Reichsmütterdienst,

the Mother Service, could be heard holding forth. The subject of that morning's talk was Love and Marriage and forty hausfraus were obediently ranked in semi-circles.

'What are the Ten Commandments for the German Woman?' barked the instructor. —

The audience must have assumed the question was rhetorical because the instructor supplied the answers herself.

'*Remember you are a German! Remain pure in mind and spirit! Keep your body pure! Do not remain single! Choose a spouse of similar blood! Hope for as many children as possible!* Anyone else know one?'

The housewife representatives wore the official Frauenschaft uniform of blue-black jacket, with matching pleated skirt and grey blouse buttoned to the neck, their faces unblemished by lipstick and their hair braided as precisely as steel cables. Most bore expressions of slavish interest as they listened, but a few had an air of absent anxiety, as though trying to recall if they had left the cooker on.

When she had first heard the Love and Marriage talk, Rosa Winter had listened incredulously. Now, sitting in the adjacent office and hearing it for the tenth time, she merely zoned out and tried to focus on that morning's task – completing data on the names and addresses of mothers in Berlin who had not yet applied for membership of the network of schools run by the Reichsmütterdienst. Membership was not compulsory, but if a woman didn't join then she would get a visit from a Nazi official wondering why, and if she still delayed joining she might find herself guilty of failing in her duty to the Reich, which was in itself illegal. The lessons of the four-month mother-training courses were pretty basic – thrifty shopping, mending, gardening, handicraft, avoiding foreign goods, making meals from leftovers – but all instruction was underpinned by the rationale underlying the regime. A mother should avoid buying imported food, if possible, to support the national welfare, but if absolutely necessary she should select goods from a country friendly to the Reich. The shortages in the shops had provided the opportunity for another brilliant example of the Führerin's ingenuity. Disturbed by stories of fighting and unpatriotic squabbling between housewives as they queued for their daily groceries, she had decided to create a whole new division called the Market Police, a crack troop of women trained up to serve on the shopping front line who would shepherd the queues and adjudicate on disputes between shoppers and shopkeepers which might otherwise turn nasty. One of Rosa's jobs was to collate the names of those whom the Führerin had chosen to volunteer and organize training sessions in cooperation with the Berlin traffic police. You had to hand it to the Führerin. She really did think of everything.

The Love and Marriage session was concluding and Rosa flinched as the roomful of women launched into the obligatory hymn to Hitler, bellowed with especial passion because everyone knew the words.

> 'Yet as once you loyally struggled for us,
> Now we are yours with every breath we draw
> You suffered alone for us so long
> The strongest heart that ever was on earth.'

The only wedding Rosa had ever attended was her sister Susi's and that union was as far from the Love and Marriage talk as was possible to imagine. Pauly Kramer was a middle-ranking official in the Reich Labour Front, a thickset man with a scalp like the pink, bristled skin of a pig who regarded Rosa with a look that seemed to combine simultaneously lust and disgust. Susi and Pauly's marriage was not so much a meeting of minds as a careful demarcation of duties, seemingly arranged so that they met as little as possible. They had one son, Hans-Otto, a slow child who at the age of five had still not learned to button his coat or lisp his numbers from one to ten.

Rosa adored Hans-Otto. She loved his wide, dreamy eyes, and

the way he sucked his thumb when she hauled him on her lap to read to him. He barely spoke and knew far fewer words than most children his age, but the emotions moved on his baby face like the clouds passing across the sky as he listened to *Hansel and Gretel* or *Cinderella*, or the king who turned everything to gold. He loved animals too, and there was nothing he liked better than to visit the zoo and watch the lion cubs writhing and squealing in their cage or run his hands through the rough hair of the goats in the petting enclosure.

Hans-Otto's dreaminess, however, was not universally admired. Recently there had been letters from the headmaster at school concerning the child's inability to tie his shoelaces and demanding an improvement. More worryingly, in the past few weeks, Hans-Otto had suffered a number of convulsions which left his little face more washed out and vacant than ever.

No wonder Susi showed little inclination to increase the Reich birth rate with a second child. Hans-Otto's inadequacies seemed to compound her general bitterness about her circumstances, which she never hesitated to express whenever she saw her sister. 'We can't all spend our lives on luxury cruises,' she had remarked resentfully when Rosa returned from her trip.

That comment caused the image to resurface in Rosa's mind, though in truth it had scarcely been out of her thoughts for weeks. She returned to it again and again, as though revisiting the scene of a crime.

The picture was frozen in her head like a still from a film set. She was standing in the gloom of the rain-lashed deck, watching the thrilling progress of the storm. A mist of spray rolled across the sea, obscuring the middle distance, but she could just see the water boiling up beneath the prow of the ship every time it veered and listed in the wind, and a mountain of violet clouds banked on the horizon. Suddenly, away to her left, came the gleam of something white, sprawled at the feet of a group of sailors. Looking closer she saw it was a young woman, hauled clumsily onto the deck like a fish. Rosa felt again the shock of seeing that delicate face, its beautifully curved lips bleached of colour like a marble Madonna, and the soaked tendrils of hair splayed across it like seaweed. The girl's sodden dress, flattened against her breasts, and the crumpled mess at the back of her skull. The sailors staring at her, agog.

She couldn't get that picture out of her mind. Why had the captain instructed her not to mention it? Why should such a tragic thing be hushed up? The fact that she had exchanged a few words with the girl gave her a sense of personal responsibility, as though she was actually involved in the death, which was plainly absurd. Surely just being a witness to a crime, if indeed it was a crime, didn't make you a participant? She, Rosa, was not responsible for what she had seen. Yet the disquiet lingered and she knew it was not going away.

Her first thought was to confide in the Führerin – that would be the proper thing to do. After all, her entire purpose on the cruise had been to assess the suitability of the *Wilhelm Gustloff* as a VIP venue and details like passengers falling overboard must surely reflect on the ship's safety record. Not mentioning what she had seen was a direct violation of her duty, and yet . . . it was hard to imagine confiding anything in the Führerin. Besides, it would only spoil the glow of approval that Rosa was enjoying just then. The Führerin was already talking about sending her on another trip, this time to explore the Prora complex, a vast holiday camp on the Baltic coast which was being built by the KdF. The place was a hulking, blank-faced high-rise almost three miles long with ten thousand rooms. It looked like Rosa's idea of hell but grandiose constructions were essential to convey the epic status of the Reich and someone needed to reconnoitre the complex for the forthcoming conference on Women and Domesticity. If Rosa confided her discovery to the Führerin it would only mar this pleasant glow of approbation. She would be bound to question why Rosa had left the incident out of her original, post-cruise report and would immediately take it up with the ship's captain, who would be likely to contradict Rosa directly, meaning that it would be the word of a secretary against that of a decorated captain of the German navy. Rosa might lose her job. Weakly, too, she remembered the words of Captain Bertram warning her that any mention of the incident would mean neither she nor her family would ever again attend a KdF holiday. Her mother would be heartbroken if her daughter's actions meant she was barred from KdF cruises for life.

Yet at the heart of Rosa Winter was an unorthodox spirit. She knew there was something wrong about what she had seen and there must be somebody she should tell. The girl's face seemed to float before her, like a photographic negative developing in its solution, standing out sharp from its blurred surroundings. The bloodless face and the empty blue eyes that just a few hours earlier on the sun deck had been looking around with a panicky air. *Is anything the matter? No. Why should it be?* Other than the few words they had exchanged, Rosa had no idea who she was. Somebody's daughter or someone's mother even. It might be that the girl's own family had no idea what had become of her, and they never would, unless someone disobeyed the ship's captain and revealed what really happened.

Chapter Eleven

The Elizabeth Arden Red Door salon on the Kurfürstendamm was the haunt of Berlin's most fashionable women. Its perfumes and potions escaped the general disapproval of foreign cosmetics because Miss Arden herself, despite being American, was a personal friend of Reich Minister Hermann Goering, and the Nazis' favourite beautician. She was the only person who had ever been brave enough to offer the gargantuan minister some useful diet and exercise tips, and he had indeed gone so far as to buy an exercise horse on her recommendation, even if he never used it. Every Christmas Goering would buy up dozens of boxed sets of cosmetics to distribute to the wives of his officers, whose photographs hung on the salon walls, alongside famous clients like Leni Riefenstahl, Olga Chekhova, Zarah Leander and Marlene Dietrich and, in their midst, Miss Arden herself, swathed in white mink and shot by Cecil Beaton. Also dotting the walls were pictures of the Arden spa, with its hooded sun loungers and Riviera striped canvas awnings, and a framed advertisement for the famous Eight Hour Cream. *Neither wind nor sunrays will alter the purity and brilliance of your complexion.* It might have been the photographs of the actresses, or the expectation of glamorous transformation, but the whole salon had the air of a movie set, from its dove grey walls and silver drapes to the gleaming marble floor and crystal chandeliers. There were French

chairs, upholstered in rose velvet and flatteringly lit mirrors surrounded by pink and blue bottles of 'Venetian Cream', cosmetics,
oils and treatments. Only the white leather treatment chairs added
a slightly clinical touch, suggesting that beauty was essentially a science and its effects could be scientifically obtained.

At ten in the morning the salon was almost empty, except for
a single elderly woman attempting in vain to stave off the ravages
of time with a bottle of Ardena Skin Tonic and a cloud of scented
steam. With the temperature already rising on the street, Clara
pushed through the door, relishing the cool air against her face,
tinged with the scent of pine and eucalyptus, and a faint trace of
Blue Grass.

Sabine Friedmann had started out as a make-up assistant at the
Ufa studios, where she and Clara had first met, but her flair and
personal charm had attracted the attention of Elizabeth Arden herself and Sabine was offered a job at the salon, followed within a
few years by a promotion to manager. Now she was a walking
advertisement for the products she promoted. Tall and striking
with suitably Aryan blonde hair, she made it her business to adopt
the Arden 'Total Look', which entailed lip, cheek and fingernail
colours coordinated with military precision. That day her face was
a porcelain mask and her mouth a cupid's bow of signature salmon
pink. Her usual effusive greetings, however, were muted. Instead
she gave Clara a quick kiss, then walked over to the door, turning
around the sign to read 'Geschlossen' and with a quick glance
round the salon ushered her to an alcove at the back, where a chair
was spread with a spotless white towel.

'We keep this seat for our special customers. They like a little
privacy.'

'I'm flattered.'

'It's less obtrusive.'

Clara cast her a quizzical glance in the mirror.

'I thought you had come by some new samples, Sabine. They
must be pretty hush-hush!'

'It's not about that exactly.' Sabine's china-blue eyes met Clara's soberly in the mirror. 'It could be nothing, but I thought I should let you know. Why don't I give you a facial?'

Rapidly Clara realized that whatever Sabine wanted to discuss, it wasn't cosmetics. Leaning back obediently she closed her eyes as Sabine poured a few pearls of apricot-scented oil into the palm of her hand, and began massaging her face with soothing, rhythmic strokes. Bending over Clara she murmured softly in her ear.

'I tried several times to get hold of you.'

'I've been in Paris.'

'Perhaps you should have stayed there.'

'What on earth do you mean by that?'

'I hope you don't mind me saying this, Clara.'

'Please . . . tell me.'

'It's very delicate. If anyone knew I had mentioned this . . .'

'Sabine, I know how to keep quiet.'

'You see, they all come here, the top wives. Frau Heydrich, Frau Goering, Frau Goebbels, Frau Ley. I hear all the talk. Not deliberately, but I can't help it sometimes. They gossip, you know. What else are they to do when they're having treatments? When you're lying on your back having a massage or relaxing with a facial, your guard is down. You talk. They assume that the person who tends to them is a servant who simply won't hear. Or perhaps they think a servant can't understand.' Her fingers fluttered over Clara's brow, smoothing the apricot oil in relaxing circles.

'Anyhow, the other day, I overheard something Frau von Ribbentrop was saying. She knows you a little, I think.'

'She does. I didn't know she was a client of yours.'

Sabine made a grimace which suggested she knew of no beauty treatment that could soften the iron mask of Annelies von Ribbentrop.

'She comes often. And she's very happy at the moment. This spring the SS took over a castle called Fuschl near Salzburg, exe-

cuted the owner and handed it to her family. It's proving to be the
perfect holiday place, apparently.'

'I pray I never get invited. What was she saying?'

'She was talking to Frau Lina Heydrich, the Obergruppenführer's
wife.' Sabine lowered her voice, though they could not possibly
have been overheard. Merely the name of the man in charge of the
Gestapo and the Sicherheitsdienst, the SS's own spy service, was
enough to provoke people to an instinctive whisper. He was called
Himmler's Hirn, Himmler's brain, because his severe meticulous
attention to detail was invaluable to his superior. His wife Lina, a
cool, Nordic beauty, was known to be a more ardent Nazi than her
husband, if such a thing was possible.

'Both ladies were here to have a treatment before the
Nuremberg rally. And they were gossiping about the Propaganda
Minister. There's always so much gossip about him. It's their
favourite topic.'

'I think the same goes for everyone in Berlin.'

'Annelies von Ribbentrop was telling Frau Heydrich that Joseph
Goebbels is so blinded by love for this actress – you must have
heard – that his judgement is quite askew. Otherwise he would
notice that Berlin is infested with English spies.'

'English spies?'

The soothing motions of Sabine's hands massaging Clara's face
were in inverse proportion to the alarm that this remark engen-
dered.

'Yes. Infested, Frau von Ribbentrop said.'

'Strange thing to say.'

'Perhaps not. You know better than me that the von
Ribbentrops hate England with a passion. Ever since he was
ridiculed when he was ambassador there. His wife is worried that
the Führer has been so blinded by those Englishwomen he hangs
about with, the Mitford sisters and their crowd, that he will let
them influence him in this Sudetenland business. He will refrain
from action out of an unfounded respect for the English.'

'If he refrains from action that's good, isn't it?'

'Maybe, but it's not that . . .'

'What are you getting at, Sabine?'

'That's just it, Clara. It's what surprised me. Frau von Ribbentrop mentioned you.'

'Me?'

'She said you might have Goebbels fooled, but you don't fool her. It was about time someone checked up on you.' Sabine lowered her voice yet further to a frightened whisper. 'Frau von Ribbentrop said Heydrich should have one of his men keep an eye on you.'

Clara opened her eyes and caught Sabine's agonized expression in the mirror. Her own face, sleek with cream, had a ghostly, impenetrable glow.

'Keep an eye on me?'

'That's all she said. To Frau Heydrich. I thought you should know.'

'Thank you,' said Clara, closing her eyes again in an attempt to suppress the panic that was rising within her.

Sabine didn't bother with platitudes about trying not to worry. Nothing could be more worrying than the attention of Obergruppenführer Reinhard Heydrich. Lean and blond with a savage, watchful gaze, of all the Nazi leaders, it was Heydrich who most conformed to the Aryan stereotype, which was ironic, given that as a child his schoolfriends had called him Issy in reference to the rumours of Jewish blood in his veins. But no one was making jokes about Heydrich now. In his immaculate black SS uniform, with the silver insignia of the SD on his arm and jackboots polished to a high gleam, the man who proclaimed himself 'as hard as granite' was considered the most fearsome member of the Nazi élite. A shadowy army of fifty thousand men were under his command and everyone in Germany lived in fear of them. Their base was an ominous cluster of buildings in Prinz Albrecht Strasse, but like a poison gas Heydrich's men were seemingly everywhere. If the grocery had run short of eggs, or a military parade held up your car, and you made an unwise comment, the man next to you might show his Party badge, demand your papers and request your appearance at the police station. It was worse when they didn't make themselves known. Heydrich's stool pigeons were always there, keeping an ear out for anyone who might betray a sympathy for Jews, Marxists, Social Democrats or Freemasons, and if they did, the details would be noted in a vast archive of files stored in the bowels of Prinz Albrecht Strasse for future reference.

One of the beauticians arrived to place a cup of steaming coffee on a tray beside Clara and Sabine stepped back, folding a towel neatly over her arm and lightly touching Clara's shoulder.

'Please. Have a drink.'

Clara took a sip and forced herself to think. Annelies von Ribbentrop was an heiress, born into a wealthy wine merchant family, the Henkells. Her family had been scandalized by her decision to marry Ribbentrop — before he had added the aristocratic 'von' to his name — yet that made little difference, because Annelies had plenty of ambition for two. With the help of lavish entertainment at their villa in Dahlem, she had angled successfully for her husband's appointment as ambassador to the Court of St James in Britain, only to find that the London posting was a disaster. English society had scoffed at the von Ribbentrops' grand attempts to impress them and were scandalized by the grandiose marble cladding at the embassy in Carlton House Terrace. Rumours spread that the ambassador was sleeping with Wallis Simpson, the American divorcee now married to the Duke of Windsor, and that he sent her seventeen red roses every day. Undaunted, Annelies had simply redirected her energy to securing her husband the job of Foreign Minister, and refocused her decorating obsession to an exorbitant refurbishment of the Foreign Ministry in Wilhelmstrasse.

She had known Clara for the past five years, and disliked her for that long too. It might have been because Frau von

Ribbentrop loathed Emmy Goering, who had been friendly to Clara, and was, like Clara, an actress, but if Clara had to guess, it was probably the mere fact that she was half English – a member of that despised race who had laughed at Annelies behind their hands, ridiculed her pretensions and gossiped about her husband's affairs.

As Sabine took up a warm flannel and massaged Clara's face, then set about perfecting her make-up, Clara was calculating the effect that Frau von Ribbentrop's comments might have. Would Lina Heydrich actually bother to relay gossip about a half-English actress who had fallen foul of the Foreign Minister's wife? And even if she did, what was the chance that Heydrich would pay any attention, given that the Nazi hierarchy was in the midst of an international crisis? When the continent stood on the brink of war, who could be bothered with gossip about actresses? Politicians, maybe, merited scrutiny and statesmen, even journalists. But who cared about actresses?

Somehow Clara managed to thank Sabine, and leave the salon with a semblance of calm, but once outside she walked along the Kurfürstendamm without seeing it. The streets were sticky with rising heat which smelt of melting tar and the sun's glare bounced off the hot steel of postcard sellers' carts and reflected in the windows of the department stores. A snatch of music issued from a bar and the cries of a newspaper seller on the corner of Joachimstaler Strasse competed with the sound of drilling on yet another new building. Yet despite the hustle of the street, Clara felt as though she was in a film with the sound locked off, cocooned in silence and her own thoughts. Sabine's comment echoed in her mind.

Heydrich should have one of his men keep an eye on you.

While the threat of surveillance was always with Clara, in recent months it had become a more low-level fear, a theoretical possibility which led her to undertake routine precautions out of habit, rather than immediate concern. She still, religiously, followed the lessons Leo had taught her. She must never carry with her the name of Archie Dyson, her contact at the British Embassy, nor should she keep tickets to trams or cinemas. Tickets were tiny, valuable mines of information that pinpointed your location and left an unmistakable trace. The only tickets in Clara's pocket should be those she had deliberately placed there. She must always ensure her moves were accountable and have a valid reason for anywhere she went. Lastly, and most importantly, she must assume she was being watched, day and night.

Despite these precautions though, since arresting her the previous year the Gestapo seemed to have satisfied themselves that Clara was nothing more than she seemed; a moderately successful actress whose ambitions lay in securing better roles, rather than securing secrets for British Intelligence. She had not dropped her guard, yet she had been able to breathe a sigh of relief. Now it seemed she would need to step up her attention again. Fresh threat lurked all around her and more than ever she would need to be at her most alert.

She came to a halt in front of a green octagonal, turreted news kiosk. The *B.Z. am Mittag* was displaying a photograph of the most famous baby in the Reich, Edda Goering, with her adoring parents. The fact that the child had been given the same name as Mussolini's daughter raised excitable gossip about her paternity, particularly since the Duce had been visiting Berlin at the time of her conception and Goering was widely assumed to be impotent. That was easy to believe, Clara thought, looking at his face like a ripening cheese, the fat wet lips and slightly protruding eyes as he bent over the child in the arms of her mother Emmy, who at forty-five might well be cradling the only baby she would ever have. The couple's joy was shared around the world, at least if you believed the six hundred thousand telegrams plus vanloads of artworks, Meissen porcelain sets and other lavish presents that had poured in. In terms of kings bearing gifts, Edda's arrival made the original Nativity look like a Bring and Buy sale.

Clara had encountered Emmy Goering many times and knew

that whenever they next met Emmy would expect her to be entirely up to date about the baby and all her appearances in the press. Like any new mother, only a hundred times worse.

Blindly, she took a paper from the rack.

'Dreizig pfennig, bitte.'

She fumbled in her purse for change and dropped the coins. Stooping to pick them up, she was beaten to it by the customer behind her and looked up to find herself staring at a familiar face. It was jovial and slightly fleshy, with beads of sweat on the forehead, crinkled lines around the eyes, and unruly, receding hair.

Cultural attaché, Max Brandt.

At once, the sounds on the street amplified as though an invisible volume had suddenly been turned up. The screech of tram wheels ripped through the cocoon of thought that enveloped Clara and she was suddenly conscious of her freshly made-up face and the trail of apricot scent that radiated from her.

'Herr Brandt! You're in Berlin? What a surprise.'

'Isn't it?' He took off his peaked cap and smiled down at her. 'People tend not to like surprises nowadays, but I say this is a remarkably pleasant one.'

'And you're in uniform.'

'Unfortunately. These things are unbearably hot, you know. But it could be worse. This is just the day uniform; our full diplomatic uniform has a dark blue tailcoat embroidered with oak leaves and a silver sash and dagger.'

'A dagger doesn't sound very diplomatic.'

'Depends what kind of diplomacy you're engaged in. Diplomats with daggers seem to be in vogue right now.' He ran a finger round his collar. 'As a matter of fact, all these get-ups are a new thing. A few years ago we Foreign Service people wore plain suits until someone had the bright idea of dressing us up like eighteenth-century dandies. They're designed by some fellow called Benno von Arent.'

'I know von Arent. He's a stage designer. He works at Ufa.'

'That makes sense. We all look like we're performing in an operetta.'

Even in his uniform there was something unruly about Max Brandt, something untamed, as though dark hair might curl mutinously from the neck of his shirt, or the buttons of his uniform burst apart. Unlike a lot of Party men who liked to shave their heads so that only a single, brutal strip remained, his own was wavy and only just controlled by brilliantine. Instead of the polished charm of a professional diplomat, he exuded a kind of insubordinate jollity. Despite herself, Clara's anxiety lifted and she laughed.

'So what brings you from Paris?'

'Just some work matters. But it looks like serendipity.'

'Are you here long?'

'A few days, probably.' Although he looked older in uniform, his eyes were still sleepy and humorous and his manner suggestive.

'As I recall, we had an arrangement to meet for dinner. What would you say to making that a firm plan? That is, if Sturmbannführer Steinbrecher doesn't object.'

Despite herself, Clara blushed at the memory of her made-up boyfriend.

'I'm really sorry. I can't just now.'

'Lunch then. It's not yet midday.'

'Again, I can't.'

'Can't today, or can't with me?'

'It's just not possible.'

'That's a shame. I thought you gave me your word.'

She hesitated. Though she felt an intense gravitational pull of attraction, the appearance of Max Brandt redoubled her alarm. Moments earlier she had been warned that Heydrich might be watching her and here was a Nazi officer on the street in front of her, claiming co-incidence. How could it be co-incidence that he should resurface in Berlin, let alone contrive to turn up right by her side at this precise junction on the Ku'damm at exactly the same time? Coincidence troubled Clara. She had learned to see it for what it was, genuine but rare, and always meriting scrutiny. Where other people saw coincidence, she tended to see patterns. *Just some work matters*, Brandt said, but how could the work of a cultural attaché have any importance at a time when the fate of nations hung in the balance? His business was opera and art, but which opera could merit his immediate return to the capital? What painting could require high-level attention in Berlin?

And yet . . . she yearned to accept his invitation.

Unbidden, her mind travelled ahead to the idea of a long lunch with Max Brandt, talking about theatre and opera, and a slow walk afterwards, perhaps culminating in a hotel somewhere, silk sheets rumpled and curtains drawn against the world. A tangle of clothes on the floor. Her cheek against that tanned chest, her naked limbs entwined with his. The smell of French cigarettes and his warm skin. The image was so scandalously real in her mind that she blushed and in that flash she perceived that similar scenes were playing in Brandt's imagination too. For a fraction of a second, the possibility hung tantalizingly between them. A stolen afternoon of pleasure, cut off from the world. Then she remembered how lonely she had felt in Paris and realized that Brandt, with his broken marriage, probably felt that way too. It didn't have to be her – he would probably have gone with any girl who might, for a few days, staunch the isolation of a solitary existence. But Clara wasn't just anyone and she was not interested in a few days' pleasure, above all not when it came to sleeping with a Nazi officer whose motives were far from romantic.

'I don't have the time.'

'Please.' There was a note of appeal in his voice. For a second it was as though the suave mask had slipped to reveal a kind of desperation. A need for contact that went beyond the purely personal. Brandt reached a hand forward to her arm and his touch seared her, but she kept her tone light and friendly.

'You see, I have an audition in Munich tomorrow so I'm taking the night train down this evening. We'll have to postpone our dinner.'

It did the trick. His mask was resumed, the languid smile back in place. 'I note you say postpone and not cancel, Clara Vine. I shall take that to heart. I won't forget.'

She rested her hand in his briefly.

'Nor will I.'

Brandt remained, watching her thoughtfully, as she headed up the street.

Chapter Twelve

In the lobby of the Ministry of Propaganda and Enlightenment, Rupert Allingham paused beside a display of priceless mediaeval cartography that had been recently pilfered from the city's museums. Since seizing power, Nazi ministers had had no qualms about helping themselves to the contents of the state's art collections, not only for home use but also to decorate their political domains. This time Goebbels had been on quite a spree. The most exquisite item in his new collection was a fourteenth-century depiction of the Kingdom of Bohemia, a vista of turrets and bears, with a glinting river running through it, crowded with fishes and ships. Rupert squinted at it carefully. He loved those old maps, the ones with dolphins plunging into absurdly crested waves, towns encircled by fortifications and cherubs in the corners blowing their trumpets. Where nations were divided into states with their own coats of arms and tiny castles nestled in miniature woods. They belonged to another, simpler world, one where history hatched national borders gently, like cracks in a shell.

Map-making was an appropriate enthusiasm for the Nazi regime, given that it was intent on revising the maps of Europe all over again. Also on the wall was a map that had been redrawn since the Anschluss to include Austria, now renamed Ostmark, and stamped with a decorative swastika whose crooked arms seemed to extend like hooks across the continent, angling for other nations to ensnare. Cartography was certainly a good career choice in Nazi Germany. That, or making battleships.

Austria had shattered him. At the age of thirty-six, with a good fifteen years in journalism behind him, Rupert Allingham no longer expected that a news story could make him weep, but the things he had seen in Vienna in the past month had brought tears to his eyes. The sound of German drums beating like an iron heart as the troops marched into the city centre. The sight of strapping blondes fighting to get a glimpse of a Jewish surgeon on his hands and knees, scrubbing the pavement with delicate, experienced fingers that had probably saved the lives of hundreds of Austrians and were now bruised and bleeding from the slashes of the whips wielded by thugs in swastika armbands. The Viennese Nazis were far more brutal than the Germans and they lost no time in jailing Jews and confiscating their property. The rich or élite Jews, like Sigmund Freud, were able to flee, but the others were stranded. Even before they crossed the border the Gestapo had assembled a hundred thousand names with Viennese addresses, and now an official called Adolf Eichmann had been put in charge of an Office for Jewish Emigration in Vienna. The trouble was, nobody else wanted them. Czechoslovakia had closed its borders to Jewish refugees. President Roosevelt had convened a conference in France to address the problem, but France, too, was making it hard for Jews who wanted to escape. The word was that since the Nazis had given up the hope of the Jews moving en masse to Palestine, they had a plan to ship them to Madagascar. All sorts of schemes were in the pipeline, formulated by fat officials behind desks in Berlin, reducing the faraway lives of thousands of people to a stack of paper. One plan had been floated to arrest all the Ostjuden on a single night and transport them at gunpoint to Poland. Canada, Angola, Haiti, Abyssinia had also been mooted. What kind of minds devised these schemes? Did they consider what it would mean for people to be wrenched away from everything they knew? It was sometimes impossible to avoid the conclusion that some of the nastiest acts of the century were being perpetrated not by evil geniuses, but by bureaucrats.

No wonder he drank.

'You waiting for something, Allingham?'

A voice cut through his reflections. It was Herbert Melcher, from the Associated Press, a quiet American with a wit as dry as a vodka martini.

'I'm waiting for the Fourth Reich to begin.'

'You might be waiting some time.'

'Let's hope not.'

Melcher had a face full of creases, like a newspaper that had been balled up and smoothed out again. He was more softly spoken than a lot of the correspondents, whose voices tended to match the size of their by-lines, but he had been around a long time, and Rupert respected him.

'Mahatma Gandhi was on frenetic form today, I thought. Determined to avoid all mention of the international situation. Incredible that he should be talking about an exhibition of German culture at a time like this.'

'Sure. If you want an exhibition of German culture, just take a walk down the Jewish quarter when a marching band's been through.'

'Heard about this reception he's holding?' Melcher asked. 'A showcase for Hollywood? A night of the stars to flatter the executives of the big American studios?'

'Can he be serious? They're never going to turn up at a time like this.'

'Don't you believe it. The invitations have gone out already and I'll bet they've all been accepted, too. What Hollywood mogul would miss a chance to drink Goebbels' champagne and eyeball his actresses? Germany's an important market for them and they'll do a lot to keep in the Reich's good books.'

'So no movies about aggressive nations marching to war.'

'Precisely. Stick to candy-floss romance. Take the public's mind off their troubles.'

'Are the press invited to this extravaganza?'

'The society columns will be for certain.'

The newspaper gossip columns were full of actresses sleeping with sports stars and countesses having affairs with gigolos at the Adlon and Goebbels always encouraged them, chiefly because they never dared mention the spiciest society gossip, concerning himself.

Melcher moved closer and brought his soft felt hat up to his face. 'Here's something you won't find in the social columns, though. You know about Goebbels' Czech girlfriend?'

'Who doesn't? The porter here told me he's had a suite installed behind his office. It has a system of bells so that no one disturbs them.'

'Might prove unnecessary. From what I've heard, the girlfriend's about to be banished from the Reich on the Führer's orders. The Minister's beside himself. He asked Hitler to make him ambassador to Japan instead, and let him leave with the girl, but Adolf said no. Went crazy apparently. Ordered Goebbels to focus on promoting the role of the family in the Reich.'

'Ah,' said Rupert. 'Hence this morning's new ordinances.'

In the twice-daily Propaganda Ministry briefings, the domestic press was issued with straightforward directives – everything from which story to carry to what line to take on each newsworthy incident and which minister to be mentioned – but it was trickier with the foreign press. Foreigners couldn't be told what to do, so they were told what not to do instead. That morning's prohibitions included a new ordinance against any negative media, film, theatre or literature comment about large families. Gross offences would result in the loss of the licence to practise journalism.

'You filing that?'

Melcher stroked his chin.

'I'm a bit busy at the moment. As if things weren't frantic enough, Chuck Lewis, you know, the chap from the *Chicago Herald*, has gone absent without leave so I'm being asked to cover.'

Rupert knew Chuck Lewis. A louche, handsome devil, with a deadly mixture of intelligence, amorality and southern charm.

'Lewis's gone AWOL?'

'Nothing serious. Woman troubles. Seems they're not confined to government ministers. Talk of the devil . . .' A bustle of uniforms burst through a set of doors across the hall. 'Here comes the poison dwarf now.'

Goebbels was barrelling towards them, a huddle of minders around him. The minders, all senior officers of the Ministry, were an ill-assorted crew, full of bluster and menace but lacking real conviction. If you were casting a movie, Rupert thought, these would be the ones who never made the recall. Melcher melted away.

'Ah, Herr Allingham. Another member of the press intent on whipping up hatred against me,' rasped Goebbels.

'Not at all, Herr Reich Minister.'

After the lengthy monologue Goebbels delivered each morning, there was a brief interval for questions. These took the form of craven queries from the domestic press and slightly bolder ones from the foreigners. Following Clara's request, Rupert had stood up and asked about the possibility of a woman falling overboard on a KdF cruise. His question had been met with incredulity, bewilderment, then anger.

'I assure you there has been no such tragedy on any of our KdF holidays. The Labour Front's commitment to health and safety is second to none. The Kraft durch Freude programme is unparalleled in the world and the pride of the Reich.'

That seemed to cover it, so why had Goebbels come after him now? Rupert guessed he was about to find out.

'I've had a thought, Herr Allingham, given your interest – might I say *unexpected* interest – in female affairs.' Goebbels paused to let this witticism reverberate amongst his minions, who chuckled nastily. In a flash, Rupert realized precisely their assumptions about his private life.

'I have decided to grant you an interview with Frau Scholtz-Klink. The Führerin will be pleased to meet at your convenience.'

The Führerin. Hadn't Clara mentioned something about her and a documentary Goebbels was making about the Deutsche Frauenschaft?

'Can I ask what exactly . . .?'

'I shall leave it to Frau Scholtz-Klink to elaborate, but I can tell you it's a very interesting initiative designed to honour German womanhood,' said Goebbels. 'I'm offering you a scoop, in fact. And a rather more inspiring one than some fictitious tittle-tattle about the KdF.'

The alacrity of Goebbels meant something, but Rupert couldn't tell exactly what. At a time when the whole world was holding its breath, when every news desk in Europe wanted articles on peace talks and ultimatums and conventions, and when ambassadors could not leave their front doors without being dazzled by the flashbulbs of the international press, the idea of wasting a morning talking about German womanhood was a crazy diversion. But refusing a direct request from Goebbels was equally crazy right now, and the Minister knew it. The best thing Rupert could do was to get this business over with as fast as possible.

'Sounds fascinating, Herr Doktor. I shall make an appointment immediately.'

'Do that.'

The Propaganda Minister limped swiftly away. If the Nazi sterilization laws had any logic to them, Rupert thought, they'd have started with Joseph Goebbels.

Chapter Thirteen

The Artists' House in Munich had a new car park. Until a few months ago, the site just off Lenbachplatz had been occupied by the centuries-old Munich synagogue, but on Hitler's orders the synagogue had been razed to the ground to create more parking spots for the patrons of his favourite club. In the past, when the Party had risen to power in Munich, the Führer had loved relaxing at the Artists' House, hosting parties there and inviting actresses from whichever show he had seen to reprise their dances or singing in a more intimate capacity. Even though international events now precluded such harmless diversions, Hitler, like Goering and Goebbels, still liked to think of himself as a tasteful sophisticate with a special regard for art. All the senior party leaders portrayed themselves as men of culture who understood that art had a role, and it wasn't just about enjoying yourself. Art was a sacred thing and the Artists' House, with its marbled halls and gilded ceilings, echoed that idea. On the outside, caryatids supported ornate gables, Neptune and Bacchus adorned the walls and the gateway was crowned by the statue of a centaur wielding a club. Inside, the ornate ceiling was spattered with gilded stars. To the casual visitor the place was like some exotic, pagan temple, and one which had witnessed equally exotic goings-on. That afternoon, however, the rather more routine business of auditions was taking place.

Standing in the gleaming marble hallway, Clara waited uncer-
tainly. Despite the fact that *Good King George* was merely a cover
for another more serious assignment, she still felt the familiar
nerves which came with any audition – even now, when she was
well established in her career.

When she had first come to Germany, and applied for work at
the Ufa film studios, she had needed to learn her craft all over
again. Until that point she had been a stage actress, but she quickly
discovered that acting for the movies was an altogether subtler
affair. It required intense control over the tiniest nuance of gesture
and facial expression. A raised eyebrow could contain an ocean of
expression. A glance was enough to convey a heart full of love or
hate. You needed rigid self-discipline to portray emotion in a
camera close-up, and the effort Clara put into her acting provided
useful respite from her secret life. It might seem perverse that being
in front of the camera should be the place she felt most relaxed,
but the spotlight was a refuge from the task she had willingly taken
on. It also provided her with an authentic cover. Clara Vine was
exactly what she said she was, an actress who devoted herself diligently to each role. Except that now, in Eva Braun's home town,
her other role suddenly felt more real and more impossible.

Having consulted the receptionist and been told to wait, she
went over to a chair at the foot of the stairs, took out a silver
enamel compact from her bag and applied another coat of her rapidly dwindling Elizabeth Arden Velvet Red. Then she found her
copy of *Rebecca* and tried to lose herself in the landscape of the faraway south coast of Cornwall where she had spent so many of her
childhood holidays, tramping through damp rhododendrons and
picking the sand out of sandwiches beside the icy sea.

'Clara Vine! Thank God. At least there's someone I've heard of
here.'

A statuesque blonde swept through the door as though pursued
by a phantom horde of pressmen touting flashbulb cameras and
notebooks. She was dressed as for a first night, complete with a hat

featuring a little bird picked out in diamanté, a taut silk dress against which her breasts strained, and perfume which trailed luxuriously after her like a mink wrap. Her face was a flawless expanse of creamy foundation and her bleached hair shone like a pale flame in the dim light of the hall. Perching on the chair beside Clara, she extracted a cigarette from her bag, lit it, took a disdainful drag and peered loftily about the hall.

Clara tried to contain her astonishment. Ursula Schilling was an A-list star, one of the country's favourites. For years her face had stared seductively out from billboards and film hoardings, and the gossip columns of innumerable newspapers and glossy magazines. It was a face simply made for the screen. Ursula Schilling could drown a man in the depths of her violet eyes and unleash a tide of contempt with a twitch of her high arched brows. She possessed a kind of sulky grandeur which made men want to kiss her or slap her, usually both. Yet here she was auditioning for a potboiler which would barely get screened at the local Munich fleapit, never mind the Ufa Palast am Zoo.

'Ursula! What a surprise to see you!'

'You can say that again, darling.'

Ursula gave Clara a sidelong look and exhaled a stream of smoke sideways out of her mouth. On previous occasions, when they had passed in the corridors of the Ufa studios, or rubbed shoulders at parties, Ursula barely deigned to speak to Clara, but now, it seemed, things had changed.

'God knows why I came. It's not my kind of film and to top it all I'm being asked to play the wife's friend. A role with about three lines! Fritz Gutmann told me she was the girl-next-door type and I had to tell him, "Fritz, I'm a movie star. That's why people come to see me. If people wanted the girl-next-door look, they could just go next door."'

'But you accepted?'

A faint shrug.

'I'm thinking about it.'

'Herr Gutmann must have been thrilled to get you.'

'He didn't show much sign of it.' Ursula flicked her hair impatiently and out of sheer habit looked around for the crowd she would usually draw.

'What about you? Which part are you up for?'

'Well, actually . . .'

Clara was saved from an immediate answer by a shout of greeting. A flamboyant man with a sweep of brown hair and a generous mouth was clipping down the stairs towards them. Though his SS uniform was personally tailored by Hugo Boss, he wore it like an evening dress accessorized with an invisible feather boa.

'Ladies! What a relief. At last we can expect some quality in this production.'

Hitler had often opined that if he had not been singled out by fate for the role of Führer and saviour of his nation, he would have chosen to be a theatrical set designer, but as it was he would have to settle for patronizing the genius of Benno von Arent instead. The pair of them would linger late into the night, poring over the Führer's own designs for sets and revolving stages and lighting techniques. As well as designing blockbusters like *Viktor und Viktoria*, *Hitler Youth Quex* and Clara's most recent film, *Es leuchten die Sterne*, the Reich stage designer also had the job of transforming *Die Meistersinger* every year at the rally into a Nazi extravaganza, complete with massed crowds, flags and banners.

He glanced curiously at Clara's book.

'I always forget you're English.'

'Half, Herr Sturmbannführer.'

'You play the German half so well. Why don't we ever see you in the Künstlerklub?'

The Künstlerklub in Berlin was one of Goebbels' recent business enterprises, a private members' club with dancing, restaurant and bar. It was full of actresses with plunging necklines and strutting Nazi officials, most notably Goebbels himself, who liked to take actresses there to discuss their work as a prelude to other matters.

When he first had the idea of creating his own nightclub Goebbels had seized on von Arent, as the Führer's favourite, and put him in charge and the choice had paid off handsomely.

Von Arent wagged a finger. 'No excuses. I insist you come. In fact we're holding a reception for the Propaganda Ministry to honour the American/German artistic friendship. I think that's what they called it. Anyhow, everyone will be there. I'll send you two ladies invitations when we're back in Berlin.'

'Which can't come soon enough,' added Ursula.

'Come, come, sweetheart, it's not that bad. This may not be Babelsberg but I shall be making you the most magnificent costumes. Get the clothes right and the rest will follow, that's what I always say. They tell me the script is an absolute disaster, but if there is any way of saving us all from total humiliation ...' He whirled round. 'And here's our director now.'

If it was true that Fritz Gutmann was preparing to flee to England, he was giving no sign of it, other than a complexion as grey and mottled as the ash from his own cigarettes and a frame as starved as a Giacometti sculpture. His green-shaded director's cap with tufts of hair sticking out reminded Clara of the ostriches at Berlin Zoo. He was not Jewish – or he would have been barred from working as a director by the Reich Chamber of Culture – but his films were hardly noted for their ideological fidelity to the Reich and were routinely branded as turkeys in the press conferences of the Reich Chamber of Film. This latest production would, no doubt, suffer the same fate. When he shook hands Clara noticed that his nails were bitten to the quick.

'Thank you so much for coming, everyone. Fräulein Vine, perhaps if we could talk first. Would you follow me?'

He led the way into a hall, shut the door firmly behind them, glanced around and lowered his voice.

'I appreciate you coming. It's not always easy to tempt actresses to Geiselgasteig any more.'

The Geiselgasteig studios, which occupied a leafy plot of land a short train ride south of Munich, had an illustrious history. During the silent era they had attracted prestigious foreign direc- tors including Alfred Hitchcock, and people began to refer to the studios as 'Los Angeles on the Isar'. But all that had changed since the Reich Chamber of Culture took over the film industry and any movies that were daring, experimental, or strayed outside Goebbels' rigid parameters were destined to be cast-iron flops.

'Have you found pleasant accommodation?'

Clara had booked a room just a few minutes' walk away in a small pension in Maximiliansplatz. It was a gloomy place with all the atmosphere of a funeral parlour. Her bedroom had a bed of heavy, Bavarian fretted wood and a tiny desk covered with an embroidered cloth, but the furniture was polished, the sheets clean and the window overlooked a leafy square decorated with terraces and stone urns and a large bronze statue of Goethe.

'Thank you. Yes.'

'You come highly recommended from London Films. I met them first when they were scouting for locations in Munich. Are you familiar with their work?'

So there was to be no overt mention of Guy Hamilton's elab- orate plan. Alexander Korda's film studios may have been engaged in a high-stakes espionage scheme, but Fritz Gutmann was not going to risk discussing it and however impatient Clara was to broach the real purpose of her presence in Munich, she knew he was right.

'I am.'

He tilted his head curiously on one side.

'Do you miss England?'

'Sometimes.'

'I hope to see it myself someday.'

A flicker of understanding passed between them,

'Soon, I hope.'

His face relaxed into a smile. 'I hope so too. I should tell you, Fräulein Vine, that I have followed your career with some interest. I remember your first film for Ufa, *Schwarze Rosen*, wasn't it? That glance you gave when you said goodbye to Hans Albers – I've never forgotten it. It was only fleeting, but you managed to express so much. That's what I always tell my cast: a good actor should be able to compress a thousand words into a momentary glance. Anyone brought up with silent films understands that, but our modern actors, unfortunately, seem to believe that a bellowing voice or clever script will do the job for them.' Snapping out of this reverie, he continued, 'Anyhow, about this part . . . '

Ushering her to the back of the hall, he continued with a rapid rundown of the film and the part of Sophia of Celle, George 1st's unfaithful wife.

'It's a wonderful story. A tale of unrequited love. You've done a few of those.'

'My speciality.'

'Indeed. Sophia spent decades in love with a Swedish count, even though she was thrown in prison by her husband on account of it. That's my only concern actually.'

'Oh?'

'It's the issue of portraying an unfaithful wife. You know how it is. The last thing we want is the Minister ordering a last minute rewrite of history.'

'He didn't seem to mind when I mentioned it to him.'

Gutmann paled visibly. 'You mentioned my film to Goebbels?'

The director could not have looked more terrified if Clara had been wearing a Gestapo leather coat instead of a Jaeger jacket and carrying a search warrant in place of her crocodile clutch bag.

'Have I caused a problem?' she said anxiously.

'No, of course not. You probably had no choice. And the script has been approved. We submitted it to the Ministry for all the usual moral, political and racial purity checks. We've ensured there's no Jewish music in the score and of course we had to observe the ban on images of political unrest, which will rule out our crowd scenes.' Gutmann was ticking off the regulations on his fingers, as though terrified to have forgotten a rule. 'But I didn't expect to attract the attention of Doktor Goebbels. Generally it's only the lowly officials who handle pre-censorship, unless something specifically catches the Minister's eye.'

'He seemed to think it was fine, as long as she dies at the end.'

'Ha! It would probably help if she could turn out to be Jewish too. No matter. With my films . . .' Gutmann shrugged. 'Let's just say, the Herr Doktor does not view my output with especial enthusiasm. But I thought I'd be safe with a historical theme.'

'I'm sure it'll be a success.'

'And I'm grateful for your confidence. But Goebbels is always a worry to me, to be honest. Film matters so much to him and he notices everything. The only time I had the experience of meeting him, he told me that the entire Third Reich could be seen as a cinematic event . . .'

He halted mid flow and straightened up. 'Excuse me, but I think there's someone who'd like to meet you.'

The slam of a door behind them caused him to halt mid-flow and Clara turned to see that another person had entered the room. It was a young woman in her mid-twenties, with a stiff raffia hat set jauntily to one side of her head and soft curls that reached her shoulders. She wore a green dress with a sweetheart neckline and carried a calfskin bag with a shiny enamelled swastika for a clasp. Though she had never seen the woman before, Clara recognized her at once.

Eva Braun.

The woman paused a moment, before stepping forward confidently and extending a hand.

'Fräulein Vine, I'm so pleased you agreed to see me.'

Clara allowed no inkling of surprise to cross her face. This was the person she had come to see. The object of her mission. The woman who, if Guy Hamilton was to be believed, was the only person on earth privy to the Führer's true plans, motivations and intentions. The girl who might hold the fate of the world in her white lace gloves.

Gutmann sprang forward as though propelled by an electric charge.

'May I introduce Fräulein Braun?'

'I hope you didn't mind me writing to you last year.' Eva Braun's voice was softer than the senior Nazi wives, gentle and hesitant compared to the confident rasp of Frau von Ribbentrop, or the husky tones of Magda Goebbels.

'I expect you get a lot of bother from fans.'

'Not at all. I was flattered to receive your letter.'

Despite the girlish façade, a single glance at Eva Braun's face told Clara there was a core of steel behind the shy exterior. Everything about her appearance was in direct contradiction of Hitler's cherished notions of feminine beauty. Her carefully styled hair was peroxided, despite his hatred of artificial colours, and her liberal use of foundation and lipstick made mockery of the Führer's famous ban on cosmetics. Clara was reminded suddenly of a character she had once played in Noël Coward's *Hay Fever* – Sorel Bliss – charming, brittle and outwardly girlish, with a glimmer of steel beneath the surface.

'*Black Roses* is one of my favourite films. Wolf and I have seen it several times at the Berghof.'

The reference to Hitler's mountain-top fortress was deliberate. As was the use of her nickname for him – Wolf. It ensured that Clara knew beyond a shadow of a doubt that the topic of the Führer need not be taboo with Eva Braun. Indeed, it might be practically compulsory.

'We watch a movie every night at the Berghof. Sometimes two. He loves movies. He says a great film has the power of a great speech.'

At last Eva Braun seemed to notice Gutmann, quivering beside her.

'I do hope I'm not interrupting, Herr Gutmann?'

'Not at all, gnädiges Fräulein,' he stammered.

Clara's mind was calculating rapidly. She may be exchanging pleasantries with the Führer's girlfriend, but there was no chance of forming any deeper acquaintance so long as Gutmann was quaking like a leaf alongside them. She needed to get Eva on her own.

'I wonder . . . Fräulein Braun. I'm longing for some tea. Would you like to join me?'

'That would be lovely. Herr Gutmann, are you coming too?'

Gutmann recoiled as though he had been asked to take tea with a rattlesnake. A shudder of horror ran through him, which he failed to disguise.

'So busy right now, gnädiges Fräulein, so many people to see . . .' he muttered. 'In fact,' he turned to Clara, 'why don't we dispense with the audition? I know you'd be perfect for the part. Filming begins in two days' time. May I assume you are interested in the role?'

'I'm interested, yes.'

'Very good then. Costume fittings start on Friday. Could you talk to my production manager about timings and so on?'

'Aren't you forgetting something?'

He started as Clara pointed at the script in his hand.

'Oh.' Almost as an afterthought he held out the wedge of paper. 'Of course.'

Before he could hand the script to her the tremor in his hand caused him to drop it and the papers fluttered to the ground like the petals of a blown rose. Gutmann scrabbled to pick them up, losing his spectacles in the process, and Eva Braun regarded him impassively, as if he were a waiter who had dropped his tray.

'I've an idea,' she said brightly. 'As we're having tea, why don't we go to my favourite café? If you've finished business for the day, of course, Fräulein Vine?'

'Please call me Clara.'

Clara picked up her bag and took the pages, wishing fervently that there was a script for the encounter to come.

The taxi delivered them to the Hofgarten, Munich's beautiful central square, and they crossed the sun-dappled cloister to the Café Heck. The fine weather had brought out the crowds and around the gravelled paths men in typical Bavarian costume – short leather trousers and knee socks, and small green hats planted on their shaven heads – strolled, accompanied by stout matrons in ankle-length dirndls and with frothy lace at their bosoms. In the centre of the square a brass band had set up base, thumping out a medley of uplifting Bavarian songs.

As they entered the café, heads swivelled and the man opposite them blatantly lowered his newspaper to stare. Eva planted herself at a window table, fully aware that all eyes were on her. Indeed she seemed to bask in the attention, pursing up her crimson lips and blowing a long stream of smoke towards the ceiling.

'Don't mind them gawping. You're lucky we're not with him,' she quipped. 'Then everyone stands and applauds.'

Clara wondered how much knowledge of Eva Braun's position she might presume. Her existence, after all, was unknown to most loyal, Führer-abiding Germans. She was a state secret, and no newspaper stories about her or pictures of her could be published. When they travelled together, Hitler ensured that she remained in a separate car, well behind his own, and even on Alpine walks she was obliged to linger behind, lest any passers-by jump to conclusions. Yet Eva had brought her here, to Hitler's favourite café, and openly referred to her trips to the Obersalzberg.

Now, she leant confidentially across the table.

'It's lovely to meet you in person, Clara. I adore the movies and I've seen all of yours. I keep loads of film stills and photographs, I collect everything. It's silly I know, but I adore it. I met Herr Gutmann at a function and I mentioned you, and I was so thrilled when he offered to introduce me.'

They ordered glasses of Orange Pekoe tea, and Eva Braun's eyes roved over a glass cabinet of cream cakes, Black Forest gateaux and puff pastries, before she settled on Kaiserschmarrn, a mess of cream and cherry sauce enveloped in a pancake.

'I don't know why I eat this. It's terribly sickly but it's Wolf's favourite. I suppose I order it out of habit. Bad habit!'

She gave a little laugh, and gestured at her waist.

'I'll need to keep my figure if I'm ever going to act myself.'

Clara almost choked on her cinnamon cake. 'I didn't realize . . . are you planning on an acting career?'

Eva fixed her with wide blue eyes.

'It's all I've ever wanted to do.'

'And are you, I mean, do you have any plans?'

'I act already.' She gave a modest smile. 'Just putting on plays with friends. I know that sounds a bit amateurish to you, but at the moment it's all he'll allow me to do. I love making my own little films and getting my schoolfriends to act in them. Wolf – the Führer – gave me a cine camera for my nineteenth birthday and I never go anywhere without it. Since then I've got lots more equipment too; an Agfa and a Leica and a Siemens movie camera. So you see I'm as much at home behind the camera as in front of it.'

'How did you first meet the Führer?'

Eva shrugged dismissively, as though she didn't want to dwell on the less glamorous parts of her career.

'I worked for his photographer, Heinrich Hoffmann, not far from here, in Schellingstrasse. I took the orders and supervised the framing and so on. I had a lot of time on my hands so I used to spend time looking through Hoffmann's drawers at all the photographs of Wolf. Not very flattering, most of them!'

Clara recalled her discovery of the previous year. An early negative of Hitler which might have dashed forever the image of the Führer, had circumstances not intervened. She wondered if Eva had ever seen pictures like that, and if so what she must have thought of them.

'One day I was serving behind the counter, terribly bored, and I looked up to see him standing right in front of me. I was so flustered; I mean he wasn't the Führer then, but he was still famous, and he asked me to the opera. It was so romantic. And after that he started taking me regularly and sending flowers. He sent so many flowers to Hoffmann's the place smelt like a cemetery.'

She wrinkled her nose.

'A shame it had to be opera he loves. I'm always nagging him to go to the ballet but he absolutely refuses. He hates it. He thinks men in tights are disgusting and he has to look away. He says it's a cultural disgrace to see people hopping about and even ballroom dancing is a stupid waste of time and effeminate. He told me Viennese dancing is the reason for the decline of the Austrian empire.'

Eva rolled her eyes in time-honoured exasperation at the waywardness of men and Clara gave a sympathetic smile. Even though she was acting on instructions from Guy Hamilton, there was something endearing about Eva Braun's girlish demeanour and the way the chatter tumbled out of her as though she was starved of social life. She had that in common with other Nazi women Clara had met. All of them lived closeted existences, circumscribed by the dictates of their men and the suspicions of a paranoid regime.

'He's very stubborn when it comes to taking any interest in my hobbies. Like perfume, for example. There's a shop in Theatinerstrasse which sells the most delicious French perfumes; Worth's *Je Reviens*, that's my favourite – awful that my favourite perfume should be French, isn't it? Anyhow, I used to love going in and trying one, then waiting until it had worn off before going in again and trying some more, but I could never persuade him to come into the shop. He'd just stand outside or wait for me in the car. That was ages ago, of course – he never comes shopping with me now and you can't get French perfumes either. But it doesn't matter because I've started making my own.'

'Your own perfume? What an ingenious solution.'

'Sounds awfully eccentric, doesn't it? But it's true. I like creating my own concoctions. Taking two completely different scents and mingling them and making something unique. Don't you think that's how incredible things happen? You pick the most unlikely ingredients and put them together and somehow they make an impact?'

She laughed lightly, wiping a little cream off her mouth, and Clara thought there was nothing more unlikely than the match between this gauche young woman in front of her and the monstrous German dictator. She must be careful not to stem this headlong rush of confidences, which tumbled out of Eva as though they had been far too long suppressed.

'There was an industrialist at the Berghof the other day who was trying to explain it to me,' added Eva. 'He said they had discovered molecules that could also be used in perfume to make them last – aldehydes, I think they're called. When you put them in perfumes the particles collide and reform into something quite different. You'd never think perfume would contain strange, synthetic molecules, would you?'

'It's amazing what chemistry can do.'

'It is, but to tell the truth, I don't really like the idea of all these chemicals. I like things to be natural. Did you know Chanel No. 5 contains a thousand jasmine blooms and twelve roses in every bottle? It's true. I know someone who works at a perfume company and they told me all about it. I decided I wanted to create a cologne for Wolf so I needed some samples. I thought the first thing to do would be to find out all about the ingredients of the famous perfumes; myrrh, jasmine, iris, violet, narcissus and so on, and how they fit together. Which ones clash, which ones suit each other. I love the idea of observing someone's personality and creating a scent for them.'

Perfect.

Clara lit two cigarettes and passed one to Eva.

'You know, I can't think of anything nicer than having a

bespoke perfume. I've always secretly wanted a scent made especially for me.'

She waited as Eva pursed her lips and tilted her head to one side, scrutinizing her before coming to the obvious conclusion.

'In that case, why don't I make one for you?'

'Make me a perfume? Would you really? What would that involve?'

'We'd need to meet again.'

'Of course.'

'Preferably somewhere private.'

Eva's eyes lingered on Clara's Velvet Red lipstick. 'I'm glad you don't refuse to wear make-up like some of those wives. Most of them have faces as wrinkled as custard skin. More lines than the Berlin U-Bahn. I couldn't bear to let myself go like that. When I was a girl I was never really considered pretty but I learnt to make the best of myself.' Her smile drooped. 'Don't know why I bother though, now. No one's allowed to take any pictures of me. Wolf has banned Hoffmann from ever having a photograph of me on the market.'

'Why's that?'

'He says no one must know what I look like. The Russians might want to kidnap me.'

'Are you scared?'

'Not a bit. How's any Russian going to get to me, surrounded by all this?' She waved her arm and Clara followed her gaze, noting the way the other customers hastily averted their eyes, pretending to devote their attention to the coffee cups in front of them.

'Does it ever bother you? The attention?'

'A little. But I have my ways of keeping my own confidences.' Her eyes sparkled secretively. 'And besides, if I'm ever going to be an actress, I'll have to get used to people looking at me, won't I?'

Clara sipped her tea and tried to take stock. Everything the man

from London Films asked of her had happened, and so much faster
than expected. Within a day of arriving in Munich she was actually taking tea with Eva Braun, who seemed quite happy to entrust
her with personal confidences. And yet what confidences was
Clara able to pass on? That the Führer hated ballet? That his girlfriend liked make-up and French perfume? Such information was
no use to anyone. Clara needed to get onto the subject of the
Führer's intentions for war.

'It must be hard for you, having to listen to him talking about
politics, night after night.'

'It is.' She made a sulky pout at the thought of it. 'He never
stops. Especially now. In the early days he used to be so much
more romantic – I'd slip little letters into his coat pocket, and he'd
reply, but now it's all politics, politics, politics. The Czechs, the
French, the English. In fact, you'll never guess what he told me the
other evening . . .'

She stopped suddenly as a man entered the restaurant and seated
himself at one of the tables sideways on to theirs. He proceeded to
open a copy of *Das Schwarze Korps* – the SS newspaper – and bury
his face in it.

'Actually, shall we go? I don't like this place any more.'

Outside the café Eva made for the road and signalled for a taxi.

'Sorry to leave so abruptly, Clara, but I can't stand all those
people spying on me and trying to overhear what I'm talking
about. Besides, I'm awfully tired. We were up late last night, and
there's another dinner at the Carlton Hotel tonight so I'll need to
get my hair done.'

'Of course. That's fine. I'd like to take a walk around.'

'I suppose you want to see the Bürgerbräukeller. Everyone
wants to see the Bürgerbräukeller. It's where the Putsch started in
1923. They should do one of those historic tours. The Führer's
favourite beer hall, the Führer's office, the Führer's apartment
block. In fact I could lead it myself. I could reveal a thing or two.
That red sofa in his office, for example. That could tell a tale.'

She gave a sardonic little laugh and pressed a card into Clara's hand. It read Wasserburgstrasse 12, telephone 480844.

'This is one place no one gets to see, though. If I'm going to create that perfume for you, you'll need to come to my home because it's where I keep all my ingredients. If you're free, we could continue our conversation tomorrow, without everyone listening. Might you be available at tea time?'

'I'm sure I am.'

'Tomorrow then.'

Clara had been telling the truth when she said she wanted a walk. She needed to process everything that had happened. She could hardly believe that she had managed to achieve so quickly and easily what Guy Hamilton asked of her. She had made contact with the Führer's girlfriend and had even secured an invitation to her home all in the space of an afternoon, yet she was increasingly doubtful about what it would yield. Eva Braun might well impart snippets about the Führer's intentions, and it might even turn out that he was in the habit of confiding his military plans to her, but would she have paid attention? Did she even know where the Sudetenland was? The men back in Whitehall would need something far more concrete to prove the extent of Hitler's territorial ambitions.

Compared with Berlin's churning hurry and its oppressive Prussian architecture, Munich's elegantly proportioned streets and stately neoclassical façades of cream and gold stone were stunning. The city seemed entirely untroubled by the air of crisis which gripped the capital. The scarlet swastika banners draping every building gave off a festive air and every hoarding was decked with travel advertisements: *Visit the Rhine! The Perfect Holiday for German Families* and *Spring in the Spreewald!* One billboard bore a gigantic picture of a cruise ship, with flaxen-haired children waving from the deck as their parents pointed joyously at a fluorescent blue sky. *Kraft durch Freude. Freude durch Reisen!* Strength through joy and joy through travel.

It was impossible to insulate oneself from the admonitions of the Party. There were slogans and exhortations everywhere you turned. As in Berlin, most public buildings seemed to have a loud-speaker lashed to them, alternating between speeches and music, and as Clara passed the State Opera House, the Führer's voice emerged staccato from a ten-foot pediment.

'*There is no greater honour for a woman than to be the mother of German sons or daughters. That is the highest honour she can attain.*'

It was appropriate that Hitler enjoyed Wagner, because what his utterances lacked in lyricism, they made up for in thundering, operatic volume.

As she crossed the Odeonsplatz, trying to ignore the three-hun-dred-and-sixty-degree bellowing of the Führer, Clara experienced a distinct, subliminal disquiet. It was an instinct she had developed, a prickling between her shoulders that told her she was under sur-veillance. Accompanying it was the acid twist of fear.

When she had first become an informer for British Intelligence she had been highly self-conscious. The glances of other people were as sharp as sandpaper on her skin, but now that self-con-sciousness had mutated into something more useful – a kind of heightened perception that told her when those around her were paying her more attention than they should. Peering over her shoulder she scanned passing pedestrians for anyone who might be out of place or have no valid reason to be there. Though a shadow would always aim to blend in, it was useful to look for a solitary figure who was not going purposefully about their busi-ness. Her glance snagged on a man crossing the square towards her, the collar of his coat turned up, obscuring the half of his face that was not overshadowed by his hat, but he turned the corner and disappeared from sight. Even while examining every face she passed, she rationalized the feeling she had. It would be entirely logical to be followed after a meeting with Eva Braun. The Führer's girlfriend was a heartbeat away from the Führer himself and there was every reason to assume that Hitler kept tabs on the people who surrounded her. Surveillance would be utterly reasonable. Yet still Clara needed to know if her instinct was correct.

It was Leo who had given her the only lessons she ever had in evading surveillance. There were the elementary things to look out for – pedestrians you had seen before, anyone who leapfrogged you in the street or avoided eye contact, cars which idled by the kerb with the engine running. Agents might wear a heavy coat which could be removed or a hat which could be changed, so it was vital to focus on those elements of appearance that were harder to change in a hurry – the shoes, for example, or the hair. She had forgotten all the technical terms for surveillance manoeuvres – piggybacking, switching, blocking – but she knew that if you turned a corner the tail would often cross the street to keep you in view and sometimes two or more agents would form a team, with one dropping back while another moved ahead. Yet while she had listened diligently to Leo's instructions, Clara had gradually evolved her own ways of throwing off potential tails. And now, as her focus tightened and a jittery tension entered her limbs, she decided to make a circuit of the city centre to see if her suspicions were right.

At an unhurried pace she crossed Odeonsplatz towards the Feldherrnhalle, the city's military memorial, where the lavish monument to the Putsch was flanked day and night by an SS guard of honour. The site had been co-opted by the Nazis as a memorial to the holiest day in their calendar, when marchers staged an unsuccessful clash with police resulting in sixteen Nazi deaths, and on solemn days the site resembled a Greek temple, complete with flaming urns. Even on ordinary days two enormous laurel wreaths were guarded round the clock by steel-helmeted sentries, requiring everyone who passed to make a right-armed salute. Noticing that some pedestrians skirted round through an alley on the far side of the monument to avoid having to give the Hitlergruss, Clara followed suit.

As she walked, she took in every detail around her. A mother dragging two children behind her, a third in a pram. A flower seller, women gossiping in a café, cakes glistening in the window of a bakery, a sweet doughy aroma issuing from the opened door – all the time Clara committed key details about her surroundings to memory. She watched for shapes as much as faces. Postures too. Slouching, lingering, any sense of not being in a hurry. Then there were the signals. Gestapo agents communicated with a rapidly evolving system of signs, like the tying of shoelaces – a single knot or a double, laces crossed or straight – or the way they wore their hats or carried their newspapers. Nothing she saw stood out, though, so Clara decided to employ the ultimate anti-surveillance technique, and the one most perfectly suited to the female agent – shopping.

There was no better place to spot a tail than a large department store. Drifting through dress rails fingering the fashions, lingering at cosmetics displays and sampling the odd perfume was a woman's natural habit but entirely anomalous to a male agent. In a beauty hall, with its infinite mirrors, glistening reflections and largely female clientele, a Gestapo agent in a leather coat would stand out a mile. And nowhere were men and women more different than in the way they shopped. Men were impatient and impulsive; browsing was anathema to them and most could not spend two minutes in a shop without being bothered by a sales assistant, whereas women could loiter for hours, sniffing, sampling and examining themselves in mirrors, which in Clara's case afforded an excellent view of what lay behind her.

After several minutes of browsing at a cosmetics counter, trying, then rejecting, Palmolive soap, Pond's face cream and a few Tosca powder compacts, then going up the escalator and down again, Clara had seen nothing to worry about. Leaving the department store on Kaufingerstrasse she ducked into Loden-Frey, which was all stuffy Tracht and Tyrolean suits in hairy green tweed, as might be expected from the official uniform makers to the SS, then exited right and crossed the central square of Marienplatz, coming to a halt beneath the impressive façade of Dallmayr's delicatessen.

Unlike Berlin, where the signs reading 'For Display Only' had been there so long they were bleached white, here the goods were piled high and in pride of place were shining packages of the store's own coffee, roasted to a special recipe on the premises. Clara paused for a moment, but the window's reflection revealed no solitary figures behind her, and the siren call of coffee was strong. It was impossible to resist, she told herself, as she counted out the marks. You would never be able to find coffee of this quality in Berlin.

Having left the shop, she returned to the Hofgarten, where the fountain's splashing water made a gauze veil, suspended in the air. The flowerbeds were packed with colour and butterflies floated above autumnal roses. Clara paused, savouring the dense fragrance of the earth and the deep scent of the flowers, made a circuit of the park, then turned suddenly back on herself and retraced her steps to Dallmayr's coffee counter, where she enquired anxiously about the possibility that she had left an umbrella. Once the apologetic assistant had confirmed that no umbrella was to be found, Clara headed north past Hoffmann's photography shop in Schelling-strasse and the smoky interior of Schelling tavern, before finally reaching Maximiliansplatz.

The light was falling as she turned into her pension. Whatever her instinct told her, she trusted her routine. She had taken every precaution. She had conducted every procedure to shake out surveillance and seen nothing untoward. The man she had seen in Odeonsplatz was an ordinary Munich citizen, who was, she hoped, entirely oblivious to Clara's suspicion of him. So why was she filled with fear, like a musical instrument vibrating with the notes of an invisible player?

She had an early supper in the gloomy dining room – leek and bacon soup, followed by chicken breast and cabbage – during which Frau Altenburger, the owner of the pension, a jovial, uninhibited matron, divined that Clara was an actress and interrogated her on the private lives of the stars like the most ruthless reporter for *Filmwoche*. Was Zarah Leander genuinely stand-offish? Was Joachim Gottschalk really married to a Jew? Was Lil Dagover Hitler's favourite actress?

Eventually Clara escaped and closed the bedroom door behind her.

Unclipping her hair she shook it out, releasing the faint fragrance of *Soir de Paris*.

'I knew someone who used it.'

She thought of Max Brandt dancing in Chanel's salon, his arms keeping firm hold of her, smiling seductively as he took his own nonchalant sex appeal for granted, and she wondered if she would be able to resist his advances so firmly if he were here now. Often, as she slid into sleep, she craved the warmth of a man next to her. She yearned for the frank pleasure of sexual fulfilment. Her body ached with emptiness.

Wearily, she stretched out on the bed and reached for her book.

Chapter Fourteen

The first thing Rupert saw, as he stood in the lobby of the National Socialist Women's League headquarters, was the face of Gertrud Scholtz-Klink glaring from the wall like a leathery gorgon guarding her lair. With the basilisk smile and a face as scoured as a pan, it was perfectly possible to believe that her stare alone, like her mythic doppelgänger, could turn onlookers to stone.

Even as he recoiled from the portrait, the Führerin herself bustled over and shot out a hand like a Walther 6.35. That morning she had foregone uniform in favour of a grey worsted jacket which looked a little warm for the weather and what looked to Rupert Allingham awfully like an Old Etonian tie, though he doubted very much she was entitled to wear one. Then again, if Reich politicians stuck to what they were entitled to, Europe wouldn't be in the state it was today. Nazi foreign policy was, at bottom, a case of a vast sense of entitlement out of all control.

She led the way into her office, talking as she went. As female Führer she was in charge of all National Socialist women's organizations, including the Women's League, the Reich Mothers' Service and the German Women's Enterprise. It was her duty to train all German women in accordance with National Socialist ideology. She oversaw the culture, education and training sections and even a propaganda department which produced leaflets for

German women living abroad detailing the inferiority of foreign races. At least that's what Rupert thought she said, but as he trailed behind her the Führerin's voice was having to compete with an entire, ill-tuned orchestra pounding in his head.

She seated herself beneath an especially hideous poster of a woman and child beneath a sun in the shape of a swastika, emblazoned with the slogan *Warriors on the Battlefield of Childbirth* and wearily Rupert pulled out his notebook.

He was badly hung over. The previous night had been emotionally wearing and you could have powered a Panzer on the amount of schnapps he had consumed. He wondered why the epicentre of German domesticity had so far failed to furnish him with a cup of coffee.

'I'm not sure if you were present at my talk to the annual rally, Herr Allingham,' said the Führerin, sliding a sheaf of paper across the desk.

'Sadly not.'

'Then you will have missed our exciting news on tax reductions. I've had some information printed out for you. No income tax at all for families with more than six children. So long as the children are racially pure and valuable.'

'I see.'

'You'll be wanting some statistics, I daresay. The figures are extremely encouraging. Marriages are up, there are only half as many divorces, and births have risen to . . .' she checked a sheet, '1.4 million this year. 19.2 per thousand head of population.' She rattled off the figures like a Lewis machine gun. 'That's up from five hundred thousand births in 1932. So National Socialist ministers have tripled the number of babies being born.'

Some National Socialist ministers more than others, if gossip was to be believed, Rupert thought.

'More cribs than coffins is my motto, and it seems the birth rate is exceeding all our expectations,' she added with satisfaction.

Babies, Rupert realized, were just another crop in the new Reich, like potatoes or wheat, to be counted, monitored, improved and lied about. Good one year, free of blight for the most part, a creditable reflection on the citizens of the Reich.

He doodled his pen idly across the page.

'Could you remind me, please, what exactly the Reichs-mütterdienst . . .?'

A flicker of irritation crossed her brow. 'The Reichsmütter-dienst is open to all racially pure women in the Reich. It prepares women for their role as housewives and mothers because the family is the germ cell of the nation.'

Rupert scribbled wearily.

'We already have hundreds of Mother Schools all over Germany, and so far more than a million and a half women have attended 56,000 courses. There are four million women in all the Frauenwerk organizations. Not to mention the Reichsbund der Kinderreichen, the league for large families.'

Rupert's head was already reeling. He had given up trying to note down the numbers. When was she going to come out with this scoop Goebbels had talked about? He had planned to give this interview no more than half an hour before proceeding to the Foreign Ministry to hear von Ribbentrop's latest threats against the Czechs.

'Are there any other recent developments you would like my readers to know about?' he enquired, flatly.

The Führerin frowned.

'We have brought about new reforms to the divorce law which allow divorce on the grounds of one partner's refusal to have children,' she volunteered. 'We call voluntary childlessness a diseased mentality.'

'Diseased?'

'A disease of the mind, rather than the body. But just as harmful to the health of the nation.'

Rupert had spent the previous evening at the bar of the Adlon drowning the world's sorrows with a group of journalists who had just returned from Prague. Now he felt the excesses of the night before return to him in a bilious wave.

'I always wonder, Frau Reichsfrauenführerin, how it is that a woman of your impressive stature can support the fact that one of the first ordinances of the Nazi party was to exclude women from ever holding a position of leadership. As I understand it, you believe that women should no longer have the vote?'

Sarcasm glanced off the Führerin like a bullet from a tank. She regarded him pityingly.

'The Führer sees the emancipation of women on the same level of depravity as parliamentary democracy or . . .' she cast around, 'jazz music.'

'Jazz music?' said Rupert incredulously.

'I think that's what he said. He believes, and we agree with him, that there is no interest whatsoever in women maintaining the vote.' Her eyes narrowed. 'I wonder . . . are there large numbers of female politicians in your own country, Herr Allingham?'

Rupert shrugged.

'Precisely. And I think you will find the reason is that women themselves prefer to confine themselves to their own sphere. They don't want to be spending their time wrangling in parliamentary chambers with men who are equipped with law degrees. They would far rather occupy themselves in their own area of expertise, which is producing children and ensuring that they are properly equipped to carry on the nation's culture to future generations. I daresay it has never occurred to the British to have their own Women's Leader either?'

The face of Lady Allingham, sorting out the estate's paperwork at the breakfast table in her reading glasses, floated into Rupert's mind. If Britain ever decided to instate a woman to micro-manage the affairs of the entire female population, he could think of the perfect candidate.

The Führerin paused. 'As it happens I've just been invited to

London next year by a very prestigious grouping. The Anglo-German Fellowship. Do you know it?'

Rupert was only too familiar with the doomed selection of the deluded and the desperate drawn from the ranks of the aristocracy and the far right who actively supported Hitler's territorial ambitions. It had been started by an associate of Clara Vine's father and some of the early meetings had taken place in the Vine family home in Ponsonby Terrace.

'There's to be a dinner at Claridge's. Lord David Douglas-Hamilton will be there. His wife is head of your Women's League of Health and Beauty and, as it happens, I'm due to welcome her shortly to Hamburg at the International Women's Fitness Congress.'

Women's Fitness? It seemed astonishing that at a time of grave political crisis such events could still be going on. The leader of Germany was attempting to annihilate Czechoslovakia and his female equivalent was planning a fitness conference. For someone like Rupert, who lived in the drama of the moment, the idea that anyone should be occupying their mind with gymnastic routines was inexplicable.

But then, glancing up at the poster, *Warriors on the Battlefield of Childbirth*, he realized that was the thing about the Nazi regime: every human activity from cradle to grave was transformed into part of the Nazi struggle. Every aspect of life would be approached with military precision. From what he had seen of the lines of BDM girls in their cotton shirts and navy shorts practising synchronized gymnastics in the Tiergarten, even an apparently innocent enterprise such as women's fitness would be carried out with the efficiency and ruthlessness of a Wehrmacht manoeuvre.

A gawky, pale-faced girl carrying a stack of papers entered the room, then immediately attempted to back out again.

'Stop! Rosa! Where have you been? Fetch coffee for Herr Allingham at once, please.'

Rupert watched with sympathy as the girl scurried away.

'Now then … about that news. As it happens, the Führer is working on something very exciting. It's been under wraps, but it's felt that now is a useful time to reveal it.'

At last. Rupert wondered how exciting the Führer's new plan would turn out to be. Most of his recent innovations had involved the destruction of nation states.

'It's a Mother's Cross,' continued the Führerin. 'To be given to kinderreich women with four or more children. Only live ones of course, and not defectives. There will be three gradations. Bronze for four children, silver for six and gold for eight or more. In fact, I think there may be plans for a diamond cross, featuring genuine diamonds, for mothers of twelve children. Anyone wearing a Mother's Honour Cross must be saluted in the street and receive a range of deferences.'

'Deferences?'

'She must be given the best seat on the bus, for example, go to the front of the queue in a shop, have the best seats at the theatre and so on.'

'Interesting idea.'

'I'm glad you think so. It's our women's equivalent of the Iron Cross. It is to be awarded every year on 12th August, the birthday of the Führer's mother. Despite our excellent figures, we need to give women every encouragement we can to reproduce.'

Which included banning abortion and contraception. One of the major contraceptive firms had been owned by Robert Ley, head of the Labour Front, Rupert recalled, but Doktor Ley's interests lay in a completely different kind of labour now.

The gawky girl returned with the coffee and handed Rupert a receptacle the size of a doll's cup, which he drained in one.

'As a mother myself I understand personally how important the birth rate is in the strengthening of the Reich,' added the Führerin. 'I have produced six children already.'

'Of course.' Rupert tried very hard not to picture her in the act of procreating them.

'Our regime promises every unmarried girl a husband. Indeed . . .' Her eyes dwelt on Rupert speculatively. 'We are establishing a chain of marriage bureaux for eugenically eligible candidates. Everyone who signs up must declare themselves willing to establish a large family.'

'Marriage bureaux?'

'That's right. It probably seems terrifically modern to you, Herr Allingham, but in Germany we have never been afraid to embrace change in the cause of national advantage. Are you married yourself?'

'Afraid not.'

She frowned, then gave a girlish smile.

'We shall have to see if we can help you!'

Horribly, it occurred to Rupert that the Führerin was flirting with him. He remembered one of those mottos Goebbels liked to come out with. '*A German woman does not marry a man of alien blood.*' He would have to keep that in mind, should it be needed.

On his way out, the plain girl was back at her desk, spectacles perched on her beaky nose, a pile of paperwork at her side. Rupert gave her a smile intended to convey sympathy with her plight in working in this godawful place and as she ducked her head in embarrassment, he saw something that brought him up short. It was just an ordinary thing, a framed holiday snap of the girl herself, with the same diffident air, although the mousy hair was sun-kissed and the arms lightly tanned. Yet it was not the girl herself who interested Rupert, as much as the cruise liner looming like an iceberg behind her.

'Isn't that the *Wilhelm Gustloff*?'

'Yes, Herr Allingham. I was sent on a cruise. For work.'

'Nice work.'

'It was important reconnaissance business,' she added hastily. 'We're staging the National Congress of Women's Fitness in Hamburg next month. The important guests will be housed on the ship.'

'Ah yes. The Führerin mentioned it. So did you have a good time?'

The girl frowned. She looked downwards, to where her hands rested on the typewriter, then she raised her face and he saw a kind of anguish and a resolve in those washed-out eyes, as though she was not just answering his pleasantry but making an important decision. She glanced around the room, checking that the door to the Führerin's office was closed, leant across the typewriter and lowered her voice.

'No, I did not, mein Herr. I did not have a good time at all.'

'I'm sorry to hear that. Why?'

She appeared to be on the brink of saying something else, but at that moment there was the sound of a door slamming along the corridor and the simultaneous ring of the telephone, which she picked up with alacrity. Rupert hesitated a second before taking a card out of his wallet and sliding it onto the desk, observing with satisfaction that the girl covered it at once with her other hand and slipped it silently into her bag.

Chapter Fifteen

Eva Braun's home was a square, red-roofed villa in Bogenhausen, an elegant suburb across the River Isar, with white shutters on the windows and a small green door at the side with panes of criss-crossed glass. It was surrounded by a high stone wall with wooden gates, and its privacy was further enhanced by a group of apple trees in the front garden, bursting with bright fruit. When Clara rang the bell, frenzied yapping ensued from deep within.

'Negus! Stasi! Be quiet!'

Eva Braun flung open the door with a little flourish, gesturing at the whirling dervish of fur that was circulating around her feet.

'I'm sorry. They're so protective. They think they're my body-guards!' The black fur separated into two Scottish terriers. 'Go on, you two, back into the garden.'

She was dressed that day in a high-necked blouse with puffy sleeves, and a full, flowery skirt, her blonde hair rolled neatly away from her face. She raised a quick hand to touch Clara's own outfit – a teal-coloured pencil dress which had originally been made for her as a costume by Steffi Schaeffer.

'I love that dress, by the way! I have one just like it!'

She led Clara proudly through into a small front room, stocked with heavy, Bavarian-style furniture, a bookcase, and two chintz-covered armchairs. Turkish rugs lay in front of the fireplace. A stack of *Filmwoche* magazines was piled high beside a chair. Eva gestured to a telephone on the sideboard.

'It connects directly with the Berghof. Isn't that something? I only have to pick it up. The trouble is, the SS installed it, which means it connects directly to an awful lot of other people too.'

She saw Clara glance politely at a couple of insipid water-colours, one of a church and another a Bavarian street scene, hanging above the fireplace.

'Nice, aren't they? Wolf painted them. Not that he ever has time to paint any more. In fact he hardly has time for anything. He bought this house two years ago, but I had to furnish the entire place myself. He was always too busy to help. He just said if I wanted something for the house I should get the money from Martin Bormann.' She gave a little, theatrical moue. 'Do you know Bormann?'

'Only by reputation.'

'Well, let me give you some advice. Never discuss home dec-orating with Martin Bormann. In a bad mood he's terrible. And he's never in a good mood. He's a horrible man. Really. He hates his brother Albert so much they will only communicate through their adjutants, even when they're in the same room.'

She looked at Clara reflectively.

'In fact, Bormann warned me against you.'

Clara gave a start and tried to disguise it.

'Me?'

'Not you in particular. Anyone really I didn't already know. He said in future I should avoid making friends with people in case they wanted to know about my relationship with the Führer. They might not be interested in me for myself, but only because of him.'

'He might be right.'

Eva laughed. 'He might, but what do I care? I hate Bormann. And I don't mind if he knows it.'

She went over to an Anglepoise lamp, drew it towards her like a megaphone and shouted into the bell, 'I hate Martin Bormann!'

Clara tried to conceal her shudder. The special telephone line was almost certainly not the only thing that the SS had installed in the house, but the thought didn't seem to trouble Eva Braun.

'Let's hope that gives someone earache!' she said, turning brightly. 'Bormann lives to prevent me doing things. He's even stopped me writing a diary. He says any kind of personal reminiscence is absolutely banned. Never write anything down, that's what he told me. Don't leave a trail. Memorize. That's what you actresses do, isn't it? You just remember?'

'It helps to have a good memory, but you can train it too.'

'What do you memorize?'

'Oh, you start with poems, and then you proceed.'

'I don't know if I could manage a poem. A song perhaps, that's different.' She began to sing a snatch of *Blood Red Roses*.

'But I'm forgetting myself. Let me make tea.'

She bustled into a minute kitchen, barely large enough to contain a porcelain gas stove with two rings, from which a door led onto a wide terrace covered with an ochre-striped awning and edged with windowboxes of scarlet geraniums.

'Would you like a chocolate?'

She opened a lavish silver box, tied with frilly ribbons, in which a luxurious pound of chocolates nestled invitingly. Despite herself, Clara's mouth watered. Luxuries like that were increasingly rare in the Reich.

'Wolf gets sent them all the time but he won't eat them. He's convinced he's going to be poisoned. I say, "Well, I'm not going to waste them! If it's my fate to be poisoned, then I accept it willingly!"'

Somehow, this idea seemed to lessen the chocolates' appeal and Clara demurred.

'How about a smoke then? If we want a cigarette, and I do, we'll either have to go outside or upstairs to the smoking room. Wolf absolutely hates smoking. He says every cigarette is a bullet in your heart. He has plans to give all cigarette packets plain packaging and have giant warnings saying "Danger! Cancer!" I told him he's wasting his time. I'm never giving up.'

She poured hot water into the pot, placed it on a silver tray with two cups and carried it out to a rickety wooden table set in the dappled shade of the fruit trees. In the corner of the lawn the dogs had momentarily ceased their yapping to tussle over a dead mouse, worrying its tiny corpse in their jaws, then each grabbing one end and pulling it apart.

'Is this all right for you, Clara?' There was still an edge of shyness in Eva Braun's voice, as though she could not quite believe that an actress she had seen on the screen was right there in her own garden. Her moods reminded Clara of a spring day, one minute cheerful, the next downcast, as though the barometer of her temperament was in constant flux.

'Your garden's charming!'

'I know.' She flipped open a packet of cigarettes and offered one to Clara, who accepted. 'I'm very lucky really. We have everything here. In fact they've only just finished installing the air-raid shelter in the cellar. It has an armoured door leading to an underground passage with radio, telephone, cupboards with provisions, medical supplies. You wouldn't believe it! The only problem is that Wolf's never here with me.'

'I suppose he must be terribly busy.'

'He is!' Eva looked up, as though Clara had had an impressive insight. 'And just now he's in a terrible state.'

'About the international situation?'

'I think it's that. All I know is, he has dark patches under his eyes and he's not sleeping. It's partly his food. He'll only eat boiled vegetables now, mainly corn and beans and asparagus, and that can't help, can it? I tell him, "Wolf, you have to eat something that gives you energy," but there's no chance of changing him. He says meat-eating is a perversion of our human nature and when we reach a higher level of civilization, we'll overcome it. In fact the other day at lunch he told everyone at the table that he's thinking of banning meat altogether.' She laughed gaily at the memory. 'You should have seen Himmler's face when he said that! It was so funny! Himmler was a chicken farmer you know. I almost hope Wolf goes ahead, just to annoy him.'

Already Clara could see how this uncomplicated girl would appeal to Hitler. Eva Braun was never going to uncover the ill-educated, provincial side of him, never going to mock the Führer's liking for operetta, or his taste in art. Unlike the other wives, her pretensions to sophistication ended at clothes and perfume. She was more likely to worry about his digestion than his dictatorship. The worst that Hitler could expect from her was a momentary moodiness if her desires were thwarted.

Unfortunately this spelled failure for Clara's own task. She thought of Guy Hamilton's remark, '*Pillow talk. Isn't that what they call it?*' But pillow talk between the Führer of all Germany and his girlfriend was never going to focus on the Treaty of Versailles. It was hard to imagine Eva listening intelligently as Hitler confided his plans for European domination and if he started talking about Lebensraum, she would probably interrupt with a reminder to straighten his tie.

She took a draw on her cigarette and tried again. 'It's impressive that the Führer has time to consider such things given all the other affairs that must be preoccupying him.'

Eva's face drooped. 'I'm so sick of politics. I absolutely pine for the Berghof but we hardly go there now. There's a cook there called Lily who he hired from the Osteria because he loved her cheese noodles. He had her brought out from the kitchen at the end of a meal and said, "Lily, I'm taking you to Obersalzberg." It's not just the food though. Everything's wonderful there. I swim in the Königssee, there's a bowling alley in the cellar and you can ski, though he hates that. In fact, he's thinking of having it banned because of the number of accidents involved.'

'He wants to ban skiing?'

'Oh yes,' she giggled. 'Along with meat-eating and smoking and lipstick and all the other things he hates. I call it his list. It's a pretty long list.'

Clara thought of Steffi Schaeffer and all the other people in Germany right then who were feeling the force of Hitler's loathing and wondered if the insouciant young woman in front of her was even aware of Hitler's other list – his persecution of the Jews, Communists, gypsies and homosexuals, and anyone else who disagreed with his politics of hate.

Eva's face clouded. 'The trouble is, even when I'm there, we're never alone because of all the guests. Some of them I don't mind. Herr Speer is nice. He talks to me when no one else does. Whenever all these actresses come to the Berghof flirting and comporting themselves like silly women – not like you, of course, Clara – Herr Speer sits with me. The wives though, they all hate me. They call me the blonde cow. Honestly, Clara, they do! Magda Goebbels even asked me to tie her shoelaces when she was pregnant. As if I was going to kneel in front of her! I rang for the maid and left the room. And Frau von Ribbentrop is worse. You'd think she was queen the way she insists that all the potatoes are the same size and she sends back a fried egg if the yolk isn't right in the middle. Can you imagine!'

Clara could. The anecdote fitted precisely with her experience of von Ribbentrop's wife.

'The others aren't so bad. I like Margarete Speer and Wolf adores their children. And Gerda Bormann's all right, even if she is constantly pregnant.' She giggled. 'Though I can't think how she manages it because he's always off. He runs after anything in a skirt.'

'What do they talk about at lunch? Is it all politics?'

Eva Braun burst out laughing. 'As if they'd try! Himmler has some idea about establishing a Women's Academy for Wisdom and Culture where high-class women would learn the social graces and how to talk about art and politics, but I could tell him right off, that's never going to work. Wolf hates women talking about politics.'

Clara's heart sank. The chances of Eva Braun having any political insights were dwindling by the second.

'What does he like then?'

'What he really likes is a woman who will sit with him and
listen to him talk. He wants companionship, I suppose. But we
never seem to get the chance to be alone. It's even worse in Berlin.
I have my own apartment at the Chancellery, it used to be
Hindenburg's bedroom, but I have to have all my meals there and
I never get to see anyone. The only place I ever visit is my dressmaker and I have to go in and out through a private entrance, in
case anyone sees me.'

Whatever she may have felt about a woman who was prepared
to love a man like Hitler, Clara felt a pang of sympathy for the girl,
shunned, isolated, treated as an embarrassing confidence, to be
kept at all costs out of the public eye.

'Do you travel much with him?'

'The Anschluss was lovely. It was my first foreign trip with him.
People were so pleased to see him, they threw flowers in front of
the cars. We stayed at the Imperial Hotel and the people stood
outside all night, singing.'

Clara glanced around her. If things went Hitler's way, Eva would
soon be having more opportunities for foreign travel.

'But I get so lonely here. He thinks I have everything I could
want – my own Mercedes and a chauffeur and Negus and Stasi –
but I don't have him. I don't understand why he never wants to
come here.'

Hearing their names, the terriers abandoned their fight and
raced across the grass, clamouring for attention with incessant
barks and jumping up at Clara's legs with their sharp little claws.
Even for a man who loved dogs, it was hard to imagine Hitler tol-
erating these two without the help of the bullwhip he carried at
all times.

A chill wind fluttered the leaves of the apple trees, stippling their
skin with goose pimples, and Eva jumped up.

'Let's go inside.'

Following her upstairs, Clara caught a glimpse of a blue-tiled bathroom then they entered a frilly bedroom, hung with the oblig-atory photograph of the Führer and an oil painting of Eva alongside it. On the dressing table a silver-backed vanity set engraved with the initials EB, stylized like a butterfly, lay alongside a jumble of bot-tles and creams. A pile of ribboned underwear lay on the bed and on the table beside it a bottle of Vanodorm sleeping tablets.

'Excuse the mess.'

Eva folded her arms and tipped her chin resolutely.

'Now, Clara. You'll need to be honest. I need to know the truth about you.'

For a split second, Clara hesitated. For all she knew the house was fitted top to bottom with listening devices, even here in the bedroom. Perhaps especially here.

'What do you mean, the truth?'

'If I'm to make a perfume for you, of course!'

'Of course! I forgot.'

'Well, I didn't. I have all my equipment.'

She gestured across to a mahogany dresser crowded with tiny, stoppered glass bottles. Even with their stoppers in, the fragrances sent a pungent, intermingled aroma into the air – floral, citrus, woody and smoky, jasmine, tuberose, violet and pine. Each flask had a label inked in a neat hand and Clara was surprised to see Eva's writing so small and precise. It suggested a meticulous streak behind her girlish frivolity, a sense of discipline and control. Perhaps an ambition to achieve what everyone around her assumed was impossible.

Eva reached forward to a larger bottle and took out the cork.

'I've prepared a few things based on what I think you're like,' she glanced shyly upwards – 'Sophisticated of course, but with a soft heart. At first I came up with this.' She waved the vial under Clara's nose. The fragrance was light and floral on top but under-cut with a deep, sweet ghost of vanilla and violets.

'But then I thought, no. Perhaps too sugary.' She picked up a second bottle. 'What about something more like this?'

The second scent had the freshness of clean linen and windows opening to green orchards, with a trail of vetiver in the background. Eva Braun put it down again.

'That seems more like you, but it's not perfect. I think I need to know more about you. Like one of those quizzes they have in *Stern*. Are you a city or a country girl?'

'City, definitely.'

'Do you prefer a film, or a night at the opera? No, don't answer that. I'm sure you're the same as me there. Do you like loud colours, or subtlety?'

'Subtlety, I suppose.'

'Do you wear your heart on your sleeve?'

'I try not to.'

'Roses or gardenia?'

'Roses, probably.'

'Then what about this one?'

She picked up a crystal decanter with a gold top and Clara saw that it was engraved again with her initials – EB, made into the shape of a butterfly.

'That's pretty.'

'Do you like it? It's my personal monogram. I designed it myself, with a little help from Speer. At first I thought of it as a four-leaf clover, which would make sense because I'm lucky, but then I decided it looked more like a butterfly. And I've always thought of myself as a bit of a butterfly! Now see what you think of this.'

The third perfume had voluptuous notes of rose and jasmine, but with a darker heart that seemed to evade definition, a haunting blend of musk and woodsmoke and leather. It hung in the air like strange and evanescent music.

'Oh, I like that. It's mysterious.'

'Do you really think so?'

'Yes. I'll wear it.'

Clara dabbed a little behind her ears.

'I'm so pleased! I'll make up a proper bottle for you. I'm going to name it *Black Roses* in your honour.'

She took out an empty bottle, carefully inscribed a fresh label with the words *Black Roses* in her tiny, meticulous handwriting, and stuck it on. But her pleasure did not last long. The mercurial weather of her moods swiftly swung back to melancholy again and her expression grew clouded and brooding.

'Is anything wrong?'

She flung herself down into an armchair, pouted and gave a shrug.

'Just about everything.'

'I'm sorry. Would it help to discuss it?'

Eva Braun glanced up at Clara. A thin sheen of tears glittered in her eyes, but she summoned a smile.

'Would you mind? It's so hard to talk, you see. Most people I'm not supposed to confide in, and my sisters get very impatient with hearing the same old problems, and I know I shouldn't speak to the wives of the senior men. But you're not anyone's wife or girl-friend, are you? I mean, not anyone important.'

For a moment Clara wondered how Eva knew this, until she remembered the stack of film magazines in the sitting room. The celebrity movie magazines of which Eva was such a devoted reader never featured photographs of Clara out with Nazi officials, or even her leading men. She was no Zarah Leander or Kristina Söderbaum to be found in the daily gossip columns. Unlike Ursula Schilling, there had never been a story about Clara's dalliance with a co-star, or any shots of her staggering out of a National Socialist fundraiser the worse for wear.

'No. I'm not.'

'But there must be someone. Come on, Clara. I can keep a secret.'

It would help, Clara reckoned, to have a secret of her own to exchange. Even if the secret was not strictly accurate.

'There's a Sturmbannführer I know. Sturmbannführer Stein-brecher. But I haven't seen him in a while. His work takes him away.'

'Poor you.' Eva pursed her lips. 'I know how that feels. Anyway, it means I can talk to you without worrying that you're going to tell all the senior men. Promise?'

'I can absolutely promise you that.'

'I really don't want Himmler to know anything about me.'

'Why should he?'

'Oh, Himmler likes to know everything about everyone. He's definitely keeping tabs on me. When my sister Ilse had an affair with an Italian officer, Himmler photocopied all her letters and then produced them for blackmail.'

'I would never tell Himmler your secrets.'

'Thank you, Clara. I didn't think you would.'

She relaxed visibly, and drew another cigarette from a silver box and perched it in her mouth to light. Taking a deep coil of smoke into her lungs, she exhaled and examined her fingernails. Then she turned over her hand and showed Clara the palm.

'When I was young, I went to a fortune teller who told me that one day I would become world famous. I used to believe it, but I don't suppose that will ever happen now,' she said tonelessly. 'You see, I just don't know where I stand. Sometimes, at public dinners, he doesn't utter a word to me all evening, then he simply hands me an envelope of money at the end. It's so humiliating. When I ask him about the future he says he has responsibilities to the nation and I must be patient. But it's more than that. He says he'll severely punish anyone who mentions my name in connection with his, for the sake of my honour. His job is like a priesthood and he's like the Pope – only in a good way – and he's taken holy orders for serv-ice to the Fatherland. At least I think that's what he said.'

She flicked a stray blonde curl from her face and pouted.

'I know I'm lucky. There are millions of women who would envy me, and I shouldn't complain, but I just can't bear this pretence. I see all those wives laughing, thinking their Führer isn't serious about me, but he is. When I tell him he just smiles and says I'm the most important woman in Germany. The most important woman in Germany? That's a joke. He says when he has achieved all that we need for the Reich, he'll marry me and we'll live in a house he has planned in Linz, where he was born, and he'll write books and I can do whatever I want but until that time no one should know about me. I have to remain a secret. That's what you're looking at, Clara.' She spat out the words. 'A great big, embarrassing secret.'

'Surely not,' said Clara, perching on the bed and crossing her legs.

'Yes! And it's all Goebbels' fault.' Her face darkened. 'Goebbels says the Führer should have no private life. No one's even allowed to know if the Führer has stomach troubles in case it affects his image, so imagine what it would do to him if people knew he had a lady friend. *Consider the effect on the German people.*' She mimicked Goebbels' bark with cruel accuracy. 'He censors all radio reports, and any journalist who dared to mention my existence would end up in a camp. *The Führer of Germany should have no private life.* That's what Goebbels says. But I'm tired of being Miss No Private Life. If anything happens to Wolf or me, I want them to know that he loved me and was planning to marry me. I'm tired of being a secret. Secrecy is exhausting. You wouldn't know. I mean, you probably don't have many secrets, do you, Clara?'

'Some.'

'Not like mine. Anyway, I'm going to tell you the biggest secret of all. When these international affairs are over, I've arranged to go to Hollywood.'

'As an actress?'

'That's right. I want to make a film about our story. How we met. I've already chosen the theme tune. It's *Blutrote Rosen* – you know, by Max Mensing's orchestra. *Blood-red roses speak of happiness to you.*'

As she spoke of her dreams, her eyes lit up with happy anticipation and Clara realized that the mere act of articulating them was
making them real.

'And would you be in this film yourself?'

'Of course. I'd play me. Eva Braun. Little Miss Nobody who fell
in love with the Führer of all Germany. It's a wonderful story, isn't
it? I'm sure people would be interested. I've told Wolf to hurry up
and decide who should play him, or I'll choose. I'm thinking of
Clark Gable.'

Clara was astonished at the extent of her self-delusion. Of
course Eva Braun would never be an actress. Hitler was the actor
in their relationship. Everything he did was stage-managed and
Goebbels controlled every single picture of him.

'My parents don't like Wolf – they say he's old enough to be my
father and ask when he's going to do the decent thing, and even
my own friends I can't trust now.' She took a disconsolate drag of
her cigarette. 'But you don't want to hear all my problems.'

Her face brightened. 'I've had a wonderful idea! Frau Goering's
giving a party on Thursday to celebrate the birth of her baby. It's
at the Bayerischer Hof hotel in the Tiki Bar.'

'Sounds fun.'

'Fun? Do you think so? It will be absolutely dreadful. Everyone
will be there. Well, not Wolf of course, he's far too busy with the
political situation, and Goering is otherwise detained and Himmler
and Goebbels are away too, thankfully. But everyone else – all the
wives – will be there. I suppose I'll have to show up, but I can't
think of anything worse. I've been dreading it, to tell the truth, but
now you can come as my guest. I'd much rather talk to you than
those old crows! Will you?'

Clara shuddered to think of it. She had been to enough Nazi
receptions to know that they demanded an unusual level of alert-
ness. They weren't anyone's idea of a party, unless a party implied
mingling with people you detested, who probably wanted you
dead. All the same, befriending Eva Braun was the entire reason

for her presence here, and if she was to find anything to tell the man from London Films, apart from Eva Braun's tastes in perfumery, then she would need to persevere.

A late afternoon sun was slanting down as Clara made her way back through the streets of Munich. She passed a pretzel seller, his wares threaded on a long stick, who smiled at her in a way that his Berlin equivalent would never permit himself, and nodded as a Wurst merchant came up beside him, holding boiled sausages in a hot, metal container round his neck.

'It's Führerwetter,' said the pretzel seller, cocking his head at the sky.

'That's because he's in town,' said the other, shielding his eyes against the sun.

It was not just the sun which had come out for the Führer. As Clara headed towards Prinzregentenplatz, she saw that a bevy of SS honour guards in black steel helmets and uniforms was positioned outside Hitler's luxurious second-floor apartment. Barriers had been erected all around the square in happy anticipation of the Hitler circus, with its drums and banners and flags, plus, of course, its star performer.

She walked quickly past, heading towards the centre of town, but as she approached, she found herself swept up in a larger crowd and allowed herself to be pulled along in its stream. There were dozens of people thronging joyfully, pouring along the street with a hum of excited anticipation. The crowd passed tall blocks with heavy wooden doors studded with ironwork and window boxes where massed ranks of geraniums stood to attention, before slowing to a halt beside the gigantic, neoclassical House of German Art. They stood there, a sea of happy faces pinned behind sleek-jacketed troops, as the air rang with shouts and the distant sound of marching boots. Black uniforms moved like an oil slick through the crowd. A man was selling periscopes with mirrors that allowed people at the back to see what was happening and a detachment of BDM girls with triangular swastika flags were arranged at the front, giggling hysterically.

Suddenly the murmuring of the crowd intensified to a roar and the people in front of Clara surged forward, arms rising, as a six-wheeled black Mercedes, as sleek and magisterial as a cruise liner, flanked by SS motorcycle outriders, approached slowly, the sun glancing off its chrome hubs. Simultaneously she registered that the band was playing the British National Anthem and saw through the car's window a bowler hat and wing collar, the sparkle of a watch chain and a pair of beady eyes peering out above a toothbrush moustache. A face as ashen as a pine coffin.

'It's Chamberlain!' cried the man next to her. 'The British Prime Minister.'

Bewildered, she turned. 'Mr Chamberlain is here?'

'He came by aeroplane this morning. He's going to meet the Führer at the Berghof!'

As Chamberlain's car approached, two women edged forward and threw something into the road and a frisson of alarm ran through the crowd until they saw that it was only a scatter of long-stemmed chrysanthemums, their white petals wheeling in a confetti of joy. Eyes travelled upwards, following the stems as they sailed into the air before they whirled back to the ground again and were crushed by the fat, oblivious tyres of the Mercedes, leaving a bruise of flowers on the road behind.

Chapter Sixteen

Rosa Winter had a new typewriter. Everyone did, in fact. All official typewriters throughout the Reich were being replaced with keys that could spell SS in Gothic script. Rosa rather liked the look of hers, squared precisely, gleaming and shiny on her orderly desk, alongside the stacked carbons and the official NS Frauenschaft notepaper with its eagle letterhead signifying the offices of the Führerin, and a row of pencils ranked in order of size. Every morning the Führerin glanced at the pencils on Rosa's desk as she passed, as though inspecting a stormtrooper honour guard, and that morning she had murmured an approving 'Ja' which would have gladdened the heart of any other secretary.

Tidiness was, Rosa knew, the main reason the Führerin liked her. To Gertrud Scholtz-Klink tidiness was not just a virtue but a political act. In fact, Rosa realized, her habit of putting everything in its correct place was a microcosm of the entire Reich. Nazi Germany was like her own orderly drawers, but on a massive scale. There was a file for every part of society – Mothers, Bund Deutscher Mädel, Hitler Youth. Everything neat and everyone in their place. An identity card for every citizen. A labour service for all ages. A Party file for every part of society. Germany was like one vast filing system, the kind the Gestapo were said to be assembling for every person in the Reich, with all citizens noted, annotated, sorted and accounted for. Every activity categorized and evaluated with a department allocated to it, or an association or a club. *Alles in Ordnung.*

Perhaps that was why Rosa liked keeping her Observations. Journalists looked at the messy parts of life, after all. The bits which didn't fit with the official picture. People who stepped out of line, or slipped through the cracks. People who couldn't be tidied away. She kept her blue leather notebook tucked at the bottom of the filing cabinet; she couldn't risk leaving it at home. Her mother rifled through her belongings routinely like a domestic branch of the Gestapo, searching for evidence of something she suspected but could not quite pin down, so Rosa brought the notebook to work every day and tucked it at the bottom of her drawer, between the files on Childbirth Targets in the Brandenburg area and a list of the Frauenschaft leaders in the local districts. It was safer that way.

Rosa didn't mind living with her parents, even if her school-friends had long since set up home with office clerks and bank managers and produced families of their own. Anselm and Katrin Winter lived in Bamberger Strasse in Wilmersdorf, a tree-lined street of beautiful, turn-of-the-century houses with elaborate decorative plasterwork and wrought-iron balconies, in an area called the Bayerisches Viertel. Their building had stucco of bone ivory with a pea-green balcony and inside a marbled foyer with a twisty walnut banister and high ceilings, swirled with plaster at the cornices like cake icing. The idea of cake was intensified by the smell of cinnamon and nuts that emanated from the Winters' stove, a marvel of blue and white porcelain tiles, mingling with the aroma of hot cotton from her mother's ironing and the musky smell of Brummer, Rosa's dog. Brummer was a cross between a Schnauzer and a louche, anonymous stray who had contributed melting brown eyes and one folded ear. By some subliminal canine instinct, Brummer knew to the minute when his mistress would be home, and would stand ready at the door to greet her, whereupon Rosa would bury her face in his neck and inhale his aroma of warm fur, which was to her the loveliest perfume in the world.

Rosa's father worked at the Prussian Academy of Sciences, an imposing building of pale, porticoed stone on Unter Den Linden, yet although he was a scientist by profession he was a great lover of literature. He had schooled Rosa in his beloved Schiller, as well as writers now considered degenerate like Heine and Mann, and when the Nazis burned these writers on the Opernplatz in 1933, Rosa's father had wrapped their books in waxed paper and hidden them in the garden, under the pretext of burying a dead pet rabbit. It was he who had first read Rosa the fairy stories that she now passed on to Hans-Otto. 'Fairy tales teach us what science and philosophy can't,' he would say. 'They teach us the mystery and the truth of life.'

It was possible, too, Rosa guessed, that Anselm Winter regarded her continued presence as mitigation against the abrasive personality of his wife, who came from a line of country farmers and considered spinsterhood an anomaly of nature. The Winters were themselves an anomaly in the Bayerisches Viertel, where most of the residents were Jewish, but Rosa's father had been a friend of Albert Einstein, who lived just streets away before he left the country, and he made no distinction between his Jewish neighbours and those who were, in the terminology of the new Reich, genuinely German. Although Herr Doktor Winter endured most of his wife's criticisms with good cheer, his refusal to join the Nazi Party was one shortcoming she knew better than to berate him for – out loud, at any rate – and she had to content herself with talking wistfully of the pleasures of various friends whose husbands had been more politically astute. When Rosa had landed the job at the Frauenschaft she had been overjoyed.

The great love of Katrin Winter's life was the cinema. She would spend hours poring over quizzes in the celebrity magazines. *Stern* was her favourite and she liked to read out items such as 'Could You Be A Star?' which centred on whether readers were 'as photogenic as Brigitte Horney', 'as expressive as Olga Chekhova' or as 'disciplined a worker as Marika Rökk'. Rosa's father endured this, but he could not be persuaded to accompany her to the cinema itself, so every week Rosa would be roped into an outing to watch whatever her mother chose – usually romantic comedies. The type of storyline Katrin preferred featured young women in reduced circumstances – singers and flower girls – who found themselves unexpectedly wooed by attractive and wealthy men. Last week's outing, *Es leuchten die Sterne*, in which a young secretary travelled to Berlin to seek work and was mistaken for a famous dancer, ending up as the lead in a star-studded musical, conformed precisely to this ideal.

In truth, though Rosa found many of the plots risible and she would prefer to be at home with a good novel, it was relaxing to sit there in the flickering dark, watching the actresses with their glamorous costumes and silken skin. They made such a contrast to the members of the Reichsmütterdienst she saw at the office every day, whose idea of fashion was flannel coats buttoned to the chin, black fedora and clumpy boots, and for whom a flower on the lapel represented transgressive glamour. Sometimes Rosa wondered what it must be like to wear a satin dress and feel it move like liquid with your body, rather than riding up and prickling against your skin as her woollen vests and underclothes were wont to do, the suspender belt digging into her waist like a mediaeval instrument of torture.

It was after one of those evenings that it had happened. Katrin Winter had already bought the evening's tickets to *Festival of Beauty*, the second half of Leni Riefenstahl's film of the 1936 Olympic Games, which was showing at the Paris Kino on the corner of Uhlandstrasse. The film had been premiered on the Führer's birthday and had tremendous reviews, but Katrin was suffering from a heavy cold so Rosa called on her sister Susi, who was busy with Hans-Otto, and in the end she decided to go alone. It had been a tiring day, so she was glad to sink down in the warmth of the stalls in a trance-like state, watching the synchronized swimmers sleek as seals in their shiny costumes and the gymnasts like statues from some ancient Greek temple, their skin like perfectly carved marble. The audience was overwhelmingly female, so a lone male was noticeable, especially one with a smart grey suit, a sharp face and a thin, pencil moustache, not unlike an American film star himself. She saw him first when they were settling down for the feature, sitting on his own a few rows back and diagonally along from her, brushing a hank of oiled hair out of his eyes. She was aware that throughout the movie he kept shooting her glances. He was there again as the crowd streamed out of the cinema into the street and when she joined the queue for the tram he came up next to her, tipped his hat and said, 'Lovely film.'

He thrust a hand towards her. August Gerlach was his name and he hoped she wouldn't think him presumptuous if he said she reminded him of Zarah Leander in *Heimat*? He hoped that didn't sound forward. Did she go to the movies often? What were her favourites? He cupped a cigarette to light it and offered her one too.

Rosa was so startled by these unexpected attentions she hardly knew how to respond. She half-wondered if the man was making fun of her, or chatting to her for a bet, but when she glanced around she could see no cohort of sniggering friends behind him so she carried on the conversation, swapping details of favourite movie stars and recent films, praying for her tram to arrive. When it came, it turned out that Herr Gerlach was travelling in the same direction, so he sat himself comfortably beside her, spreading out on the seat and obliging her to shrink to avoid physical contact. She reasoned that maybe he was lonely. People who weren't used to being on their own did, apparently, find it difficult and would seek out anyone, even strangers, for the sake of human company. Rosa had never remotely felt that way, but she supposed she could sympathize, even if on closer acquaintance Herr Gerlach, with his hard-edged face and loud laugh, looked more at home in a beer cellar than a Hollywood love story.

Chapter Seventeen

There was only one costume in the Third Reich as popular as the brown shirt, breeches and jackboot ensemble, and that was anything from the era of Frederick the Great. Movies glorifying Frederick the Great – Hitler's longtime hero and role model – formed a genre all of their own, and no fancy dress party was complete without several guests parading in silken crinolines, embroidered frock coats, white stockings and Prussian wigs. Hermann Goering thought nothing of raiding the costume rails of the Ufa studios for his own dressing-up parties, and any actor cast in an eighteenth-century movie knew that at the very least they would have plenty of charming outfits to choose from. But as Ursula Schilling waited alongside Clara in the costume department of the Geiselgasteig studios a few days later, it was another kind of fashion that was occupying her.

'You've seen this, I suppose.'

Ursula was holding a magazine at arm's length, as though it was something unpleasant she had picked off the pavement. Clara saw it was the current edition of the Nazi women's magazine, the *NS-Frauen-Warte*.

'I never miss it.'

'Don't joke, I mean it. Take a look.'

She pointed a disdainful crimson fingertip at a two-page spread

of actresses who had appeared in recent films. On one side were
vamps and chorus girls, platinum blondes who made up for in cosmetics what they lacked in clothing, cavorting in deliberately
sleazy poses. On the other side were ranged young women in
peasant costumes and braids with faces as blank and clean as
starched cotton. Beneath this group a caption read, *You think:*
boring, We think: healthy and beautiful!

Clara leant across and read the accompanying editorial.
'*Contemporary films do not pay enough attention to idealizing the family,*
and there are too many childless women featured. The demi-monde type,
hostile to marriage and family, is the living embodiment of the sterility of
the previous epoch of decay.'

It was the kind of thing Joseph Goebbels dictated in his sleep.

She shrugged. 'That's just the usual, isn't it? We've all heard it
before.'

'That's not the point. Take a closer look.'

Clara did. And on closer inspection she realized the problem.
One of the sterile vamps, poised on a barstool against a painted
background of a cocktail bar, staring at the camera with smoul-
dering eyes and clad in nothing more than a top hat, black
stockings and a pout, was Ursula herself.

'That's me done for.'

'I can't believe it.'

'It was freezing the day we did that shoot. A studio lot in
January. I almost died from pneumonia. If I'd known this was
going to happen I would never have bothered.'

Clara took the magazine from her in amazement. For all the
years she had been at the Ufa studios, Ursula Schilling had been
a rising star of the Reich, a goddess whose picture graced the foyer
at Babelsberg and whose voluptuous figure was a staple at every
Nazi reception and society party. Her curves, Schwarzkopf-dyed
blonde hair and wholesome Aryan looks had made her a natural
for the syrupy confections that were turned out like candy floss by
the Ufa studios with the intention of taking the population's mind

off butter shortages and wars. She had a wardrobe full of mink coats and her photograph in a thousand soldiers' wallets. She had been the ultimate pin-up of the Ufa studios, and now she was the poster girl for the scheming vamp.

'It's astonishing. But then, I have been wondering . . .'

'Why I agreed to take a bit part in this dump?' Ursula took out her patent leather handbag and lit a cigarette, then passed one over.

'I suppose I ought to tell you.'

She gave Clara a look of scrutiny, as if assessing whether she could trust her, exhaled a long stream of smoke and said,

'It started around a month ago. I had an unwanted visit. They turned up first thing in the morning, and it had been a rough night. Two of them, with faces like a wet Wednesday. I thought they were asking for my autograph so I slammed the door on them, but it didn't work because they just stood there knocking until I opened up again.'

'Police?'

She lowered her voice to a husky murmur. 'That was my first thought too. But they said they weren't policemen at all. They described themselves as civil servants.'

'Civil servants?'

'They worked for the government, apparently.'

'What did they want?'

She crossed her perfect legs and flicked a languid tower of ash into a nearby hatbox.

'They wanted to know if I had ever received a sexual advance from the Propaganda Minister. What kind of question is that for a girl at six o'clock in the morning?'

'My God. What did you say?'

'What do you think I said? I said of course I have! What girl hasn't? It's like breathing to him. Our Minister likes conquering women the way the Führer likes conquering countries.'

'You actually said that?' Whether Ursula was immensely brave, or entirely reckless, Clara couldn't decide, but she couldn't help being impressed.

Ursula sighed and raked her fingers through her ice-blonde locks.

'I told you, it had been a rough night. I'd only had a couple of hours' sleep. I was barely conscious.'

'What happened?'

'By the time they'd barged into my apartment and stamped their muddy boots all over my cream carpet, I'd come to my senses. I mean I'm used to giving interviews, but not the sort which end with a warrant for your arrest. I told them I had nothing more to say.'

'Did they accept that?'

'They said if I refused to talk it would constitute a refusal to help a government department with its enquiries and I might find my own activities investigated.'

'Your activities?'

Ursula fitted another cigarette in her mother-of-pearl holder and raised a pair of exquisitely plucked eyebrows.

'Precisely. You see the flaw in their argument, Clara. I have no activities. Not off screen anyway, and now it looks like I'll have precious few on screen either. I knew I should have kept quiet. Remember poor Renate Müller?'

How could Clara forget? Renate Müller was a rising star who had the misfortune to come to the attention of the Führer himself. An evening alone at the Reich Chancellery with Herr Hitler had proved so eventful that Renate dined out for months on the eye-popping details, until Goebbels placed her under Gestapo surveillance. Eventually the girl was found dead, having fallen from a window in a clinic where she was being treated for anxiety.

'I don't want to go the way of Renate Müller. Or Helga Schmidt for that matter.' She gave Clara a meaningful look.

'I knew if I said a word about the Herr Doktor it wouldn't go well for me. We all owe our careers to him and we're fooling ourselves if we think otherwise. Anyhow, it turned out I was right – there's been not a whisper of work since. Why else would I be playing in a low-budget historical romp? And today I see this.'

She stared mournfully at the magazine again.

'It's a message from him. He might as well have sent me a post-card.'

'I'm sure you're worrying unduly,' said Clara, who wasn't sure. 'Goebbels has plenty of other things on his mind at the moment.'

'Him! The one thing you can say about him is that women are always on his mind.'

Ursula laughed, but there was fear in her eyes. She was far too skilled an actress to allow it to dominate, but there was too much fear in Germany now for Clara not to recognize when she saw it. You could read the signs like a gambler's tell; the tremble of the hand which made Ursula replace her coffee cup too swiftly in its saucer, the toss of the head which disguised a discreet glance around the room.

'It's probably safer being a soldier than an actress these days. Whoever guessed we were signing on for such a dangerous job? If I'd known I'd have gone into something more secure. Stunt flying, perhaps, or doing the high-wire trapeze.'

'What actually happened with Goebbels?'

'Oh, that. It was fine to start with.' She flexed out her fingers in front of her like a cat's paw and studied the nails. 'The day after our first . . . encounter . . . at the after party for one of my films, he called me to his office and said he had great plans for me. I was perfect material for the Reich – material, that's what he called me, not flesh and blood – except that I needed to be "refashioned". I liked that idea because it sounded, well, it sounded rather pleas-ant, you know? I love fashion, and clothes, what girl doesn't, and the way he said it made me think I was going to get a whole new wardrobe. Ha!'

A frown snagged her ivory forehead. 'It turned out he wanted to refashion my image. I was to represent the woman of the new Reich. I was not to resemble a little American vamp any more. Instead I should say I dreamed of owning a farm in the country and riding horses.'

'Horses?'

'Horrible, isn't it? Filthy great beasts. Don't you just hate horses?'

Actually Clara loved them. She'd had a horse back in Surrey, a dappled bay called Inkerman, a creature of infinite patience and intelligence, and the smell of him – warm leather and horsehair – came back to her in a rush. All the same, it was hard to think of Ursula cantering through the Tiergarten with a flush on her cheeks.

'You could probably get to like them.'

'Never. Just think what riding does to the thighs. Besides, darling, horses were just the half of it. Goebbels wanted *Stern* to take pictures of me in the kitchen, whipping up a stew. I had to contribute my favourite recipe to a stars' cookbook. My dear, can you imagine me with a recipe? I couldn't boil an egg. If I could find an egg to boil, that is.'

She shook her head as though Goebbels had asked her to split the atom rather than perform a perfunctory domestic task.

'Besides, I had other plans.'

She gave Clara a look, as if assessing whether to trust her, and leaned forward.

'I'd had an approach from Hollywood. A man called Frits Strengholt, the head of MGM – you must have heard of him.'

Vaguely Clara recalled a dough-faced bureaucrat who had been snapped at Hitler's right hand during a number of screenings.

'He's very close to Goebbels. He sacked all the Jewish staff in the MGM offices at the request of the Promi and he even agreed to divorce his wife because she was Jewish and Goebbels complained. Anyhow, Strengholt said I would be a knockout in the States. I was a second Garbo and had a face to die for. I wasn't complaining. It felt like it was my turn. Everyone's been going to Hollywood and back for the past decade – name me a single star who hasn't been there – Emil Jannings, Lilian Harvey, Olga Chekhova, there's no end of them, so why not me? Only when I applied the bastards at the Chamber of Culture refused to recommend me for an exit visa.'

'On what grounds?'

'Too many actresses are jumping ship. It looks embarrassing. It's bad enough that Marlene Dietrich, the most famous German actress in the world, won't come back. So now they've slapped a ban on any other actresses crossing the Atlantic. I'm cursing myself. I would have left last year if it wasn't for . . .'

'Wasn't for what?'

Something in her face had wilted, so that her eyes were huge and woeful, and a dab of wetness smudged her mascara. She frowned at Clara, as though she was about to continue, but at that moment the costume girl appeared, hovering behind them, bearing two powdered wigs.

'Oh, never mind. I'm pinning my hopes on this evening at the Künstlerklub that von Arent's invited us to. It's for the benefit of the Americans, to showcase the Ufa stars, and all the big cheeses will be there. I'm going to have another try with my MGM man. See if I can persuade him to sort things out for me.'

Turning to the costume girl she fixed her with a beaming smile and said, 'Darling, could you fetch me another coffee? As black as sin and as hot as hell. That's how I like it.'

Then she tossed her head, dried off her eyes, and turned her attention to Clara.

'Enough of my troubles. You're doing fine. Kaffeeklatsch with the Führer's girlfriend, that's a good start.'

'Shh.' Clara looked around her. 'Your voice carries, you know.'

Ursula laughed. A rich, husky, knowing laugh.

'You imagine they don't know already? They know everything, Clara, and anything they don't already know, they're going to find out. They know everything you think, even before you've thought it. There's no point having secrets here. Secrets in Germany are like butter; they don't keep. You've heard the saying: the only person with a private life in the Reich is the person who's asleep, but that's not enough for them. Goebbels wants to control your dreams.'

She shrugged. 'What I want to know is how you do it. I've seen the way they hang around you, all the men at the studios, and yet you've managed to keep out of Goebbels' clutches. How've you pulled it off? Are you in love or something?'

The question brought Clara up short.

'Why do you ask?'

'You have that look about you just now. As though you're thinking about a man.'

'I am. I'm thinking about my godson Erich. He's fifteen.'

Ursula sighed, a long, world-weary sigh.

'Ah well, fifteen or fifty, men are always a worry. Don't I know it?'

After the fittings had been completed, and they had spent the afternoon in the rehearsal room, the cast drove back to Berlin for dinner at the Hofbräuhaus, the former royal brewery adopted by Hitler in the Twenties for the inaugural meeting of the newly launched National Socialists. By that time in the evening the place was already loud with the drinking songs of boisterous men in leather Bavarian jackets and fur-edged Tyrolean hats. Barmaids balancing great steins of beer blithely ignored the men's ribald remarks as they placed huge dollops of sauerkraut and sausage on their plates. In the past Mozart had drunk there, and Lenin, but no one remembered that now, when the riotous alpine flowers painted on the ceiling were entwined with ornate blue swastikas, and the buxom waitresses had Nazi symbols embroidered on their dirndls.

As she sat with the cast Clara wondered again if the feeling she had – that a man was on her tail – had been correct, and if so whether someone might be following her even there. It would be hard to spot a watcher in a crowd – the place was packed to the rafters – but after a while she decided to relax. If a shadow was there, then good luck to him. He wouldn't be up to much surveillance after a couple of steins of the Hofbräuhaus's finest, strong Bavarian beer.

Back in the pension in Maximiliansplatz Clara sat for some time at the little desk in front of the window, watching a moon of pale bone climbing the sky. It was true that she had been thinking about Erich. She had not seen as much of him recently as she would like and she was dismayed that his first experience of foreign travel had been marred by that incident on the *Wilhelm Gustloff*. She wondered if Rupert had taken the chance to find anything out about it.

She had meant to write a postcard to Erich, but instead she sat, abstracted, making shapes on the letter pad as a tapestry of thoughts wove through her mind. She picked up *Rebecca* and tried to read, but the descriptions of the Cornish landscape only reminded her of Joachim von Ribbentrop saying that Cornwall was his favourite part of England, with the unspoken implication that if ever the Nazis were obliged to invade, Cornwall would pretty much be his. It was terrible to think of her beloved Cornwall, her childhood holiday home, in his hands. She thought of sitting on the gritty beaches and cutting her feet on the flinty rocks. Of walking through rhododendron woods, fragrant with moss and damp earth, in the early days of her childhood.

The thoughts stirred memories, and on impulse she went over to her suitcase and picked out a locket. It was a pretty thing, Victorian probably, with a design of entwined flowers and leaves and a filigree silver clasp, and all she possessed of her mother's apart from a fox fur coat. Inside was a photograph of her mother and herself at the age of six – her mother's watchful, luminous eyes and high cheekbones repeated with uncanny precision on the child beside her. Clara dimly remembered that she had been trying to copy her mother's air of reserved self-control, a look that she had eventually perfected. She realized that she must be the same age now as her mother was in the picture, and wondered what her mother would have made of her current situation. Would she urge Clara to return to the safety of London, as Leo Quinn had, or would she acknowledge that her daughter had made a new life in a foreign land, just as she had done herself?

For a long time after she died, the image of her mother on her deathbed had been the one that dominated Clara's thoughts – her wasted, bony hand on the eiderdown, her searching, brown eyes with violet smudges beneath them, and her long hair, wired with grey and tied in an incongruously girlish plait. But eventually earlier memories returned, many of them bound up with her mother's attempt to recreate her German youth. Though Helene Vine was self-effacing in public, hating for people to notice her German accent and always quick to defer to their father, at home she had tried ardently to recreate her Hamburg childhood, teaching the children to sing *Stille Nacht* at Christmas time while she played the piano, and ordering gingerbread from Harrods. She encouraged the children to leave their shoes out for presents on St Nicholas Day, and told them about Black Peter who beat bad children with his stick. On Christmas Day she baked Stutenkerl, little men made of sweet spiced dough, and they ate goose and red cabbage for lunch. Probably she expected Clara to follow in Angela's footsteps. To be married in England by now, with children perhaps, her acting career long behind her and a dull, blameless, housewifely life ahead. Would that be so bad?

After Helene Vine died, her daughters might have grown closer, but instead grief seemed to drive a wedge between them. Angela's politics had veered to the right and she had adopted her father's pro-Nazi sympathies, while Clara came to Berlin. Despite their differences though, Angela remained an inveterate letter writer, covering pages of notepaper headed Elizabeth Street, SW1, in her round, curly handwriting, spiking her political sympathies with arch humour. She wrote punctiliously once a month, with news of a world that Clara had long since left behind. How Angela's husband Gerald had been put up for White's club by their father and the three of them had been invited to Nancy Astor's place in Cliveden. Frequently she enclosed clippings of herself from *The Tatler*, grouse shooting or attending a charity ball, but while her face may have worn the myopic, glassy expression which had made her such a successful model before her marriage, the mind behind it was as sharp as a whip. Angela prided herself on her ability to tell what her younger sister was thinking – indeed it was probably having Angela as a sister that had honed Clara's ability as an actress.

Though Angela had plenty of friends who studied music and flitted between castles in Bavaria and art in Berlin, she maintained a relentless campaign to persuade Clara to return to England. She had tried again when she visited the previous year. '*I've never under-stood why you felt you had to leave us and spend all this time abroad. I know you have your career and everything, but you must miss England, surely? All those people you used to go round with. Ida McCloud. The Cavendishes. And you didn't even make it for my wedding! What is it about Germany?*'

In that moment Clara had been badly tempted to tell her: of her discovery that their grandmother was Jewish, and that they them-selves were a quarter Jewish, a fact which had been kept from them all their lives, as though it was something to be ashamed of. But she could never be truthful with Angela; the intimacy they had once shared was over and instead she said nothing, leading her sister to deduce that Clara's affection for Berlin must be connected to her love life.

'It's a man, isn't it? Anyone special?' Angela enquired in her knowing, elder sister voice. Then, more softly, 'Whoever it is, you want to get a move on, Pidge. Men don't wait around forever.'

Pidge was a childhood nickname. A reference to the time when an eight–year–old Clara had found a pigeon with a broken wing, a mess of fright and clotted feathers, and insisted on nursing the bird in a cardboard box until, inevitably, it expired. The memory stung Clara into denial.

'It isn't a man. There's no one special.'

It felt like a lie, but perhaps it was true.

It was hard to unwind. Even when she undressed and lay between the cool sheets, Clara couldn't sleep. Angela's question, '*Anyone special?*' ran through her brain, along with her advice, so casually dispensed, '*Men don't wait around forever.*' That was true. The splinter of pain left by Leo was a lingering reminder of that. She recalled what Eva Braun had said about perfume, that sometimes the most unlikely things, when the particles paired and collided, could have a dramatic effect. Then the face of Max Brandt came to her, talking of how perfume stirred olfactory memory – the kind which went to the deep seabed of the brain and unlocked the images buried there. Of the hundreds of strange ingredients in perfume, and the exotic names they had. '*They don't work so well in German of course; you have to say them in French.*'

But Max Brandt was not to be trusted, no matter how attractive he might be. That brown gaze and seductive smile was concealing something, she was sure of it, and every instinct Clara possessed warned her to be wary. All the same when she eventually fell asleep she dreamed of the collision of unlikely particles and of dinner with Max Brandt, speaking softly to her in French.

Chapter Eighteen

Rosa Winter reached for Adolf Hitler and idly flicked his right arm up and down into a salute. He looked faintly risible, standing rigidly in his Mercedes 770, with his moustache reduced to a mere dab, and cheeks as rosy as a case of diphtheria. The Führer figurine was one of several stationed on her desk in preparation for a talk to be given that afternoon to the senior officials of the cultural section of the Reich Mothers Service. Already several of the women had begun to arrive, in their frumpy grey coats and flat black boots, notebooks and pens at the ready for the lecture on the importance of promoting the correct German playthings. Toy production in Germany had been severely curtailed in recent years, but the Elastolin company was still doing a roaring trade with its replica soldiers and action figures. As well as Hitler, you could buy Goering, Hess, Goebbels, Himmler, von Schirach, Mussolini and Franco, though the figurine of SA leader Ernst Röhm had been discreetly discontinued after Hitler had him assassinated in 1934. The figures were made of plastic now because all metal was needed for aeroplanes, but Joseph Goebbels had recently instructed that the heads of the most important figures should in future be crafted out of porcelain, to look more realistic. Rosa wasn't sure it made much difference. Making Himmler more lifelike was hardly going to make children want to play with him.

Traditional German toys, preferably made of wood, were essential to convey the correct ideological conditioning, the Führerin believed, so along with the action figures Rosa had that morning been sent out to buy puzzle games with pieces of wood that spelt out the words Adolf Hitler, a spelling book – A is for Adolf, B is for Bormann etc – and a mobile with the face of Hitler to hang above a baby's cot. There were card games too, like the one where players competed to collect the top Nazi leaders, with Hitler, of course, worth the maximum number of points. All these toys would be demonstrated to the women's leaders in their session on Childhood Indoctrination, and everyone would be allowed to examine them more closely, though not, of course, play with them.

The Führerin had indicated that, as a perk of the job, Rosa might like to take home the Hitler figurine for Susi's son, Hans-Otto, when they had finished with it. Already Rosa was imagining Hans-Otto's wide face lighting up as he saw it, the vacant blue eyes sparking with delight when she gave it to him that night.

Thursday evenings were when Rosa looked after her nephew while Susi went to her weekly Mutterdienst meetings and Pauly was off drinking with his friends from work. As soon as she had finished for the day, Rosa took a tram to the dingy, pockmarked block in Moabit where the Kramers had their apartment, and climbed the stone stairs to the fourth floor. But as soon as Susi opened the door, it was clear she would not be leaving the house. Her eyes were pink and blotchy with crying and she was wearing her apron. She held up a handkerchief to her face, ushering Rosa inside with a tired wave.

'Is it Pauly again?' During their rows, Pauly was known to resort to physical force to give his argument more emphasis.

'No. But I'm not going out tonight. I have to stay in with Hans-Otto.'

'What's wrong?' said Rosa with a surge of alarm. 'Is it another fit?'

'It's worse.'

As Susi shunted her sister into the kitchen, Rosa suppressed a gag. The claggy moisture of a cabbage stew hung in the air, mingled with the heavy damp of drying clothes stacked on an ironing board and underwear soaking in a bucket. Hans-Otto was sitting on the floor, playing lethargically with a cardboard box, still dressed in his school uniform of a short-sleeved shirt buttoned to the neck and tucked into his trousers. His face had a dazed expression, as though he was listening to music that only he could hear, but as soon as he saw Rosa he held out his arms for a hug.

Susi returned to the sink and resumed savagely scrubbing potatoes.

'You know how he is at school. You've seen him, haven't you?'

On the occasions when she had collected him from school, Rosa had watched Hans-Otto amongst his classmates, and winced inwardly at how he hung back while the other boys scampered around the schoolyard, faces flushed and yelling their lungs out. He didn't properly come alive until they reached the pet shop on the way home, where he would smile at the puppies and place his palms flat on the window as their wet noses nuzzled the glass.

'Well, now we've had this.' Susi fumbled in her apron pocket and thrust a letter towards her. It was a thin blue envelope, marked with the official stamp of Hans-Otto's school office, and contained a terse note, outlined in the finest National Socialist officialese.

Dear Herr and Frau Kramer,

I am writing with regard to the episode suffered this week by your son. This episode, as well as difficulties observed by your son's teachers, has alerted us to the possibility of congenital weakness. Under the law for prevention of Genetic Diseases, 1933, I am required to report any signs of weakness or potential

disability to the requisite authorities. Please be advised that unless
you can provide medical evidence that your son is free from any
disease of heredity the school will report his case for examination
by a Heredity Health Court which will evaluate his condition.
The school awaits your response.
    Heil Hitler!

'I don't understand it,' said Susi, half despondent, half angry. 'All that jargon.'

'What are these difficulties they're talking about?'

'You know. It's just Hans-Otto. He's not like other boys. He's slow.'

'He's a dreamer. That's what Vati says. Hans-Otto is dreaming up great things. Vati says Einstein didn't talk until he was four.'

This remark only seemed to upset Susi more.

'Einstein! He's not Einstein! Look at him!'

Hans-Otto was holding up the figurine of the Führer and gazing at it with a seraphic air, as though observing the transit of invisible angels.

'You don't know what he's capable of,' said Rosa stoutly.

'I know what he's not capable of. The teachers are supposed to report any child who seems abnormal and according to Fräulein Blitzer that includes not being able to button a coat, doing badly in sports, or failing an exam. Hans-Otto hasn't taken any exam yet, but he certainly can't button his coat and that fit he had the other day has made everything so much worse. He sits there in a trance. I'm desperate, Rosa.'

'What's this Heredity Health Court they're talking about?'

'A type of health board.'

'But what does health have to do with a court? It's nothing to do with the law, is it?'

'I don't really understand it either. Apparently it's a place where they investigate an inherited disease.'

'But having a fit isn't inherited.'

Susi's face seemed to contort with suppressed rage and fear.

'Pauly's father had fits. Pauly's brother has had them too. It's something called epilepsy. But Pauly absolutely refuses to accept that Hans-Otto is suffering from it. And he insists that his brother's fits were just a consequence of too much beer.'

'What about Doktor Eberhardt?' The family doctor was a kindly man with a practice in Keithstrasse, who had tended the entire Winter family since Rosa and Susi were children.

'I've seen him, of course. He said he would prefer not to examine Hans-Otto.'

'But why?'

'He would be obliged to pass any information about Hans-Otto to a central archive and he doesn't want to do that.'

'Not even to see him, though?'

'I'm glad. I don't want Doktor Eberhardt to write anything about Hans-Otto down. I don't want anything about my son on some file in someone's archive.'

'So what can you do?'

Susi folded her arms defiantly.

'It's you who need to do something, Rosa. You understand the way these things work. You talk to these people. You work for the Führerin after all – the most powerful woman in the land – you must be able to ask her for help.'

'But . . .' It was impossible to explain to her elder sister just how adamantly the Führerin was opposed to any form of nepotistic advantage. Giving Rosa the toy that day was the nearest to official corruption that the Führerin had ever come, and Rosa knew she would probably have reimbursed the office later from her own pocket.

'I will. Of course I will. I'll see what I can do.'

She cast a glance at Hans-Otto, who was now bashing the Hitler toy with a gentle rhythm, up and down, up and down, on its head.

'Susi, why don't you go tonight anyway – you need the break. Let me stay with him for a couple of hours.'

Once Susi had left, Rosa opened her bag and drew out the book she had plucked from the library before leaving work. The very few children's stories available were all on the recommended list for National Socialist teaching and followed correct ideology. By far the most borrowed was Holst's *The Dragon Slayer,* in which Hitler was pictured as a prince battling to free the princess who was Germany, but Rosa had chosen a book with a deep burgundy cover and a line drawing of a wizened, old dwarf on it, decorated by a title in black Gothic script: *The Household Tales of the Brothers Grimm*. Women on the Mother Service course were encouraged to read fairy tales to children on the grounds that they embodied the correct folkish values and the characters in them bravely struggled to find racially pure marriage partners, but Rosa didn't care about any of that and, obviously, Hans-Otto didn't either. She just loved the stories.

She tickled Hans-Otto's cheek.

'Shall I tell you a story?'

A dreamy nod.

She settled on the warm chair next to the stove, hauled Hans-Otto onto her lap and flicked through, searching for an appropriate tale as his small body snuggled up to hers. Most of the fairy tales in the NS Frauenschaft version had soldiers in them, like the stormtrooper who came to rip open the belly of the wolf who ate Red Riding Hood, or the SS officer who arrested Cinderella's Slavic stepsisters, and there was plenty of violence too. But Rosa disregarded anything too gory, like *Snow White*, where the Jewish Queen was made to wear red-hot shoes, or *The Jew in the Brambles*, in which a magic violin made the merchant dance in a thicket of thorns, and carried on searching until she came to one of her favourites, *Rapunzel.*

'*There was once a man and a woman who had long in vain wished for a child . . .*'

Hans-Otto sucked his thumb and with his other hand held the Hitler doll up against his cheek. His limbs were entirely relaxed and his eyelids drooping. It was hard to tell if he was listening or not.

Chapter Nineteen

The Tiki Bar at Munich's Bayerischer Hof hotel was an eccentric testament to the craze for Polynesian culture which had swept Germany a few years earlier. The basement bar was done out entirely in colourful island fashion with fishing nets draped from the ceiling, teak beams decorated with the evil eye supporting it, and coconut and conch shells studding the bar. The lamps were made from dried blowfish and bamboo, and the cocktails were Mai Tais and Pina Coladas. Island music was piped through the loudspeakers in the wall and the entrance was flanked with totem poles carved with the grotesque visages of gods and demons. But none of them could compete with the faces of Frau Emmy Goering's soirée.

Clara was not looking forward to the party. She had already walked twice around the centre of Munich in an attempt to soothe her nerves. Her relationship with Eva Braun depended on attending this event yet the prospect of coming face to face with Frau von Ribbentrop, who had so recently denounced her as a spy, and Frau Heydrich, who may have repeated that accusation to her husband, was daunting and it would take every acting skill she possessed to retain an outward calm. Might the women take the opportunity to have her arrested there and then? And if so, could Clara count on Eva Braun to vouch for her? Eventually, after attracting the whistles of a pair of stormtroopers, who assumed that the attractive lady in high heels and a fox fur coat was parading the streets for their benefit, Clara braced herself and entered the throng.

The cream of the master race was out in force that night; sweaty men with short necks and only a brutal dusting of bristles on their scalps, squeezed into SS dress uniforms that were bursting at the seams. They were loud, competitive and flushed with drink and their demeanour was aggressively alert, as if they were assembled for a brawl rather than a high society cocktail party. As was usually the case at Nazi events, male guests vastly outnumbered the female, and the men tended to prioritize the chance of professional advancement over the opportunity to make small talk with other people's wives. In this case they were all vying for the choicer spots next to the more senior officers, jostling for position in the Nazi pecking order.

Swiftly Clara scanned the room, checking which VIPs were present. National Socialist cocktail parties were the opposite of the ordinary kind – you sincerely hoped there would be no one there you knew – and it seemed she was in luck. She recognized very few people and no one so much as gave her a glance in return. Nor was there any sign of Eva Braun.

The room was packed and oppressively warm and she felt a strong temptation to turn tail and slip away. No one would notice and she could always make her excuses the following day. Yet she forced herself to remain – it was essential to excavate some more cogent information from the Führer's girlfriend. Mr Churchill and all those people in Whitehall who were presumably aware of her mission had no interest in Eva Braun's views on perfume, or that she was planning a Hollywood biopic of her love affair with Hitler. They wanted concrete insight into Hitler's military plans.

As Clara was thinking this, two things happened. A waiter thrust a vivid green cocktail into her hand and a large, plump woman elbowed her way through the crowd to greet her. Her hostess,

Emmy Goering, the wife of Germany's second most powerful man, was decked in diamond earrings and a matching necklace that cut into her heavy flesh. Just like her husband, whose love of jewellery and outlandish uniforms suggested many happy hours with the dressing-up box, Emmy never stinted on extravagant displays of satin, velvet and lace. That evening bulky Wagnerian braids framed her face and enough taffeta to rig a ship was ruched around her considerable frame, topped with the pelt of a sizeable fox. The whole ensemble could not have looked more out of place amid the tropical island décor of the bar. The thicket of SS men parted like the Red Sea as she made her way across the room.

'Clara Vine! Fancy finding you at my little party. Come and talk to me,' she said imperiously. 'I've not seen you since the baby was born.'

'I meant to say, Frau Goering, many congratulations.'

'Thank you. It's tremendously fulfilling having a child. You should try it. We're holding the baptism next month at Carinhall. The Führer's to be godfather and I must say he's overjoyed. If he's not to be blessed himself it's the next best thing.'

'They say he loves little girls.'

For years there had been regular photographs in the papers of the Führer at the Berghof holding the hand of a small blonde poppet who shared his birthday and was often invited to tea. Once Martin Bormann's investigations uncovered the child's Jewish grandmother however, the little girl's invitations dried up and Hitler was advised to take tea with his Alsatian instead.

'You should see the gifts, Clara! Everyone's been so generous.'

That was no surprise. The christening of the child who was already being called the Princess of the Reich would almost certainly involve piles of art treasures ransacked from city museums and enough crowned heads of Europe to fill a stamp album.

'The Luftwaffe's promised to build a full-scale replica of Sans Souci palace in the orchard, complete with a little theatre for her plays. Isn't that charming?'

'Adorable.'

'Though if she's going to be an actress, one does hope she sticks to the stage. The film world these days seems to attract the absolute dregs of society, saving your presence, of course, Clara.'

Clara laughed. 'Of course.'

'So what have you been up to? We missed you at the rally.'

Yet again, Clara had succeeded in avoiding the annual Nuremberg rally, an affair which actresses as well as international visitors were aggressively encouraged to attend.

'I was working and I just couldn't make it. But I saw the news-reel.'

It was hard to miss. No one could visit the cinema in September without sitting through a news documentary devoted entirely to the Party rally, whose theme this year had been Forward Planning. Goering had focused on 'The eternal mask of the Jew devil' while Hitler followed up with his usual incandescent rant, concluding that the Sudetenland must return to the Reich 'no matter what'.

'It's no good saying you've seen the newsreel. The newsreel's no substitute for the real thing, as I hardly need to tell you, dear. It can never capture the atmosphere. It's like film compared to theatre.' As a stage actress who had never made it into films, Emmy Goering was prone to trumpeting the superiority of theatrical performance over all other dramatic work. She was especially given to criticizing Ufa films as low-brow and lacking in artistic value.

'Anyhow, as we were all down in Nuremberg, it made sense to come on to Munich before heading back to Berlin, which is why I thought it was the perfect opportunity for a party. And nearly everyone's here.'

Clara glanced around the flushed faces and the bare shoulders glittering with jewels. It was true that any assassin planting a bomb in this basement bar would take out most of the top tier of Nazi society.

'Apart from the Goebbels, of course. But then Magda, naturally, is in no state, poor woman.'

'Is she unwell?'

'Not physically.' Emmy Goering gave her a significant look. 'Her problem is more of the marital kind. She's not alone, of course.'

She nodded towards a dumpy woman standing on her own with an orange juice, whom Clara recognized as Marga Himmler, the former nurse turned chicken farmer, who obeyed the Nazi ordinance against cosmetics like holy writ.

Emmy Goering drew closer, her dense perfume enveloping them both like a rotting lily.

'Doesn't Marga look miserable? Do you think it's because her husband is off with little Hedwig Potthast, his secretary, or because she thinks she might have to talk to Lina Heydrich?'

Clara felt her stomach clench.

'Is Frau Heydrich here?'

'Oh yes. Didn't you notice?'

She cocked her head towards a patrician ash blonde arguing vigorously with a cowed-looking man whose uniform identified him as an SS Sturmbannführer. It was likely to be a one-way argument – no Sturmbannführer was going to risk disagreeing with the wife of SS-Obergruppenführer Reinhard Heydrich.

'She's suffering a lot of stress. Reinhard is drowning in paperwork, they haven't had a holiday for ages and they have barely any social life in Berlin. She says it's difficult to make new friends because she never knows when her husband might have to arrest them.'

Emmy gave a knowing smirk.

'To cap it all, she had a frightful falling-out with Marga. Apparently Marga told her husband to persuade Heydrich to divorce Lina.'

'Divorce his wife? But why?'

'Marga thinks Lina is unsuitable for someone of Reinhard's stature. Lina was fit to be tied, as you can imagine. And Marga won't give an inch. How difficult for two senior men to have wives that hate each other. At a time like this, too. Some women are so selfish.'

Clara glanced over at the stout figure, nursing her orange juice. Alone among the crowd, Marga Himmler had eschewed evening dress in favour of a dirndl.

'It seems such an unlikely intervention.'

'Oh, Marga's like that. She may play the humble hausfrau but she can give as good as she gets. She had someone arrested the other day for overtaking her on the autobahn.'

As she spoke, Emmy Goering was eyeing up Clara's pale pink dress with its collar of frosted fur.

'So why are you here in Munich then, if not to attend the rally?'

'I'm making a film at the Geiselgasteig studios. With Ursula Schilling.'

'Ursula Schilling?' Emmy took a long draw of her cigarette and narrowed her eyes. 'From what I'm hearing, the only kind of spotlight that woman will be under in the future is a Gestapo interrogation lamp.'

A jolt of anxiety shot through Clara, which she forced herself to suppress. It was always best to affect ignorance when it came to the Gestapo, but to hear Ursula mentioned in this casual way made her heart race with alarm.

'Really? I hadn't heard.'

Emmy raised her eyebrows and lowered her voice.

'They say she's been consorting with asocial elements.'

Clara managed a carefully calibrated expression of surprise – enough to suggest innocence of Ursula Schilling's private life, but not enough to imply that she was in any way close to her fellow actress. That was a familiar demeanour just then. People were as cautious with their expressions as they were with their butter. In Nazi Germany excessive emotion was reserved for marches and Party rallies.

'Asocial elements? Surely not.'

'Let's just say, for the sake of your film I hope she has an under-study.'

Privately Clara resolved to find Ursula as soon as possible and warn her.

'Anyhow,' Emmy Goering retrieved the maraschino cherry from the bottom of her glass, speared it on a cocktail stick and ate it. 'You didn't say. Who invited you tonight?'

'Actually, it was Fräulein Braun.'

Emmy Goering paused mid-swallow, her face a cartoon of astonishment.

'Really? The Führer's ... I had no idea you two were acquainted.'

'Fräulein Braun is very interested in film. She sent a note of her – appreciation – to the studio, but though she invited me, she doesn't seem to have come herself.'

Clara scanned the room again. There was indeed no sign of Eva.

'Oh, she's a law unto herself, that girl. She's probably having another photo session.' Emmy smiled cruelly. 'Eva's always having her photograph taken in a white dress – it's a hint the Führer never seems to take.'

'Herr Hitler only likes being with her because it means he doesn't need to think,' came a familiar voice.

The voice cut through the smoky air like a draft of ice. Clara did not need to turn to know it belonged to her greatest enemy, the person who above all others in Germany regarded her with suspicion and distrust; the wife of the Foreign Secretary, Annelies von Ribbentrop.

The woman who wanted Clara investigated as an English spy was that evening resplendent in imperial purple with a frosting of tiny black hairs on her upper lip and blotches of rouge on her cheeks. She took a puff on her gold-tipped Egyptian cigarette and gave Clara a narrow stare.

'If, as you say, she invited you, it seems strange she's not here.'

'Perhaps she's off playing with her perfumes somewhere,' said Emmy Goering.

'Her perfumes?'

'Didn't you know? It's her hobby. The Führer's obliged to put up with it, even though he despises perfume. She plays around making different concoctions and gets people from perfume companies to supply her with ingredients. That and frivolous films seem to be her only interests. I heard she gets her dressmaker to run up copies of dresses she's seen on screen, so she can feel more like a real actress.'

Clara recalled Eva admiring her dress. *I have one just like it!*

'I suppose it gives her something to do,' reasoned Frau von Ribbentrop. 'Now that she's given up the shop work.'

Clara was not surprised to hear Eva Braun subjected to this barrage of scorn. No one would dare disparage Eva in Hitler's presence so they made up for it when he was not around and evidently they reasoned that there was no problem in revealing their feelings in front of Clara. Yet despite the triviality of their conversations, and the torrent of bile they unleashed on the mistress of their beloved Führer, it was important to listen to what they had to say. If the people back in England had identified Eva Braun as a potential clue to Hitler's thinking, there might be a nugget of gold in this river of mudslinging.

'So, Fräulein Vine,' Annelies von Ribbentrop folded a canapé into her large jaw like a boa constrictor ingesting a mouse, 'how interesting to see you here.'

What could that mean? Had an order already been put out for her arrest? The Foreign Minister's wife gave the flicker of a smile.

'I suppose you know your Prime Minister has visited the Berghof?'

It was not the first time Annelies von Ribbentrop had referred to Chamberlain as 'your' Prime Minister as though Clara were not half German, but she knew better than to rise to it.

'I saw his car go past yesterday.'

'He only stayed a few hours,' said the Foreign Minister's wife, leaning closer. 'From what I hear, the Führer was not too impressed with his arguments. He says it's time England stopped playing governess to Europe.'

Though Frau von Ribbentrop liked to imply she was confiding a state secret, Clara had managed to gather this much from the copy of *The Times* she found at the studios. Chamberlain's mission had changed nothing. It was widely reported that Hitler had blackmailed Chamberlain with the threat of immediate war and that the Czechs had been betrayed. One commentator compared Chamberlain to a curate visiting a pub for the first time, imagining all the customers were as decent and honourable as himself.

'I feel sorry for Chamberlain actually,' Frau von Ribbentrop continued. 'Poor old man. He's very weak and troubled by his health. Did you know that until this week he had never flown in an aeroplane before? Extraordinary, don't you think?'

This was an enjoyable fact. It fitted with the notion of Britain as hopelessly backward-looking in comparison to Germany, with her gleaming Dorniers and Junkers and her ranks of gleaming Panzers preparing to roll east. But Emmy Goering was glazing over. Politics bored her. She had once confided to Clara that she wished Goering had made his career on the stage, rather than the grubby and frankly dangerous world of politics.

'Fräulein Vine was just telling me she's acting with Ursula Schilling,' she interrupted.

Annelies von Ribbentrop gave a fastidious little sniff.

'That foolish woman. She's probably regretting all that time she spent cultivating Joseph Goebbels now.'

Clara's alarm was confirmed. Had something happened to Ursula since they had been together the previous day? She was desperate to ask more but forced herself not to.

'How about you, Clara?' Emmy turned to Clara with an air of innocence. 'Have you seen Herr Doktor Goebbels recently? In the course of your work, I mean.'

Clara knew there was nothing these two wives would like better than to bracket her with the actresses who were said to have slept their way to the top. The best response was an entirely neutral one.

'I saw him and his wife in Berlin the other day.'

Frau von Ribbentrop suppressed a snigger.

'Not in the same room, surely?'

Emmy Goering cast her a disapproving glance. Goebbels was ridiculous and the public state of the couple's marriage was pitiful, but there were limits. She pursed her lips primly.

'Was it about a new film?' she asked.

'Yes. The Herr Doktor wants me to voice a documentary about Frau Scholtz-Klink and the place of the German mother.'

The prim expression turned to disgust.

'That harridan. I can think of one place this German mother would like to put *her*.'

Half an hour later Eva Braun still had not appeared and the gossip about Ursula Schilling, plus the strength of the Mai Tai cocktails, combined to give Clara a raging headache. With a swimming head and unsteady feet she was no longer able to resist the desire to escape so she forced herself to dally another five minutes, before slipping out of the bar.

Outside on the hotel's red carpet other women who had enjoyed one cocktail too many were wobbling on their high heels into taxis on the arms of SS officers. The doorkeeper attempted to hail a cab for Clara but she demurred and turned left, heading not to her pension, but to Ursula's hotel. Though she wanted nothing more than to collapse in bed, first she needed to see if Ursula was all right.

Moonlight lent a silvery glamour to the streets, which thanks to the presence of high-ranking international visitors, had been swept until they gleamed. Munich looked as perfect as a film set – one of the old Expressionist films made by Fritz Lang or Robert Wiene, with shafts of brilliant street light puncturing the blackness of the night and inky alleyways leading off the main streets to small squares glittering with cobbles. As she threaded her way through the side streets, unfamiliar buildings loomed up and faded again like movie scenes and Clara could not help thinking of what Fritz Gutmann had said about Goebbels. *He sees the whole of the Third Reich as a cinematic event.*

At Ursula's hotel the night receptionist had only just come on duty, so he couldn't vouch for Fräulein Schilling, but he was only too pleased to direct Clara to her room on the second floor. Clara picked her way through the honour guard of jackboots that lined the corridor, waiting outside every room for their nightly polish like a phantom squad of stormtroopers on permanent watch, and hoped she would not run into their owners.

But there was no answer to her knock on Ursula's door.

Chapter Twenty

In the corner of the Friedrichshain Volkspark, a group of Arbeitsdienst lads armed with spades were attacking a roped-off area, hacking deep into the turf. They were constructing a bunker in case enemy bombers should fly over Berlin and demolish the houses. If that happened, a siren would sound and everyone would have to go to their nearest shelter or risk certain death as the bombs rained down and fires started. At the same time, anti-aircraft guns on all the buildings would shoot into the sky, hitting the bombers and bringing them crashing down. The whole city would be lit up by livid flames and the sound of machine guns. It sounded pretty exciting. Like most boys at school, Erich was looking forward to it. He hoped it would happen before he was due to start his own Labour Service. It would be far more exciting to enrol directly into the airforce than spend six months digging trenches and latrines and draining marshes for the Arbeitsdienst.

Even though his godmother Clara was half-English, it was plain that Britain needed to be taught a lesson. They had studied it in Geography.

'Schmidt, name the chief enemy of the Fatherland!'

'Great Britain, sir.'

'Who are the villains of the Versailles Treaty?'

'Britain, France and America, Herr Kinkel.'

'What is the greatest enemy of the civilized world?'

That one was easy. Bolshevism.

Herr Kinkel had got his pupils to draw a large swastika in pencil on the cover of their exercise books and write the list of Germany's enemies on the first page. When he discovered that Erich had met Ernst Udet, the air ace, he had been visibly impressed. He was mad keen on fighting and Erich's class often got him talking about the forthcoming war to distract him from the work they were supposed to do.

Erich rolled over in the warm grass and inhaled the deep green scent. No matter how exciting war was going to be, he didn't mind waiting a bit longer. He loved this park. He used to come here a long time ago with his mother when she was alive; on fine days they had sunbathed and there was a pond with swans and a skating rink and a café. It was a popular place for parents to take children, partly on account of its famous fountain, the Märchenbrunnen, surrounded by stone sculptures representing characters from traditional German fairy tales – Cinderella, Tom Thumb and the rest. They didn't mean much to Erich; as a kid he had preferred the life-sized ones they had in the KaDeWe windows at Christmas and he preferred stories about crime like *Emil and the Detectives* – indeed he'd rather fancied becoming a detective for a while until he decided to join the Luftwaffe. The best stories, though, were the ones his mother told him about her film career. Mutti knew all the movie stars and she'd met a lot of important Party people too. If she'd lived she would most likely have been as famous as Marlene Dietrich. She used to tell him all about the parties and the stars she met – Emil Jannings, Hans Albers, Gustav Fröhlich – with gossipy details of who was in love with who, though most of them seemed to be in love with her. Sometimes, if Mutti had been to a party, she would keep a few of the chocolates they served with the coffee for him, and smuggle them back in her handbag. He swiped away a tear. Now all he had was Oma. His grandmother was devoted to him of course, but she was just a plain old nurse who went off every day to the red-brick Gothic Charité hospital and returned at night smelling of sick and disinfectant and nagging him about school. Oma hated Erich talking about war. There was his godmother Clara, who had been friends with his mother, only they talked about his mother less and less now. Often he wished they could talk more about her, and that Clara would add to his little stock of memories, which were in danger of dwindling, but he didn't like to bring the subject up in case it upset her.

Normally he saw Clara on a Saturday afternoon but she was away now, and the day's HJ session had finished, so he had jumped on a tram and come to the park just to get out of the apartment.

A soldier passed, walking arm in arm with his girlfriend, and Erich tracked them, watching the girl flick her long, creamy plaits flirtatiously across her shoulder as the man's hand caressed her waist. With a painful stab he was reminded yet again of the woman on the ship, Ada. He kept wondering what had really happened to her. He knew she hadn't disembarked at Funchal, whatever the captain said. They had talked after the ship left Madeira. Oma said he had got muddled, but young people didn't forget things like adults did – their minds were still fresh and sharp. It might be that Ada had gone off with a man – that was obviously what Clara thought – but Erich knew something worse had happened. He knew she was dead, and he guessed that he was the only person in the world who cared.

What would she look like if she had fallen into the sea? Would they even be able to identify her body? He had heard of bodies being pulled out of water – he had even seen one once, a woman being dragged from the Landwehr Canal, shockingly white, with her dress ballooning on the surface of the water. Someone joked that it was the corpse of Rosa Luxemburg, the communist, who had been shot and dumped in the canal alongside her revolutionary comrade. Erich knew that drowning would disfigure a person –

you were bloated beyond recognition and your flesh was eaten away by fishes – and he hated to think of that happening to Ada. He almost felt like praying for her, only he knew praying was wrong.

He wondered if Clara had discovered anything, as she promised, but he guessed she was just fobbing him off. She was always too busy acting now to focus on him. Erich was proud, of course, of her acting – it meant he got to meet celebrities like Ernst Udet, which boosted his status at school, but he didn't talk about Clara's acting work too much because actresses were not entirely respectable. He had watched Clara act once, at the studio in a scene with Gustav Fröhlich. It was a love scene, in which Clara had to tell Fröhlich that she was leaving him, and it made Erich feel awkwardly uncomfortable. He hadn't realized that film actors had to repeat the same scene over and over again, while the cameras stood just inches from their faces, until the director decided they had got it right. As Erich peered from the shadows of the set, the great hall seemed to shrink so that only Clara and Gustav Fröhlich existed, facing each other in their little pool of light. After each take Clara wiped the emotion from her face and faced him again with a fresh smile. But when she told Fröhlich the sad news, her face crumpled in the same way, and real tears came to her eyes. Erich wondered how Clara knew what it felt like to tell a man you were leaving him. She didn't have a boyfriend, as far as he knew, so did that mean she was making it up? And if she was, how was it possible to look like you meant it each time? How could you summon the emotions and control them, so that your face only said what you wanted it to say?

Sitting up, he felt for the satchel by his side and took out the cigarette album. Everyone collected cigarette cards now, all the boys at school. It was the number one craze, and at break time the playground was full of kids trading their cards to get a complete set. The albums came in different colours – golden, red and blue – and there was a text underneath the space where the card would be pasted, or secured beneath plastic sheets. Erich had completed several albums already, despite the fact that, unlike most of his friends, he didn't even smoke. There were always adults willing to hand out the coupons for the cards, which were high-quality reproductions on a variety of themes from Old Masters, to sports cars to castles, and you had to pay extra for an album to collect them in. So far Erich had collected *The Portraiture of Northern Europe*, sports stars, flags, *Germany Awakes*, and most recently, *The Life of Adolf Hitler*. Even though the company which issued these cards was not her usual brand, Oma had bought several packets of cigarettes until they got the full set.

Now he looked down at the cigarette card album in front of him. *Stars of the Ufa Studios*. It was a smart, red and gold cardboard creation with the title in twirling gilt on the cover and thick, heavy-gauge leaves inside, with spaces for photographs of forty-eight actors and actresses whose names were inscribed underneath. The album was Ada Freitag's. She had the complete series. They must have taken some time to collect and he could tell it was a prized possession by the way she had handled it, which made it all the more odd that she had never come back for it. Once she had disappeared, Erich had intended to return the album to Ada's cabin, but when he looked the whole place had been cleared, the bunk stripped and the cupboards emptied. None of Ada's possessions remained and there was a choking smell of disinfectant in the air. So instead he had brought the album back home with him, stashed in the bottom of his bag, along with the green and blue silk scarf she had left. He hadn't told anyone. Flicking through it, he paused at number 37. Clara Vine. She looked different in pictures, smooth and artificial, her pearl-grey skin shimmering and her eyes veiled; nothing like the real Clara with her quick smile, her eyes sparkling with interest and her habit of tilting her head to one side when you talked to her. When Clara came back he would show her the album and remind her that Ada Freitag had been one of her fans. Perhaps that would prompt her to do something.

Chapter Twenty-one

Hours after she had fallen asleep, Clara jarred awake with a pre-monition of doom. Why did Eva ask her to the party at the Bayerischer Hof if she was not going to be there? What could have happened to stop her attending? In the gap between sleep and wakefulness, when reasoning took second place to subliminal instinct, she realized for certain that something was wrong.

Pulling on the blue dirndl dress Steffi Schaeffer had made, and slipping a trench coat on top, she made her way out of the still sleeping pension.

Dawn was breaking and iridescent clouds streaked the grey sky like mother of pearl. With the sharp breath of morning in her throat Clara set off at a rapid pace, trying to rationalize her alarm. She barely knew Eva Braun, so had no real idea whether her absence signalled a dramatic departure from habit, or merely a skittish approach to arrangements. For all Clara knew, the Führer may have ordered Eva to Berlin, or perhaps she had felt simply unable to face the venom of the Nazi wives and girlfriends. That would be perfectly understandable. It was hard to forget the scorn in Frau von Ribbentrop's face as she dismissed the Führer's girlfriend: *Perfume and frivolous films seem to be her only interests.* Yet Clara's first instinct persisted. Something had happened to Eva Braun; something bad.

It took twenty minutes to reach Wasserburgstrasse, and as she walked, the sounds of the city waking up filled the air – the screech of trams and the plodding of a milk carthorse, newspaper men stacking their kiosks and the clatter of iron shutters as shop-keepers opened up. Nearer Eva's home, in the residential streets, families were waking, making breakfast, children squabbling and preparing for school. At Eva's villa, however, the curtains were drawn. Pushing through the high wooden gate she went to the door but the bell clanged emptily in the hall, provoking the dis-tant barking of the dogs, which were, from the sound of it, confined in the back garden. Clara rang again, received no answer, and stood back to stare up at the shutters.

After what seemed like an age, though it could only have been a few minutes, a shuffling figure loomed through the glass panels of the door and after a couple of attempts undid the latch. Eva Braun, wearing a pale blue, soiled, quilted dressing gown, her face naked and washed out, stood for a moment swaying, then stag-gered back into the living room, and half-sat, half-fell, into an armchair. Clara followed her and surveyed the scene. There was a stuffy, fetid atmosphere and the room was littered with discarded clothes and magazines scattered on the floor. Several cups of coffee stood half drunk on the table, alongside a bottle of cognac and a small framed photograph of Hitler, the glass of which was cracked. As Clara half-opened the curtains, allowing a wash of sunlight to penetrate the gloom, Eva Braun winced and turned her face away. She had the greenish, sickly tinge of drunkenness and her eyes were half closed. Without make-up she looked much younger and her dyed hair, showing dark at the roots, hung greasily over her face. Clara unplugged the lamp and the telephone and shut the door. Then she knelt down close beside her and spoke quietly.

'What happened, Eva? Did you drink too much?'

Eva groaned. Yet no telltale smell of alcohol issued from her.

'Would you like some water?'

Another, softer groan.

'I'll fetch some.'

Forcing Eva to sip a cup of water, Clara reasoned, might bring her to her senses, but when she returned, balancing the cup on the side of the coffee table, something else caught her eye. An opened bottle of Vanodorm sleeping tablets, with a few remaining tablets scattered across the table. Eva was not drunk. She had taken an overdose. Just like she had done before.

'My God, Eva. How many have you taken?'

There was a whispered croak. 'I didn't count. I took twenty last time and it didn't work so I reckoned I'd take more.'

'We need to get you to hospital.'

'No!' The force of her resistance caused Eva to sit up and open her eyes. As she did, her complexion grew greener and she produced a small amount of vomit and some of the pills were ejected.

'Sorry.'

Clara found an abandoned cardigan on the floor and wiped her mouth with it.

'Don't worry. It's going to be OK.'

Eva sank back against the chair. 'I'll never be OK. Never again.'

'What do you mean?' Her mumble was barely audible, so Clara drew closer. She reasoned that it was vital to prevent the girl lapsing into unconsciousness again before she could fetch help.

'He'll never marry me now.'

'You don't know that.'

'I do. Not after what I've done.'

'What have you done?'

Eva turned her face away and issued another groan.

'Besides, I have it from his own lips.'

'He told you that?'

'Oh, not directly. That would be too brave. He did it a different way. He told his old girlfriend, and she told me.'

'Who is this girlfriend?'

'Mimi. Mimi Reiter. She was his first girlfriend. She was sixteen when she met him and he was thirty-seven. They were walking their dogs in the Kurpark in Berchtesgaden. She said Wolf wanted them to have a host of blonde children and she was his ideal woman.'

Eva gave a choked laugh.

'It wasn't true, of course.'

'Of course not.'

Clara reasoned that the best thing was to keep Eva talking. She scrabbled in her bag for a cigarette, lit it, and placed it between Eva's parched lips. She inhaled, then coughed, sat up and inhaled again. A flicker of life came back to her face.

'They broke up years ago but she's always showing up at the Berghof as if she owns it. And now they've met up again.'

'Why did they break up?'

'She used to laugh at him. He hates anyone to laugh at him.'

'So how do you know they've met up again?'

'She came to his apartment here,' she slurred. 'In Prinzregentenplatz. She's married now, to an SS officer, Georg Kubisch, so she's Frau Kubisch now, but it doesn't seem to have made any difference. She had the nerve to call on Wolf in the hope of staying the night. When I accosted her about it she told me Wolf had said he was not happy with me. He's known from the day we became intimate on that red sofa in his office that it would never last. He's forty-nine now. He thinks he's too old for me.'

'Don't take any notice of her. She's jealous. That's no reason to attempt something silly like this.'

Eva groaned again. Fear darkened her eyes. She buried her head in her hands.

'It's not just that. It's something else. I can't tell you. Something awful. When I discovered, I realized I might as well be dead.'

'It can't be that bad.'

'It is . . . he'll be so angry with me. They all will.' She stared at Clara, then looked dully away. In the vivid sunlight her complexion seemed almost translucent, with a bluish colour around the mouth. She dropped the cigarette into an ashtray and slumped down further in her chair.

'It would help to talk,' insisted Clara, attempting to prop her up.

'It would help to die.'

She retched again and a realization came to Clara in a rush – the haggard eyes, the feeling of doom, the dreadful discovery – they all told the same tale. Eva Braun was pregnant. She must have hoped it would encourage the Führer to marry her, and instead she learned that he was tiring of her. If the Führer really was planning to dispense with her, as Mimi Reiter said, presenting him with an unwanted child would surely only hasten the impending rejection.

With another sigh, Eva's eyes drooped shut and her head fell back. Clara realized she needed to act quickly. She eased the sleeping girl onto her side, plugged the telephone back in and dialled the operator.

'I want to speak to the police.'

Chapter Twenty-two

In the apple trees outside, the birds, untroubled by the gravity of the moment, sang their hearts out. The milky morning light had clarified to promise another sunny day and Stasi and Negus, indignant at being confined to the garden, issued a continual volley of barks to indicate that breakfast was long overdue. The minutes passed agonizingly as Clara stood in the small sitting room, watching the slow breaths of the comatose figure beside her and waiting for the police to arrive. It must have been a full five minutes before, with a wave of relief, she heard a car screech to a halt outside and footsteps hasten up the path. When she opened the door, however, it was not a policeman on the step but an officer in black tunic and cap with a death's head emblem and smartly pressed breeches tucked into jackboots. It took a moment for her to swallow her amazement because the man standing in front of her, kitted out in the full uniform of Heinrich Himmler's SS, was Max Brandt.

Ignoring Clara's astonishment he pushed past her into the sitting room, taking in the scene in seconds, walked over to Eva Braun and picked up the bottle of sleeping pills by her side. After a glance at the label he took off his gloves, felt Eva's pulse for a moment, then let her wrist fall. He strode to the door.

'Get in the car right away.'

There was no longer a jocular amusement in his eyes. The languid charm had vanished, to be replaced by a curt urgency. Clara's astonishment at the sight of him mutated to an icy apprehension. There was no doubt about it now. The fears she had about Brandt's true motivation were justified and his intentions towards her were plainly malign.

'What are you talking about?' Clara glanced at Eva and lowered her voice. 'She's taken a bottle of pills. She could die if we leave her. I've just called the police.'

'I know. They'll be here in less than five minutes. That's why you need to leave.'

'I'm not going. I have to look after Eva.'

'They'll know what to do. They've done it before often enough.'

'I don't care. I'm going to wait for them.'

'If you do, you'll find yourself in custody.'

'What do you mean?'

'They'll arrest you.'

'Arrest me? But I was the person who found her.'

'Do you really believe you're going to be congratulated for saving the Führer's girlfriend? This news is going to be rigorously suppressed, especially at a time like this.'

'A time like what?'

'Don't be a fool, Clara. The eyes of the world are trained on Munich! Negotiations to preserve the peace of Europe are at a delicate stage. Even if you're very lucky and they don't arrest and charge you with breaking and entering, there's every chance they'll keep you in custody until the meetings of foreign leaders are passed. Do you have any idea how serious this would look if it gets out? The Führer's mistress attempts suicide for a third time. What does it say about a man, when his girlfriends keep trying to kill themselves?'

'It won't stop his enemies appeasing him.'

'There's no time for this. Did you give the police your name?'

'They didn't ask.'

'Thank God for that. We need to get you out of here.'

He held the door open and gestured to a long, streamlined saloon with gleaming chrome and white-walled tyres standing outside. Its engine was still running.

'Now.'

Clara cast a look behind her to where Eva remained unconscious in the chair. Brandt seized her arm, pulled her out of the house and into the car, shutting the door behind her with a thunk and pulling rapidly away, the expensive engine purring beneath them.

For a moment they didn't speak as Clara sat, trying to assess her situation. How much did Brandt know about her and why should he want to prevent the police arresting her? Where was he taking her now? She glanced around the car in confusion.

'It's an 853A Horch cabriolet,' said Brandt tersely. 'I borrowed it.'

'I wasn't thinking about the car. I was thinking about Eva. What did you mean when you said that his girlfriends keep trying to kill themselves?'

'It's a habit they have. One of his first girlfriends tried to hang herself in the garage. Mimi Reiter, I think she was called.'

Mimi Reiter. The woman Eva had talked about. The one who visited the Führer just days ago.

'Then his twenty-three-year-old niece Geli shot herself in the heart with his own Walther pistol. People say he never got over that one. He was obsessed with her. And Eva herself tried to do the same with a gun, though not very convincingly. She had another try with pills a few years ago. The Führer has not been lucky in love. It's one of the perils of mixing with women half your age.'

Clara bit her lip and looked away. She had known Eva Braun for all of a week, and what had she deduced? There was a gaucheness about the girl, and a devastating naïvety. She was not like Magda

Goebbels, who had become infatuated with the National Socialist creed, or Annelies von Ribbentrop, who was more of a Nazi than her husband. Least of all like Lina Heydrich, who shored up the cruelty in her husband's soul. Instead, the woman closest to Germany's Führer seemed to have no political interests whatsoever. Yet how could that be possible? Was Eva Braun guilty of innocence, or deliberate ignorance? It seemed grotesque that a girl as young and deluded as her should forge a relationship with a man like Hitler. With her girlish, foolish hopes, Eva Braun was like a blonde child in a German fairy tale, who enters a forest and discovers something terrible at its dark heart. Had she felt no foreboding at all when she first encountered the man who introduced himself as Herr Wolf?

'Why do you think she did it?'

'Who knows? She's unbalanced.'

It's something else. I can't tell you. Something awful. When I discovered, I realized I might as well be dead. Clara was more certain than ever. Eva Braun was pregnant.

'Do you think she'll be all right?' she asked.

'Those bottles of Vanodorm hold twenty-five tablets. She hadn't taken all of them. And I noticed she had coughed up quite a few. So I suspect she'll be fine once they get it out of her. A little groggy perhaps, but no damage done.'

He gave a sidelong glance.

'Nothing worse than a few Mai Tai cocktails could do, at any rate.'

Clara remained staring out of the window, trying to analyse the remark he had just made. So Max Brandt knew about the party at the Tiki Bar. Perhaps he had been there too. How could she have missed his distinctive figure in such a confined space?

'How did you know where I was this morning?'

'A stroke of luck.'

'You can't expect me to believe that. You turned up a few minutes after I had called the police. Who told you?'

'I happened to be at the police station when you called.'

'You happened to be there? Why?'

He shrugged.

'Perhaps I lost my dog.'

'Don't joke.'

'All right. I was on official business. I happened to be there when you made your call.'

Official business. What kind of official business did a cultural attaché have at a Munich police station? Clara didn't need to wonder long because the truth was perfectly evident to her, and as sharp as a knife in the heart. Brandt, the man who had danced with her so tenderly in Paris, whose charm had been so seductive and whose kiss she had dreamed of over so many nights, was the instrument of Heydrich she had been warned of. The man who had been sent to check her movements and build a case against her. What else could explain why he had turned up at her side in Berlin? Or why she had sensed surveillance in Munich? Why else should he have appeared, out of the blue, at the home of Eva Braun, ordering her into his car? And most damning of all, why should he now be wearing the uniform of the SS, when he had previously told her he was an attaché in the German diplomatic service?

Glancing sideways she saw the tense jut of his jaw, and his eyes, which she had once considered melting, were now steely. Brandt looked old. Perhaps he didn't like what he was doing. What honourable man would? Maybe he regretted deceiving her. Perhaps he hated himself for the role he was carrying out, and for what was about to happen to her. Clara shut her eyes momentarily, dreading what lay ahead. A year ago she had been interrogated in Prinz Albrecht Strasse, the headquarters of the Gestapo, and the memory of that night and day, the casual brutality meted out by Hauptsturmführer Oskar Wengen, a man with the eyes of a snake, still woke her regularly with a racing heart.

Yet the thought of that night also served to focus her. If Max

Brandt was Heydrich's man, she was now in his car, powerless, so
the best she could do was to give nothing away. He could have no
idea that she had been warned of surveillance. She must remain
resolutely in character – an actress with no conceivable interest in
politics.

She shuffled herself deeper into the cream leather seat, smoothing her dress over her knees and checking her face in the overhead
mirror.

'Where exactly are you taking me?'

He glanced at her and said gruffly, 'It's a social event.'

'A social event?'

'Precisely. I have to go, so you may as well come too. It's about
a hundred miles from here.'

He glanced in the mirror behind him.

'It'll take up most of the day, if that's all right with you.'

'I don't suppose I have much choice. Where exactly is it?'

'The Berghof.'

The address, uttered so casually, caught the breath in her throat.
The Berghof. Hitler's mountain residence. The heart of his
domestic base, and the place where, above all others, the Führer
felt at home. High in the Obersalzberg mountains where, away
from the hustle of Berlin or Munich and surrounded by his inner
circle, Hitler liked to relax and plan the next stage in his strategy
to enlarge the German Lebensraum.

'Hitler's house? Herr Brandt, I can't.'

He lifted an eyebrow.

'It's an honour, you do realize.'

'I know. I just don't feel . . . I mean I don't know if I could cope
with that. Just now. After what I've seen. I mean, the Führer's girlfriend.'

'You'll cope fine, as long as you give no word of what has just
happened. You need to stay completely silent. Don't let on to
anyone – and I mean anyone – about Fräulein Braun's mishap.'

'But the Führer . . .?'

'The Führer's not there today. He's in Munich with Doktor Goebbels.' For the first time, he allowed a terse smile. 'I'm only going because I have a little cultural duty to perform.'

The familiar ironic lilt entered his voice. 'I've been summoned by Reichsführer-SS Himmler.'

Himmler, head of the SS, the élite of the Nazi party, whose carefully picked members wore the same striking black uniform that Brandt was wearing now.

'He wants to brief me on his plans for a celebration of Teutonic culture with reference to the operas of Wagner. My task is to appear as enthusiastic as possible.'

'I thought Wagner was the Führer's special interest?'

'It is. But Teutonic mythology is Himmler's passion. He has a castle in Wewelsburg for his SS leadership school dedicated to the Teutonic order. It's a most extraordinary place. It's triangular in shape and full of mosaics decked with mythic significance. All the rooms are named after the Grail legend – King Arthur, Siegfried, Parsifal and so forth. The crypt is called Valhalla and there are all sorts of stories about what goes on there.' He winked. 'Don't worry. Women aren't allowed in. Except for SS wedding ceremonies, and I don't imagine you're about to participate in one of those.' He paused, and a glimmer of the old, sardonic manner returned. 'Unless Sturmbannführer Steinbrecher has plans, of course.'

Outside, it was brightening into an exquisite morning. Clara sat in silence, staring out of the window as the Munich buildings with their cream and gold stone slipped by and the powerful car purred southwards, through the outskirts of the city, until the houses gave way to fields and the autobahn stretched out before them. Perhaps it was the beauty of their surroundings, but Brandt himself seemed to relax a little; his brow unfurrowed, his shoulders dropped and he stopped checking his mirror.

'So is that the official business that brought you to Munich? Himmler's celebration?'

'Not exactly. I had some other issues to attend to, but I found myself invited to lunch at the Berghof, and as you can imagine, that kind of invitation is difficult to refuse.'

He gave a wry smile.

'How did you come to be Himmler's expert on Teutonic culture?'

'Good question. I was a lawyer before I joined the Foreign Service. I went to law school in Königsberg, then I worked briefly in a magistrates' court in Berlin and began to specialize in civil rights.'

A dry laugh.

'Good job I switched professions or I'd have found myself redundant. Civil rights lawyers are about as useful as handlooms or spinning wheels in Germany today. Anyway, I'd always had a hankering for foreign travel. I had an uncle who'd been an ambassador and he struck me as far more civilized and worldly than the dull lawyers populating the other branches of my family. We're a family of lawyers, all upstanding men, of course, minor nobility, we've been running the Prussian justice system for generations and I was all set to follow in their footsteps. But I always secretly cherished the idea of living an exotic life, like my uncle. That was how I saw it, anyway, so I sat the exams for the German Foreign Service and passed them.' He grinned. 'Though I realize life as a Nazi cultural attaché probably doesn't sound too exotic to you.'

'You joined the Party?'

'Of course. I knew that was going to be essential if I was to progress. I was lucky with my first embassy – I was posted as an attaché to Budapest – but I served in a couple of less salubrious places before I landed Paris. I can't deny I was very fortunate to get the French Embassy. 78, Rue de Lille is the address of Foreign Service dreams.

'Anyhow, my heavy exposure to opera, as you so acutely noticed, must have rubbed off. Himmler takes me as a cultural connoisseur of the highest order. I've had to bone up because whenever I see him he asks about Wagner. It would be enough to terrify a lesser man, but as it is I have a gift for bluffing. It's probably my greatest talent. Perhaps my only one.'

Casually, he added, 'He was so pleased with me he's awarded me an honorary rank in the SS. I've had to change uniforms.'

'I noticed.'

'What do you think?'

'I preferred the other one.'

The roads had emptied out now and they had passed into the Bavarian countryside. The air was fresh and clean. Pockets of forest were intersected with fields of intense, luminous green, and here and there white-faced houses with green shutters and red slanting roofs stood, bursts of crimson geraniums frothing at their windows. Cows gazed indifferently at a gate. It was a landscape of idyllic calm, but it was not enough to soothe the anxiety thrumming through Clara's body.

Affecting a nonchalance she did not feel, she said, 'Do you have any idea who will be at this lunch?'

'Hardly anyone.' He paused. 'The Bormanns. Himmler, obviously.'

'And Heydrich?' she asked, before she could stop herself.

He gave her a quick, curious glance, as if assessing her interest, and said,

'Perhaps. If he's not detained by other business in Munich.'

Clara quailed. The thought of Heydrich's eyes, as grey and pitiless as a frozen North Sea, meeting hers across the lunch table, terrified her. Fear narrowed her throat, making it hard to speak.

'Heydrich intrigues you, doesn't he? I can understand why. He's an interesting figure. He's a very talented violinist,' said Brandt musingly. 'He plays in a quartet with Frau Canaris, the wife of the Abwehr chief. Strange to imagine, isn't it?'

'I suppose.' Actually, she could just about imagine Heydrich submitting to the discipline of practice, applying himself to a piece day after day with military rigour until he had mastered every note of it precisely. But imagining a soul inside that cadaverous frame, thrilling to the beauty of Strauss or Beethoven, would take a greater imagination than hers.

'He's a surprising figure all round. When Himmler first interviewed Heydrich he was impressed by how much he knew about intelligence affairs. He never discovered that Heydrich's grounding in espionage matters came entirely from reading British spy novels. John Buchan, Erskine Childers and so on. Heydrich always wanted to be a spy. They say he was obsessed with spy fiction even while he was still in the Navy. He signs his internal documents with "C" because he's read that's what the head of the British Secret Service likes to do. Whether he does or not, I wouldn't know.'

Clara gave an obligatory laugh. She did know, but Brandt must never discover that.

'Heydrich knows all the secrets of the Third Reich. He knows where all the bodies are buried. He even dug up and interviewed the residents of the Viennese flophouse where Hitler lived in 1910. Can you imagine that? Extraordinary efficiency.'

Seeing her face he added, 'Don't worry. With any luck you won't need to talk to the men. You can gossip with the ladies. I'm sure that's the kind of intelligence-gathering you prefer.'

The road was winding upwards now, and the landscape was becoming mountainous. Ahead, the crags of the Bavarian Alps were silhouetted against the morning sky, lilac and grey, towering into a light net of mist. Snow lay in the folds of their peaks, and in their valleys, deep silver lakes were captured. Despite her apprehension, Clara was awestruck. These mountains had inspired so many artists, from Caspar David Friedrich to Wagner. They encapsulated the sublime and lent themselves to the wildest flights of fantasy. King Ludwig had built his fairy-tale castle, Neuschwanstein, amongst their southern foothills, determined to recreate the Germanic legends of Tannhäuser and Lohengrin, and Hitler was merely the latest leader to be transported by their romantic grandeur. This was a landscape that tugged at the heart of the German soul, though the feelings it aroused were not to be trusted. Something lay deep within these daunting cliffs, something as sharp and unforgiving as the crags themselves, which dwarfed ordinary human beings and made them seem utterly insignificant.

After a while the road narrowed and they passed into a pretty little town, with a sign announcing itself as Berchtesgaden. Brandt gestured to a freshly built station, furnished with grand pillars in monumental Third Reich style, which looked freakishly out of place in the quiet Alpine surroundings.

'The Führer's architectural tastes always tend towards the grandiose. His offices look like railway stations and his railway stations look like churches.'

'What do his churches look like?'

'Heaps of rubble, if our leader has anything to do with it. He doesn't like churches at all. He prefers rally grounds to cathedrals.'

Past Berchtesgaden the road began to wind upwards, beneath a banner stretched across the road which read, *Führer, wir danken Dir!*, and out towards more fields. Occasional walkers alongside the road waved and gave the Hitler salute, peering avidly through the windows of the gleaming car on the lookout for celebrities. The men were dressed in traditional leather jackets and Bavarian hats, with knee breeches and socks, the women in starched dirndls, aprons and white, knitted socks and hobnailed boots. Some of them carried baskets of flowers.

'They're hoping for a sight of the Führer. He always comes out when he's here. Sometimes the women tear open their blouses as he passes.' Brandt grimaced. 'It's extremely unbecoming.'

'I take it the Führer averts his eyes.'

'I'm sure he does. Unfortunately, the passions he provokes can prove more dangerous. It's been known for girls to throw themselves at his car in the hope of being injured and then comforted by him.'

Eva Braun's pallid face came again into Clara's mind. Once it might have seemed astonishing to her that women would risk physical injury for their leader, let alone their lives, yet this man carried death around him wherever he went. Suddenly, the thought of where they were headed caused fear like a surge of nausea to catch in her throat and she wound down the window to gulp the fresh air. It was as sharp as diamonds. The bright alpine sun made everything shimmer with iridescence.

'The air's extraordinary here, isn't it?' Brandt commented. 'It's to do with the salt deposits in the mountains, apparently. The Führer says it makes him feel well again. Ah, here we are.'

They had come to a ten-foot, double layer of barbed wire surrounding a roped-off area of the mountainside. The car crunched over the gravel to a stone guardhouse where the guards stiffened to attention. One ducked his head in and Clara and Brandt showed their identity cards. Further on she glimpsed more guards, patrolling with dogs.

'Security here is second to none. A few years ago an SA man named Kraus was granted permission to present a petition personally to the Führer and he fired at him. He was killed by the guards of course, and reprisals were taken immediately, but ordinary people can be just as much trouble. They like to collect the gravel on which the Führer has set foot and take home parcels of it in muslin bags. It annoys the SS immensely.'

They passed a barracks and several parking lots until the road wound round and the house itself came into view.

The Berghof might once have been a charming country home, a white-faced chalet-style construction set into the slope of the hillside, yet now the simple mountain house had been extended to form the hub of an entire Nazi complex, a gated community for the National Socialist élite. All villagers who had lived within sight of the house had been forcibly removed, and their chalets and farmhouses transformed into luxury homes for Goering, Goebbels, Hess and Speer, or, if they were too humble, into barracks for soldiers. The entire compound was ringed with anti-aircraft guns and deep underground bomb- and gas-proof bunkers had been built.

The entrance to the house itself was preceded by a steep flight of wide steps, the same steps that just a few days ago Neville Chamberlain himself had mounted.

For a moment, as Brandt pulled the Horch to a stop, Clara froze. Being here, in the jaws of the Third Reich, had never seemed so real or so intimidating. There was no escape here or refuge from scrutiny. She wasn't in the middle of a city, where she could turn tail and disappear, or in a film studio, surrounded by people who cared only for their work. She was not among friends, but at the beating heart of the Nazi regime, with officers who were apt to look on strangers with particular scrutiny. The only person she could trust was Max Brandt, whom she knew she must not trust. Fear moored her to the seat, turning her limbs weak and immovable. She wanted to beg Brandt to turn the car around and drive back fast the way they had come. Then two SS guards leapt forward, in black jackets with swastika armbands attached, opened the doors and gave the Hitler salute. Brandt raised his right hand, turned to Clara and said softly,

'Ready?'

'I'm not sure.'

His expression was strange, unreadable.

'Relax. You of all people know how to put on a good show.'

He led her up the steps, then another flight, and there, in front of them, was the most famous view in Germany.

Every citizen of the Reich was familiar with the vista from the terrace of the Berghof. Every cinema-goer had seen newsreel film of the Führer, strolling with Himmler or Albert Speer, playing with the flaxen-haired children of his aides, sitting beneath a striped parasol with his loyal dog at his heels while beyond him lay the panoramic vista of the Untersberg mountain with Salzburg Castle

in the distance. Some way away was the Eagle's Nest, the Kehlstein-
haus, commissioned by Bormann and formally presented to Hitler
on his birthday that year. Immediately beneath the terrace, mead-
ows rolled into distant forest, above which soared the mountains,
veined with snow like a garland of blossom at their peaks. In that
mountain range across from the Berghof Charlemagne was said to
sleep, waiting to restore the glory of the German empire. This
craggy romantic landscape could not be less like the military geography of Berlin, with its squares of stone and steel and its ranks of
marching soldiers. Yet in different ways they both expressed the
indomitable ethic of the Nazi soul.

The terrace, which wrapped itself around three sides of the
house, was furnished with cane sun loungers, white wooden chairs
and tables. The pale stone shimmered in the sharp Alpine air, and
lounging against the wall on the far side was a group of men, some
in SS uniform, others in field grey and a couple in suits, chatting
to women over pre-lunch drinks. Two little girls in perfectly
smocked dresses and plaits like chunks of woven corn played with
an Alsatian, hanging garlands of daisies around its neck as the dog
patiently endured the little fingers digging into his fur. As she
watched the knot of people chatting and laughing, Clara's only
consolation was that all the women were wearing dirndls. What
luck that in her blind panic that morning she had chosen the dress
with puffed sleeves and dirndl neckline to wear. And her silver
necklace with the picture of her mother inside. Her clothing, at
least, would not give her away.

Brandt strode confidently towards the group and clicked his
heels before dipping his head to hand-kiss the female guests, and
then gestured to Clara.

'Fräulein Clara Vine, you may know, from the Ufa studios,' he
said, with a tone that implied that even if they had not heard of
her, they should have. He introduced the entire group, the men
giving Clara a curt bow and clicking heels, the women a handshake. He ended with a buxom blonde.

'And this is Frau Mimi Kubisch.'

Kubisch. Clara recognized the name immediately. She knew, as Brandt did, that this was Hitler's first girlfriend, the one who had been Mimi Reiter, yet Clara also knew that this woman had visited Hitler at his apartment just days ago and if Eva was to be believed had been told by Hitler that his relationship was ending. Like the others, Mimi wore rustic, Bavarian fashion, which on her translated as a tip-tilted red hat, a puffed-sleeve blouse beneath a red bodice, thick white socks and brown lace-up brogues. She gave Clara a broad smile.

'Have you been here before, Fräulein Vine?'

'Only in the Ufa Tonwoche,' said Clara lightly.

'Then you'll be longing to see around! Would you like a tour while the men talk?'

The Berghof might have been inspired by Hitler's passion for Wagner, but there was nothing Wagnerian about the interior, unless Lohengrin had a penchant for flocked wallpaper or Tannhäuser liked to relax in a chintz armchair. Everywhere stolid bourgeois taste prevailed, with fretted wood, fringed lampshades and slightly threadbare sofas piled high with embroidered cushions. Mimi followed her gaze.

'There must be fifty cushions with *Ich liebe Sie* and *Heil mein Führer!* stitched on them. He won't throw a single one away. He says each gift is precious to him but I say why can't people think of something more original than *Heil mein Führer!*'

Mimi led the way through a vaulted corridor into a vast room, fit for a mediaeval banquet, with a gigantic window to one side giving a panoramic view of the mountains. It was grander here. The walls were covered in Gobelin tapestries and the floor laid with red velvet and Persian carpets. Portraits of nude women hung over the fireplace and a gigantic eagle crouched over the bronze clock. At one end a grand piano was clustered with silver-framed photographs of foreign royalty, including a shot of the Duchess of Windsor, smiling up at Hitler as he took her hand on the steps of the Berghof the previous year. Like so much of Third Reich architecture, the main function of the room was not comfort or convenience, so much as making everyone feel small.

'This entire place was rebuilt a couple of years ago. He's terribly proud of it. All the swastika tiles on the floor are hand-painted and every evening that tapestry over there lifts up to make way for the screen. They show films every evening; several, usually,' she smiled merrily. 'Nothing's allowed to get in the way of the Führer's screenings. When Mr Chamberlain came here recently, the Führer cut the meeting short so he could watch an Ingrid Bergman movie!'

'I heard he liked *The Lives of a Bengal Lancer.*'

'Liked it? He's seen it ten times! He's made it compulsory viewing for the SS because it shows how Britain gained her empire. And every night when the movie's finished, he gives his opinion to an adjutant who wires it over to the Propaganda Ministry in Berlin.'

'That sounds amazingly efficient.'

'It's terribly important, the Führer says. He's been watching a lot of American films recently – Tarzan, Mickey Mouse, Laurel and Hardy and so on, because he wants to learn about American culture. He loved Laurel and Hardy. Gave them a standing ovation, actually. Oh, here they come . . .'

The door opened at the far end of the room and a group of men entered, deep in conversation. Their German was harsh and guttural and Clara was only able to catch the occasional word and phrase. 'Rabble' was one and 'essential preparations' was another.

Clara shivered.

'Cold, isn't it?' said Mimi. 'It's always freezing here. He actually bought the house because it's orientated to the north. He doesn't like the sun, you see, but it does mean the house is constantly in shadow and it always feels like winter. You need to bring a fur coat, even in the warmest weather.'

The group at the end of the room erupted in laughter and Clara nodded at them casually.

'What are they talking about, do you suppose?'

Mimi shrugged. 'What do you think? They say Adolf Hitler is the guest at every party. Even when he's not here. Want to go back outside? I'm dying for a cigarette and no one's allowed to smoke anywhere indoors. You won't find a single ashtray in this entire place, not even in the bedrooms. He has them inspected regularly to check.'

They lit up and leant over the balustrade. In the driveway below Clara could see a soldier polishing Brandt's gleaming Horch, buffing its sleek lines as meticulously as if it had been one of his own jackboots. Further on, the little girls were throwing the Alsatian's ball into the flowerbeds and watching the animal trample the flowers while a guard, rifle slung over his shoulder, tried ineffectually to prevent them.

'What do you think of the view? It's tremendous, isn't it? You never get tired of a view like this.'

'It's breathtaking.'

'We have Bormann to thank for it.'

She pointed behind her to a squat man with no neck and clothes that hung on him like flabby skin.

'Bormann ravaged this place,' said Mimi more softly. 'Fifty houses were taken down, and a sanitarium. He burned down a farm to make way for a place big enough to accommodate his ten children. It was pretty hard for the families who lived here. My own family knew a lot of them, but even if they'd been here for generations, Bormann wouldn't let them stay. Security reasons.'

She turned round and rested her elbows on the terrace ledge as she surveyed the group of men in the hall, pointing at them with the tip of her cigarette.

'I don't suppose you know many of these people. That one's Julius Schaub, the Führer's valet.' She indicated a man with bulging eyes and a pronounced limp. 'He limps because several of his toes were amputated for frostbite in the war.'

Clara had heard of Schaub. All the actresses knew him. He was in charge of visiting theatres and cabarets to hand-pick actresses and dancers for quiet evenings with Hitler.

'And that's Albert Bormann, Martin's brother. And my husband Georg,' she added, a trifle dismissively, pointing to a horse-faced man with broken veins spidering his cheeks. 'Herr Brandt of course you know.'

As Clara looked across, Brandt caught her eye and winked. He was a good actor. It was dreadful to think that this man, with his dark jokes and teasing smile, might be in Heydrich's pay.

At that moment the doors of the dining room were opened to reveal a phalanx of white-jacketed waiters carrying silver trays.

'At last!' Mimi exclaimed. 'Lunch is here. I'm famished. Come on, sit next to me.'

They seated themselves around a long table set with white linen tablecloth, crystal glasses and solid gold cutlery engraved with the initials AH. Despite the lavishness of the table settings, there was a distinct parsimony where alcohol came in. No cognac or champagne was in evidence – instead the men were served beer and the women made do with the Führer's favourite Fachinger mineral water.

The company applied themselves to their meal with relish but Clara had no appetite. The situation was so strange that she could scarcely believe it. She was at the Berghof and sitting at the Führer's dinner table, though thankfully without the host, whose seat at the end of the table had been left conspicuously empty.

'Bad luck that he should be away on your first visit,' said Mimi, following her gaze. 'He may come later this evening. Are you staying tonight?'

'No,' said Clara, a little too quickly.

'That's a shame. But even if you did, you might miss him. He doesn't normally get up till noon.' Mimi leaned closer with a smile. 'Even then, the servants always have to let us know what mood he's in. And there are some advantages to him not being here.' She picked up her fork and turned towards the servant behind her bearing a tray of warm ham. 'It means we can eat meat without it being called carrion. And we don't have to listen to long descriptions of the insides of slaughterhouses. Ugh.'

'What does the Führer like to eat then?'

'Hardly anything!' Her face mimed disgust. 'His favourite dish is Hoppelpoppel – fried eggs with potatoes – but there's so many things he won't eat. Mushrooms, for example, because he's frightened of being poisoned. Like a Roman emperor, you know? And of course, he drinks apple peel tea, never alcohol.'

A stiff brandy was the only thing Clara wanted to consume just then, but Mimi carried on, seemingly oblivious of Clara's silence.

'Of course, him being away also means we don't have to have any after-lunch entertainment. The Führer likes to get Blondi, his dog, to sing. It's so funny, watching this dog howling away, but we have to keep straight faces. I'm laughing just thinking about it.'

Even the picture of the Führer's singing dog failed to relax Clara. Every moment she expected a call would come, bringing news of Eva's suicide attempt. Yet there was nothing.

The waiters were just clearing the first course when the conversation suddenly hushed and faces turned towards a door at the back of the room. A slender figure had entered and was surveying the company impassively. He was wearing grey woollen trousers hanging wide at the thigh and tucked into black jackboots, beneath a grey tunic with a wide black belt. On his collar three silver oak leaves glittered. He seemed, in his uniform, like a dark silence, a hole in the air drawing all the laughter and ease and energy from the room, as though his mere presence had physically lowered the temperature.

Party member number two, Reichsführer-SS Heinrich Himmler.

It would be hard to find a more unlikely physical specimen of the Aryan race than Himmler, unless you counted Hitler himself. His blinking eyes behind round wire-rimmed glasses gave him the appearance of a malevolent owl and only a narrow outcrop of hair survived on top of his severely shaved skull. The pudgy face and weak, receding chin were in ironic contrast to the stiff silver death's head gleaming from the cap of his uniform.

Acknowledging the lunch guests with a curt nod, he sat down, calling over a servant who brought him a humidor shaped like a little hunting chest and decorated with stag horn tips. Taking advantage of the Führer's absence he removed a Cuban cigar that he lit up with hands that were small, and strikingly delicate.

Himmler's arrival cast a chill over the lunch. Like a sinister, invisible toxin in the air, his presence poisoned the company and changed the tenor of the conversation. The men forewent the attentions of the women and competed with each other to entertain the SS-Reichsführer, while the women censored the gossip from their conversation, as if conscious that they must dwell on more serious matters.

As soon as lunch was over, Clara escaped back to the Great Hall, secreting herself in one of the corners by the fireplace. Just as Mimi had said, the shadow of the mountain had fallen across the house, and the servants had lit a fire to combat the autumnal chill. Trays of coffee and cake were placed on small tables. Clara buried herself in an armchair and stared into the flames, wondering what the next few hours might hold. She felt paralysed by uncertainty, both about the intentions of Max Brandt and the suspicions he must harbour. She was more certain than ever that Brandt's motivations were not romantic ones, but as to what game he was playing, and how she should respond, Clara was frighteningly unclear.

A shadow fell across the fire and she looked up to see a figure gazing speculatively down at her. Clara sat upright and tensed. Heinrich Himmler stood with a cigar in one hand and the other hooked in his pocket, rocking back on his heels, regarding her quizzically.

'Is it true, Fräulein Vine, that the English upper classes always eat porridge for breakfast?'

'I don't think it's a hard and fast rule, Herr Reichsführer.'

'I understand that's the reason for their good figures.' He paused, perched on the arm of the chair opposite and crossed his legs. 'I think it's a good idea, actually. I have instructed porridge to be served at every one of my Lebensborn homes.'

The Lebensborn homes were Himmler's pet project. A series of homes where unmarried women who could prove Aryan descent through four generations could bear their babies. After birth, they could choose to donate them to the SS. They were generally places of female misery and desperation. Clara had seen inside one the previous year and found it hard to associate babies with a place of such joyless sterility.

Himmler took a draw on his cigar and exhaled, allowing a miasma of smoke to coil around him. Other guests had gathered round and Clara felt their eyes on her, as if trying to divine how she had drawn Himmler's attention. They balanced brandy glasses, conversations hushed as they tried to catch the SS-Reichsführer's quiet rasp. It was a technique Himmler shared with many of the senior Nazis – starting out softly so that people had to strain to hear them.

'Producing high-quality children is a science, like any other,' he continued. 'Nutrition is just one element in a precisely calibrated process. I know this from my own experience. Some years ago I used to breed chickens at my farm in Waldtrudering. It was an enlightening process, matching poultry, mating the correct blood-lines, improving the stock; it taught me a good deal. Sometimes, one needed to make firm judgements to attain the highest qual-ity of birds. If one wants to create a pure new strain from a well-tried species that has been exhausted by crossbreeding, then one needs to be selective. Eradicate inferior material that could taint the flock. Pick out the unhealthy ones, the weaklings, those whose diseases render them incurable. Be ruthless in purging the flock of mutant elements. There's no place for bleeding hearts. We can learn a lot from livestock.'

He had a low, insidious voice, quite different from the Führer's guttural tones or the harsh scrape of Goebbels' address. Cruelty came off him in waves, like body heat.

'Or examine, if you will, the actions of a nursery gardener. If he wants to reproduce a strain of plants that has been corrupted he will weed out all those which are stunted or malformed. And we are grateful to him, because we will all enjoy finer flowers and fruit. It is my conviction that a well-conceived breeding plan must stand at the centre of every civilization. Unless one plans a population with scientific exactitude, then that population can never be truly, morally pure.'

Clara's silver locket, with its photograph of her Jewish mother, burned on her throat. Though Himmler was known to have forsaken Christianity in favour of his mystic blend of Nordic paganism, he had a Jesuitical air about him, as though he could never quite shake off the Catholic faith he was born into. She found herself gripping the arm of her chair with unnatural rigour and forced herself to relax. It took everything in her to meet that cold, penetrating gaze and hold it.

'The biological laws that operate with animal and plant life also apply to humans. Animal breeding and plant cultivation can teach us much about racial hygiene. Nature is perfectly unsentimental. It expels the degenerate and the alien because it understands that they weaken the species.' He blinked. There was a dreadful dissonance between his manner and the substance of his speech. The crackle of the fire sounded unnaturally loud in the silence of the room.

'Sometimes, our human instincts get in the way. Our senses tell us that we should pity the weaklings. Empathize with them. So one of our greatest tasks will be to harden ourselves against the soft language of sentiment, and follow what we know to be right. The sentimentalists would argue for sparing the young, but nature knows that it is better to start with the young. The earlier that the degenerate young are eliminated, the more resources remain for the healthy stock. And once you have that healthy stock, it becomes imperative to increase it. Childbearing is a woman's highest duty to her Fatherland. It is only when our childbearing is both scientific and sacred that the nation will flourish with eternal life.'

He paused, ground out his cigar in a saucer, and placed the stub in his pocket. Outside, the shadow of the mountain crept further across the Berghof, casting the terrace into deeper shade, and inside, the glimmer of the fire enclosed the pair of them in its glow, whilst around them the other guests looked on.

Himmler retrained his focus on Clara, eyes flickering over her breasts and legs as though assessing her sexual potential. Never, in all the time she had met or mingled with Nazi officers, had she seen a more clinical, sadistic gaze.

'You have no children yourself, Fräulein Vine?'

'I'm not married, Herr Reichsführer.'

'That need not be an impediment in a woman of good blood.'

For a second she was puzzled until she understood the implication and shuddered. Himmler was suggesting that it was her duty to Germany to bear a child. Husband optional.

'What age are you?'

'Thirty-one.'

'It seems curious that a woman of your age is still single.' He waved a hand in a slight gesture of concession. 'On the other hand, perhaps you serve the Reich in other ways.'

'Thoughts of the Reich are at the very heart of my work.'

He gave a colourless smile. 'Of course. You are one of Doktor Goebbels' protégées, I understand. I'm sure he appreciates . . . well, everything you do for him.'

The way his pince-nez glinted in the flames of the fire made him all the more inscrutable. Clara knew the only safe response was impassivity.

'The Minister has been kind enough to ask me to voice a documentary about Gertrud Scholtz-Klink. There's an announcement he wants to make concerning the birth rate and a reward for prolific mothers.'

At this, a wince of irritation crossed Himmler's face.

'Does he indeed? That must be my new decoration for kinder-reich mothers. I didn't know the Herr Doktor had taken it upon himself to publicize it already.'

He turned crossly, knit his hands behind his back and stared out of the window where the distant mountain loomed purple and indigo in the lengthening shadows. After a few moments, in which he seemed to be collecting his thoughts, he said,

'So what do you make of the Berghof, Fräulein Vine?'

'It's very beautiful.'

'We made it that way. It was a mess before we took it in hand. Squalid little huts and chalets everywhere. Residents milling around interfering with the Führer's privacy. It had to be cleared, but I must say, that was no easy task. One resident who had a pho-tography shop on the mountain had the impertinence to approach the Führer himself and hand him a letter begging to be allowed to keep it.'

'And was he allowed?'

The ghost of a smile twitched his thin lips. 'Let's just say we found him alternative accommodation. Two years in a camp.' A sniff. 'But it was a lesson to us. After that, all approaches to the Führer were halted forthwith. The price of liberty is eternal vig-ilance. I forget who said that.'

'An American, I think, Herr Reichsführer,' said Max Brandt. He had come up to them and was watching Clara, assessing how well she was coping. Her eye caught his and she held it without a flicker.

'Ah.' Himmler turned. 'It seems your Sturmbannführer Brandt is eager to leave.'

'So soon?' Clara managed.

Brandt's smile was as jocular as ever, but she noticed that beneath the black tunic, his shoulders were rigid.

'Indeed. Again, my apologies, Herr Reichsführer.' He bowed slightly, reached for Clara and gripped her arm, his fingers digging into the flesh. There was a grim light in his eyes. 'You remember, my dear, I have a dinner engagement back in Munich.'

He clicked heels to the assembled gathering, and Mimi Kubisch grasped Clara's hand in farewell.

The SS valet brought the Horch round to the front. Brandt ushered Clara in and drove sedately down the mountain, but once he had turned the corner out of sight of the Berghof, he accelerated along the winding road as if pursued by Valkyries.

Chapter Twenty-three

The Berlin Police Headquarters in Alexanderplatz – known universally as the Alex – was an extensive blank-faced block of pale stone which occupied the entire length of the square. With its arched doorways and cupolas, surmounted by a dome, it was a building which exuded power and authority, and just like all the other buildings in his life which had done that – Winchester College and Christchurch College Oxford, and, for a brief while, the Palladian building off Trafalgar Square which housed his uncle's merchant bank – it provoked in Rupert an urge for rebellious dissent. It was an urge he was obliged to quell that morning as he arrived for a meeting in the Police Museum with his only contact in the Kriminalpolizei, or Kripo, Kriminalinspektor Alfred Bremer.

It was at a barber's shop a few doors down from the Alex that Rupert had first encountered Bremer. The barber's was a place where policemen went for a relaxing shave after a long night of beating people up and, being sleepless and vulnerable, the policemen were liable to treat the barber's chair as a kind of confessional. The conversation Rupert had with Bremer that first morning had continued, off and on, for the past five years in a gruff acquaintance of mutual admiration which was never overtly expressed. Bremer was a sensitive, intelligent individual, and thus lacking in

the basic job requirements for the Kripo, and he cherished a sen-
timental vision of England as a land of bowler hats and peasoupers
that Rupert had no desire to disabuse. He had invited Rupert to
dinner at his apartment in Kreuzberg, where his plump wife Grete
made the best schnitzel Rupert had ever tasted and Bremer puffed
away on an old-fashioned briarwood pipe. In the privacy of his
home Bremer had felt free to moan about the horrors of the Kripo
takeover by Himmler's Gestapo. He was getting on for retirement
now, and had a beer barrel gut and a face like a walnut from a lifetime of nicotine and frowning.

The Police Museum was an echoey hall of glass cases showcas-
ing an array of forensic detritus – jackets with bullet holes in,
knives, guns and fragmented skulls – which had led Berlin's finest
to crack their historic crimes. Chill northern light slanted in from
the high windows onto the cases, where photographs of celebrated
murder victims were accompanied by the implements responsible
for their demise and a brief explanatory text, like a miniature
crime story. The Kripo liked visitors here; no doubt because they
preferred to focus on old-fashioned methods of detection rather
than the kind now practised with rubber truncheons in their basement cells. Rupert peered at a ripped satin dress dappled brown
with blood and displayed on a mannequin like something from the
couture department of KaDeWe, which had belonged to one
Sophie Kleist, a victim of the 1934 Cabaret Killer. Her case had
apparently been solved after two years of painstaking police work.
It seemed strange, he thought, to spend so long investigating a
single crime at a time when Germany was planning a crime against
an entire nation in the space of a weekend.

The international situation was becoming daily more febrile.
After his inconclusive meeting at the Berghof, Chamberlain had
returned for a further session at Bad Godesberg, a resort on
the west bank of the Rhine, but there was no sign that Hitler
would back down. Rupert remembered his first glimpse of the
Führer, years ago, shaking hands with Hindenburg, and he was

still astonished at how that little figure bowing to the old Field Marshal like a head waiter receiving a tip had grown immense enough to terrify an entire continent. As far as avoiding war went, Rupert could see no hope. He tried to remember what he had felt last April, walking through Victoria with Leo, looking at the sunset over Green Park and hoping the sun wasn't sinking on everything he held dear. At the time he had been annoyed at Leo's suggestion that he leave the *Chronicle*, yet now he saw that Leo had been prescient. Every day Winstanley spiked more of Rupert's stories, while never making clear what he wanted instead. Whatever it was, though, it wasn't pieces about missing girls on transatlantic cruises.

Rupert had only begun asking questions about the girl on the cruise ship as a favour to Clara, but his original instinct to dismiss Erich's story as part of a young boy's overactive imagination had changed when he met the secretary at the Führerin's office. That grey-eyed, imploring stare she had given when he asked her about her trip on the *Wilhelm Gustloff* had lit some battered journalistic touch paper within him, with the result that he had met up with Bremer in a Kneipe beneath the arches of Friedrichstrasse S-Bahn and asked him to look through the Missing Persons file.

He could tell now, from the ponderous way Bremer crossed the hall towards him, heels slapping reluctantly on the parquet, that the search had uncovered something. He came up to Rupert, gave him a handshake that could crack nuts, and stroked his fine, handlebar moustache.

'Any luck, Alfred?'

'I think I've found your girl. Or rather, I haven't found her.'

'Bit cryptic for me.'

Bremer refilled his pipe and underwent the habitual pantomime of combustion, before expelling clouds of noxious smoke while Rupert did his best not to flinch.

'The other day, when we met, I came back to the office and looked through the files as you asked me and there she was. Ada

Freitag, age twenty-three. Notified missing by her parents – nice couple – Viktor and Hilde Freitag of Wedding, on August 12th. Never returned from a cruise on the *Wilhelm Gustloff*. She was their only daughter and she'd never been in any trouble before. High-spirited, is what I think they called her, but no reason to think she would abandon her old parents without a word, even if, as the captain said, she disembarked at Madeira. I had to attend to another matter so I put the file back, meaning to return, but when I went to look this morning, it was gone.'

'So perhaps the case is being looked at?'

'The case? Who said there's any case?'

'You mean it's not being investigated?'

'I mean it doesn't exist.'

'Help me here.'

Bremer looked unhappily around.

'I searched for the file, though I didn't want to make too much noise about it, but it's simply disappeared. Nobody took it, and nobody I've asked knows anything about it.'

'What does that mean?'

'Perhaps the girl's been found.'

'But you don't think so.'

Bremer's voice sank so low it was barely detectable. For some time he stared into the glass case beside him, as though transfixed by Sophie Kleist's evening dress, then said,

'What does it matter what I think? Maybe old guys like me don't know best. In the past, we Kripo detectives prided ourselves on being out of politics – we were the professionals; the career detectives. Look around you.' He waved a phlegmatic arm at the glass cases. 'All this was our work. But now, these Gestapo men have come and they're all lawyers and administrators and they have – what do they call it? – different skills. Protective custody, intensified interrogation. Us old-timers have weekly training sessions telling us that the Kripo must undergo a change in our criminological theory.' His eyes dulled as he reeled off the list. 'We must learn a new definition of crime. Concentrate on habitual offenders, lags whose racial roots lead them towards crime. We need to protect the moral fibre of society from professional criminals, vagrants and prostitutes. It's the Gestapo men who decide what's a crime and what's not.'

'But when I raised the case at the Propaganda Ministry . . .'

'You did what?'

'I asked Goebbels if he knew of any young woman missing from a KdF cruise.'

'My dear fellow,' Bremer took his arm, his face aghast, 'isn't there enough to be going on with, with the Czechs and so on, that you can't stick to international questions? Why do you need to be worrying about a girl on a ship?'

'So because we're about to go to war with the Czechs, a missing girl doesn't matter?'

Bremer's kindly face was deadly serious.

'Let's just say, the girl is missing, her file is missing and in my professional opinion, my dear chap, unless you want to learn the Gestapo's definition of crime for yourself, I advise you not to ask another question about it.'

He turned and trudged slowly out of the hall.

Chapter Twenty-four

'So this is the dinner engagement, Sturmbannführer Brandt?'

He winced at her use of his rank.

'Don't call me that. I told you, it's honorary. Himmler awarded it to me on account of my extraordinary knowledge of Parsifal. Please call me Max.'

They were seated in Max Brandt's fifth-floor suite at the Vier Jahreszeiten Hotel. Outside, evening traffic sailed down Maximilianstrasse, and inside, the curtains were drawn on an opulent room of brocaded upholstery, walls hung with still lives of half-peeled fruit, and a vase of lilies with yellow stains at their heart. Clara was being handed a glass of champagne that tasted of vanilla and wet stone.

'Thank you then, Max.'

Brandt's tension had all but disappeared. He smiled, and leaned languidly back in his chair.

'After all, you made me wait long enough.'

Clara sipped her champagne. The cut glass sparkled in the candlelight and she felt the bubbles tilt at the back of her throat, sharp as diamonds.

He chuckled. 'It seems a long time since that night at Coco Chanel's salon. I've looked forward to this ever since. You know, I still can't believe the way you ran rings round me in the streets of Paris. Anyone would think you were practised in evasion.'

'Surely not.'

'It's true. And you certainly managed to evade any awkward moments with the Reichsführer too. You handled him very well, if I may say so. There are plenty of SS officers who could learn from you. Himmler is not an easy person to make conversation with.'

'It seems he likes to make most of the conversation.'

'If you can call it conversation.' The jollity had vanished from his eyes. 'All that stuff about breeding.' He shook his head.

There was a knock at the door. Clara froze, but Brandt smiled.

'Relax.' He called, 'Komm!' and a waiter entered, bearing a trolley stacked with dishes. A platter of oysters bedded on ice. Two dishes, topped with silver covers, glasses and side plates. Delicious smells emanated, of rich sauce and meat, and the waiter removed the covers with a flourish to reveal golden Wiener Schnitzel, crispy fried potatoes, spinach and carrots. Beside them was a plate piled with grapes and peaches. Clara felt a wave of hunger sweep over her.

'Here, as promised, is dinner! I hope you can manage some after that lunch we had.'

'I don't think I ate a mouthful.'

'Nor me. There's something about the Berghof that drives all thought of food from one's mind.'

'There are oysters!' she exclaimed.

'They don't look much, do they?' He prised open a shell and offered it to her with a spritz of lemon. 'But they say it's the least distinguished ones that contain the pearls. There. Eat it in one.'

She felt the oyster slide down her throat, like the purest, distilled essence of the sea. She shut her eyes to savour it and when she opened them he was smiling at her.

'I like watching women eat. It's as if they're devouring life.'

'I enjoy eating. Believe me, it was hard for me to decline dinner with you before. I'm always hungry.'

'Good.'

A fire was burning in the grate, and its wavering flames caught in his eyes, illuminating the amber shards in their depths. The light seemed to draw both of them into its soft, enclosed circle, shutting out the shadows beyond, as though they were in one of the paintings on the walls, with the fruit and oyster shells beside them posed like a still life and their own faces lit up from inside with a painterly glow.

'I think we should all live more sensuously.'

'What does that mean?' she laughed, taking another oyster and dabbing at her dripping chin.

'We should listen to what our senses tell us. We should be alive to our feelings.'

'That's pretty much the opposite of what Reichsführer Himmler was saying.'

'Sounds about right then.'

She smiled.

'Although Himmler was correct in one regard.'

'Oh yes?'

'It seems curious that a woman like you is still single. Can I ask why?'

She fiddled with her glass then gazed at him directly.

'I suppose because the only man who ever proposed to me made it a condition of marriage that I move back to England. If I'd done that I would have lost any chance of parts at the Ufa studios. And my work was important to me. Is important to me, I mean.'

'So this man asked you to choose between your work and love?'

'In a way.'

'And you chose . . .'

'As you can see, I chose.'

'Still.' He finished the last of his schnitzel and beamed. 'You don't need to worry about old flames any more. Not now you have Sturmbannführer Steinbrecher. Tell me about him. He sounds a nice chap.'

She took another sip and dipped her eyes.

'A good upstanding servant of the Reich?'

'Of course.'

'Would you marry him?'

Marry him? Clara wished fervently that she had never invented him. Evasively, she rummaged amongst the grapes on the tray.

'Far too early for that.'

Cautiously, she drank her champagne. There was a mystery about Brandt. Something unknowable. She could see why he was in the diplomatic life because, despite the odd glimpses beneath the mask, such as his urgent desire to escape the Berghof, there was a smooth imperturbability to him. His eyes were ranging over the remnants of the dinner tray.

'This fruit is quite something.' He sliced a peach into six neat portions, offered her one and she bit into it. The flesh was sweet and intense and she felt a pulse of pure pleasure.

'Good, isn't it?' he said. 'And I suppose we should make the most of it, in the circumstances.'

'The circumstances?'

'Given that we don't know what's coming . . .'

A shadow crossed his eyes. He jumped up, gesturing at his black tunic with its glistening silver buttons and its insignia.

'Would you excuse me? I'd like to change out of this.'

'Of course.'

He disappeared into the adjacent bedroom, leaving the door ajar, and Clara remembered the image she had conjured back in Berlin, of a half-made bed, with drawn curtains, rumpled sheets, and hot bodies entwined. An anonymous hotel, somewhere like this, closed against the eyes of the world. Why had that image so stubbornly refused to leave her mind? She fortified herself with another sip of champagne and when she looked up again he was leaning against the doorframe, wearing an open-necked white shirt which revealed dark curls against a golden skin.

'As far as I'm concerned the less time I spend in uniform, the better.'

As he came towards her he turned off the overhead light, leaving only the glow of a pink-fringed lamp, and sat opposite her, smelling of Eau de Cologne and lemon soap, their knees almost touching. As he did, Clara felt a surge of attraction so strong she was almost faint with it and as an automatic response to what she was feeling, she said,

'Tell me about your wife.'

Brandt blinked, stiffened and looked away.

'Clara Vine. You have the most extraordinary ability to . . .' He drew a hand across his eyes. 'All right, if that's what you want, we'll talk about my marriage.' He leant forward, his elbows on his knees. 'I come from a close family. My father was a lawyer, as I said, and my mother was musical, and they were untypical of their generation in that they loved to spend time with my sisters and brothers and me. We had a family boat and we would go sailing down the Havel and took holidays on my grandfather's estate outside Potsdam. They were very cultured people. We would stage family concerts and I suppose I got my love of music from them. Anyhow, I expected that sense of security and predictability to continue when I myself was married. Closeness, loyalty, sharing. Those were my expectations. I thought that was what family was.'

Clara couldn't help a wry sympathy. Her experience of family had been of bereavement, estrangement, and buttoned-up English unhappiness. She had learned that if you didn't expect much, you wouldn't be disappointed.

'Unfortunately,' Brandt continued, 'my marriage was not like that at all. Gisela loved the outdoor life, but she disliked music and theatre, and most of all she hated travelling. That was, perhaps, the only way in which she was out of step with our leadership. They enjoy the idea of European travel. They've made it their mantra.'

'Do you have children?'

His eyes clouded. 'No, sadly. I wanted children but it seems

Gisela couldn't have them. She became pregnant shortly after we married, then lost the child. For years, we tried and nothing happened, until one day she told me she was expecting for a second time. I begged her not to go out riding but she wouldn't listen and she lost that one too. I was still grieving for it, when she told me it hadn't been my child anyway. That seemed to seal it.'

'So . . . you live in Paris now?'

'Yes. Though I keep an apartment in Charlottenburg. Clausewitzstrasse, just off the Ku'damm, for when I'm in Berlin. It's been in the family for generations. It fell empty after my grandmother died. It was strange, at first, being apart from Gisela, and being back in a place I associated with childhood, but in another way, it has helped clarify my ideas of who I am and what I believe.'

'What do you believe?'

'I have a sense, how to describe it? It's like what they call in the Bible "The end of days". And if it is the end of days, then perhaps we should, as the Romans say, as I said once before, *carpe diem*.'

'Seize the day?'

'That's right.'

'How gloomy you sound.'

'You're right!' His voice had a way of shifting from melancholy to humour in the space of a single sentence. 'What kind of man darkens a dinner with a beautiful woman with talk of his ex-wife and the end of days? That's the kind of thing I should reserve for my psychiatrist.'

'Do you have one?'

'I did once. I fired him.'

'Why?'

'He talked too much.'

'What do you mean when you say it's like the end of days?'

'I suppose I mean it may be the end of one era and the beginning of the next.'

'You mean war?'

'Perhaps. At times like these everything is changed, isn't it?'

He was staring at her intently, and to break the spell Clara got up and went over to the tray to refill her glass. Brandt came up behind her and very gently lifted the hair from the nape of her neck, leaned forward and kissed her there. She felt his breath burn her skin, moving across her hair, and she turned to face him. His eyes were serious and tender and his thumb moved roughly across her face like the harsh caress of a cat's lick.

He fed her another piece of peach and her mouth drowned in sweetness. There was a slow deliberation about him, as though he was prepared to enjoy everything, every sensation and every smell, like a man who might be living his final day.

He cupped her face in his hands and looked at her seriously.

'Let's not talk about the past. Nothing's predestined. We all have the power to affect our own destiny and make our own choices, don't you agree?'

Clara felt herself melting. Why should she not respond to him? Sexual allure was a weapon, but it was also real for her. At that moment she saw both of them with a sudden vividness as if from above, everything in minute detail, the food on the tray beside them, the shards in his eyes, the delicate powder on the inside petal of the lily. Her situation, and the choice she faced, was cast in intense clarity.

Max was right to say people should make their choices, but Clara had made hers. What was she thinking of, letting her guard down and giving in to the urge for a moment's pleasure? She moved across the room.

'Something's the matter,' he stated, baldly.

'Of course it is. You're not what I think you are, Max.'

He crossed his arms.

'Is that so? What am I then?'

'You're in the SS for a start. That doesn't happen by chance. It takes something to be in the SS.'

'Certainly it does. Aryan heritage going back to 1750, at least twenty-three years in age and five foot six and a half inches in height. Oh, and at some point I'll need to get my blood type tattooed onto my arm. At least that's what it said in the booklet. I didn't read the small print.'

'You know that's not what I mean.'

'What do you mean?'

'It takes a certain kind of person. Someone who's working for Heydrich.'

For a second he stared in amazement. Then he burst out laughing. After a minute he recovered himself and wiped a hand across his eyes.

'I shouldn't laugh. It's no laughing matter. But what the hell makes you think that?'

'The rank. The uniform.'

'I explained the uniform.'

'It's more than that. I have an instinct about you. You've not been honest with me. You're concealing something.'

There was a moment of silence. She could see his face calculating, his mind turning before he spoke. He moved slowly across and poured himself a shot of brandy and soda, and when he turned back to face her, his eyes had lost their humorous gleam.

'You're right. I've not been entirely honest. But then, my dear Clara, neither have you. You, too, are not what you seem. I've known that for some time. Since the first evening I met you, in fact.'

There was a moment of stillness in the room and time seemed to expand, as if the two of them were poised on the threshold of some deeper understanding.

'I don't know what you're talking about.'

'Don't you? I think you do. I knew there was something about you in Chanel's salon. You confirmed it for me when I followed you back to your hotel. You told me that you're a British agent.'

Her entire body became rigid with shock, but she managed a laugh and, to deflect his scrutiny, coolly withdrew a cigarette from her bag.

'What an extraordinary suggestion. I never told you any such thing.'

He pulled out his lighter and the flame leapt up to touch her cigarette.

'Oh, not overtly of course. You're far too skilled for that. Far too clever to make any number of little slip-ups. You're cautious. I've seen you check the street around you for shadows. I've noticed the way you assess a situation before you progress. You have that alert intelligence in your eyes that lets nothing escape you. You're always listening, even when you seem to be far away. And you speak several languages. To speak another language fluently is to inhabit an entirely different character, don't you think? But the fact is, you told me what you were the instant you mentioned your lover's name. Sturmbannführer Steinbrecher. I recognized that name at once. I know him actually.'

'You know him?'

'Very well.'

'Oh. I see.'

'I don't think you do. You see, that's my name.'

'Steinbrecher?'

'Shall we say my codename. The British gave it to me. When I first made contact with them.'

As she stared at him he sank down into the armchair, gazing into the fire, and then leant forward, hands clasped together and elbows on his knees. There was no smile in his eyes any more, just deadly seriousness.

'It was about a year ago when I first made contact with members of the British Foreign Office. I volunteered my services and privileged information to a foreign power in what is effectively treason, or would be, except that I regard it as pure patriotism. You see, Clara, I no longer recognize the Germany I love. I see these brutes strong-arming a small nation like Austria, and now threatening Czechoslovakia, because they can and no one will stop them. I see them running riot with the rule of law – Germany, whose legal system is the greatest in the world, which has always stood for justice and right. And when I see this gang of thugs flooding the streets of my beloved country with tides of blood, I feel hatred swelling inside me and I think damn them all, these savages who are making our country a pariah. Damn these men like Himmler and Heydrich who are sadists of a kind I can hardly bear to imagine. I hate this false Germany, as much as I love the real Germany. And I intend to do something about it.'

'What can you do?'

'I'm part of a conspiracy, a plot to overthrow Hitler. We intend to mount a coup.'

'A coup?' The word seemed to ring out in the silence of the room.

'More an act of self-defence. Defence of Germany against an aggressive madman.'

His face sideways on seemed older, anxiety etched into the lines.

'I mean it, Clara. Someone needs to tell the truth about Hitler before it's too late. We've been waiting for the opportunity for an overthrow. And now I think the time has come.'

'We? Who is we?'

'I can't tell you that right now. To be honest, it's not safe to give you that information. It would compromise you, as much as them. But one thing is certain, Clara. We need Britain to understand our resolve. If Britain believes there's serious opposition to Hitler among the German military, she will be empowered to take a stronger stand against him. Then if this madman proceeds to attack Czechoslovakia, he will face an Anglo-French alliance on one side and a Czech force, perhaps allied with Soviet air power, on the other front.'

Clara tried to control her conflicting emotions. The relief, that Brandt was not the tool of Heydrich she had feared, the growing admiration for his bravery and, underlying both, the potent attraction she felt for him.

'Why are you telling me this?'

'I wanted to. I couldn't bear you thinking of me in the same light as them. Some black-shirted gangster who thinks ethics belong in ancient Greece.'

He reached forward and brushed a curl of hair from her forehead.

'And there's another reason. There's something you could do for us, Clara.'

She had a sinking realization that this was the culmination of what he had been planning since the moment he met her.

'What could I do?'

'I'm torn. Part of me doesn't want you to be involved with this in any way. I don't want to put you in danger, any more than you might be already. I was already thinking about how you might help us when I met you on the Ku'damm that day . . .'

'Which wasn't a coincidence?'

'No. I went looking for you. Even then, I hadn't quite decided whether to approach you. But when I discovered you'd met the Führer's girlfriend, I realized the opportunity was too good to miss.'

'So what do you need me to do?'

'If, as I assume, Eva Braun recovers from her little cry for help, she will be returning to Berlin with the Führer. That's where we'll need you. I can't yet tell you how, or even when, but you'll get adequate warning.'

'What sort of warning?'

'I can't tell you that either. Not yet.'

He ran a single finger in a line down her cheek.

'Do you know why I chose the name Steinbrecher? It's one of our native flowers – a stone breaker. It grows in the Bavarian Alps. It's nothing much to look at, this little flower, but it's vigorous and strong enough to break paving stones apart. It makes its way up through the cracks in the rock and fragments them. It's a fragile thing, yet it has the power to tunnel through granite.'

'It suits you. You're brave.'

He reached out his arm to her.

'If I were really brave I would make love to you, as I've wanted since the moment I saw you. I would not hesitate because, after all, you came here willingly and a woman who comes alone to a man's hotel room must have a pretty good idea of what he would like to do with her. I would pick you up in my arms and carry you through to that bed – it's what I was planning from the moment we arrived. I would persuade you that it was the right thing to do, even though I know there's something holding you back. And I know it can't be Sturmbannführer Steinbrecher.'

His hand followed the contours of her body, as his voice wound through her mind.

'Perhaps you can't bear to sleep with a Nazi officer. Even if he detests the Party. Is that it?'

'I've done it before.'

'Then you find me too old, too unattractive?'

'No.'

'I'm still married. Is that it?'

She shook her head.

'There's someone else?'

'There's no one. I think I'm meant to be alone.'

'If you're not waiting for someone, then it's only your past that's stopping you. And we shouldn't cling to the past, Clara, we should seize the day. Isn't that what we said?'

Something yielded in her. She was lonely, wasn't she, and what was the point of refusing the most basic human solace? Whatever her thoughts about Nazi officers, Max Brandt was a decent man. Surely you should cling to the good you found, like a pearl in the harsh rubble of oyster shells? And he was right. It wasn't as though she was waiting for anyone.

Brandt sensed the give in her and pulled her closer. His hands reached to her shoulders and caressed her arms, before his full, soft lips met hers. His strong fingers loosened the buttons at the back of her dress and let it fall, and his hand found its way to her stocking tops, plucking at the suspender belt.

'I've taken off my uniform. Why not slip out of yours?'

She arched her body against his chest, and felt the warm circle of his arms around her.

From outside came the sharp screech of car tyres against the road. Brandt cocked his head and put his hand against her mouth.

'Hush.'

He moved over to the window and lifted a narrow aperture, then let the curtain drop. The lights of cars passing in the street outside reared up, making scissor shapes across the ceiling and picking out his face in the gloom. Clara came up behind him.

'What is it?'

'There's a particular car in the street down there. I noticed it before.' He turned.

'I saw it this morning, in Wasserburgstrasse, when I went to find you. I wonder if it might be you they're following. Do you have any reason for thinking the Gestapo might be on to you?'

'Frau von Ribbentrop told Lina Heydrich she didn't trust me. She advised Lina Heydrich to tell her husband. But I didn't think Heydrich would pay attention. Not at a time like this.'

He contemplated this. 'It never does to underestimate them. And von Ribbentrop knows his wife is twice as intelligent as him. If the Führer allowed women in his cabinet he would do well to sack the Foreign Secretary and instate his wife.'

'Do you think they'd arrest me?'

'If they saw you go into Eva Braun's house, almost certainly.' He began to pace the room. 'The only thing is . . . if they know you're here, I would expect them to come straight in. It's not like the local Gestapo to wait around.'

He regarded her solemnly.

'You need to go back to your hotel and pack. You must leave Munich. There's no alternative.'

'There certainly is. I've a part to learn. I've got a film to make. I can't leave Fritz Gutmann in the lurch.'

A shadow passed over his eyes.

'I'm afraid Fritz Gutmann is in a worse place than that.'

'What are you talking about? I saw him only the other day.'

'He was arrested yesterday at dawn. He is being questioned on suspicion of assisting foreign powers.'

'That's impossible!'

'Remember I mentioned I had a little cultural business to attend to? I went to the studios to warn Gutmann, but it was too late. I blame myself. I got wind of it a couple of days ago, then I was held up in Berlin. I should have left immediately. As soon as I discov-- ered I went to the police station. That was how I happened to hear of your call from Fräulein Braun's house. I had an inkling the caller might be you. There's nothing I could do to help Gutmann. Now another fine man is destined for the attentions of Heydrich.'

'What will they do with him?'

'Work him over first, ask questions later. That's the way they usually operate.'

Clara could not help herself reflecting on what Fritz Gutmann knew. If his association with London Films had been detected, the entire operation was compromised. And even if he did not know exactly what Clara did, he had arranged for her to meet the Führer's girlfriend. If Gutmann was interrogated and confessions flooded out of him, there was no telling how many people his knowledge might threaten. Interrogations were like throwing a stone in a lake. The consequences of confessions rippled far. And the Gestapo liked throwing stones.

'So what will happen to the film?'

'Nothing, for the moment.'

Brandt's face was absent. Calculating.

'I've changed my mind. We'll leave right away. You can't go back to your hotel. You're coming with me and we're catching the first available train.'

'But . . .'

'It's dangerous for you to stay here. There isn't any time to lose. You're coming back with me to Berlin.'

Chapter Twenty-five

Villages and towns sped past as the train made its way northwards in the six-hour journey to the Anhalter Station. Dawn was gradually lightening the fields and forests and in the farmsteads, cherry, apple and nut trees were in fruit. Mist was rising from the grass as it was warmed by a low morning sun.

They had taken window seats in an ordinary second-class compartment. Around the carriage photographs of the Bavarian countryside were framed on the walls alongside a sign decreeing 'Nicht Raucher'. Max Brandt sat opposite her in his Foreign Service uniform. Clara was still wearing the previous day's clothes. The only other occupants of the compartment were a kindly-looking elderly couple in Bavarian costume unwrapping hot bacon rolls whose smell quickly filled the carriage and piqued Clara's senses.

They had already agreed not to talk openly, so Clara occupied herself by gazing out of the window at the fields, the odd cluster of farmhouses and occasional small church. They passed a youth camp, with little wooden huts, and a banner over the entrance reading, *We were born to die for Germany*. Looking out at the fat, uniform squares of corn rolling into the distance, glinting in the morning sun, Clara couldn't help but be reminded of the shots of the Nuremberg rally, with hundreds of thousands of people ranked in the rally ground, stretching as far as the eye could see.

At one stop, a young man entered the carriage, hauled a heavy suitcase up onto the baggage rack and settled himself in a corner. In sharp contrast to the traditional costumes of the old couple, he wore a floppy cravat and a suit with a wide stripe. The savoury fragrance of the bacon rolls caused him to dab his moustache fastidiously with a handkerchief, before he extracted a newspaper and fenced himself off.

Brandt sat with his jackboots stretched out and occasionally his legs touched Clara's. When a tunnel plunged them momentarily into darkness, he reached over and felt for her hand, only to withdraw it again when daylight flooded back.

The train clattered and groaned, and the gentle swaying on the tracks was soothing, yet Clara's mind was churning. She was still reeling from Brandt's revelation of the plot to oust the Führer. The coup would take place very soon, within days perhaps, and they – the plotters – wanted her involvement too, though they could not yet explain how. She was also shaken by his casual comment that she was being followed, which meant that Sabine's warning was justified and her instincts, as she moved around Munich, had been entirely correct.

They had made their arrangements hastily, on the way to the station. Clara would go to Brandt's Berlin apartment the following Sunday, where he would explain precisely what they wanted of her. He made her memorize his address in Clausewitzstrasse – *Prussia's greatest military strategist, appropriate in the circumstances, don't you think?* – then warned her not to utter another word, not on any subject, not even the movies. Yet though they had agreed not to talk, she continually caught Brandt's glance on her and felt his probing eyes. Despite her anxiety about the plot, another question was running through her mind. Was he right about the instinct that had caused her to draw away from him?

If you're not waiting for someone, then it's only your past that's stopping you.

Every so often the train halted at a platform long enough to see newsstands hung with bright magazines and newspapers pegged to their sides. *With Hitler and Chamberlain for peace!* Country-women were selling fruit, and tubs blazed with scarlet geraniums. Other stations they sped through too fast to catch more than a blur of faces on the platform, and in between fields unfolded, occasional lakes shimmering like silver lamé in the bright morning and great tracts of deep German forest, as mysterious and impenetrable as any fairy tale from the Brothers Grimm. Clara remembered a report about an impassioned farmer who had managed to plant silvery saplings in the shape of an enormous swastika amongst the pines on his land, so that foreigners arriving in Berlin by plane would see even the ancient woodland bearing Hitler's mark.

Just before Berlin they passed a succession of trains full of munitions and artillery, and then an airfield, where a flock of sleek silver planes stood beside their hangars. Shortly afterwards the train began to slacken and came to an unscheduled stop. There was a banging of compartment doors and the sound of boots coming down the corridor as three men in SS uniform, followed by the train's own guard, shouldered their way along the carriages, demanding identity documents. Immediately, a subdued tension pervaded the carriage, as everyone sat up and braced themselves for scrutiny.

A guard slammed open the compartment door with a surly announcement. 'Identity check.'

He was a burly character, with a prominent gut and a thick, creased neck encased in olive-green uniform. He passed his eyes over the old couple's papers so swiftly he could barely have registered their names, then turned to Clara.

'Your papers, Fräulein.'

Without a word, Clara handed them over, her heart hammering.

The guard looked at the photograph on Clara's red identity document, then at her face, then at the document again. He took his time, twenty, thirty seconds, as a look of blunt puzzlement formed on his florid countenance. She reminded herself that she need not be unduly concerned. This often happened, when policemen who checked her papers happened to be film fans too. Frequently Clara would have to endure a conversation about her latest movie, as well as some gratuitous film criticism of the kind that Goebbels himself had recently banned. But normally she would see recognition dawning in the policeman's eyes, not the bridling suspicion she detected now.

'Can I ask where you boarded this train?'

'Munich.'

'And what was your business there?'

'I was making a film.'

'A film?'

'At the Geiselgasteig studios. I'm an actress.'

That was superfluous. Why had she said that? It was as though she was undermining her own authenticity, inviting him to distrust her.

'What film?'

'It's called *Good King George*.'

God forbid that they knew of Fritz Gutmann's arrest. She wondered if Max would intercede if she was arrested.

Eventually the guard grunted and returned her papers, then turned to Brandt, who handed his own documents over with languid confidence. Noting his rank, the guard clicked his heels.

'Thank you, Sturmbannführer Brandt.'

The young man with the cravat then furnished his documents. His sallow complexion had paled further and a line of sweat had formed on his upper lip. There was a slight, barely detectable tremble in his hand. The guard read the papers, but did not return them. His failure to find fault with Clara seemed to make him more determined.

'You are travelling to Berlin, Herr Honigsbaum?'

'That's what it says on my ticket.' The young man was trying to sound authoritative, but merely sounded arch.

'May I ask what your business is?'

Honigsbaum offered a smile around to his audience – *What kind of question is that?* – but the audience did not respond.

'I live there.'

'So I see. Rykestrasse, 131. Do you have luggage with you?'

'Certainly.' The young man inclined his head towards the luggage rack.

'Open it.'

Clara remembered Steffi Schaeffer's comments about Jews being searched on trains, right down to their tubes of toothpaste. *It pays to be very careful if you're going to conceal something.*

Honigsbaum hauled his leather case down from the rack with shaking hands and made several attempts to undo the clasps before he succeeded. The guard bent over and rifled through the contents with a rough hand. A bottle of pomade. Underwear. A wrinkled shirt. He extracted a novel – stared at it, then held it by the spine and shook vigorously, as if notes might be concealed. Then he seized on a pair of worn brown shoes, tapped the heel and, reaching inside, peeled back the insole.

'Is there anything I can help you with, officer?' ventured the young man, unwisely. His voice was reedy and educated in comparison with the guard's thick Bavarian accent.

The request only spurred the guard to further efforts. He opened the bottle of pomade and shook it, so drops splattered on the floor, then turned a pair of gloves inside out. The young man stood immobile, but his face was running with sweat. He would not dare to protest against this invasion of his dignity by disparaging the guard; even to query the search might suggest some criticism of the authorities, so he said nothing. But there was a terrible eloquence in his silence, and an ominous tension amongst everyone in the carriage. The fat neck of the guard was blocking her vision but suddenly Clara saw him withdraw a pocket knife from his tunic and with a swift, practised movement, run it through the blue satin lining of the case, cramming his sausage fingers inside and withdrawing something that looked like a deck of greasy cards but on closer sight proved to be a wad of notes.

A look of cruel satisfaction broke across the guard's face at this trophy.

'What's this?'

'My savings. Where am I supposed to keep it, with this new ruling about bank accounts? I'm not breaking any law.'

'That's for us to say.'

The guard slammed the case lid shut, and stood at the door.

'Come with me.'

'Why is that?' asked the young man, his show of indignation entirely failing to mask his fear. He offered an imploring smile round to the rest of the carriage. 'I've done nothing wrong.'

'That is what we need to establish,' said the guard, keeping hold of the suitcase. 'Come quickly. We don't want to keep these people waiting.'

He slid open the door and took the young man's elbow.

'Heil Hitler!'

Everyone responded.

The guard proceeded to escort the young man down the train and Clara watched him being marched along the platform, his white face mouthing protest, his hands gesticulating as other guards came forward to meet them. Then there was a piercing whistle as the train moved slowly off again, and as they passed, the young man glanced directly at Clara, with an expression of imploring anguish on his face.

Brandt did not even look up. His eyes remained trained on his boots as the scent of the spilled pomade rose accusingly from the floor. The elderly woman alongside Clara observed her distress and reached a comforting hand to her arm.

'Er Jude war,' she said, consolingly. He was a Jew. It explained everything.

As the train swayed on, Clara recalled what Steffi Schaeffer had said about the men who were arrested at dawn and taken away. Loaded onto trains, but not like this one, more like trucks, and transported to camps all around the country. What happened to them there? She had no idea. She knew no one who had been in a camp, at least no one who had returned from one.

The lift was out of order again at Winterfeldtstrasse and the bulb was out on the stairwell so she walked up the seventy-two steps – she knew exactly how many steps to the fifth floor – in semi-darkness, listening to the sounds emerging from the closed doors as she went. There was a blast of dance music from the school-teacher on the ground floor and the sound of raised voices from the young couple on the first floor. Excitable squabbling from the children in apartment four. But when she reached the top of the stairs next to her own door, an unfamiliar figure loomed in the dim light.

'May I introduce myself? I'm Franz Engel, your new neighbour.'

He was a slender man – in his forties perhaps – with a precise, professional demeanour and a gaunt clean-shaven face that was at once humourless and forgettable. It was the kind of face you could see anywhere, behind a desk or a bank counter, in a school or an office, but never be able to recall. A face that was always going to stick to the rules.

'I just wanted to say hello.'

Surprise made Clara abrupt.

'What's happened to Herr Kaufmann? Is he OK?'

He shrugged. 'I'm afraid I don't know. The lease of this apartment has been assigned to me.'

Through his opened door she caught a glimpse of the apartment behind him. Drab grey paint, cheap, practical wooden furniture, no distinctive features.

Herr Engel gave a bureaucratic smile and although instinct told Clara she should engage him in conversation and enquire after his job, perhaps, where he had last lived, or at the very least comment on the weather, for once her Englishness failed her and she remained silent. Her lack of response seemed to forestall any further pleasantries, so in his clipped voice Engel said,

'Anyhow, I just wanted to let you know I had moved in.'

He vanished quickly into his apartment and shut the door.

Perhaps it was fatigue, or the alarming events of the past twenty-four hours, but the encounter shook Clara. Who was Franz Engel? To judge by appearances alone, he might have been a teacher or a civil servant or a clerk, some kind of professional anyway, yet he could be any of those and still be a Gestapo spy. That was the genius of the Gestapo – its strength lay almost entirely in its network of informers. They fanned out through Berlin like a giant spider's web, connecting every strand of society, no matter how far from the centre. If, as Sabine said, the orders had gone out that Clara should be watched, what better method than to take the empty lease on the adjacent apartment and install a man within? Listening out for whether Clara tuned to foreign radio stations, watching who visited, how long they stayed, observing her daily routine and eavesdropping on her conversations through the wall. It couldn't be easier if you were stationed right next door.

She went over to her window and looked out across the rooftops to the arched dome of Nollendorfplatz U-Bahn. She had always loved this place, ever since her friend Mary Harker was ordered to leave Germany and allowed her to take over the lease on the apartment. Nollendorfplatz had been the vibrant hub of the old Weimar Berlin, packed with nightclubs and cabarets at the time that the Nazis came to power, and even though they had closed down the clubs and replaced the Expressionist repertoire of the famous Metropol Theatre with operetta and light revues, it was still possible to feel the old racy pulse of the city running through these streets. The buildings with their scrollwork and plaster ornamentation bore witness to a lingering Weimar charm and the crash of bottles being collected from bars in the small hours suggested that some traditions hadn't changed.

Winterfeldtstrasse was her home, but now, for the first time since she moved in, she realized she might have to leave.

Chapter Twenty-six

The second most important woman in Germany, Gertrud Scholtz-Klink, was in a more than usually filthy mood. She was engaged in a battle over territory – not quite as frenetic as that over the Sudetenland – but just as heartfelt. The Führer, she had told Bormann, despite his fulsome tributes at the Nuremberg rally, was simply not sparing time to meet her. There had now been three hundred thousand applications from women in the Sudetenland to join the organization, and that was on top of four hundred and seventy thousand from Austria. Yet she was still not getting the official recognition or encouragement that she deserved.

As the Führerin paused for breath, Rosa looked around her office – a place of utilitarian drabness that was a perfect outward expression of her boss's personality. There was no mirror, there being no need for cosmetic adjustments, and the sole touch of luxury Gertrud Scholtz-Klink allowed herself was a row of leather-bound speeches of Adolf Hitler with lettering picked out in gilt. On the wall, by way of decoration, was a tapestry bearing a pronouncement from the Führer, stitched in elaborate Gothic letters in black thread:

Woman's world is her husband, her family, her children and her home. We do not find it right when she presses into the world of men.

When eventually Gertrud Scholtz-Klink finished dictating the letter to Reichsführer Himmler and flounced out for a meeting with the Faith and Beauty League, Rosa moved swiftly. Her boss would not be back for a good hour, giving Rosa the chance to attend to the matter that was preoccupying her.

The light in the windowless library was dim and the air smelt musty and unused, reflecting how few visitors it received. This was not a place many people came to browse. The couple of shelves of books were outnumbered by rows of tall steel racks containing thousands of files, organized under sections including Family Policy, Marriage and Race Hygiene. Rosa gave a quick smile to the librarian, a mountainous woman whose job afforded very little exercise, and received a sour nod in return. Rosa's position as secretary to the Führerin lent her a certain status, but the librarian was under-employed, and liked to flex what little authority she possessed to the full.

'Can I help you, Fräulein Winter?'

'I'm just looking in the files for something on racial science.'

The librarian inclined her head towards the shelves beside the chart explaining differences between the Nordic, Alpine and Baltic races and the inheritance of tainted blood through the generations. The chart was a baleful thing, illustrating the progress of the bad blood with red arrows pointing in various directions, like a diagram on a detective's wall to follow the movements of a crime.

'Anything particular you need?'

The woman was more like a guard than a librarian, as though, if not vigilantly protected, her files might be accessed by any passer-by in search of light reading.

'It's fine. I'll just have a quick browse.'

Rosa needed to find what happened when children were reported to something called a Reich Health Board, but she had no idea where to start. She thumbed through the files at random, her fingers trembling, the contents blurring before her eyes. Tiny puffs of dust rose up as she browsed, suggesting that no one had felt the need to access any of this information since the day it was stored.

She withdrew a pamphlet entitled *Mate Selection Guidelines* with chapter headings like 'You and the Question of Blood' and 'What is Race?' She skimmed a little:

'*Since normal and sick hereditary factors are passed on equally to the offspring, the knowledge of hereditary factors and the duty to intervene – to restrict and to promote them for the formation of coming generations – are of enormous importance. At conception, the essence and worth of a person for his folk and his race are already determined. Hence the responsibility for the next generation lies with us.*'

It concluded with the triumphant announcement,

'*Everything weak or inferior is annihilated.*'

It read like gibberish. Rosa couldn't see how any of this rhetoric could possibly apply to Hans-Otto, but she sensed the librarian peering suspiciously in her direction and guessed she would have to offer more information.

'We just needed to clarify an item of law. About Reich Health Boards.'

'Why didn't you say then? It will be Hereditary Health you need.'

The librarian heaved herself to her feet and progressed along the length of another shelf, her fat fingers flicking expertly through the files.

'Better let me help you. I don't want anything getting out of alphabetical order.'

She pulled out a drawer and plucked a pamphlet entitled *Law for the Prevention of Genetically Diseased Offspring, 1933.*

'You'll need to start with this.'

Rosa read it through. The law concerned anyone who suffered from any of nine conditions assumed to be hereditary: feeble-mindedness, schizophrenia, manic-depressive disorder, Huntington's chorea, genetic blindness, genetic deafness, severe physical deformity, chronic alcoholism and epilepsy.

Epilepsy.

The pamphlet was illustrated. Rosa gazed appalled at the grisly portraits of the mentally weak, easily identified by their slack, empty expressions and lolling tongues. They reminded her of a newsreel she had seen once, in the cinema – a documentary screened before the main feature which argued that some people led 'a life unworthy of life', and were doomed to rot in institutions. The Fatherland should be rid of such 'burdens on the German worker'.

None of this, though, surely, had any connection to the note from Hans-Otto's school. She felt sweat prickling under her blouse and sensed the librarian's eyes boring into her, as though this was the most interesting thing that had happened all day. She was compelled to explain.

'I'm just trying to remind myself of the details of the Hereditary Health Boards for children.'

'Oh those. They're new. You want to look under Proposals for Registration of Diseased Offspring.'

'If you could show me.'

'They've just come through. A letter's been sent out to all the schools so I filed it under Education.'

The woman heaved her way across the room and extracted a piece of paper, stamped with the crest of the Reich Interior Ministry.

'*A decree has been enacted compelling all physicians, nurses and mid-wives and other professionals involved in the care of children to report infants and children who show signs of mental and physical disability. The prescribed registration form is designed with the intention of giving increased medical care. District doctors will send the completed form to a National Committee for observation.*

The aim is to prevent the neglect of healthy children in a family through excessive care of the sick. Details of any child who might warrant registration under the scheme will be forwarded to the Health Board unless sufficient authority is given for such registration to be suspended.'

The letter finished with the touch that was the hallmark of all Nazi bureaucracy, a combination of promise and threat.

'*A reward of two Reichmarks will be given to the teacher or health administrator who furthers a name to the register. Failure to register any such infant will be subject to investigation.*'

The final salutation, however, was unambiguous.

'*Heil Hitler!*'

Rosa thanked the librarian and made her way back to her desk. She had a stack of typing to complete, but although her fingers flitted across the keys mechanically, her mind was full of the letter, with its ominous circumlocution and evasive terminology. *Disability. Registration. Increased medical care. Excessive care of the sick.*

Each one was a dagger of ice to the heart.

Rosa had a special reverence for words. She had always thought that words were instruments of enlightenment and that if you chose the correct words in the right order they would help you to see the world in a more beautiful and perfect light. That was why she had wanted to be a writer in the first place. It was why she worked away at her Observations in the privacy of her bedroom every night, trying to recapture the things she had seen that day in precisely the right language. Finding words that would make her experiences leap out from the page. But now she understood that words could be used to obscure, as much as elucidate. Abstract words and ugly official phrases grew up like a thicket of thorns around an idea. Walls of bland bureaucratic jargon could hide horror. Rosa saw that words were dangerous, and powerful. If you used the right words, you could do anything.

Chapter Twenty-seven

For days now the city had been alive with politicians. Hurrying down the Wilhelmstrasse, burning the midnight oil in the embassies. Making so many foreign calls it was almost impossible for the wiretappers to keep up. At street level the bars and cafés buzzed with rumours and all night the dull rumble of convoys, lorries, tractors and tanks kept people awake in their beds. Police car sirens wailed through the streets. Chamberlain had met Hitler twice now, yet there was stalemate. Berlin felt like a city poised on the edge of something, uncertain whether the speeches of politicians represented the wind of change or mere bluster. History hung in the balance like a charge of cordite in the air.

Admiral Wilhelm Canaris, head of German Military Intelligence, five foot three with white hair, a ruddy complexion and bushy eyebrows, liked to project an air of professional inscrutability. In his Abwehr office he had statues of the iconic three monkeys fashioned to exemplify Canaris' personal motto: see all, hear all, say nothing. He was a workaholic, perhaps on account of an unhappy home life, so he spent most of his time in his office on the Tirpitzufer, where he could be seen arriving at the crack of dawn and leaving late at night. Although the wily Canaris managed to camouflage his precise feelings about the Führer, his discontent with the direction of the Reich's foreign policy was suspected and the gap between himself and Hitler was apparent to everyone in the know. Probably the only thing that Canaris did share with Hitler was his devotion to dogs. He could not be friends with anyone who disliked animals and took his two wire-haired dachshunds everywhere. He would book twin-bedded hotel rooms on his travels so that they could sleep beside him and when he was in Berlin he arrived at Army High Command carrying them tenderly under each arm in the black government Mercedes.

Sitting in the Casino Club opposite Canaris' granite-faced headquarters, sipping a vodka and tonic, Rupert wondered yet again if the whispers he had heard were true. That a section of German generals, calling themselves the Black Orchestra, had launched a desperate mission to the heart of the English government and Canaris himself was aiding and abetting those who wanted to bring Hitler down.

This astonishing information had come to him the previous day, at the Stadtbad Mitte on Gartenstrasse, where he swam regularly with Dieter Adler, an army officer who had become a friend. The swimming pool was a handsome Bauhaus place, and its great glass windows which echoed the lively splash of swimmers made it the perfect place to talk. No one could possibly eavesdrop on two men engaged in a leisurely length of breaststroke even if they wanted to, which was why Adler had selected it for their regular meetings. All the same, Adler was a slow swimmer – he had suffered an injury to his leg in the war – so Rupert kept having to decelerate to catch his words.

'There's something up, Rupert. A stirring of something. A lot of the army are made up of Prussian aristocracy. They regard Himmler and Heydrich as despicable thugs and they're extremely exercised about the idea that Hitler will take the Sudetenland by force.'

'What can they do?'

'That I don't know, but I get the impression that something is planned. Unless, of course, your Chamberlain stands up to Hitler.'

'I wouldn't bank on that. You've heard the joke. "Chamberlain takes his weekends in the country. Hitler takes a country at the weekend."'

'That's the problem with you British. You're always making jokes. No one can tell when you're being serious. A sense of humour is a dangerous thing.'

'On the contrary, Dieter. A sense of humour is a valuable defence. No country with a sense of humour could have elected Hitler as Chancellor.'

Adler finished his length and hauled himself from the pool.

'Whatever you say, Rupert, this is no joking matter. I think very soon it will be decided – one way or the other.'

These ruminations were interrupted by Clara, coming through the revolving brass doors of the club wearing a fetching cream jacket and skirt. Though the suit fitted her like a glove, she was thinner than usual and looked, even to Rupert's jaded eye, worn and tired. She had brushed rouge into her cheeks, but there was no mistaking the dark rings round her eyes.

'I've never been to this place before.' She took a swift, automatic look around the dimly lit room. 'Isn't it full of army officers?'

'And some of my best contacts.' He slid another vodka and tonic across the table to her and was gratified to see her drink it down without demur.

'To what do I owe the pleasure?'

'Actually, Rupert, I had a little request to make.'

'I suspected you wanted something more than the sheer enjoyment of seeing me.'

'I need to place an advertisement in the *Chronicle*.'

'For a friend, I take it?'

'That's right.'

Rupert wasn't surprised. The Situations Wanted columns of the *Daily Chronicle* were full of requests from German Jews for any work, in exchange for the guarantee of fifty pounds sponsorship to cover the passage to England. '*German couple need position, preferably together, all housekeeping and gardening possible.*' '*Hanover family seek work, anything considered.*' '*Young lady, modest, hard worker, urgently looks for position with English family.*'

'It's to go in next week. Thursday's edition.'

'I could get it in sooner.'

'No. That's the day they want. There's a lot of readers for the Thursday edition, apparently.'

Rupert extracted his notebook.

'Do you have the wording?'

'*Berlin lady seeks London employer. German and Latin tuition possible. Tel: Berlin 1845.*'

'Latin? Really? Is she an intellectual, this friend of yours?'

'She's a keen learner.'

'And no name?'

'She prefers it that way.'

'Probably wise. I wish her luck. They're all trying to make it to England now. It's hard enough even to get to the coast. The stations in Paris are crammed. It's impossible to get a ticket on the boat train.'

'It's going to be worse for those who stay.'

'I don't doubt it. I heard that von Helldorf, the Berlin police chief, wants to construct a ghetto for wealthy Jews in Berlin, charging the Jews themselves to construct it.'

'What do you think will happen, Rupert?'

The revolving doors ushered in a blast of cold air and a detachment of Wehrmacht officers, which, Rupert observed, seemed to make Clara uneasy. He folded some bills beneath the ashtray and they walked out up Bendlerstrasse, past army headquarters and round the corner along the Landswehr Canal, a swollen channel of khaki with a rainbow of oil shimmering on its surface.

'You asked me what I think will happen. I'd say Hitler is nervous beneath that swagger. He must be worried – he's had two flak wagons attached to his special train and arms stationed on

the carriage roof. And Goebbels is planning a major rally at the
Sportpalast to prepare the Party faithful for war.'

He turned towards her.

'It's looking rather grim, Clara. In London the schoolchildren
are being evacuated. They've mobilized the Fleet. They've given
out gas masks. My mother had to stop her cook from testing her
mask by putting her head in the oven.'

Clara gave a brief smile at the idea of the formidable Lady
Allingham in a gas mask.

'I know, it sounds funny. But it's serious. All the parks are being
dug up. Hyde Park is bristling with anti-aircraft guns. The hospi-
tals are being emptied so they can accept war casualties and the
Archbishop of Canterbury has called the nation to prayer.'

'I've heard nothing about that here.'

'Are you surprised? Goebbels is doing a miraculous job of keeping it out of the press. Unfortunately my editor has the same idea.'

'Is Winstanley still spiking your pieces?'

'He's convinced that Hitler has no aggressive intentions beyond
the Sudetenland. He won't listen to anyone saying that Hitler has
designs on the whole of Czechoslovakia. He asks me where is the
proof? No one has ever managed to find a document with Hitler's
signature on it that suggests he has any aggressive plans at all. Until
you find that, there's no persuading them. If I were you I'd be
thinking about leaving.'

Clara longed to confide in him about the plot, but she would
never have chanced it. It pained her that this man to whom
she felt so close, the person who had first suggested she come
and try a career in Berlin, knew barely anything of her private life,
nor she of his. They shared so much, after all – an English childhood, mutual friends, and Leo Quinn. Leo most of all. His
shadow seemed to walk between them – never mentioned, always
there.

'Nothing's going to happen, I feel sure of it.'

How bright and optimistic her voice sounded. She looked at

the windows they passed and wondered how long before they were covered with Herr Feinmann's blackout cardboard.

Rupert seemed to accept this. He'd probably guessed already that Clara would stay put.

'And there was me thinking you wanted to check my progress on the cruise ship girl.'

'Oh, I did. I'm seeing Erich tomorrow and he's sure to ask me.'

'Turns out Erich was right. A woman did disappear off that ship. Ada Freitag, aged twenty-three. Her parents reported her missing, according to my friend in the Kripo. He found her Missing Persons file.'

'So they are looking for her?'

'Apparently not. When my man went back for the file, it had disappeared. If this girl is dead, it seems someone's very keen to keep it a secret.'

'Because it's bad publicity for the KdF?'

'Perhaps. But I can't help suspecting something more. When I asked a question about your Ada Freitag in a press conference at the Promi, Goebbels sought me out straight afterwards and offered me an exclusive on his Mother's Cross. That's not like him. I know he was trying to distract me. And when I told my man at the Kripo that I'd raised it with Goebbels he nearly had a heart attack. He advised me to stick to questions on international affairs. But why should it be more dangerous to ask questions about a girl on a cruise than the advance on the Sudetenland? It makes no sense at all.'

Chapter Twenty-eight

Rosa was finding it impossible to concentrate on her work. Every time she started a letter, her thoughts would return to the telephone call she had received earlier that day. She recognized the voice at once, and had almost dropped the phone in shock.

'Is that my favourite Zarah Leander lookalike?'

It was Herr August Gerlach, the man from the cinema, and he wondered if Rosa would like to meet up.

She wondered how he had managed to track her down. She must have told him she worked at the Führerin's office, though she didn't recall it, but in all other respects he was exactly as she remembered. The brash, confident voice. The jocular tone underlined with an edge of aggression. His request took her so much by surprise that she didn't know what to say. She didn't really want to meet him, but nor was she quick enough to refuse. Stepping into the silence, Gerlach suggested a wine restaurant called the Ganymed on the banks of the Spree near Friedrichstrasse and gave her the address. He would be there at seven o'clock that evening if she was free.

At the end of the afternoon she escaped to the lavatory and stared at the peeling poster on the wall.

Though women are armed only with the soup ladle and the broom, our impact must be as great as other weapons.

No opportunity for propaganda must be lost. Even in the lavatory.

Regarding herself quickly in the tiny mirror, she twisted her hair savagely back into its braid. When she was young her father had called her a stork, because she was tall and skinny, and although she still practised the gymnastic exercises she had learned in the Bund Deutscher Mädel, she remained as stork-like as ever, only now she had thick glasses too, which concealed her lively, expressive eyes. There was a gap between her teeth and her clothes felt dull and frumpy. Freckles were scattered liverishly across her pale face. Yet this man had seemed keen to meet up, so there must be something about her that he liked. She checked her stockings for runs, feeling glad that she had worn her best pair that morning, then mortified at what such thoughts implied. She drew out of her bag a tin of Khasana cheek colour and lipstick and applied them surreptitiously, praying that she would not encounter the Führerin on the way out. If the Führerin ever saw a staff member wearing cosmetics she would stop them on the spot, whip out a handkerchief and wipe it off there and then.

In truth Rosa had simply no idea how this encounter would turn out because it was her first proper date in ages. There had been occasional outings when she was much younger with the cousin of a friend, but they had always been in a group, and Adam was a nervy, religious boy, far too inhibited to seek intimacy. Since then Rosa rarely met any men, unless they were Party functionaries visiting the Frauenschaft on business, or friends of her father's who were ancient and only interested in chess. Although the BDM was nicknamed the League of German Mattresses for the frequency with which girls found themselves pregnant after social outings with the HJ, Rosa's experience had been one of excessive athletics and blameless chastity. Her Arbeit Service had been spent with a gaggle of other girls on a potato farm north of Berlin, and now she found herself at the Frauenschaft, in a world run for women by women, and despite everything the Führerin said about raising the birth rate, Rosa could think of no way that she was ever going to meet a man. Sometimes in Germany it was as though politicians wanted to keep men and women in entirely separate compartments, like sugar and flour, or dynamite and matches, not to be mixed.

As she hurried down Derfflingerstrasse towards the Kurfürstenstrasse U-Bahn she wondered what Herr Gerlach would talk about. Susi had led her to understand that men mostly wanted to talk about themselves, which was fine by her, but she worried that she might need a few conversational topics just in case. Not politics, obviously, and not work either. Gerlach didn't look like a man who was too keen on literature, and she didn't want to risk discussing an author who might turn out to be degenerate. It would have to be movies. That, or dogs.

With a shudder she remembered the motto of the Love and Marriage talk. *Keep your body pure! Do not remain single! Choose a spouse of similar blood! Hope for as many children as possible!* They didn't seem to be very specific guidelines for a dating situation. She wished she had taken some tips from Susi, but her sister said Rosa was immature – that she saw the world in terms of fairy tales and lived a kind of fantasy life which prevented her from seeing the world as it really was – 'one long disappointment'. Rosa needed to grow up, Susi said, or she'd never find a man.

In the U-Bahn a wave of nausea engulfed her. The smell of sweat, old cooking oil and worse reeked pungently from the crowds on the platform. That was the worst thing about the shortage of soap. Straphanging on the train, up close to your fellow citizens, it was almost impossible to forget that Berliners were now forced to wash their clothes in plain water, if they bothered at all, that was. Rosa wanted to press a handkerchief to her nose but she was far too polite, so she took out a copy of *NS-Frauen-Warte* magazine and tried to focus on an article about Marlene Dietrich in a velvet trouser suit in Hollywood. Rosa wondered what America was like. Everything she knew about America came from the movies and Karl May's Westerns, mostly involving deserts, Red Indians and bears. Karl May's cowboy adventures were the Führer's favourites; he had spoken about them on the wireless. The stories gave him courage and he recommended them to all his top men.

Gerlach was leaning against a lamppost outside the restaurant. When he recognized Rosa, he straightened up and flicked away the butt of his cigarette, a slow smile spreading across his thin mouth.

'I hoped you'd come.'

Almost immediately she wondered why she was there. She felt no excitement or pleasure at all at seeing August Gerlach, more a vague feeling of disappointment. He looked older than he had at the cinema, at least thirty-five she guessed, and the film star glamour he had possessed beneath the cinema's neon lights had faded to a scrappy moustache and wolfishly prominent canines. He wore a sharp grey suit, a slightly grubby fedora, and his sleek, oiled hair glistened beneath the lamplight. She fortified herself by thinking how pleased her mother would be if she said she had had a drink with a man. Perhaps it was normal to want to walk away again as fast as possible.

Gerlach took her elbow and she tried to stop herself flinching at the unexpected touch as he led her to one of the outside tables which lined the Spree, facing Friedrichstrasse. Dusk was falling and the bright, arterial pulses of neon rippled like diamonds on the water. Above the S-Bahn arch opposite, a train tore through the air, heading out into the suburbs, and Rosa looked up at the faces in the lighted windows, wishing she were among them.

August Gerlach spread himself out, elbows on the table and, as anticipated, began talking about himself. The company he worked for was being Aryanized and the Jewish owners were leaving, meaning that there were plenty of job opportunities coming up.

'It's all about being in the right place at the right time, but I'm sure you know all about that,' he said, favouring Rosa with a broad smile. 'You're a clever girl, getting yourself a job in the Frauenschaft. You're obviously going places.'

She smiled, awkwardly.

He leaned over, encouragingly, towards her.

'You've really got under my skin, you know, Fräulein Winter. Rosa. As soon as I saw you at the cinema I thought you looked very . . .' He searched for the correct phrase. 'Intelligent.'

'Thank you.' Being called intelligent was not exactly a compliment in the Reich, not for a woman, but Rosa took it as one and she liked the fact that he seemed to think so too.

'You're quite a looker as well. That's a lovely suntan you have. Been somewhere nice recently?'

'I went on a cruise on the *Wilhelm Gustloff.* To Madeira and Portugal.'

He blew out his cheeks in an impressed sigh.

'Aren't you the lucky one?'

'I suppose so.' In an instant Rosa was transported back to the spray-lashed deck, smoking a cigarette and enjoying the bracing feeling of the water needling her face. Then, through the rain-drenched air, the sight of the girl's body pulled from the sea, her sundress clinging to her icy flesh.

'Bet you enjoyed yourself. I've heard those cruises are for the special ones. The VIPS.'

Stung by this suggestion, she frowned.

'Not exactly. There were all sorts on board.'

'Not the likes of me, I'll bet. More the teachers' pets.'

'No really, that's the thing about the KdF cruises. They're for everyone.'

'If you say so, sweetheart. Wish I could have been there with you. It sounds fabulous.'

'It was. I would have enjoyed it more, only . . .'

'Only what?'

'There was an accident on the ship. It rather spoiled the trip for me.'

He was scouring the drinks menu.

'Say, that's a shame. What happened?'

Rosa hadn't really wanted to tell Herr Gerlach what she'd seen. It was bad enough to be sitting there in the company of a man with whom, she swiftly realized, she had absolutely nothing in common, let alone to sully it further with talk of dead bodies and the terrible sight that had haunted her for weeks. Yet, she reasoned to herself, she had already decided that she was going to tell somebody, and she didn't have much else to talk about. Besides, Gerlach was paying for her drink.

'All right, I'll tell you, if you really want to know. It was an awful accident. A girl died. She fell into the sea.'

'My God. That's hard.' Gerlach gave a shrug which conveyed his absolute disregard for dead girls. 'Accidents can happen anywhere, though. Even on cruise liners.'

'I know. But the thing is . . .' Rosa leant forward across the table, even though no one was listening. 'The more I think about it, the more I believe . . .' The girl's white face came back to her, the bloody mess on the back of the head. 'The more I believe that she didn't just fall.'

He looked up.

'What are you saying?'

'I think someone pushed her.'

'Pushed her?' Gerlach exhaled a stream of smoke, a little smile dancing on his lips. 'You sound like a girl with a vivid imagination.'

A vivid imagination. That was what her father always said. But when her father said it, he meant it as a compliment. Gerlach made it sound like a crime.

'I'm not imagining it. I'm absolutely sure of it.'

'This isn't some fantasy that's got into your pretty little head? Not been watching too many movies?'

'Not at all,' she retorted. 'I saw the body with my own eyes.'

That made him sit up. He ground out his cigarette and steepled his fingers.

'You saw it?'

'Yes. When she was taken out of the water.'

'And you saw her being pushed in too?'

She allowed a little shrug.

'Not exactly.'

'What's that supposed to mean?'

'I think she *was* pushed. Or worse. But . . .'

'But what?'

She was beginning to regret ever mentioning it.

'I probably shouldn't tell you any more. In fact, the Captain came to see me and advised me not to talk at all about what I'd seen.'

Gerlach raised his eyebrows.

'Exactly,' said Rosa. 'But . . . why would he do that, if he wasn't trying to cover something up?'

'Wait a minute, let's get this straight.'

Gerlach lit himself another cigarette and flicked the match over the railings to immediate extinction in the Spree.

'You saw a dead body and you think this girl was murdered? And you think the Captain of the *Wilhelm Gustloff* was involved in a conspiracy to cover it up?'

Rosa was bitterly wishing she had never brought the subject up with August Gerlach, who obviously thought she was some kind of fantasist. When he put it like that, it did sound melodramatic and she felt compelled to convince him that she was not crazy.

'I'm not making this up. It's a feeling I have. Anyway, I'm trying to decide if I should tell anyone.'

'How many people have you told so far?'

'None.'

'Well, that's not true, is it? You told me quite happily. And we've only met twice.'

'I said, I've told no one.' She looked sideways, towards the sluggish waters of the canal, and couldn't help thinking of the bodies that they said were found floating there too, mushrooming up from the gloomy depths. Miserable relicts of humanity reduced to puffy white flesh, pulled up by the bargemen at dawn.

'You don't seem that bothered about what the Captain said.'

A spark of alarm flickered through her.

'What are you? A policeman or something? Obviously the Captain had a reason for asking me not to discuss it, and it might have been simply that he didn't want to alarm the other passengers. But it could have been something else.'

'Which is why you're going to discuss it with all your friends.'

Rosa was not going to mention that she had very few friends. The women at work tended to avoid her, wrongly believing that she would repeat their gossip back to the Führerin.

'I would never do that.'

'Perhaps not.' He was cool, now, rolling his cigarette between his fingers, scrutinizing her with his head on one side. 'But how about your parents?'

'It would scare them.'

'The rest of the family?'

'We don't really have that kind of conversation.'

'You told me, though. Despite the fact that the Captain specifically asked you to keep it confidential.'

Rosa felt a hot rush of indignation rising within her. Who was August Gerlach to lecture her?

'Well, I'm sorry. You seemed like the kind of person I could confide in.' He didn't of course, but she could hardly say that.

This remark made him smile. He looked out across the canal, as though contemplating her conundrum, and exhaled a stream of smoke, watching it curl up into the air.

'Want to know what I think, Rosa? I think you're a nice girl. Perhaps you watch too many detective movies, but you're a bright lady and you have good prospects. You should keep your nose out of this business.'

The waitress interrupted, bringing their drinks, and Rosa took a huge gulp of her beer, in the interests of finishing it quickly.

Gerlach's eyes followed the tight skirt and shapely legs of the wait-ress as she retreated, then turned back to Rosa.

'So are you going to follow my advice?'

She nodded. She was desperate to let the subject drop. She had no idea how long she would have to sit here before she could get away. When a man invited you for a drink, did it actually mean just a single drink?

Gerlach reached across to her hand and patted it.

'Don't look so worried, sweetheart. I'm just looking out for you. Let's not spoil any more of our evening talking about dead bodies. Not when there are movies to talk about. On the subject of which, I took the liberty of getting tickets for *The Divine Jetta*. It stars Grethe Weiser as a cabaret singer wooed by a Tyrolean count. Tuesday evening at the Kino Sportpalast. How about it?'

Chapter Twenty-nine

It would be a relief, in a way, to see Erich.

He had called the day before and although Clara always did her best to keep any telephone conversations from her apartment to a minimum, nothing that Erich ever said could possibly arouse the suspicion of the hidden army of listeners at the telephone exchange who eavesdropped on the calls of every foreigner, or even half-foreigner, in Berlin. Erich wanted to give her something, apparently. Perhaps a gift from his holiday that he had forgotten. They arranged to take advantage of the last vestiges of warm weather and go to the Strandbad at Wannsee.

The beach at the Wannsee was an old favourite of Erich's. A short walk from Nikolassee Station on the S-Bahn, down a sandy, pine-fringed lane, the beach, lapped by the shallow fresh waters of the lake, was a welcome relief from the dusty heat of the city. Jetties protruded into the Wannsee and yachts could usually be seen tacking their way in the distance, framed against the gloomy pine fringes of the eastern shore. Bathers could hire deckchairs or hooded seats in white wicker called Liegestühle, from which to survey the view. With its sausage and beer stalls, the Strandbad offered an entirely egalitarian experience for Berliners, unless of course they happened to be Jewish. As Clara and Erich made their way down the steps to the beach they passed a sign announcing

Badeverbot für Juden am Strandbad Wannsee. Jews should not even think about using the beach. Clara, of course, thought about that sign every time she passed it, but on this day she had more on her mind than the possibility that her Jewish self should be discovered defiling Aryan sand.

Erich, as he always did, plunged straight into the water and swam a strong circuit, while Clara queued for a couple of bottles of lemonade. As this was likely to be the last opportunity before the approach of a Berlin winter made such diversions impossible, the beach was well populated with groups of Hitler Youth and Bund Deutscher Mädel flirting and showing off, families commandeering rings of deckchairs and lovers admiring the caramel smoothness of each other's bodies. Loudspeakers, lashed to the lampposts, broadcast a medley of light and military music, interspersed with the odd homily from Joseph Goebbels. As she queued, out of the corner of her eye Clara noticed a man buying a copy of the *Völkischer Beobachter* at the kiosk, and thought he was looking at her, before glancing down and realizing that his gaze might just have more to do with her tanned legs in their bathing costume.

She returned to her spot on the beach and sat staring out at the sparkling lake and the dark fringe of the Grunewald beyond. How incredible it was that she should be sitting in this lovely place, surrounded by the carefree laughter of Berliners relaxing, while back in the city a group of plotters were preparing to mount a coup on the Reich Chancellery. Clara was glad she was wearing sunglasses or her face would surely betray the anxiety that was thrumming through her mind and Erich would ask her what was wrong. She wished, more than ever, that she could share her thoughts with him, the person in Berlin who cared the most for her, yet she knew it was impossible. Some secrets were too heavy for a boy his age to bear, and besides, Erich's sense of duty and patriotism were bolstered daily by his sessions with the Hitler Youth.

That was just how it was for boys now. The speeches and slogans and marching songs they learned at the age of ten in the Pimpf were repeated for all their formative years in the HJ, followed by the service year and then the armed forces beyond. Everyone knew Hitler's motto: 'The weak must be chiselled away. A young German must be as swift as a greyhound, as tough as leather and as hard as Krupp's steel.' Children were no different from cars or aeroplanes on the Führer's production line and if it came to a conflict between his beloved godmother and his adored Hitler Jugend, who knew what Erich would say or do?

He came and flung himself on the sand beside her, scattering icy drops of water like a dog.

'Nothing's as good as swimming in the Wannsee.'

'Not even the Atlantic Ocean?'

'No. There were pools on the cruise ship, but I prefer our lakes.'

Erich rolled over, propped himself up on his elbows and squinted up at her with Helga's dark, quizzical eyes.

'I wanted to ask you, Clara ... Did you find anything out about that woman? Ada Freitag. Like you said you would?'

Clara wondered how to tell him that her enquiries about Ada Freitag had reached a dead end. What had Rupert said? *Someone seemed very keen to keep her death a secret.* Keen enough to alter the ship's log to suggest that the woman had left the *Wilhelm Gustloff*, rather than falling overboard. Keen enough that the Kripo's own Missing Persons file on her had been disposed of. Was that merely an instance of traditional Reich paranoia, mounting a cover-up to conceal an official mistake? To avoid any stain on the glamorous reputation of Strength Through Joy, which was right up there with the Luftwaffe as a source of Nazi pride? Or was it something more?

'I did ask a few questions, Erich. I got a journalist contact of mine to make some enquiries at the police station, and I saw him the other day to follow it up. But so far there's not much ...' She decided in the circumstances a lie couldn't hurt. 'Obviously they're investigating the situation.'

'Good. Because I was meaning to tell you, she left some things.'

He sat up and felt for the satchel at his side.

'Remember I said Ada was a fan of yours? And she had a complete collection of the Ufa stars series? Well, the last time I saw her, when she said she had to go off for a few minutes, she asked me to look after her belongings.'

Out of the satchel he drew a silk scarf, patterned with green and blue rhombuses which contained within them the interlocking double C of Chanel – and a large book.

'She left this scarf.'

'It's lovely.'

Clara examined it closely, looking at the hand-stitching and the rolled edges, wondering what kind of young woman came by an expensive silk Chanel scarf.

'And this. I tried to give them back, but when I went back to her cabin all her stuff was gone and the place had been cleaned. So I thought I'd look after them for her. I mean, I don't want anyone to think I was stealing. I would have given them back.'

'Of course you would.'

'But if you're going to be finding out about it, perhaps you should have them. They could help the police investigation. Here.'

He tucked the scarf into Clara's bag and opened the gilt and scarlet album. Clara turned the pages dutifully.

'You're Number 37.'

She smiled briefly. That made sense. Everyone in Germany had a number.

Erich reached over and pointed Clara out to herself. It was a wistful shot of herself gazing skywards as Gretchen, the part she had played the previous year in *The Pilot's Wife*. She recalled so clearly the day it had been taken. It had been easy to look sad, because she had just heard of the death of a Luftwaffe pilot, Arno Strauss, who had become a friend. Indeed it was a miracle she wasn't crying.

'I remember that day.'

'Ada said she was a fan of yours. I'm sure she'd be glad that you have it. Will it help the investigation, do you think?'

'It might. You never know.'

A bank of cloud passed over the sun and the bathers on the beach gave a collective shiver. Faces turned as one to the sky and bodies tensed, assessing whether it was a passing chill or if the darkened sky meant this long spell of fine weather was finally breaking.

'Fancy a Wurstsemmel?'

Erich nodded and Clara headed back up the beach towards the concrete parade where a line of booths sold beer and snacks and ice creams. Queuing for a couple of sausage rolls she glanced around her and as she did, the feeling came, the one she knew so well, that said someone was watching her. She had no idea how she knew it, yet she recognized pursuit the way a wild animal recognizes the presence of a predator. It was as if some current in the air – not sound or smell but something infinitely lighter, driven along the same particles, like a pheromone, alerted her to danger. She looked about carefully, studying the faces of the people around her, and that was when she noticed it. The man whom she had seen buying the *Völkischer Beobachter* at a newspaper kiosk earlier – the one who had glanced at her legs. He was there again, standing with his back to her as he chatted to the girl behind the counter. There was something wrong about him, but what could it be? He was in his thirties, with a sharp-planed face, steel-rimmed spectacles and wiry hair, wearing shirt sleeves and braces, and a jacket dangling over his arm. He had a deep tan but there was no sign of sand on his trousers or his lace-up shoes. What kind of man came to the beach in office clothes? As he handed over his change, tucked the paper beneath his arm and sauntered off down the parade, Clara realized what it was that disturbed her. It was the newspaper. No matter how exciting the news from the continent, what man bought two copies of the *Völkischer Beobachter* on the same day?

Alarm washed over her. Everything she had feared since that day

in Sabine's salon was confirmed. Max Brandt was right. There was
a shadow after her and she had finally set eyes on him. As the
metallic taste of anxiety rose within her, she walked slowly back
to Erich on the beach, gave him his sausage roll and said, 'It's getting cold now. I think it's time to leave.'

They took the S-Bahn back to Friedrichstrasse. Clara chose the
seat in the corner with a view of the entire carriage and Erich,
buoyed by his swim, sprawled across the seat, chatting constantly.
Clara stared out of the window, trying to filter out his conversation while she worked out what the newspaper man might signify.
The glimmering reflection of the window afforded her a good
view of the other inhabitants of the carriage, most of them fellow
day-trippers, with swimming costumes bundled into baskets and
canvas bags, but a few minutes into the ride the connecting door
of the carriage clanged and a man entered, taking up a seat as far
as possible from her own. The wire-rimmed glasses were unmistakable. Like Clara, he gazed studiously out of the window. She
glanced across at him a couple of times but his gaze didn't flicker.
It was almost a relief to have set eyes on him at last, but was he one
of Heydrich's men? Were they planning to arrest her?

At Friedrichstrasse Station she parted from Erich, made her way
down to Leipziger Strasse and crossed the green slug of the canal,
heading for Nollendorfplatz. Then she paused. There was no point
leading the tail straight to her apartment. From there she would
have no idea who was watching her, or why. And she needed to
know. She turned on her heel and headed north.

Potsdamer Platz was its usual tumult of traffic and Clara paused
on the pavement, as though waiting to cross, while she took stock.
Bicycles wove in and out of the tram tracks and pedestrians milled
around the green clock tower stationed on a patch of grass at the
centre of the square. Neon advertising slogans shouted at each
other above people's heads and late Saturday shoppers poured into
the Wertheim department store. On impulse Clara dipped into

one of the cast-iron octagonal lavatories, known as Café Achteck
in Berlin vernacular, slipped from her bag the Chanel scarf that
Erich had given her, and tied it round her hair. When she emerged
she jumped on the first tram.

The tram took her to the far east of the city, to areas she rarely
visited, past tenements with dank courtyards where hawkers and
vegetable sellers parked their carts. She glimpsed the insides of blocks
with dingy whitewash and peeling plaster, occupied by the type of
family where the men would spend their wages drinking and fighting, before coming home for a repeat performance. Disembarking,
she walked along and saw little notices everywhere pasted onto gates
and doors. *To be sold. Carpets in good condition, furniture, other items.*
Utensils. Jews who fled, or 'evacuated' in the official terminology,
were obliged to leave all their possessions behind, and these belongings, everything from china to sheets and armchairs, were itemized
and listed and passed to the state, so it made sense to sell as much as
possible before you left. How dispensable people were, Clara
thought, and how trifling the possessions they had spent a lifetime
acquiring.

She continued at a purposeful pace, neither too fast nor too
slow. She had developed a way of making herself intensely aware
of the sounds and sights around her, stilling her own thoughts to
register every sensation that occurred – the high screech of a train
running above the buildings out to the suburbs, blue electricity
flashing in the dusk. A man pouring a zinc bucket of water into
a drain, a child hauling her toy pram up some steps. At one point
a cat approached, rubbing against her legs, and she stooped to
caress it, feeling the push of its silky head in her hand. As she
stroked it, she glanced around, but there was nothing behind her,
no one out of the ordinary, no figure slipping from the edges of
her vision like a shadow.

On the corner of Knaackstrasse she stopped in a café, choosing
a table in the way that Leo had taught her – halfway along the
room with her back to the wall and clear sight of the exits – and

ordered a pot of coffee. The window afforded a view across a wide intersection, and as she watched the people and the traffic going past, another phrase of Leo's came into her head.

Examine the territory.

It was a lesson he had drawn from birdwatching. Most people see only a fraction of what they look at – a few outstanding features of a street or a room. They see what they think they will see, but the spy must look for what she is not expected to see. Like the dappled feathers of a bird that have been designed through eons of evolution to blend precisely into a tree trunk, or the speckles on its breast which match the flinty texture of a ploughed field, the spy must focus on whatever blends into the environment. Because it will be there that the anomaly lurks.

Once she started looking it was easy to see him. He was directly opposite her on the other side of the street, lost in a crowd of people at a stand-up noodle bar, with a carton of food in hand and a clear line of sight to her. She had no idea if he realized she had caught sight of him, but a truck momentarily obscured her view and when it had passed he had disappeared.

She forced herself to concentrate, staring at the menu while her mind ordered its version of events. Everything that Sabine had warned of had come true. She was being followed – almost certainly by a man sent from Heydrich – but if Heydrich suspected her of spying, why did he not simply arrest her? It must be that they were still waiting and watching, checking who she met, where she went, what she did.

She half-turned her back on the window, took out her compact and applied a layer of Velvet Red, watching the street behind her in the mirror. She repeated the action regularly over the next half hour, revealing nothing, but a man on the table next to her who, perhaps assuming her regular cosmetic checks were for his benefit, began to grin over the top of his newspaper. He was reading about the failure of the talks at Bad Godesberg and seeing her glance flicker over the headlines, he commented softly,

'We have bad luck in our leaders.'

Clara didn't answer. If the man was genuine, he would soon find himself arrested for remarks like that and if he was a plant and she responded, she would be the one to be arrested for treasonous comments. It was safer to say nothing, so she gathered together her things and left the café.

By the time she made her way back up Leipziger Strasse she was shattered. She had walked miles. Her feet hurt and she was shivering in the flimsy dress and cardigan she had worn for the beach. Approaching Potsdamer Strasse she became aware of something strange – a distant rumble in the air – and tilting her head she detected a murmuring din from the direction of Unter den Linden. The sound rose and people began to turn in its direction. It must be a motorcade of some kind, or a rally. There was nothing unusual about a rally in Berlin – they were almost a daily occurrence – yet it was odd that one should take place so late in the evening. Generally motorcades were staged in the daytime for full public display. As the shoal of people moved forward, she allowed herself to drift in their wake.

The sight that greeted her, as she rounded the corner of Wilhelmstrasse, was astonishing, even by the standards of war-ready Berlin. Rank upon rank of soldiers were marching in a seemingly endless line down the street, field guns mounted on motor trucks, followed by motorcycle outliers and heavy motor-drawn cannons. Rows of Panzers, engines roaring and tracks clattering on the asphalt, made their way up past the British Embassy to the spot where a couple of hundred people were gathered in the square outside the Reich Chancellery, its boxy frontage lit up with spotlights, swastika banners fluttering like standards at a mediaeval tournament. Burying herself in the crowd, Clara watched as the seemingly unending parade rolled by, a frank, propagandist statement of a regime readying itself for war, brashly illuminated by arc lights from an Ufa Tonwoche crew. As she tried to fix on individual soldiers' faces, white blurs against their black and field-grey tunics, the sky darkened and in deafening counterpoint squadrons of Luftwaffe planes were roaring above them, causing heads to crane upwards at the sky and a shudder to pass through the crowd like wind through the leaves of a tree. Staring at the tanks, imagining the contrast between their steel and iron and the fragility of the human lives inside them, Clara pictured the troops in their helmets and the planes overhead spreading through Germany in a vast wall of men and metal, rolling and gravitating inexorably towards war.

Generally crowds in Berlin were pumped up and feverishly excited, but this one was dejected, mutinous even, like a football crowd whose team is losing, and whose supporters begin to slink away early. If this display was designed to intimidate the populace, or prepare them for an imminent war, then it was failing miserably.

Once the troops had passed, leaving only a ghost of exhaust fumes and clatter in their wake, the crowd began to break up, but Clara remained, watching the last vestiges of the motorcade disappear down the street. Beside her, two drunks who had stumbled out of a bar to see what all the commotion was about stared openmouthed at the vanishing parade, then shook their heads. Behind them, a man with a pot of glue was posting up an advertisement for the Winterhilfswerk, the winter relief charity. It was the usual kind of picture, little children at their mother's knee and a slogan reading,

No one will feel hunger or cold.

'So even that's verboten now,' quipped one drunk.

The poster-painter ignored him.

'Call it relief?' added his friend. 'The only people relieved are us and we only get relieved of our money.'

A few people around them exchanged glances, as if daring each other to say something, but no one had the inclination and within minutes everyone had drifted away.

Chapter Thirty

A rattle at Clara's door revealed a small girl with a red bucket and a tray of Nazi Party lapel pins. Every Sunday householders could expect callers asking for a 'voluntary' contribution to Party funds. They would have the names of every occupant of an apartment block, and beside each name, the sums that they had given on previous occasions. Often the sheet of paper would be proffered so that you could compare how much you gave in comparison with your neighbours. The youth leaders chose Sunday for these collections because it meant the children would be too busy to attend church. Christianity was not approved of – Erich had earnestly advised Clara in the past that Christ was a Jew – and now only a trickle of elderly people attended services while children were sent on marches, or collecting missions. Yet the strange thing was, Clara thought, that their earnest, shining-eyed insistence on the HJ gospel, and their unrelenting commitment to proselytizing it, was exactly the same as those missionaries who once used to knock on apartment doors, Bible in hand, in an effort to save your eternal soul.

On that day the girl's tray held small round wooden pins of the Reichsmütterdienst, formed in the shape of an alpine flower. Clara picked one up, gave a mark for it, and watched the child move on to the next door to rouse Herr Engel.

Nerves had dulled her appetite, so after drinking a quick cup of tea – black because she had forgotten to buy milk – Clara headed out. In the streets, sandbags had been piled up, and a couple of children were playing with one that had split, scooping handfuls of it into their own little fortresses. The railings alongside had been removed, for melting down into aeroplanes.

The city was at its most beautiful that day – the trees were flushed with gold and the first autumnal edge had entered the air – but beneath Berlin's distinctive smell of buses and trams, asphalt and pine, there was another scent now – the smell of fear. It was pressed into the walls and trapped in the streets, lurking behind the impassive faces. It was there, although everything was doing its best to look normal. Even though the Ku'damm still hummed with the bustle of people out on a Sunday stroll, girls window-shopping the smart stores, ancient men with cracked leathery faces and fur rugs over their knees, sipping steaming coffee with pursed lips, sparrows bobbing on and off the tables, bicycle bells ringing and Zoo station rearing like a great botanical greenhouse behind them. It was there in Clara herself, who forced herself to walk at the same, unhurried pace as the Sunday strollers, hoping that yesterday's shadow had not resumed his task.

As she walked, Clara thought about the message she had sent to London Films and calculated what she had achieved in the past couple of weeks. She had done what they asked her to do. She had got close to Eva Braun, and even rescued her from suicide. She had learned that Hitler was intemperate, liable to wage war at any moment, but other than that, she had no valuable detail. Now she was about to be drawn into a plot against Hitler staged by Germans themselves. What would the men back in London make of that?

Clausewitzstrasse was a tree-lined street leading off the smartest end of the Ku'damm in Charlottenburg. The expensive, nineteenth-century buildings with their white stucco faces and mahogany-panelled halls housed doctors and lawyers, many of

them Jewish, judging by the Meyers and Grossmanns on the brass
nameplates by the bell which Clara rang. At the top of the block
a curtain twitched at a window.

Max Brandt opened the door, but he was no longer the passionate, seductive figure who had wooed her with oysters and
champagne in his Munich hotel room. His eyes were bloodshot as
if he hadn't slept and a bluish tinge of stubble darkened his cheeks.
He wore a crumpled, open-necked shirt and braces and smelt of
alcohol and cigarette smoke. For a moment he hesitated and she
thought he would embrace her, but instead he waved her inside to
the drawing room where a man in immaculate field-grey uniform
was standing in the centre of the room.

'Ulrich Welzer. Clara Vine.'

Welzer stiffened with Prussian instinct and clicked his heels. He
must have been around forty, with features finely chiselled by generations of Prussian breeding and a wave of immaculate blond hair.

'Ulrich wanted to meet you briefly.'

Welzer grasped Clara's hand and fixed her with a penetrating
stare. She could sense him taking her in, his eyes sweeping over her
cotton blouse and tweed skirt, noting the cut of her hair and the
colour of her eyes. He even glanced down at her shoes – black
leather T-bar – and then up again to the silver locket at her throat.
She had the impression that he was committing every part of her
to memory and she returned his gaze unwaveringly.

'All too briefly, I'm afraid, Fräulein Vine,' he spoke with precise,
upper-class diction. 'I'm due to drive out to the country for lunch
with my mother today, and she will not look kindly on me if I'm
late. But believe me when I say, I am very pleased to make your
acquaintance.'

'And I yours.'

'Ulrich works at the Abwehr, with Colonel Oster,' said Brandt.

Clara frowned, uncomprehendingly.

'I'm sorry, Clara. We've been up half the night talking. I forgot
that you know nothing of this. I'll explain.'

'And perhaps we can make a better acquaintance when this enterprise is over,' said Welzer gallantly. 'I have seen many of your films, Fräulein Vine. In happier times. I would far prefer to discuss movies than army manoeuvres.'

With a nod at Brandt, he crossed to the door and was gone.

'Did I interrupt something?'

'He just wanted to get a good look at you. So he'll recognize you when he sees you again.'

He turned on the wireless – an act which had become automatic for any Berliner planning a private conversation. It was one of the 'People's' sets, the Volksempfänger, which were universally dubbed Goebbels' Snout. A blast of dance music drifted out.

'In England they have a record label called His Master's Voice. I suppose the Goebbels' Snout must be Our Master's Voice.'

The orchestra was playing a sweet, lyrical ballad called *Adolf Hitler's Lieblingsblume* which was wildly popular just then. Adolf Hitler's favourite flower. It had the tendency, once heard, to embed itself in the listener's mind for hours.

'High on steep cliffs blooms a flower,
To which the Chancellor turns his thoughts.
Adolf Hitler's favourite flower
Is the simple Edelweiss.'

Brandt listened for a moment.

'Do you like this one?'

'No. It's dreadful.'

'You're wrong, my dear. It's brilliant. Goebbels thought of it. Adolf Hitler's favourite flower. Hitler doesn't give a damn about flowers of course, I know for a fact, but Goebbels thinks of everything. Whatever else you say about him, Goebbels is a tailor. He tailors people to be the way he wants them. Sit down or take a look around while I fix you some coffee.'

Clara walked slowly round the apartment. It was luxuriously

equipped, the antique furniture burnished and gleaming, the walls covered in paintings she could tell were valuable; an engraving of a hare, a still life of flowers, and one of a dead partridge. Another wall was devoted to bookcases and the floor was covered in deep Persian rugs. A bronze copy of the Brandenburg Gate's quadriga stood on the mantelpiece and there was a low Chinese lacquered table piled with more books. In the corner, a cabinet of burled walnut was clustered with bottles – brandy, cognac, vodka – and a cocktail shaker, and above it hung watercolours of a German lake. Behind the radio on a chest of drawers was a photograph of two small boys in sailor suits, accompanied by a young woman in white lace, whose dark curls and shy smile marked her out as Brandt's mother. Beside it was a glass bottle containing a ship in full rig spreading its sails. Clara bent down to inspect the meticulous modelling of the decks and the steelwork. Tiny passengers could be seen on deck and through the windows of the cabins. Like all German products, it was engineered to a high standard, a perfectly reproduced nineteenth-century sailing ship, correct in every detail.

Brandt returned with two cups of steaming coffee. It was the real thing, Clara could tell from its aroma. He flung himself down onto the sofa and spread his arms across the back.

'That's my mother you were looking at. I miss her every day. Do you miss yours?'

'It's been more than ten years, but yes, I do.'

'Were you alike?'

'Physically very much, and I think in some aspects of character too. But my mother kept her cards close to her chest and that meant I never felt I knew her properly. The reason I came to Berlin originally was because I wanted to feel closer to her and understand the country she'd grown up in but . . .' Clara scratched a pensive fingernail along the sofa's arm, 'though I miss my mother, it sounds wrong, but I feel angry at her too.'

'For dying?'

'I've never told anyone this, but her death left me feeling abandoned. That's monstrous of course to my dear mother, but her dying when I was sixteen left me with a sense that you can't ever rely on anyone. Or that anyone you do love will desert you. And in some ways, that's become true in my life.'

Brandt was gazing at her fixedly.

'It will only be true if you allow it to be. You can protect yourself from love, Clara, or you can take a chance and risk being hurt.' He touched her hand fleetingly. 'And everything I know about you tells me you're brave enough to take risks.'

She blinked and turned away, fixing her attention on the ship in the bottle.

'It's a beautiful thing, isn't it? My father was in the Navy and he made that ship for me. I loved it as a child – it symbolized the idea that one day I might escape.'

'You mean travel?'

'Travel, certainly. But escape too. It's why I joined the Foreign Service – the idea of other countries was always appealing to me, no matter how much I loved my own. I never wanted to be tied down by national boundaries. But now, I suppose, is no time to be talking about travel . . .' He leant forward grave-faced, suddenly businesslike. 'Things are moving fast. There's no time to lose.'

Clara replaced her coffee untouched, and sat attentively.

'Remember when we last talked I told you that it was crucial for us that Chamberlain takes a strong stand against Hitler's threats to the Sudetenland? So that Germans understand their Führer is a warmonger? Well Chamberlain's back in London and it seems Hitler has no intention of backing down from his plans. Welzer has just informed me that Hitler has secretly moved his troops into attack formation along the Czech border. The resistance has decided it's now or never.'

A chill ran down her spine.

'What does that mean?'

'It means I need to give you a little more information about our plans. This has been a long time in the preparation. A few weeks ago Ludwig Beck, the Chief of Staff, resigned as a Wehrmacht officer in protest at Hitler's plans to take Czechoslovakia by force. Since then, an entire provisional government has been drawn up. Under the plan, Beck will be regent in the post-Hitler regime. The plotters will arrest and try Hitler. They've compiled a file of Hitler's crimes and will prosecute him in a people's court. They've lined up a neurologist to testify that he's insane and they've found that he and his parents are descended from a line of highly psychotic people. The plot goes right up to Canaris, the head of the Abwehr.'

'Canaris? You mean German Military Intelligence is behind a plot to oust Hitler?' She stared at him, trying to grasp the magnitude of the endeavour.

'Canaris has all the files on the Nazi leaders, he knows everything, but it's too risky for him to play a leading part, so he's promoted a young colonel to be his deputy, Colonel Hans Oster. Oster is a Christian. He hates the SS. He's obsessed with getting rid of Hitler, so he will mastermind the coup.'

'How will it happen?'

'They've been planning this for a long time. They have a string of safe houses around the Reich Chancellery, stashed with arms and ammunition. The aim is to occupy the government quarter, take over the government communication centres and neutralize the Gestapo and the SS. The Gestapo has camouflaged its buildings well – they're mainly quite innocuous outposts but Arthur Nebe, the Gestapo's head of criminal investigation, has provided a map of all the Gestapo bases in Berlin. Count von Helldorf, the head of the Berlin police, is also involved.'

Canaris? Arthur Nebe? And the head of the Berlin police? Clara was stunned at the level of the people involved.

'The idea is, if we raid the Gestapo, SD and SS offices, we should turn up enough evidence to try all the key players and provide legitimacy for the coup to the rest of the world. At the same time we'll have a ready-made list of names and addresses of Gestapo informers to be rounded up and arrested.'

He stubbed out his cigarette, and immediately lit another.

'They've decided that tomorrow's the time to strike.'

'Tomorrow!'

'It has to be. The country must be on the brink of war before a coup like this could succeed. That's the only circumstance in which army officers could be persuaded to rise up against Hitler. Only a lunatic would underestimate the force he exerts on the minds of the people. The only way they will accept their Führer's arrest is as an alternative to dragging us into a senseless war. And it looks very much as though that is what Hitler has in mind.'

'So what will happen?'

'Captain Friedrich Heinz, a colleague of Oster's, has a commando unit of twenty men who will assemble at dawn at army headquarters in Bendlerstrasse. They will be issued with grenades and guns with instructions to take the Chancellery by force. The commander of the Berlin military district, General von Witzleben, will be escorted to the Chancellery by a unit of thirty active army officers to perform the arrest of Hitler.'

Clara thought of the impenetrable wall of black-suited SS who formed around the Führer at all times.

'But surely Hitler's protected by his own bodyguard. They'll die before they give him up.'

'The Leibstandarte Adolf Hitler consists of thirty-nine men and three officers. They are all specially selected and personally approved by the Führer himself. Only twelve are on duty at any moment. There is one security guard at the main entrance of Wilhelmstrasse 78, and one at Hitler's residence at number 77. There are other armed guards around the Chancellery and special security officers who work at reception. They look like ordinary reception officers but they are trained to recognize people of interest. Potential assassins. However, that number of guards is not an overwhelming security force. A commando raid of twenty would certainly be able to overcome them.'

'And what then?'

'The 23rd infantry division is based in Potsdam. They will be ordered to march on Berlin and occupy all key ministries, radio stations, police, Gestapo and SS installations. They'll seize Himmler, Goering and Goebbels. We will need to occupy all the transport and communication centres in Berlin. For the purposes of this operation Oster's codename is Uncle Whitsun. Hitler is Emil, the Reich Chancellory is Mount Olympus.'

Brandt's eyes rested on her, tender and probing, and suddenly he clattered the cup down on its saucer and got to his feet.

'Forget this coffee.'

He strode over to the decanter and filled a glass, gave it a squirt of soda and turned to face her.

'This is where you come in.'

Until this moment, Clara was too astonished by the details of the plot to question why she herself was there but though she remained entirely still, she felt a pulse of alarm at the confirmation that her role in this audacious attempt had already been decided.

'How exactly?'

'The coup is timed for eleven o'clock. We have a civil servant from the Foreign Ministry who will unlock the double doors of the Chancellery from the inside so we can get to Hitler's quarters. Welzer will be inside already, but he's leading a squad of men who will come through the private entrance to the Reich Chancellery. You probably didn't know about the private entrance.'

Clara recalled Eva Braun's comment. *I have to go in and out through a private entrance, in case anyone sees me.*

'Eva Braun mentioned it.'

'It's a side door that barely anyone knows about. It was put in in 1935, at the same time that they built the bunker under the ballroom. It's accessed through a concealed door in the ballroom

wall. You go down some steps but instead of entering the shelter, you turn right, up another flight of steps, and the door
is there. It opens onto the Chancellery garden. From there,
there's an entrance onto the Wilhelmstrasse, just between the
Agriculture Ministry and the old Presidential palace. It was
put in place in case Hitler ever needed to make a quick exit. Very
few people know about it and it's always kept locked. Only a
few people have the key and one of them is Fräulein Braun. We
need you to go to the Chancellery in the morning and find a
pretext to encourage Fräulein Braun to open the entrance.
Although preferably you'll obtain the key from her and do it
yourself.'

'What if she's not in?'

'She will be. They arrived in the Führer's train last night. You
need to be at the main entrance of the Chancellery at ten o'clock
and say you're visiting Fräulein Braun.'

'And if I find her? What then?'

'Get the key from her and take it down to the entrance. Make
sure the door is unlocked by eleven o'clock. Then leave. Nothing
else.'

His attitude had changed now. He was no longer protective, but
intensely focused.

'What will happen to Eva?'

'Initially, she'll be arrested.'

'And then what will they do with her?'

'Precisely what the Nazis do with their enemies. Shoot her,
most probably.'

Clara recoiled. Eva was a twenty-six-year-old woman, as girlish as the perfume she wore – violets and vanilla shot through with
a touch of steel and self-pity. She was privy to the secrets of a
monstrous dictator. But did she deserve to die for it? *A bit of a butterfly.* That was how she described herself. Who broke a butterfly
on a wheel? Observing her hesitation, Brandt came to sit beside
her.

'It's the only way, Clara. This is no time for sentimentality.'

'It's not sentimentality. Eva Braun's guilty of no crime. You can't visit the sins of the men on their women, not when the women are as naïve and gullible as Eva is. She isn't part of what he does.'

'She's part of his game.'

'But life's not a game. It's not like chess. It's not all about black and white. There are grey figures too.'

He took her hands and gazed at her searchingly.

'There's no room for grey figures now. You're either for us or against us. These people would kill you at the drop of a hat. In fact you'd be lucky if they killed you straight off. If you are going to be able to fight them, you need to be able to kill too.'

'You and I are fighting for a state that upholds the rule of law. A state that doesn't execute people without trial. Promise me, Max, if you have any influence, you'll prevent them shooting her. Don't let her come to harm.'

He rose abruptly and walked back to the cocktail table, where he helped himself to another draught of whisky and stood for a moment, gazing down at Clausewitzstrasse below. Then he turned.

'All right. I understand. In fact, I agree with you. We should never stoop to the level of these gangsters. I give you my word. You'll need this.'

He felt in his inside pocket and passed her a tightly folded piece of flimsy tracing paper, the size of a playing card.

'What is it?'

'A floor plan of the Chancellery. I've marked the location of the private entrance and of Eva Braun's room.'

Clara took out a bullet-shaped gold tube of Elizabeth Arden Velvet Red lipstick from her bag.

'What are you doing?'

'It's almost finished, unfortunately.' She folded the paper and rolled it tightly. 'And like everything else now, there's a shortage of it.'

She inserted the paper into the empty tube.

'I am being followed, Max. You warned me, and yesterday I saw the man for myself. He tailed me halfway around the city before I managed to lose him. If I'm arrested, I don't want to have a floor plan of the Reich Chancellery in my hand. This is not ideal, but it'll have to do.'

He smiled as she returned the lipstick to her bag.

'You're right. They'd have to be very thorough to check a woman's lipstick.'

'What if we don't succeed?'

For the first time a flash of fear crossed his face and she felt a corresponding spark of fear leap inside her.

'Our people have been driving around Berlin, seeking out escape routes through gardens and across rooftops, just in case things turn nasty. I would advise you to think very carefully about a route yourself. And perhaps a place to stay, if you can't go home.'

He reached over and touched her cheek. His gaze was serious and intense.

'There's still time, you know, if you don't want to take the risk, to say. No one would blame you.'

'I do. I'll do it.'

'Be brave, darling Clara. It's better to have tried and failed, than not try at all.'

On the Ku'damm, the last vestiges of warmth had gone and worry whipped the streets like a dry wind. As Clara threaded through the crowds the weight of the huge secret she possessed pressed down on her. By this time tomorrow, if all went well, the horror that engulfed everyone in Germany could be over and the arrests and persecution would come to an end. She passed a cabinet housing the latest editions of *Der Stürmer*, which on that day, as so often, bore the banner headline *Germany Awake! The Jews are our Misfortune*, and she imagined Steffi Schaeffer's daughter Nina kicking it until it shattered – and then kicking in every *Stürmer* cabinet in Berlin so that a crystal carpet of glass would spill across the street. The graffiti and Party slogans would be washed away, along with the fear and apprehension in people's eyes. The Hitler Youth would disband and she could make a visit to England with Erich. She would take him to see the sights – the Houses of Parliament, a play in the West End. She would introduce him to her family. It would be a fresh beginning. Germany would awake, as if from a bad dream.

Back in her apartment she took out the flimsy floor plan of the Reich Chancellery that Brandt had given her and pored over it, trying to fix the route from Eva Braun's bedroom to the private entrance in her brain. Along the corridor, turn left, down two flights of stairs, cross the ballroom to a door in the panelling three quarters of the way along the right-hand wall and then through an underground corridor to the private entrance. She ran and reran the route in her head. Something about it reminded her of one of those Greek myths Leo used to talk about – Ariadne, she thought it was, who used a piece of string to find a way out of the maze. Suddenly she was no longer able to stem the tides of memory and gave in to wondering what Leo was doing back in England. Was he in an office somewhere, or digging an air-raid shelter in his garden? Trying on a gas mask? Might he even, at that moment, be wondering about her?

She shook her head. She needed to stop thinking like that. Leo was in the past, she was not Ariadne and she had nothing to rely on except her memory. Fortunately her memory rarely let her down.

Eventually, when she was satisfied that she had imprinted the twists and turns of the Reich Chancellery interior into her brain, she took the map to the stove in the kitchen, added some charcoal and watched the flames leap up and consume it.

Then she made herself some toast and black tea, put a Bach symphony on the record player and twiddled the dials of her radio until she found the BBC, keeping the volume set to low and craning her ear against the set. Through the ether came a sepulchral voice, at once solemn and regretful, like a professional undertaker. The Prime Minister Neville Chamberlain was broadcasting to the British Empire.

'*How horrible, fantastic, incredible it is that we should be digging trenches and trying on gas masks here because of a quarrel in a faraway country between people of whom we know nothing.*'

His polite curate's voice ran on, incapable of believing any ill of other human beings. '*I realize vividly how Herr Hitler feels that he must champion other Germans. He told me privately that after the Sudeten German question is settled, that is the end of Germany's territorial claims in Europe.*'

How gullible he was! Could he honestly believe that Hitler had no intention of going further?

Mr Chamberlain wanted Britain to know that he would not rush to war for the sake of the Czech nation.

'*However much we may sympathize with a small nation confronted by a big and powerful neighbour, we cannot in all circumstances undertake to involve the whole British Empire in war simply on her account. War is a fearful thing and we must be very clear before we embark on it.*'

Clara felt the sour taste of dismay. If Chamberlain wanted to signal to Hitler that there would be no British opposition to his seizure of the Sudetenland, he could not have done it more clearly.

Eventually, she took a bath, trying to relax, and lay resolutely in bed, waiting for sleep to come and sweep her into oblivion. She was longing for the next day to dawn, and dreading it at the same time. There were just hours to go before Brandt, Oster and his men breached the Reich Chancellery and arrested Hitler. In safe houses strung like an invisible noose across the city, men were preparing for the dawn, rehearsing their movements, making last-minute checks before they slept. Knowing that the next day held the difference between a new start, or arrest and certain death. Clara, too, needed sleep if she was to keep her wits about her, but sleep took a long time to come, and when it did it was torn by fractured dreams, of Leo and Ariadne and herself, following the floor plan of the Reich Chancellery like a maze, trying to find the way out.

Chapter Thirty-one

Rosa waited until lunch hour, when the Führerin had left, and felt in her pocket again for the card she had kept there.

Rupert Allingham
Bureau Chief
The Daily Chronicle
Kochstrasse, 50
Berlin-Kreuzberg

She had liked the English journalist. Apart from their brief exchange she knew nothing at all about Herr Allingham, but the Führerin had been much taken with him, perhaps because of his handsome blond looks, and he was a journalist, which gave Rosa a kind of fellow feeling. Moreover, he was the only person in Berlin – apart from August Gerlach – who had shown the slightest interest in what she had experienced.

Despite the fact that it was a weekday, there was a dejected air on the streets. The newsstands carried reports of the latest atrocities perpetrated against Germans in the Sudetenland. People seemed to avert their eyes as they walked, as though seeking to insulate themselves from the world and all the bad news it contained. But no matter what was happening beyond the country's borders, in

Berlin Hitler's building jag continued unalloyed. As Rosa skirted around the rubble of a construction site, she looked down at the card in her hand to check the address once more.

The newspaper district in Kreuzberg was familiar from her days of tramping around, applying for journalistic jobs. The small grid of streets housed the offices of the hundreds of titles, from the giant Ullstein and Mosse publishers, which had now been certified as Jewish enterprises, to the Scherl publishing empire, as well as the offices of countless printing companies and photographic agencies. For a long time Rosa had deliberately avoided this part of town, but the sight of Mosse House, Erich Mendelsohn's striking, modernist building which housed the *Berliner Tageblatt*, sent a fresh thrill through her. With its sensuous curves of aluminium and glass, as though a spaceship had landed in the midst of the city, it seemed like a taste of the future, even if the *Tageblatt* itself, hated by Goebbels, was rapidly becoming part of the past. Mosse House was so much more exciting than Angriff House, the dour headquarters of the Nazi propaganda sheet, with its billowing black banner outside. To Rosa it seemed that everything about the district, with reporters rushing through revolving doors, motorbikes arriving with the latest copy and photographers carrying cans of film, pulsated with life.

She found Rupert Allingham at his desk, eating a bread roll and a couple of sausages. When she opened the glass-fronted door he looked up eagerly, as though he was expecting someone else, but when he saw it was her, his face fell. His eyes were bloodshot and his face speckled with stubble and she sensed he had no recollection of her at all. She flourished his card to jog his memory.

'Thank you for seeing me, Herr Allingham. I feel a bit of a fool. Taking up your time when you could be doing something more important.'

'Not at all.'

He gestured towards a chair, and she had to brush a little cigarette ash from the worn plush before sitting down. The office was nothing like any of the places Rosa had visited in her pilgrimage around the newspaper district. It was far dingier and more chaotic. It contained only two chairs, a cheap-looking desk and a filing cabinet sagging half open like a broken jaw, spilling its contents. A tower of yellowing papers was stacked precariously against the wall, beneath a calendar featuring Brandenburg Scenes tilting drunkenly, and manila files of cuttings were piled everywhere. The mantelpiece was stacked with cards and invitations, several deep, and in a bookcase to one side she noticed books by authors she was sure had been ruled degenerate.

He gave the décor a desultory wave.

'I'm afraid my office assistant has left me to get married. She seemed to think her husband required her presence more than I did. Hence,' he nodded weakly at the chaos, 'all this. Entropy, I think Mr Einstein called it, though I doubt even he could make sense of what I find in these papers. Do you read many newspapers? You wouldn't believe how many I have to plough through, though frankly I prefer the arts pages. They're so much less depressing, especially since our far-sighted Propaganda Minister banned negative reviews. However, if you know any fine young woman who would enjoy running a newspaper office, let me know, won't you?'

'I will.'

'Though God knows how long I'll be here for. If Winstanley proves awkward, I might be off to Prague. Damn.'

He flicked away the trail of ash that Rosa had already noticed down the tweedy lapel of his suit.

'Savile Row, though you wouldn't know it.'

Rosa smiled nervously. She had no idea what Savile Row was, but she could see that the suit, though decrepit, was beautifully cut.

'I've given up sending my clothes to the cleaners. They're always out of laundry soap, and once they go I never know if I'll see them again. But then I suppose that's a common problem in this city. Unexplained disappearances.'

This rambling discourse, which seemed to be directed at himself as much as at her, was interrupted by a spasm of coughing sounding like a motorcycle engine that had failed to start, and once he had finished Rupert reached across for a cigarette, tilted his chair back and regarded Rosa quizzically.

'So. The lady from the Führerin's office. I hope your boss hasn't sent you to check up on me.'

'Of course not.'

'Not trying to get me to one of her charity events?'

'I don't think so.'

'I wish I had something to offer you but ...' He tilted the sausage carton towards her. 'We're all out of coffee. And I don't suppose you fancy a brandy?'

She shook her head.

'It's a little early, perhaps, but I won't tell if you don't.'

'Really. No. I'm fine.'

Falteringly she began.

'When you visited our office the other day, you asked me about the cruise ship I was on this summer. The *Wilhelm Gustloff*. You asked if I enjoyed it, and I told you I didn't. But I want to explain to someone why it was. You see ...' she shuffled closer in her chair, 'something happened on that ship, and I saw it, but the Captain informed me that if I told a single soul, I would never be permitted on a KdF cruise again. I would probably lose my job too. So I did nothing.'

Rupert's posture remained languid but his blue eyes were alive with interest. He flicked a pen between his fingers as she talked.

'Something happened, you say.'

'Yes. A bad thing. And I think something should be done about it.'

It was the second time in the last couple of weeks that a woman had sat in front of Rupert with that expression of earnest appeal on her face. He no longer knew what to do about the missing Ada Freitag, but there was something endearing about this young woman. She reminded him of a bird, a mistle thrush perhaps, with her beaky nose and freckles and self-effacing air. Absently, he began cleaning the barrel of his pen with the silk lining of his tie.

'It's been weeks, and I can't stop thinking about it. I've decided I just have to tell someone. Who do you think I should tell?'

'Why don't you start with me?'

'Do you mean that?'

'Certainly.'

She fumbled in her bag and brought out a leather notebook, with a handwritten label that read *Observations*.

'I took some notes. Would you mind if I read them to you first?'

Rupert winced. The world was teetering on a knife edge and here he was contemplating a story about a girl who had fallen from, or been bumped off, a cruise ship belonging to the Nazis' much loved Strength Through Joy. Was he out of his mind? He could practically see Winstanley's face crumpling in distaste. That bland sneer. Those prim Methodist eyes behind their pebble glasses, roving over Rupert's suit, calculating precisely how many drinks he had sunk at lunchtime.

The thought of it only encouraged him.

'Please. Go ahead.'

Chapter Thirty-two

For a second, when she woke, Clara opened her eyes slightly, letting the soft grey dawn seep into her soul. Then she sat bolt upright. The apartment was awash with pale morning light. From outside came the customary rattle of shops running up their shutters, trams beginning to clatter and footsteps of pedestrians disembarking at Nollendorfplatz. Everywhere people were waking, dressing and preparing for another, ordinary working day, with no hint of the events that were shortly to unfold. Across Berlin, the raiding party would have been issued with their arms and grenades, ammunition would have been loaded into automatic weapons and final preparations for the coup put in place. She imagined the click of guns quietly loading in rooms and apartments around the Reich Chancellery, the shuffling of boots, the final cigarettes and the last nervous coughs among the plotters while Hitler and Eva Braun slept on unawares.

Her head was throbbing from tension and lack of sleep. She went into the bathroom, blinked in the harsh light at the washed-out face staring back at her from the mirror, then swallowed a couple of aspirin. She dressed quickly in a burgundy wool skirt and jacket, a look that felt smart but unostentatious, and made herself up more fully than usual, in case some form of feminine persuasion was needed, brushing a hint of rouge across the apple of her cheeks and applying a quick spritz of *Soir de Paris*. Neat pearl earrings and her silver locket at her throat. Picking up her coat, she checked the pockets in a reflex action for anything that might incriminate her and then shut the door behind her.

At precisely two minutes to ten she was crossing Wilhelmplatz, past the Kaiserhof Hotel, and facing the Wilhelmstrasse entrance to the Reich Chancellery, a blaze of banners spilt like scarlet ink across its sombre limestone façade. She paused at the U-Bahn entrance next to a kiosk, pretending to consult that morning's edition of the *Berliner Tageblatt*, while she battled back the stage fright that threatened to overwhelm her. She was aghast at the magnitude of what she was about to do. Fear that the plot might go wrong, or that she herself might be arrested or killed, moored her to the spot. She repeated her plans over to herself in her head, the way she used to rehearse her lines when she was standing in the wings during a play. *Go directly to Eva Braun's room. Obtain the key. Open the private door beneath the ballroom and exit through the Chancellery garden.*

Here, so close to the seat of power, the tension in the air was palpable. In front of the enormous double doors cars were already drawing up at the front steps, disgorging Wehrmacht officers, foreign diplomats and their entourages. Ministers and Party officials were passing through with a reflex Hitler salute to the waiting sentries, preparing for a day of crisis meetings and military discussions. The febrile atmosphere coming from the Chancellery transmitted itself to passing pedestrians, who glanced across apprehensively as they hurried by. Even the breeze seemed nervous, chivvying the leaves along the gutters and putting the news vendor's kiosk in a flap.

The eighteenth-century Reich Chancellery, once occupied by Bismarck, was in the process of being rebuilt. Hitler hated the Wilhelmstrasse extension, declaring its dingy grey frontage fit 'only for a soap company' rather than the headquarters of a greater German Reich. He wanted a stage set of imperial majesty. A building vast enough to intimidate visitors and reduce foreign diplomats to a sense of impotence and awe. A personal office the size of a football pitch to match the dimensions of his ego. Therefore all the buildings on the northern side of Voss Strasse had been demolished to make way for a monumental, modernist block designed by Albert Speer, with a courtyard and ionic columns hung with iron lanterns and a gigantic golden eagle. Six thousand workers had laboured day and night for a year. The enormity of the enterprise was clearly visible, rising from the last vestiges of scaffolding like a great warship, its granite façade the colour of dull steel. Like everything in the Reich, it combined overwhelming ambition with a breathtaking attention to detail. Inside, an immense gallery modelled on Versailles was hung with Gobelin tapestries, beyond which stretched a Great Mosaic Hall, a kind of pagan chapel for the Nazi regime, resembling a glowing cliff of blood-red marble inlaid with glass and gold. Everything about the severe architecture and seemingly endless corridors was designed to intimidate and disorientate.

Clara crossed the street, passed through the heavy bronze doors and crossed the Ehrenhof, the Hall of Honour. The vast courtyard, flanked by stone pillars, led to a gateway, guarded by twin ten-foot bronze statues, representing the Party and the army. Clara's heels sounded on the stone flags as she made her way to the reception, where a black tunic-ed guard waited behind a glass-partitioned desk.

'I'm visiting Fräulein Braun.'

He extended a hand for her documents, then another guard leaned over. Both wore black uniforms set off by white belts and scarlet Party armbands. They must be, she recalled, the SS special guard. What had Brandt said? *They look like ordinary guards but they are trained to recognize people of interest.* She fixed her attention on the man in front of her, focusing on the gleam of his head through the shaved prickles of his scalp.

'One moment, Fräulein.'

He reached over and picked up a telephone, closing the glass partition so that she could not hear the conversation. Clara's pulse sounded so loudly in her ears she could swear it was audible. It was freezing inside the Chancellery, several degrees colder than outside, and even with a coat and woollen jacket on, she was shivering. She hoped it was not noticeable.

The guard replaced the receiver and continued to scrutinize her cards with a furrowed brow. He gave her a penetrating look.

'What is your relationship with Fräulein Braun?'

'I'm a friend.'

'Is this your first visit?'

'Here, yes.' She tried a broad smile, but the cold and the shivering made it harder.

'And what is the nature of the visit?'

A light-hearted shrug.

'What do most women do when they get together?'

The guard didn't know, or if he did, he wasn't letting on, so she added, 'We chat! We always have so much to talk about. And she likes to ask me about my films.' Was that reckless? Did it identify her as a member of the cultural élite, perhaps one of those dangerous free thinkers who might pose a danger to the Führer's innocent girlfriend? There was a glimmer of suspicion in the officer's eyes and he seemed poised to question her further, but at that moment a detachment of officers and politicians arrived up the steps, demanding his attention, and he gave Clara a nod.

'This officer will escort you.'

The second guard detached himself and strode ahead of her, leading the way across the endless polished marble floor.

It would be hard to find a greater contrast to the rustic simplicity of the Berghof than the severe classicism of the new Reich Chancellery. It was like being in a great, marble-lined cathedral to some austere god. The cavernous recesses of the hall bounced the echo of their footsteps back at them like rifle shots. They passed bronzes of athletes rippling with muscles and vases two foot high filled with chrysanthemums. Grand pianos and candelabras groaning with crystal. Everything was finished in minute detail, from the mosaic-inlaid floors, the gilded pillars, and the lintels inset with sculpture, to the wrought-iron mediaeval sconces. At the far side of the hall Clara glimpsed a lavish ballroom abutted by a winter garden, a fixture in every grand German edifice, with tropical leaves crowding the glass. She walked swiftly, hoping to offset her shivering, conscious at every second that a single, routine security inspection might mean the end of her.

Yet nothing, that day, was quite routine. Despite its impersonal size, there was no mistaking the tension that filled the chilly recesses of the Chancellery. The front hall was as crowded as the Anhalter Bahnhof at rush hour. Knots of diplomats and ministers milled in the corridors, and army officers with braided uniforms bustled swiftly past as Clara followed the guard up a wide staircase to the first floor. As they crossed the gleaming halls she craned her head curiously to see into the rooms they passed and glimpsed a dining room being set with cutlery and white napkins, and through another door an antechamber decked with crimson hangings leading to a vast entrance guarded by an SS adjutant standing on a mat to protect the marble floor from his boots and rifle butt.

At the end of the corridor a sleek group of officers stood chatting and as she approached one of them peeled away and Clara saw with a jolt that it was Ulrich Welzer. Their eyes locked for a moment and she discerned in his face an animal fear, that the plot would be discovered, and that before the day had passed they would find themselves chained in the bowels of Prinz Albrecht Strasse, before an ignominious end at the guillotine at Plötzensee Prison. Another second and he was gone.

They marched up another flight of stairs and turned right into the upper floor of the Old Chancellery. In this wing, Clara knew from the floor plan, was the Führer's private domain, where his bedroom, private study and bathroom, as well as Eva Braun's own suite, were located. Here the corridors were carpeted and the dark green wallpaper gave off the faded grandeur of an expensive hotel long past its prime. The walls were hung with dull, gold-framed still lives of fruit, half-peeled oranges or blown roses, and landscapes of valleys and village churches, inoffensive reminders of a Germanic past.

At the end of the corridor, the guard stopped sharply at a heavy wooden door and rapped.

'A visitor, Fräulein Braun.'

Eva Braun loved to dress in bold colours, and the patterned tea dress in vivid yellow and blue she wore that morning was no exception, but it was the only lively thing about her. Her face, beneath freshly bleached hair, was pale and her eyes puffy, as though she had been recently crying. She looked hardly any better than the last time Clara had seen her, slumped in her Munich sitting room with half a bottle of Vanodorm sleeping tablets inside her.

The guard clicked his heels. Eva nodded listlessly and closed the door behind Clara.

'Well. This is a surprise.'

Clara smiled warmly and took her hands. 'I'm sorry, Eva. I should probably have telephoned first. But I wanted to see how you were . . . after the other day.'

'Then I suppose I should thank you.'

Eva led the way into her quarters.

'See what I mean about this place?'

It was easy to see how this room might have suited the former president of Germany, the octogenarian Hindenburg, who had occupied it until five years ago. Everything in the décor, from the heavy, gilded oil paintings and dull curtains to the massive furniture, was eighty years out of date. It was an old man's domain, painted in heavy cream, and dominated by a giant portrait of the man himself, with baggy poached-egg eyes, handlebar moustache and chest groaning with medals. Eva's make-up and hairbrushes, scattered untidily across the Biedermeier dressing table, looked like a doll's things, and her clothes were a colourful jumble inside Hindenburg's vast wardrobe. Even her perfume smelt sweetly incongruous in that gloomy air. The bed, its clammy sheets topped with a canopy of tassled emerald damask, looked about as inviting as a funeral bier. The only thing not out of the nineteenth century was the light dance music issuing from the wireless.

Eva went over to the dresser, clicked off the wireless and took up a packet of cigarettes, pausing to light one and offering it to Clara.

She pulled a wry face. 'Sorry. I didn't mean to sound rude. Actually I'm terribly glad to have a visitor. You've no idea how awful it's been since we arrived.'

She curled up in an armchair, tucked her feet beneath her, and motioned Clara to sit in the chair beside her.

'I hate it here. He wouldn't let me bring my friend Herta, so I'm all alone. It's bad enough being in this horrible room and never seeing Wolf, but I can't even go out when I please. He says it's a difficult time and I need to be invisible. Imagine that – I can't even walk out of the door.' She pouted mutinously. 'He got his aide to tell me I had to stay in my room all day today. Cooped up all day! Because there was important political business going on. Anyone would think I was a schoolgirl sent to her bedroom. I feel like Rapunzel in the tower. I wouldn't be surprised if I died here. I tell you, I used to go to boarding school – it was a horrible Catholic place outside Munich and I loathed it – but this is far worse.'

'Perhaps you should have stayed in Munich.'

'He insisted I came. I don't know why. Because when I get here it's always the same story. I sit here waiting while my whole life slips by.' She ran her fingers through her hair defiantly.

'I've a good mind to march downstairs and start playing the piano in front of the lot of them. That would show them.'

Clara knew she would do no such thing. The fires of rebellion burned weakly in Eva, and any act of mutiny would most probably be visited on herself. No doubt that was why Hitler had brought her here – to keep an eye on her. Just in case she was tempted to have another episode with the sleeping pills.

'I worried about you, Eva. After the other day.'

'Thank you for that. I was silly. I shouldn't have. It was just that I felt so wretched.'

Cautiously, Clara probed further. 'You said you'd done something terrible. That no one would forgive you?'

Eva picked at the hem of her skirt and did not reply.

'I wonder,' said Clara. 'I mean, I think I've guessed what the problem is.'

Eva looked up, startled. 'You guessed?'

'You're pregnant, aren't you?'

For a second a jolt of horror crossed Eva Braun's features, then she laughed, a wild, hysterical laugh, which eventually caught in her throat and made her choke.

'I'm sorry . . .' She wiped her eyes as she recovered herself. 'You don't know how funny that is. Except it's not funny at all.'

'What do you mean?'

'There's something you don't know about me.' She took a deep drag of her cigarette, exhaled sideways and fixed Clara intently, calculating if she could be trusted.

'I have Mayer-Rokitansky syndrome. It means I have no womb. I was born without one. So I couldn't get pregnant if I tried.' Her voice wobbled. 'I can never have children.'

'Oh Eva, I'm so sorry.'

She sniffed and blinked away the glitter in her eyes.

'I've hardly told anyone. I take . . . you know . . . precautions like any other woman and I swore my mother to secrecy. But I love children. I adore playing with all the kids of the top men when we're up at the Berghof, which makes it so much worse.'

'Does the Führer mind?'

'He doesn't know.'

'So if he doesn't know . . .'

'Goebbels found out,' she said flatly.

'You told the Herr Doktor?'

'Are you mad? I wouldn't tell Goebbels the time of day! I've no idea how he discovered. I think perhaps Dr Morell told him. I made the mistake of consulting Dr Morell once in Munich. Odious man. Not about this – it was something else – but doctors can detect things, I suppose. Though he never manages to detect what's wrong with Wolf. Anyhow, when Goebbels found out he was utterly hateful about it.'

'What business is it of his?'

'He says every aspect of the Führer's life and image is his business. And I'm part of that.'

That sounded like Goebbels. Eva dragged a handkerchief from her sleeve and sniffed.

'Now I'm terrified that he'll tell Himmler.'

'Why would he do that?'

'It might be that Himmler has a secret on him, and he gives Himmler my secret in return.'

'Would that really matter?'

Tears gleamed on her pallid cheek like rain on wet stone.

'It would be the end of me.'

Though Clara's nerves were straining for sounds of activity in the building below, she found herself transfixed by Eva Braun's predicament. Marooned in her private misery, the Führer's girl-friend seemed entirely impervious to the world around her.

'Himmler despises any form of physical imperfection. He would tell Wolf that I was unsuitable to be the wife of the leader of the Reich. Wolf is always talking about what women are for. And what they're not for. Women are not for politics, they're not for talking at the table. They are for looking pretty and doing their best to appeal to their men. But the main thing women are for is having babies, and that's the one thing I can't do. Himmler says child-bearing is the only purpose of women. That's what he tells his SS men. Women are about safeguarding racial purity and providing the

next generation. The other day at the Berghof he told me his latest
idea is that women who can't bear children should never be allowed
to marry. And men who are married to barren women should be
permitted to divorce them immediately. What would that mean for
me and Wolf?'

Gently, Clara said, 'But you're not married to the Führer.'

'Not now. But Wolf has said he will marry me. I finally got him
to promise and he said he would after . . . well after . . .' She tailed
off.

'After what?'

She shrugged. 'After some time has passed.'

Clara checked her watch. Ten forty. Her entire body was tensed
for sounds of action. Very soon she was going to have to persuade
the unhappy girl in front of her to hand over the key to the private entrance. Suddenly she couldn't stop herself getting up,
pulling aside the heavy damask curtain and glancing out of the
window down to the Wilhelmstrasse below. Just yards from here,
in a string of secret apartments and houses, men were preparing to
launch an audacious coup. Soldiers were mustering, waiting for the
signal to strike. Officers were readying weapons and grenades.
Colonel Oster, Ulrich Welzer and Max Brandt were bracing
themselves in their uniforms, gathering the surge of courage they
needed to make their move.

She scanned the windows, looking for evidence of telescopes
trained on the Reich Chancellery, and then looked up and down
the street, searching for signs of approaching men, but there was
nothing to see.

Eva sprang up skittishly, and squeezed Clara's arm.

'Sorry I was a bit off earlier. I'm so glad you're here. It's wonderful to have company.'

'Does anyone else visit?'

'Hardly. Wolf suggested I read, but there's nothing to read here
except great tomes about . . . I don't know, Bismarck and people.
And no one ever visits me here except the girl from Ludwig

Scherk's. I had her come over a few months ago because I wanted a fragrance for Wolf and I needed her to bring some samples, and we got quite friendly. She told me some fascinating things about perfume. But even she hasn't been for a while.'

The chime of the clock outside cut into Clara's thoughts. Fifteen minutes to go. Beneath them, cars were still drawing up at the Chancellery entrance, delivering more participants to the mêlée below. The distinctive figure of the French ambassador, François-Poncet, in homburg and spotted bow tie, hurried from his car.

Eva followed her gaze as they looked down on the traffic of grey uniforms and peaked caps.

'It's busy today.'

'It seems so.'

'It's something to do with the Czech crisis. That's why he's put me in Schutzhaft.' She meant it ironically. *Schutzhaft*, 'protective custody', was the term the Gestapo used for brutal detention without trial.

'You won't tell anyone, Clara. About my problem.'

'I promise I won't.' Clara took Eva's hands in hers. 'I won't tell anyone, Eva, on one condition.'

Eva reeled away from her, shock writ large on her face. Could it be true that the woman in whom she had been confiding should now be attempting to strike a bargain? Dismay and fear clouded her eyes.

'One condition? What do you mean, Clara? I thought I could trust you!'

'You can.'

Eva's face was beginning to contort in a hysterical spasm. 'You're one of Goebbels' spies, aren't you? One of those actresses he sleeps with? You must be, you've had so many roles. They say all the most successful actresses have to sleep with him. Is that why you made friends with me? Is that why you came to the house when I'd taken the pills?'

'Of course not! Don't be silly.' Clara was soothing, desperate that Eva's raised voice might attract the attention of the guards. 'I'm not Goebbels' spy. I came to your house that day because I had a feeling.'

'People don't have feelings.'

'Some of us do.' Clara smiled. 'Don't worry, Eva. You're getting upset about nothing. I'm only asking for a little thing. Just between women. You remember that Sturmbannführer I was talking about?'

Eva's face relaxed.

'Steinbrecher? The one who's sweet on you?'

'That's him. Well, I noticed him in the lobby downstairs. And to be honest, it's a bit awkward.' She gave a wry smile. 'I don't want to encounter him again. For personal reasons.' She paused to let the feminine implications sink in. 'And I remember you saying you use a private entrance to the Reich Chancellery.'

'That's right. I have to. In case anyone sees me.' She pulled a face. 'In case Magda Goebbels or that bitch Emmy Goering or any of the other wives discover that little Miss No Private Life is in town.'

'So would you mind if I borrowed the key?'

Eva frowned.

'Are you sure? The entrance is rather awkward to find. You have to cross the ballroom and find a door set into the panelling, but I can't show you the way. I don't dare. Wolf has absolutely banned me from leaving this room.'

Clara shook her head, the route to the private entrance seared into her mind.

'Don't worry. I can always ask.'

'No! You mustn't do that! The private entrance is confidential. Only a very few people know it exists. Hardly anyone has a key. If you said you were going there it would cause all sorts of fuss. They'd probably arrest you. It's a security issue.'

'I'll be very discreet.'

Eva frowned at her doubtfully, then shrugged.

'OK. It's a door set into the panelling exactly two thirds of the way down on the left-hand side of the ballroom. There's no handle, because that would spoil the line. You have to know exactly which panel it is and push it. Then it leads out into the garden. You can borrow the key. I'm not going anywhere today. You must drop it back in later though. Mark it for me and seal the envelope tight and leave it with the guard at reception.'

Clara wondered what the next hour would bring for Eva Braun. Arrest, almost certainly. And terror. Perhaps pain. She felt a stab of guilt at her part in the young woman's fate, but reminded herself of Steffi Schaeffer and her daughter Nina, and everyone else who had suffered or was suffering under the regime of Eva's beloved Wolf.

'I promise.'

'Don't bother to promise. I've learned not to believe anyone's promises.'

Nonetheless, she gave Clara the key and allowed her to slip out of the door.

Clara moved swiftly along the corridor, her footsteps drowned in the deep carpet. The floor plan seared into her mind told her that she needed to pass the library and descend two floors by the main staircase, then turn left and thread back through the ballroom. The key weighed in her pocket as she forced herself to slow down. By her reckoning she had precisely two minutes to find the door and open it. Even now, the infantry would be making their way from Potsdam and the Chief of Staff would be escorted from the Bendlerstrasse to arrest Hitler himself.

She descended the first set of stairs and saw, immediately opposite, a sentry guarding a door framed by a pair of caryatids. On the sleeve of his black uniform was embroidered in silver 'Adolf Hitler', identifying him as a select *Leibstandarte* bodyguard. As he stiffened she felt fear pushing against the inside of her skin like something alive, but he didn't challenge her so she passed quickly along the corridor until she reached the second set of stairs. As she stood at the top of the steps, she became aware of a level of frenetic activity, like a hive which has been stirred, an angry mixture of adrenaline and excitement that transmitted itself through the air. All around the marble hall were echoing voices, slamming doors, the sound of telephones ringing in distant rooms.

She crossed the cavernous hall with confidence, making for the corridor that led northwards, towards the ballroom. Suddenly, from up ahead came the sound of hurrying footsteps and she saw a group of officers approaching, at their centre the figures of Goering and Ribbentrop.

Fighting an immediate urge to retreat, Clara attempted to slow her racing heart. What if she was recognized? It could not be more terrifying to enter Hades and meet the god of the underworld, than to encounter Ribbentrop, the man who suspected her of spying, in the nerve centre of the Nazi regime. Yet the men were advancing, occupying the entire width of the corridor, their conversation a harsh jangle which resounded off the marble walls. There was no chance that she could avoid them. Clara froze, hearing her own heartbeat, hard and heavy in her chest as a piece of iron.

Forcing herself to remain calm, she opened the door immediately beside her and stepped inside.

The room was dominated by an enormous table, set as if for a meeting, with paper pads, ink, blotters and ashtrays. Each chair was decorated with an eagle and swastika on its back and around the walls a library of sorts was ranged. This must be the cabinet room. The place where Hitler's cabinet met to debate, in the days when there was still any semblance of debate about the Führer's aggressive plans.

The air seemed to solidify, making it hard to breathe, and Clara reminded herself that she had every excuse to be in the Chancellery. Eva Braun would vouch for her presence. She was making a friendly visit. It was all perfectly plausible. But for what possible reason would a casual friend feel the need to hide in the cabinet room?

The footsteps halted outside the half-opened door and from her vantage point Clara could see a slice of Goering, his vast bulk swathed in Luftwaffe grey, his huge feet in polished shoes, and beside him Ribbentrop, with his back to her. The swell of voices grew louder. They were talking about war. What could they mean?

It dawned on her that they must be intending to enter that room. Every fibre in her body froze, except for the tiny muscle next to her left eye, which flickered its alarm. Against every possible rule she had come out with no real cover story, other than the one she had spun for Eva about not wanting to bump into an old boyfriend, and how likely was anyone else to fall for that?

As she shrank behind the door, it was clear that Goering and Ribbentrop were having an argument. She strained to hear the substance of the conversation, but caught only occasional phrases: *'Luftwaffe power is entirely inadequate to destroy London'* and then a little later, *'There's no money for war.'*

Suddenly, Goering's voice rose to a bellow, and he shouted,

'You're a warmonger and a criminal fool, Ribbentrop. I know what war is, and I don't want to go through it again! I tell you, if war breaks out, you can sit beside me in the first bomber!'

His footsteps strode off down the corridor, forcing his followers to keep up. Ribbentrop, too, marched away. Clara realized that she had been holding her breath and let it out in a great sigh.

Checking her watch again, she knew that she needed to reach the private entrance now, or the raiding party waiting for access would be halted in the garden. But as soon as she entered the ballroom, she saw it would not be as easy as she had imagined.

The ballroom was a relatively recent addition – created to accommodate the increasing numbers of visitors invited for receptions. It was hung with grand chandeliers and the walls were clean and white as an iced wedding cake. Great pillars of blood red marble flanked each side of the room and in between the pillars was a blank of ivory panelling, perfectly regular, stretching the length of the room. The door was, Eva said, set two thirds of the way down on the left. Or was it three quarters? The panelling looked as smooth and untrammelled as a sheet of snow. Forcing herself to concentrate, Clara made her eye sweep the length of the wall, searching for anything that might stand out. It took several scans before she saw it. A slightly thicker panel, with the shadow of a dark slit at the top. She crossed the room quickly, pushed it, and a door opened.

The contrast between the ballroom she had just left and the corridor she found herself in could not be more stark. It was pitch dark and icy cold. The trademark cast-iron wall sconces that Hitler favoured in his nostalgia for some mediaeval Germanic past were unlit, and there was no sign of any light switch in the wall. The brickwork was as damp as a dungeon and the sour smell of wet concrete hung in the air. Fumbling along, she almost tripped when she reached the first in the flight of ten steps that led steeply down towards a heavy steel door. That had to be the air-raid shelter. Turning blindly right, she fumbled for a second door, and grappled in the dark until she found a chill steel handle and with her fingers located the keyhole.

She turned the key and walked up another ten steps into the light.

Clara must have passed the Reich Chancellery in Wilhelmstrasse a hundred times, yet it was still a revelation to find several acres of garden behind its walls. The garden was designed on the same monumental scale as the Chancellery itself, more of a park than a garden, with spacious lawns bisected by gravelled paths and rose beds running the length of the block from Wilhelmstrasse right through to Hermann Goering Strasse. On the far side a barracks had been built to house Hitler's personal guard and flanking the terrace were two giant bronze horses. Directly opposite them, facing Hitler's study, was an orangery – more of a small glass palace in reality – dedicated to the cultivation of the Führer's vegetables. The only actual gardening going on was being performed by a young man about a hundred metres away, hoeing a bed of roses around the base of an ornamental pool. Of the raiding party, there was no sign.

Slipping the key back in her pocket, Clara stepped into the garden, leaving the door ajar. She had not thought properly what she should do at this point. She had simply assumed that Welzer's party of soldiers would be ready and waiting for her. Instead, it now looked like she would need to find the exit Brandt had talked of, that led onto the Wilhelmstrasse.

She threaded along a gravel walk skirting the back of the old presidential palace, directly beneath what she knew was Hitler's bedroom and private study. She compelled herself to walk calmly, as though she had every reason to be strolling in Hitler's private garden on a busy weekday morning. God forbid she should encounter the Führer himself, hands clasped behind his back, in his habitual stroll. She scanned the surrounding area, nerves jangling, until she detected, at the far side of the garden, a sentry emerging from the guardhouse with a black dog tugging against his tight leash, his long pink tongue lolling. He had not noticed her, and the pair seemed to be heading away from her, but how long would it be before that dog scented her presence, and alerted its owner to a stranger?

Eventually, at the end of the palace wall she saw it, a narrow aperture that formed a claustrophobic alley, barely two feet wide, running along the side of the Agricultural Ministry building. It extended more than a hundred feet between the two buildings, culminating in a wrought-iron gate. She passed along and pushed the gate open, to find herself back in the bustle of pedestrians and traffic on the Wilhelmstrasse.

She hesitated as the sounds of an ordinary weekday morning rose up around her, and glanced swiftly down the street, scanning for any signal that could indicate the approach of troops. At that moment a man exited the bronze double doors of the Chancellery to her right and marched purposefully towards her.

Ulrich Welzer's chiselled face was an impenetrable mask. Fear was coming off him like an electric current as he came up close to Clara, avoiding her eyes.

'Thank God,' he muttered, under his breath.

She glanced behind him in bewilderment.

'What's going on?'

The words escaped his mouth like a gasp. 'It's all off.'

'Has something happened?'

Suddenly his face shuttered, and a movement behind Clara drew her attention. She turned her head to see another uniform approaching and it took less than a second to recognize the razor-blade cheekbones and the aquiline profile. The mathematically slicked fair threads sitting above a face that was not so much horse-like as lupine. Obergruppenführer Reinhard Heydrich.

Fear insinuated itself, trailing down her spine, turning her insides liquid, as Heydrich's narrow eyes ranged over her.

'Well? Don't keep us all waiting, Colonel Welzer. Has something happened?'

Welzer seemed to jerk himself from paralysis to click his heels and give a knife-sharp salute.

'Wonderful news, Herr Obergruppenführer! News has come from Britain that Chamberlain has agreed to fly to Germany. Herr Mussolini wants Hitler to postpone mobilization for twenty-four hours and the Führer has agreed. The British ambassador Nevile Henderson has just arrived at the Reich Chancellery and the word is that the conference will be held tomorrow morning in Munich. The Führer is heading down to meet Mussolini tonight.'

'To Munich?' Heydrich queried, his face alive with calculating tension, his eyes already scanning the Chancellery doors.

'Herr Mussolini won't come to Berlin. The Führer will leave from the Anhalter Bahnhof within hours.'

Heydrich swivelled and marched off towards the Chancellery without a word. Welzer turned stiffly to Clara.

'And now I should let you leave, Fräulein.' He held her gaze. 'It's indeed wonderful news, isn't it?'

'Yes,' she repeated numbly. 'Wonderful news.'

Chapter Thirty-three

When Clara closed the door of her apartment behind her and looked at herself in the mirror a ghost stared back at her. Her lips were bloodless and as a delayed reaction to the tension, a violent shaking ran through her body.

So Chamberlain was making an eleventh-hour trip to dissuade Hitler from military action. How could he be so blind as to believe that Hitler posed no further threat to Europe? If only there was some kind of documentary proof of Hitler's ambitions. Something that could prove beyond question what he was planning.

Inside her pocket the key to the Reich Chancellery private entrance weighed ominously. How long would it be before Eva Braun guilelessly mentioned that she had given away her key to the private door? And even if she didn't, what would happen when some part of the plot was rumbled and everyone who had been in the Reich Chancellery that day was arrested and interrogated? Clara thought anxiously of Max and prayed that he was lying low somewhere, keeping all traces of his involvement well hidden.

She paced around the apartment with jittery limbs, unable to settle. She knew it was only a matter of time before the actions of that morning caught up with her. It could be days, but it might only be hours. Her only hope was that in the rush to board the Führer's special train to Munich, Eva would be too busy to worry about the key. Too busy joyfully packing up her clothes and perfume samples, delighted to escape her Berlin prison. The thought of Eva's perfume samples recalled something else – a remark which had been hammering at the doors of her mind since she heard it. Eva Braun's comment about her only acquaintance in Berlin. *The girl from Ludwig Scherk's.*

Scherk's was one of the biggest cosmetic companies in Berlin. Everything about it was successful, even its headquarters – a red-brick modernist building in Steglitz – had won a clutch of architectural prizes. Advertisements for bestselling Scherk products like Arabian Nights perfume, a concoction of sandalwood and amber, or the Mystikum powder compact, could be found in every glossy magazine. But its cosmetics weren't limited to women. Scherk's Tarr pomade was Goebbels' favourite and according to Magda, in one of her periodic fits of jealousy, he had selected an especially pretty salesgirl to bring his personalized supplies to the Propaganda Ministry. Could that be a coincidence, or might Goebbels have recommended his own salesgirl to Eva? Clara was prepared to take a bet on it. What better way to spy on the Führer's girlfriend than to have a young woman befriend her and report back, with all the snippets of gossip and the confidences that involved?

This was Eva's life. Spied on from every quarter. Unable to bear children for her Führer. Befriended on all sides by people who would happily betray her.

Clara went over to her desk and took up the bottle of *Black Roses* that Eva Braun had made for her, inhaling the deep, voluptuous scent. Perfume was Eva's small act of mutiny against a lover who hated cosmetics of any kind, but it was nothing to the real dissent that existed beneath the surface of this country. All over Germany people were carrying out their own individual acts of resistance against the regime, from the Munich citizens who skirted round the alley to avoid having to salute the Feldherrnhalle, to Helga Schmidt who had loved repeating jokes about the Führer until she was silenced, and even little Nina Schaeffer kicking down the cabinets of *Der Stürmer*. But what did any of those acts of defiance amount to, when even men like Admiral Canaris, the head of the Abwehr, and Count von Helldorf, the chief of police, had failed to unseat Hitler? All resistance was destined to be crushed like flowers in the path of a Panzer tank.

If Hitler was to be stopped, it would have to come from further afield. From England or France. From the men at their desks in Whitehall that Guy Hamilton had spoken of, with their calm assumption that Clara would carry out whatever task they asked of her, no matter what risk to her personal safety.

'*It's what you do, isn't it?*'

Instantly her thoughts turned to the meeting she had set up for the following day. If London Films had found her message in the *Chronicle* and read it correctly, the contact should be waiting at the Siegessäule at 6.45 p.m. to hear the results of her encounter with Eva Braun. Yet what would Clara be able to tell them? Apart from the fact that Eva had tried to kill herself and was unable to have children and was more interested in the affairs of film stars than in her lover's aggressive intentions in Europe.

A knock on the door caused her to freeze. Had a security check identified her as a visitor to the Reich Chancellery? Had Eva already mentioned that the actress Clara Vine had borrowed her private key? It seemed she was about to find out.

She opened the door to find the lean figure of Herr Engel, rimless glasses glinting, and a smile on his smooth, professional thin-lipped face. Faint layers of baroque music, which Clara recognized as Telemann's piano suite in A, issued from his opened door. He cast a curious glance round what he could see of her room.

'I hope I wasn't interrupting.'

She wedged herself in the doorway, to block his view.

'Did you want something?'

He looked slightly taken aback at her hostility.

'I thought I should let you know. Some visitors called for you.'

'Visitors? Did they say what they wanted?'

'I didn't think it was my business to ask.' A small wince of elaboration. 'I think they may have been policemen.'

'Oh? Did they say so?'

'No.'

'Then what gave you that impression?'

'Just something about them.'

Lowering his voice, as if by instinct, he bent towards her.

'Forgive me, Fräulein Vine, for presuming, but I said you were out. I explained you were probably away filming and I wasn't sure when you would return, but I advised them not to bother coming back for the next few days.'

Why had Herr Engel said that? He had seen her only the previous evening.

'I said if I saw you I'd let you know someone had called. I asked if they wanted to leave a message, but they said it wouldn't be necessary.'

Clara heart plummeted within her, but she endeavoured to maintain a tone of polite curiosity.

'So when exactly was this?'

He frowned. 'It must have been about ten this morning.'

Ten o'clock? That was impossible. It was before she had even set foot in the Chancellery. An hour before the coup attempt. How could the Gestapo have predicted her involvement?

'Are you sure?'

'Yes, I'm sure. I know because I was listening to the wireless. I would normally be at work, but my rounds don't start today until one.'

'Your rounds?'

'I'm a doctor.'

'A doctor?' she repeated dumbly.

'Yes. I'm Doktor Engel actually. I work in the children's department of the Charité.'

Looking at the gaunt figure with his apologetic smile, she realized that she had been entirely mistaken in Herr Engel. She had taken the thin-lipped, severe-looking stranger for an informer, and assumed that his arrival in the neighbouring apartment was just another hazard to be watched for, when instead he was a doctor who had fobbed off the policemen who called, who worked with children, who played Telemann on his gramophone, and gave every indication of being on her side.

Relief, and the stress of the day, came together, and she felt tears spring to her eyes. Politely, he looked away.

'Are you all right, Fräulein Vine?'

'Yes. Of course. I've been working a lot recently. I'm tired.'

'Don't let me disturb you then. I simply wanted to let you know.'

'Thank you Herr – Doktor – Engel. I'm very grateful.'

'Not at all. Just being a good neighbour. Any time.'

He smiled kindly, and disappeared. That was the thing about Berlin. Everyone was playing a part, but it was impossible sometimes to know what part they were playing.

Chapter Thirty-four

At Tempelhof airport, Dansey's man hauled his brown leather valise into the back of the cab and gave directions to an address in Wilmersdorf.

The flight from London had been full of worried faces. In the rapid ebb and flow of diplomats to Berlin in recent days, it was easy to arrive relatively unremarked. There had been no attempt to check his credentials as he made his way past the border guards, and he had no concern that he would be followed or taken as anything other than one more international bureaucrat, attempting to solve the insoluble puzzle that Hitler had set them.

Travelling through the English countryside on his way to the airport, he had seen the last of the summer ebbing away. From out of the train window he had noticed a couple picnicking on a tartan rug, a farmer and his sheepdog, and two boys up a tree, scrumping for apples, in scenes of such utter ordinariness that the idea of nation states readying themselves for mass conflict seemed quite fantastical. Even in town, there were sunbathers on deckchairs in Green Park, queues for the Test Match and a full programme at the Albert Hall.

Now, as his cab approached Berlin Mitte, he gazed hungrily out of the window. It was extraordinary being back here, as though Time had folded in on itself. These streets had once seemed as

familiar to him as his own skin, littered with remembered incidents. Berlin had entered and become part of him, its parks and
buildings and pavements grey as damp newsprint beneath the gun-
metal German sky. He marvelled again at the enormity of the
scarlet banners, pinioned to the giant stands erected along Unter
den Linden and draped, with operatic grandeur, between the
arches of the Brandenburg Gate. Pariser Platz was populated by
gleaming, patent leather crows with white helmets, strutting their
path through the square as if they owned it. As the cab passed
Wilhelmstrasse he glanced down it to see a fleet of Mercedes, sleek
and ominous as a shoal of sharks, making their way accompanied
by motorcycle outriders, and in an instant he remembered the
faces of women turning towards Hitler when he passed, like flowers to a dark sun.

Berlin was so different, and visually at least, so much more
glamorous than the London he had just left. More clean and
modern than his Georgian terrace in Bloomsbury where the
houses stood like shoulders perpetually braced. Or the anonymous
Edwardian mansion block in Victoria that he now frequented in
working hours, and the dingy warren of the offices on the top
floor of Bush House in the Aldwych, serviced by a rattling cage
lift. Londoners greeted the prospect of war with weary endurance.
Every morning, standing on the Underground platform in a
whoosh of warm air, he would join the crowd shuffling into the
carriage, then opening their newspapers with anxious faces as the
train hurtled them onwards into the darkness.

The previous weekend he had been at a friend's house in
Wiltshire and at dinner an argument had been started up by
another guest, a bold young man who claimed that the British
could not afford another war. They weren't militarily prepared for
one and besides, Hitler was no more than a school bully. He had
tried not to respond. With immense forbearance, he had left the
room as soon as possible and gone into the garden for a smoke.
Only it wasn't forbearance, he realized, once the calming nicotine

had entered his veins and the evening air had cooled him. It was weariness. Exhaustion even, for what was to come, and a good dash of fear.

He had a couple of reasons for being back in Berlin. There were new contacts who needed sounding out, a man with an import-export business and reliable routes to Switzerland and a car salesman from Charlottenburg who might prove useful. He was also preparing to perform a little handholding, because a recent, disastrous arrest had shaken a lot of people, worried that their entire network might be compromised.

But really, there was only one reason on his mind.

As the cab edged round the southern fringe of the Tiergarten, heading for the Ku'damm, memories ambushed him again, as they so often did, and one memory in particular. A minotaur memory, hiding in the labyrinthine coils of his brain, that emerged when he was least expecting it. Anything might trigger it – a line of poetry, a snatch of women's perfume. It was an image that had sustained him for years, one he ran over and over in his mind the way a pilgrim polishes the image of a saint, and sometimes he frightened himself that the act of thinking might wear it out, so that like the features of an icon it would be gradually erased.

It was her face. The subtle poetry of her face. Where others might see calm, he saw a bright tension, like a lute string soundlessly vibrating. She was so alert to the world and its nuances, it was as though there were some register only she could hear. Sometimes it expressed itself as abstraction, the kind of air that led children to be chastized for daydreaming, which he was sure must have happened to her as a young girl, but really it was a deep, instinctive connection to the world around her – the kind an animal needs to survive in the wild. She had the unpredictable quality of a wild creature too, like a rare bird that might fly off without warning.

He liked to re-imagine her minutely, as though drawing her from top to toe; the slender legs, with their slight tracery of blue

veins across the shin bone, the concavity above her hip bones
when she lay stretched out on the bed, the line on her neck where
the sun met the skin and the network of lines around her eyes
which testified to her smile. At other times his thoughts were
drawn more by desire and the memory of it, so he thought less of
her eyes and more of her breasts pressed against his chest, her legs
wrapped around him and her body beneath him.

He remembered with painful tenderness the last time he'd seen
her. Coming behind her and encircling her waist with his arms,
feeling her slight, instinctive tilt towards him. The warm, com-
plicated smell of her and her hair, like spilled flowers, on the pillow
beside him. Then, when he left, her face framed in the pure
northern light that poured in from the window and her wave,
blurring into the distance.

Without her the world had acquired a drabber, more serious
tint, unrelieved by any intimacy. He felt as if his life had faded to
black and white. Often he watched himself as if from above, carrying on his work, trying to submerge his own little grief beneath
the sea of troubles around him. Work, and yet more work, had
been the answer.

He felt sick with anticipation.

The cab had drawn up before a tall, ornately decorated house
in Fasanenstrasse. He jumped out, and rang the bell.

Chapter Thirty-five

Berlin's Victory Column, the Siegessäule, a two-hundred-foot monument to Prussian military victory, had not escaped the mania for architectural reorganization that gripped the rest of Berlin. The tower, on its base of red granite, had been hauled up from its position in front of the Reichstag, where it had stood for more than sixty years, and relocated to the Grosser Stern roundabout at the centre of the Tiergarten. It was all part of Speer's plan to create a great alley running from east to west in the new Welthauptstadt Germania, culminating in his giant dome. No matter how grandiose Hitler's plans though, how durable the steel and granite of his monuments, they were no match for the wit of his citizens. Berliner humour was sharp enough to undercut the tallest building and the joke going round the studios was that the golden angel which stood on top of the column was the only virgin left in Berlin, because up there on her tower she was the only one safely out of Goebbels' reach.

At twenty minutes to seven Clara approached the monument quickly, her coat belted tightly and her hair bundled up beneath an anonymous grey trilby. Under one arm she carried a copy of the *Berlin Illustrated* and in her pocket was her fallback, a ticket to a KdF concert at the Volkstheater Berlin on Kantstrasse. The events of the previous day and the last-minute failure of the coup had shattered her.

That morning the conference had been held in the Führer's apartment in Prinzregentenplatz. The *Berlin Illustrated* carried pictures of Hitler, a red carpet rolling out from the steps of the Führerbau for the signing of the Munich Agreement, and Daladier, Mussolini and Chamberlain sitting on the same scarlet sofa where Hitler and Eva Braun first became lovers. They agreed that Hitler's annexation of the Sudetenland should be permitted. By 10th October Czech troops would evacuate the Sudetenland.

The photograph of Chamberlain waving the paper in the air at Heston Aerodrome had gone round the world. Chamberlain and Hitler had signed an agreement 'never to go to war again'. The way he waved it reminded her of the autograph hunters who congregated outside the Ufa Palast after a premiere, waving their books in triumph with the signature of their favourite star. Chamberlain and his wife had appeared on the balcony of Buckingham Palace with George VI and Queen Elizabeth, and outside the palace people stood ten deep, cheering. Three vanloads of flowers had been delivered to Number Ten.

Hitler's popularity had never been higher.

The Siegesäule was a popular meeting place and there were several people milling around the base of the tower, but no sign of anyone who might be from London Films. Clara scanned the faces quickly, focusing on single men who might possibly be her contact, and fixed on a man with a briefcase looking twitchy, until he was joined by a woman in a trench coat and swung his arm jubilantly round her shoulders. Although the nights were drawing in and the light falling, there were still plenty of people taking an evening constitutional with their dogs among the Tiergarten's winding gravel paths, but she identified no remotely likely candidate. No single figure, hesitating in the shadows.

As the traffic swirled round the roundabout, Clara made a couple of circuits of the monument and checked her watch. It was exactly 6.45 p.m. She would give it another few minutes and then leave. After a couple more circuits she was about to pivot away when a drift of air from behind caused her to look around.

Her heart turned over.

'Max?'

'Clara. I need to speak to you.'

The vigour had left him and he seemed tense and drained. An errant lock of hair fell down into his eyes.

'What are you doing here?'

'I might ask the same of you. I was on my way to your apartment and I saw you crossing Pariser Platz so I followed you. I hardly recognized you. Are you meeting someone?'

'It doesn't matter. Why are you here?'

'I wanted to see you. It might be the last time. Come with me.'

He drew her away, so they crossed the road and headed into the comparative shelter of the trees. Clara cast a swift glance back at the Siegessäule and decided that the contact from London Films would have to wait.

'Let's walk quickly. We need to be careful. The place is teeming with agents.'

'My God, why?'

'Heydrich's men, the SD, have an operation on this evening – they're aiming to catch a Czech agent who has a rendezvous in the Tiergarten – so all the agents have been dressed as gardeners and equipped with rakes.'

Despite herself, Clara scanned the park, looking for the blur of a face or the glint of metal under the canopy of trees. She was shocked that her own checks had been so careless. Max Brandt took her arm as they walked, leaning closely into her.

Some distance into the park, a rose garden was laid out – a souvenir of the original eighteenth-century French-style modelling of the Tiergarten – and as they passed, the pale blur of roses stood out in the gloom, their fragrance swallowed up in the chill evening air. They progressed to an avenue flanked with bronze statues of Prussian statesmen and mythological creatures.

'I don't have much time.' Brandt's tone was low and urgent. 'I need to leave Germany. The Gestapo is on my heels. I'll be given a safe berth in England, of course, just so long as I can get past the border, but they've put an alert out to arrest me on sight.' He laughed bitterly. 'They say Hitler is Europe's greatest travel agent because he has everyone on the move. That's certainly the case for me.'

Alarm cascaded through her.

'Has something leaked?'

'I'm glad for your sake, Clara, that this has nothing to do with the plot.'

'But then . . . why?'

'I have Madame Chanel to thank for my situation.'

'Chanel?'

'Remember that evening in Chanel's salon?'

'How could I forget?'

'There was a man there. You asked about him.'

Clara pictured the salon again, and tried, through the dancing couples and the dazzle of jewels, to visualize the person she had noticed there, a handsome officer with thick hair brushed back from a broad forehead and an easy smile.

'Walter Schellenberg, you said he was called.'

'SS Oberführer Walter Schellenberg. A very charming diplomatic intelligence officer. He's just been promoted actually, not that his rank is strictly relevant. It's more significant that he works in Heydrich's Sicherheitsdienst. He's Heydrich's number two. It seems Chanel reported her suspicions of me to Schellenberg and he took them back to his boss.'

'He came all the way to Paris to check you out?'

'Oh no. I was just unlucky. Schellenberg was not in Paris to expose a treacherous cultural attaché – he was on an entirely different mission. A very specific request for Coco Chanel. Heydrich had overheard Fräulein Braun talking at a dinner about her plan to create a cologne for Hitler.'

'That's right. She told me about it too. And Heydrich wanted to help?'

'How sweet you are, Clara. Heydrich's motives are never the kindly ones that people like you imagine. No, Heydrich became aware that Eva Braun had asked a young woman to bring samples of perfume into the Reich Chancellery.'

'I know about that. It was a girl from Ludwig Scherk's. I think Goebbels may have recommended her. He gets his own toiletries from Scherk's.'

'Well, Heydrich was not so sanguine. There's no motive so innocent that it can't be turned into treachery in a mind as devilish as his. He got the idea that perfume would be an ideal method of poisoning the Führer.'

'Poisoning him?'

'Exactly. What could be better? A perfume that was also a poison. Something so innocent, so intimate, yet with the power to penetrate the human dermis. Heydrich knew nothing about this young woman except that she was turning up regularly at the Reich Chancellery with samples and bottles for the Führer's mistress, so he immediately suspected a plot to kill the Führer. Extraordinary, isn't it, that he should see plots where there were none, and miss the one that was going on under his nose?'

'Is it possible to poison someone with perfume?'

'That was precisely Schellenberg's request. He was sent to ask Chanel if a perfume could also be a poison.'

Clara's mind was racing. She recalled Eva Braun's comment to her in Munich. *You'd never guess that perfume would contain strange, synthetic molecules. I mean, you can't see what's in a scent.*

'And what did Chanel say?'

'Chanel said she knew nothing about poison, but there was no better thing than perfume to get under a person's skin.'

'Did you know all about this that night in Paris?'

'No. Not until much later. It was Canaris who told me all this. Canaris' family have always been friendly with my own and I've long regarded him as a decent man. When I first heard rumours of a plan to unseat Hitler in late August I made straight for Berlin and sought him out. It turned out to be the right decision. Canaris welcomed my involvement and announced he was bringing me into the Abwehr, claiming my contacts in France would be useful to Military Intelligence, but in reality, it was so that he could afford me some protection while we made our plans. He introduced me to the officers here who were preparing the coup and that's how I got involved.'

'But this woman with the perfume? Was she really planning to poison Hitler?'

'Who knows? She was obviously planning something because Heydrich placed a man in her workplace to watch her, and he reported back her gossip. Apparently she told a workmate she had some great scheme concerning the Führer's girlfriend.'

'So why didn't Heydrich arrest her at once?'

'He would have done, but she left town in a hurry. She disappeared off on a cruise ship and hasn't been heard of since.'

'A cruise ship?'

Despite their pace, Clara almost stopped in her tracks. The invisible pattern that her mind had been searching for leapt out vividly before her, like a tapestry with its last stitch in place. She understood.

'They had this woman followed,' continued Max. 'But nothing came of it.'

Nothing came of it, because the girl from Ludwig Scherk's was Ada Freitag, the girl Erich met on the *Wilhelm Gustloff* and whose disappearance had caused him such anxiety. That was why Rupert had been warned not to pursue the story any further. It explained why the Kriminalpolizei said the missing girl should stay missing.

'I just . . .'

'What?'

Clara stopped herself. There was no point burdening Max with this knowledge. The more you knew, the more risk you ran, when Heydrich was on your tail.

'It doesn't matter. But it seems wild to imagine this woman might have been planning to poison Hitler.'

'Who knows? She had some ulterior motive, Canaris said. No one makes friends with Eva Braun for the sake of her company. You of all people should know that.'

He gave her a meaningful look, then glanced around him. They had reached the fringes of the Königsplatz, where the smoke-blackened Reichstag building, which had never been fully repaired since the fire five years previously, gleamed like a dirty fossil in the lamplight.

'As it happens, I did learn something though, that evening in Paris. Walter Schellenberg had a secondary purpose. It hasn't escaped the Nazis' notice that Chanel is supremely well connected with the British establishment. Before I met you that evening he had held a quiet talk with me. He wanted to know if I thought Chanel would be useful as a go-between for the German and English ruling classes.'

'Coco Chanel?'

'Strange, isn't it, the power of fashion? Chanel is a small woman, but her influence is enormous. She knows so many of the English ruling class – Churchill, the Duke of Westminster, perhaps even your father.'

Clara remembered the chill, appraising glance that Chanel had cast over her. Was she assessing exactly how much Clara knew, and how useful she might be to the Nazi cause?

'Now Schellenberg is planning a different kind of talk with me. And he won't be using any diplomatic charm.'

She pressed his arm closer, as if to comfort him.

'Perhaps you're worrying unduly.'

'I don't think so. I met my neighbour, Frau Hanke, in the KaDeWe food hall. She mentioned, quite casually, that she had noticed my door needed mending. I understood immediately what she meant – someone had entered my apartment when I wasn't around. It was all I needed to know; I realized at once that I can't go back there.'

The image of her own visit rose in Clara's mind. Had she been sighted visiting Max Brandt? But she pushed the thought away – angry at her selfishness when Brandt was in such immediate trouble.

'Where will you go, Max?'

'I don't know. Canaris can't help me – he's told me not even to contact him. I thought of going to my ex-wife, or my former in-laws, but it would only bring them problems and besides, I'm not sure Gisela wouldn't denounce me herself. Ulrich Welzer's elderly mother offered to hide me at her country estate, but if anyone got wind of that, it would only attract attention for Ulrich too. I need to get to Switzerland or Holland as soon as possible, but I don't know how the hell I'm going to do that. Schellenberg has supplied my name to the border points and put a watch on the stations.'

'I think . . . I might know someone who can help you.'

Steffi Schaeffer.

The idea of a half-Jewish woman helping to hide a senior diplomatic attaché, a member of the Nazi regime, from the forces of his own Party, seemed horribly illogical. But Berlin, the city where logic and rationality were once most prized, had lost sight of its philosophical heritage. Surrealism was more in vogue. And the thought of Max alone, unable even to trust his former wife, caught at her heart. If she couldn't take him in herself – which would indeed be suicidally dangerous – then she had to help him however she could.

'It's a dressmaker I know. She works out of the Scheunenviertel. Her group have safe houses all over Berlin and exit routes established. They're part of the resistance, Max. They'll help you disappear.'

'What can she do?'

'Trust her. She's helped other people.'

'And where would I find this miraculous woman?'

'Her address is Rosenthalerstrasse 31 and her name is Steffi Schaeffer.'

He gave a weary smile. 'Does she welcome in every Nazi officer who turns up at her door?'

'She'll trust you if you tell her I sent you.'

'That would be foolish of her. I'm not sure I'd want to rely on security like that.'

'Ask her how her little girl Nina is doing. Ask if she's been kicking any *Stürmer* kiosks recently. Steffi will know what that means.'

He took her hand.

'Enough of me, Clara. You must be worried too. Even if our activities have gone unremarked, you need to be thinking about your own future.'

'Don't worry about me.'

He stopped and turned to her, reaching a hand to her face.

'Why wouldn't I? This isn't the kind of ending I imagined for us.'

'So you did imagine something for us then? What did you imagine?'

'Something like this.'

He bent to kiss her and for the first time she reciprocated fully, giving in at last to the impulse she had first felt that night in Paris, leaning into him and responding with a deep, lingering embrace.

He looked at her tenderly.

'You choose your time, Clara Vine.'

'Max . . .'

He put a finger on her lips. 'Don't.' He smiled, sadly. 'You didn't want me, I know, or you would have kissed me like that before. You had the opportunity in Paris, even in Munich, but I knew there was someone else . . .'

'I'm alone, Max. There's no one.'

'Perhaps. I believe you, of course, and maybe we'll see each other again – in England, I hope. Though I still think we should have taken our chances in Paris. We might have visited the Mona Lisa and the artistic ape. We could have spent a whole day seeing the sights, and a whole night forgetting them.'

She saw the glint of a tear in his eye and to distract him she said, 'That ape – the one that makes his own drawings – sounds awfully intriguing. What on earth does he draw?'

'Ah.' Brandt recovered himself and stood upright, bracing his shoulders with a wry smile. 'Now that's an interesting question. I'm so glad you asked. It's rather sad really. This animal makes clever pictures, but he only draws one thing. He draws the bars of his own cage.'

He kissed her again and his eyes burned into hers.

'Goodbye, Clara.'

With the glimmer of a smile he walked quickly away. Ordinarily Clara would have melted swiftly back into the shadow of the trees but this time she remained in the same spot, still as the statues around her, for several minutes more. The Tiergarten might be full of agents that evening, but her heart was too full to care who might be watching.

Chapter Thirty-six

When Benno von Arent followed up on his invitation to the Künstlerklub, Clara knew better than to turn it down. The club was based in a stately villa on Skagerrak Platz. Light bloomed through the windows, and the glare of flashlights from waiting photographers dazzled the arriving guests as SS guards in rubberized capes held open umbrellas against the patter of rain. A small crowd of celebrity-spotters looked on as a line of gleaming cars curved into the driveway, their headlights slicing through the darkness, and disgorged a succession of actresses, perched on the arms of their consorts like beautiful, jewelled birds of prey. All the major actresses of the Reich were there that night – Lilian Harvey, Brigitte Horney, Kristina Söderbaum, Lil Dagover and Zarah Leander. The moguls of Hollywood were being wooed by Goebbels' own galaxy, his very own stable of stars.

Inside, the curved wooden panelling of the building, pink rosewood inlaid with mahogany, seemed to emulate the curves of the female clientele. Intricately carved mirrors reflected the soft glow of candelabra and beyond the entrance lay a winter garden, a dance floor and a beer cellar. In the corner a jazz band played and a beautifully lit aquarium was set into the lush furnishings. Waiters slid through the throng bearing trays with Sekt and bowls of nuts and olives for the men from Twentieth Century Fox, Paramount and

MGM. Gossip journalists circulated with their notebooks and bare-shouldered actresses with reddened lips swapped air-kisses. The entire scene was like Erich's cigarette card album come to life.

Clara took a glass of Sekt and pressed into the throng. Goebbels certainly knew how to hold a party. For his Olympics party two years earlier he had taken over an entire island in the Wannsee, filled the bushes with butterfly lights and spread sumptuous tables out beneath the trees. This evening he had again spared no expense. Although his new emphasis on family values obliged him to bring Magda, who was touring the room shaking hands with an expression of frigid misery more appropriate to a disaster scene than a celebrity gathering, Berlin's best-known singers and musical acts had also been summoned, and to complement the magic of the movies Goebbels had hired a real magician, Alois Kassner, the top illusionist of the day.

Clara gave a quick scan of the room and her eyes lit on a man with a humourless, pudgy face and hair shaved two inches above his ears whom she recognized as Frits Strengholt, the head of MGM. This was the man who was supposed to be sorting things out for Ursula. Quickly she scanned the throng for her friend, yet she could see no sign of her. Had Ursula's party invitation been withdrawn at Goebbels' request, or did Emmy Goering's remarks presage something more serious?

A fusillade of flashbulbs lit up the entrance of Olga Chekhova, a regally beautiful star who was one of the regime's most famous actresses. With her ivory complexion and hooded eyes heavy with kohl, she slid through the phosphorescence of the flashbulbs like a glamorous ghost. La Chekhova was half Russian and the niece of Anton Chekhov, which meant that rumours constantly circled about her Bolshevik sympathies, but Hitler was a big fan of her films and that was better than an SS bodyguard and golden Party medal for imparting a sense of security. Despite her lofty status, she had proved remarkably friendly on the shoot for *Bel Ami* in Paris that summer and now she came straight over to Clara's side.

'If I have to spend this evening listening to Hollywood producers telling me Doktor Goebbels is the greatest cultural champion the world has seen I think I'm going to scream. How are you, Clara? You're looking very lovely.'

'Olga. I wonder, have you by any chance seen Ursula Schilling?'

The diva's creamy face darkened, and instinctively she lowered her voice.

'Clara, my dear, I thought you knew. When did you last go to Babelsberg?'

'I've been in Munich. Why?'

She grimaced. 'It's all round the Ufa studios. No one can talk of anything else. Ursula Schilling was taken in for questioning a few days ago.'

Clara felt a sinking dread.

'About what?'

'She's being investigated for allegations of sleeping with a Jew.'

Clara recalled Ursula's face in the costume department at Geiselgasteig. *I would have left last year if it wasn't for . . .*

'Contrary to the Nuremberg laws, as I don't need to remind you. Maximum sentence several years in jail.'

'Who is he?'

'Quite a surprise actually. Not what you would expect at all. He's called Joachim Haber. Terrifically good-looking and a little younger than her. He's a sound engineer.'

'A sound engineer!'

'I know. Quite a surprise, isn't it? Rather an ordinary sort of fellow. He worked at the studios before the Aryanization, and since he lost his job he's been making ends meet with all sorts of low-paid electrical jobs, nothing remotely grand. They had a plan to leave Germany and settle in California, but until then he was living in an apartment out in Steglitz – when he wasn't at Ursula's home in Neubabelsberg, that is, doing all her washing and cooking. He's not at all what you'd expect for a girl like her.'

She paused, and looked at Clara musingly. 'But then people can be so mysterious, can't they? You never know what's going on underneath. And we actresses are especially good at that, I suppose.'

'Who denounced her?'

Olga shrugged. 'Her cleaner reported her, apparently. But it could have been anyone, darling, couldn't it?'

She laid a white-gloved hand on Clara's arm and that single satin touch seemed to communicate something important.

'I'm never surprised when I discover an actor has a secret, are you? We so love to be in the spotlight, but where there are spotlights, there will always be darkness too.'

Was Olga Chekhova suggesting that she knew the truth about Clara? Or that she herself had something to hide? Whichever it was, Clara knew she must end the conversation at once.

She gave Olga a quick smile and moved towards the stage where Alois Kassner was performing. She recognized him from the poster pasted outside her block in Winterfeldtstrasse. *Kassner makes a girl vanish!*

Magicians were everywhere in Berlin just then, from chancers performing the three-card trick on street corners, to celebrated variety artists on the bill at the Wintergarten. Like acrobats, contortionists, escape artists and illusionists, magicians' acts had taken over from the political songs and risqué humour of the cabarets that had been swept away in the early days of the regime. Perhaps, at a time when people were daily disappearing, it was a relief to focus on fantasy, on women who levitated and rabbits that vanished from hats. Watching a girl disappear in a wooden cabinet or a man unravel himself from chains was a reassuring distraction when escaping from a tricky situation was a subject on everyone's mind.

That evening Kassner was performing some kind of card trick. He had laid out a deck of cards in lines in front of him on a table covered in crimson velvet and was moving the cards faster than the eye could keep up with, flipping and whirring, spinning them into a hundred different positions. Clara found herself automatically attentive, the blur of flashing cards fixing in her memory with mechanical precision, and as she watched, the magician called out to her.

'Fräulein, can I ask your assistance? Would you please pick a card?'

Still abstracted by thoughts of Ursula, she complied.

'The King of diamonds. An excellent choice for a beautiful queen. Would you replace it, please?'

Clara gave the card back and watched Kassner rotate it with impossible speed around the table. She was aware of people gathering around her, trying and failing to follow its progress.

'Now could you remind me, Fräulein, which card was yours?' said Kassner, expecting her to fail. Before she could stop herself, Clara had pointed it out.

'A remarkable guess. Perhaps you would try again.'

She picked the ten of diamonds from the deck and again the cards whirred in his hands as he shuffled them around the table. Again, she managed to follow its progress and identify it with ease. Murmurs of admiration came from the people who had gathered around to watch.

'What an eye you have, Fräulein.'

'Again!' said the people looking on.

'Perhaps a different trick this time,' decreed Kassner, sensing competition. 'The lady has an excellent eye, but memory is another matter. In a moment, I will show the audience my ability to memorize an entire deck of cards in any order. Maybe,' he smiled, holding out a hand of cards to Clara, 'you would like a try at that?'

Clara was about to demur, but the sight of the cards brought back her rainy teenage holidays, when her family would while away the hours as the rain hammered down on the Cornish fields outside. One of Clara's diversions had been to memorize cards by using pictures from her own life. The Germans had a word for this memory trick, *Eselsbrücke*, literally Donkey Bridge, because it was a technique that made a mental bridge between one part of the mind and another.

'All right.'

Kassner fanned out ten cards on the velvet.

'A gentle start. I will give the lady thirty seconds to commit just ten cards to memory in order.'

Clara looked down, and saw her childhood open out before her. First came the three of clubs and she saw the three of them as children, with the queen of hearts, their mother, playing in the avenue of tall trees in their Surrey garden which resembled the ten of spades, alongside the Jack of diamonds, who looked mischievously like their dog Jip. The nine of clubs were the muddy prints of Kenneth's boots when they came in from outside. Then came the four of diamonds, four hearts shattering into jagged pieces when her mother's illness was diagnosed and the ace of spades, which was the darkness that descended over their lives.

She carried on the story in her head, until Kassner swept the cards up and fixed her with a challenging stare.

'Enough time, Fräulein?'

'The three of clubs, the Queen of hearts, the ten of spades, the Jack of diamonds, the nine of clubs, the four of diamonds, the Ace of spades, the two of diamonds, the King of clubs, the Ace of diamonds.'

A couple of people clapped, and Kassner's eyes widened.

'Bravo, Fräulein. Shall we try with a few more cards?'

Clara was about to agree, but she had glimpsed a figure out of the corner of her eye.

'I'd rather not, thank you.'

'Go on!' The people in the crowd thought she was teasing. Kassner raised an eyebrow.

'Come now. Fifteen cards this time. Surely, you could manage that?'

'Yes,' said the audience. 'Fifteen cards!'

'I couldn't possibly.'

Kassner mimed a courtly bow, and felt for something by his side.

'Thank you, then, for your participation. And perhaps you would do me the honour of accepting a ticket to my next performance?'

As Clara took the proffered envelope, a voice came in her ear.

'But you were doing so well!'

The voice was sinuous but brimming with malice, like a razor blade dipped in honey. It belonged to the scrawny, dinner jacketed figure of Joseph Goebbels.

'You have an excellent memory.'

'No better than any actress, Herr Doktor.'

'I beg to differ. And I think you are far more than an actress.'

He was exceptionally dapper that evening, in an evening suit with a camellia in the buttonhole, and his handmade, built-up patent leather shoes polished to a high shine. He dipped his head to kiss her hand. Compared with their last meeting, he was cordial, if not jubilant.

'How charming to see you again, Fräulein Vine. Don't get too thin, will you? It's not good for an actress's image.'

He seemed gleeful. As though something more than the Munich triumph was motivating him.

'I understand you were obliged to leave Munich early.'

'Unfortunately, yes.'

'No matter. As it happens, your film has been cancelled. Herr Gutmann is currently residing in Dachau.'

Clara willed herself to remain expressionless. She saw Goebbels searching her face for reaction.

'I'm sorry to hear it.'

'He was found to be consorting with undesirables.' For a moment Goebbels left the ambiguity lingering in the air as if to imply that, perhaps, Clara herself was the undesirable. Then he said,

'He's also charged with exchanging information with the

Führer's adversaries abroad. So far he's not been especially forth-coming in explaining himself, but I told them, that's just like his films! Completely unintelligible, don't you find?'

He chuckled a little at his own wit.

'Still, I'm sure they'll come up with something to make him more loquacious.'

Clara felt a deep pang of sorrow for Gutmann, and a hope that his cadaverous frame and narrow shoulders would withstand what his interrogators had to offer him.

Goebbels took a languid sip of Sekt, then added,

'Herr Gutmann introduced you to Fräulein Braun, I think?'

'She had written me a letter actually.'

'Of course. A fan letter, I'm sure. But it interested me. Why a man like that should involve himself by introducing an actress to the Führer's girlfriend. What did you make of her?'

'I thought she was charming.'

'I think so too, though many would disagree. But it's my view that your charming young penfriend has more to her than meets the eye. You know, I wonder sometimes whether the Führer is too insistent on his plan to be married to Germany. I've begun to think that Fräulein Braun might make a more satisfactory spouse in some regards. At the very least, she should receive more public recognition.'

Clara frowned. Surely this was the opposite of what Goebbels believed. The Minister removed a silver cigarette case from his jacket, offered Clara one, then lit it with his special lighter which bore Hitler's initials.

'I know what you're thinking, and indeed until quite recently, I would have agreed with you. I was the first to say that our leader should be regarded as a man with no private life. The adulation of the public stage is enough. He needs to devote himself to his destiny and so forth.' He waved his palm to indicate the platitudinous waffle the public was obliged to endure.

'Yet now I realize there's a lot to be said for the family man.

Perhaps we do need to see our Führer in human terms, as well as a great leader.'

Clara remembered what Brandt had said about Goebbels. *He's a tailor. He tailors people to be the way he wants them.* That applied to Eva Braun, as much as to Hitler himself. Looking at Goebbels' clever, calculating face, she understood precisely his motivation. If Hitler had ordered Goebbels to behave more like a family man, then shouldn't Hitler, too, be seen in more human terms? And Eva Braun was his raw material. Like some grotesque Pygmalion, Goebbels was planning to fashion Eva Braun to be the human side of Hitler.

'Remember how your British press made no mention of the touching love story between the Duke and Duchess of Windsor? What did that avail?' he mused. 'They still married, happily, but England lost a great monarch in the process. No, I think it's a shame Eva Braun needs to remain a secret.'

He tilted his head and exhaled a stream of smoke.

'Still. We all have our secrets, don't we, Fräulein Vine?'

'If you say so, Herr Doktor.'

From the direction of the band rose the plangent voice of the Marlene Dietrich classic.

Falling in love again, never wanted to, what am I to do, I can't help it.

Goebbels winced.

'We can't talk with this racket. Come with me.'

He stalked briskly across the room and opened a door which gave into a small dressing room, with a large mirror on one wall surrounded by lights, and a dressing table on which he perched, legs crossed. He gestured for Clara to close the door behind her.

'There is another matter that has been on my mind. A delicate matter.'

'Herr Doktor?'

His eyes never left her face.

'I heard that you may have been on the end of some unwanted attention.'

Clara remained impassive, waiting for him to elaborate.

'To make myself clear, I understand you've suffered some unnecessary official interest.'

'Forgive me, Herr Doktor ...'

'Don't be dense, woman. Someone's been following you.'

'I'm not sure I understand.'

He rolled his eyes, as though dealing with a starlet who was being deliberately obtuse. 'Really? Don't you? Then let me explain. I've heard that you, quite wrongly, have been the target of some official interest from the officers of the SS-Reichsführer.'

Himmler?

'What would the SS-Reichsführer want with me?'

'It's a case of misplaced innuendo. Coarse minds. It's quite revolting what filth some imaginations can conjure.'

'But I'm not sure precisely what they think ...'

'It doesn't matter *precisely what they think*. If these goons are even capable of thinking. The fact is that a rogue section of our security forces has been assembled for a quite outrageous task. They've been involved in wiretapping my hotel rooms and so on, intent on laying spurious allegations against me which could only be of help to our enemies. They've been selecting certain innocent women and following them, then inviting those women to be interviewed at the Lichterfelde Barracks. I wanted to know if you had received a visit?'

'What kind of visit?'

'An early morning one.'

Understanding was dawning on Clara with a great exhilarating rush of relief. The people who had followed her for the best part of the month – who had come to her apartment just the other day – were not Heydrich's men suspecting her of espionage at all. They were a special division of the Gestapo commissioned by Heinrich Himmler, and the crime they suspected of her was adultery. Adultery with the Minister of Propaganda. Clara almost laughed out loud. It must be the first time anyone had been relieved to be followed by the Gestapo.

'As a matter of fact, Herr Doktor, I did have a visit the other day. Two men called for me, but I was out.'

Goebbels' relief was visible.

'I'm pleased you were spared the trouble. And don't worry about a repeat visit – it won't happen. I've taken action to prevent this nonsense in the strongest possible terms. You should find yourself free from bother, but if anything does happen, I shall take it as a personal affront. I want you to contact me instantly.'

'Of course.'

His face twisted with anger. 'It's monstrous that members of the Reich Chamber of Culture should be interrogated about their every move. I, and no one else, am in charge of the lives of artists in the Reich.'

'I assure you, Herr Doktor, if I get any more calls, you'll be the first to know.'

His anger abated, he flashed his wide smile.

'You've done well, Fräulein Vine.'

He looked her up and down.

'When we first encountered you in – when was it, 1933? – we worried that your looks might be a little ... dark for a National Socialist actress. You seemed, if you'll forgive the slur, a touch non-Aryan in appearance, not to mention half-English, which is hardly something to boast about. Yet your performances have won us over.'

'Thank you, Herr Doktor.'

'And I've not forgotten that documentary you're to voice about the Frauenschaft. The film will be ready to dub at the Ufa sound studio any time now. I shall have them call you to discuss it.'

He straightened his lapels and brushed some invisible dust from his jacket, as though mentally dismissing the whole sorry matter, and started for the door.

Clara hesitated. 'Since you ask, Herr Doktor ... there is another member of the Reich Chamber of Culture who would very much benefit from your help.'

'Oh yes?'

'Ursula Schilling.'

Goebbels' eyes flickered over her, but he didn't answer.

'I think she's in great need of your protection. She's been a victim of that misplaced innuendo you talked about, and even worse, I've heard she's been arrested.'

Goebbels gave her a dyspeptic look.

'Fräulein Schilling is accused of consorting with a Jew.'

'Yet her enemies are suggesting so much more.'

Her heart was in her mouth. How had she dared to allude to Ursula's harassment by Goebbels? In the Reich Minister's scrawny face, conflicting imperatives were at war. Goebbels' hatred of Jews was competing with his fury over Himmler's interference in his affairs. Which would win out?

He rubbed his hands together and shrugged.

'I'll look into it.'

'She'd be extremely grateful.'

'As I said, I'll have a look. But I take a dim view of artists who are known to have prostituted themselves with Jews.'

'I wondered . . .'

He sighed and drummed his fingers on the table. She was trying his patience now.

'What did you wonder, Fräulein? I do have a houseful of Hollywood executives waiting for me outside.'

'That's just the thing. As it happens, Ursula Schilling has been approached to work in Hollywood and I know the Chamber of Culture is generally against our actresses leaving to work abroad at a time of national unity. Yet I wondered, perhaps, whether it might be worth making an exception in this case? The British have a saying, "Out of sight, out of mind." Maybe if Ursula had an exit visa and went to America she would be out of everyone's mind?'

He grunted.

'Perhaps you're right. The Reich would be well rid of a Jew-lover like her. Anyhow, I have to leave now – I need to be away by eleven. In such momentous times it is more vital than ever that I complete my diary. Did you know I keep a diary?'

She did. She had once, on a visit to his home, even managed to get a glimpse of it.

'The Frau Doktor mentioned it.'

'Did she? Well, I'm proud of it. I write it every evening. It's a document of immense historical value. I keep the past volumes photographed on Agfa glass plates and stored in a special underground vault at the Reichsbank because if, God forbid, war should come, they're far too valuable to be allowed to fall victim to an air raid. My diaries provide a record of my entire life and times and if fate allows me a few years for the task, I intend to edit them for the sake of future generations.'

'I'm sure your diaries would be of interest to a lot of people.'

'Exactly. It takes a certain skill to write a diary. I treat mine as a work of literary art – I like to include observations, detail and colour. It gives texture to history, I think.'

Sometimes, his ambition still amazed her. Not content with directing the thoughts of an entire nation through their newspapers and radio programmes and horoscopes, Goebbels wanted to direct posterity too. His unseen editorial hand would live on through his diary, editing history the way he wanted it.

'Some people see their diaries as a kind of snivelling receptacle for every little woe, but that never reads well. Posterity doesn't want to know about that. I always think there are some diaries that should be preserved in a vault and others that should never see the light of day.' He nodded briefly.

'I'll say goodnight.'

Clara was longing to find Rupert, but as she threaded back through the crowd there was no sign of him. He had definitely been there earlier, talking to the American journalists, but he must have gone. As she left herself, the band struck up a familiar tune, the hit song that she had heard in Paris.

'*J'attendrai, le jour et la nuit, j'attendrai toujours ton retour.*'

I shall wait for your return. Sometimes, Clara felt as though she had been waiting for something for years, yet she was still not quite sure what it was.

Rupert plucked another glass from a passing tray and leant against the bar. He had already been there for an hour and the initial effects of the alcohol were wearing off, leaving only a light nausea and the habitual sense of doom. His brain was foggier than the Spree in November and the usual brass band was marching through his head. He wished he had never come. He has missed the chance of talking to Clara. He had seen the limping figure of the Propaganda Minister approach her, and knew better than to draw attention to himself, and then he saw the two of them disappear from the room before he had had the opportunity to say what he wanted to tell her.

The news from London, that Chamberlain had capitulated to Hitler's demands over the Sudetenland, made him feel sick. He laughed to himself as he remembered Lord Halifax's faux pas on meeting Hitler at the Berghof last year – how he had taken the diminutive man in the black coat for a servant and almost handed him his coat, before realizing in the nick of time that he was the Führer of Germany. Yet now Chamberlain had mistaken the Führer in a far more fatal fashion. People in London were saying that war had been averted. Reginald Winstanley had no interest at all in Hitler's designs on eastern Europe, though it was clear to Rupert that war was more certain than ever.

He thought of his daily frustrations, the distance between what he had hoped for and what he had achieved. The things he believed in – a certain kind of Englishness, a resilience, a tendency to laugh at authority, a quiet determination of the sort that Leo possessed – what was it worth? He wished he had not asked Clara to intercede with her father now because his days in Berlin were numbered, anyone could see that.

His friend Melcher approached, accompanied by a pink-faced Obersturmbannführer with a poker up his arse.

'Hello, Rupert. Herr Freiburg here has been explaining to me how the Jews are secretly running the world.'

'I wish they would.'

The Obersturmbannführer frowned at Rupert for a moment, then stubbed out his cigarette as though grinding it into bare flesh, and turned on his immaculately polished heel.

'They'd make a better job of it than the National Socialists,' added Rupert, to his retreating back.

Melcher was regarding him with wry admiration.

'Sometimes, Allingham, I think you actually want to be on the next train out of here.'

'I have that in common with much of the population of Berlin.'

'I can't understand you. You're in on the biggest story in Europe and you give them every excuse to get rid of you.'

'Perhaps I'm just making up for our Mr Chamberlain.'

'You mean the peace-maker? Our office is full of admiration for the way Chamberlain handled those negotiations. It's just been decided that Adolf Hitler will be *Time* Magazine's Man of the Year for 1938.'

'Would that be for tearing up the Treaty of Versailles, rearming Germany to the teeth or persecuting the Jews?'

'Mostly for his handling of the Anschluss. A war of flowers, they're calling it.'

'Ah yes. Herr Hitler, the patron saint of florists,' Rupert observed. 'I suppose it wouldn't interest them to know that he also recently referred to the United States as a Jewish rubbish heap?'

'Probably not. The thing is, there are certain people in the States who would agree with that. Like those Hollywood chaps over there. They're busy patching up a Nazi-Hollywood pact. They're happy to see Jewish employees fired in their German studios. They let the German censors dictate cuts to their films in every respect. Well, almost every respect – American audiences do need a happy ending.'

'Not something that's ever troubled the Nazis.'

'And besides, Herr Hitler has promised to stop at the Sudetenland.'

'Hadn't you noticed, Melcher? Hitler doesn't keep his promises. It's only his threats he keeps.'

'You going to write that?'

'Much good it would do. Hitler could spell out his intentions in giant neon letters and hang it all the way down Friedrichstrasse and my editor would say it's a matter of debate.'

Hearing his voice in his own head like a worn-out record he paused.

'By the way, I saw Chuck Lewis earlier. I thought he'd done a bunk?'

'Ah. That was a case of *cherchez la femme*. Turns out he was due to meet some woman in Lisbon but she never arrived. Same old story.'

Rupert cocked his head towards Goebbels, who was making a grand tour of the room, bidding farewell to the female guests with hand-kisses as Magda stood by.

'How's our Minister's own love story?'

'You heard he tried to get Magda to agree to a *ménage à trois*?'

'Sounds a little Parisian. I thought we were supposed to be shunning all things French?'

'Hitler thought the same. Magda informed the Führer and now Goebbels is in the doghouse. He's furious about losing his status with his beloved boss. Apparently he's determined to do something to regain his popularity.'

'Something nasty, I assume.'

'Another attack on the Jews, probably.'

'So if Joseph unleashes one of his pogroms Magda only has herself to blame.'

'Here's another thing.'

Melcher leaned closer.

'Apparently Himmler has been taking full advantage of Goebbels' predicament. He's been compiling a list of actresses who have received advances of a sexual nature from the Propaganda Minister. His men are conducting interviews with these ladies at the Lichterfelde Barracks and getting together a dossier.'

'A *dossier*? The Reichsführer-SS is compiling a dossier against the Propaganda Minister? What for?'

'Bedtime reading for the Führer, presumably, if Goebbels puts another crippled foot wrong. Hitler hates sexual impropriety.'

'It beggars belief.'

'Oh, they're all at it. Goering hates Goebbels, Himmler despises the pair of them. It's a miracle they can focus on the international situation considering the number of internal wars they've got going on in the Party.'

'Any idea when Himmler plans to present this dossier?' Rupert asked.

'Not just yet. He's still assembling the evidence. Keeping his powder dry, and waiting for the right moment to pounce.'

Rupert shook his head.

'You have to hand it to them.'

Out of the corner of his eye, Rupert noticed Obersturmbann-führer Freiburg approaching with two guards.

'It is required for you to leave immediately.'

The guards took him under each arm and Rupert winced as he was hoisted in the air like a tailor's dummy, and half dragged, half carried into the road outside, where for the entertainment of the assembled celebrity-spotters he was unceremoniously dumped, and given a few sharp kicks in the ribs as a souvenir. He rested on the pavement for a short while until someone helped him to his feet and then he progressed down the street, declining the offers of a charming lady in a shop doorway, until the cold air sobered him up and somehow he made his way home.

Chapter Thirty-seven

The Sportpalast on Potsdamer Strasse was a great white palace of a place, built in the early years of the century with an ice rink and shops and a stadium capable of holding up to fourteen thousand people. It was a popular venue for boxing matches – the cream of society turned out for fights featuring the celebrated heavyweight Max Schmeling – as well as beer festivals, concerts and cycle races. But in the past five years it had become the venue for an even more popular form of entertainment: Nazi Party rallies. Perhaps because only the Party faithful were invited, the Hitler Youth leaders and the local Party divisions, these tended to be lively affairs, one of which had taken place just a few days ago, according to tattered remains of a flyer on the wall: *For one night only: The Führer: A Man of Peace!*

Rosa wished she had never mentioned meeting a man to her mother. Already Katrin Winter was making preparations in her head while Rosa's father had an edge of worry in his eyes when his daughter explained that she had no idea where the man lived, who his family was, or exactly what he did. But he had faith in his daughter's good sense, and besides, it was very difficult to tell a twenty-five-year-old woman whom she could and could not meet for a date at the cinema. To disguise her trepidation as she waited, Rosa watched the people around her, thinking that it might make one of her 'Observations'. There was a couple next to her, obviously married from the tone of their conversation, which was mostly an argument about their chances of ever owning a new Volkswagen car. Two elderly ladies, one large and one thin, walked past, exercising dogs that were the precise mirrors of their owners. Across the forecourt a pair of workmen were attempting to free a swastika banner that had become entangled in a streetlamp. One man held the ladder while the other lunged fruitlessly at the rope, before abandoning the attempt and leaving the banner hanging limply, like a noose. The couple next to her began laughing at the pantomime, but it still wasn't enough to distract Rosa from the meeting with August Gerlach.

She saw Gerlach before he saw her, heading across the road with a determined hunch to his shoulders, wearing the same grubby fedora and natty grey suit as before. Lost in thought, the jocular demeanour was nowhere to be seen and instead his narrow blade of a mouth was a grimace and the bristles on his jaw cast a blue shadow on his face. Rosa had a tendency to see the animal characteristics in human beings and she often privately entertained herself by attributing the appropriate creature to each person she met. Everything about August Gerlach, from his purposeful stalk, looking neither left nor right, to his lean frame and sharp nose, had a lupine quality. There was something of the wolf about August Gerlach – he had that beast's clever eyes and alert, predatory air. Yet even as she thought this, Rosa reprimanded herself for being what Susi would call immature and summoned an enthusiastic smile.

'Hello, sweetheart. Pfennig for your thoughts.'

'I was just thinking of a story.'

'A story you know, or one you made up?'

'Just something I wrote.'

Gerlach led the way to the bar area where he bought her a cup of hot chocolate and a glass of schnapps for himself. He took off his hat and looked around.

'I was here, actually, the other night. The Führer was on magnificent form. You should have heard him. He went on for hours. He's very angry about the Czechs.'

'Why are they always so hysterical at the Sportpalast?'

'Hysterical?' he sounded testy. 'Why do you say that?'

It was the word Rosa's father used. Whenever the speeches came on the radio at home, Anselm Winter would turn them off and put music on the gramophone instead, but sometimes, from another room, she would hear him listening to the Führer's shriek, when he thought no one else could hear.

'Over-excited, I suppose is what I mean.'

'There's plenty to get excited about.'

'Is there? I don't feel excited. But perhaps I don't read the papers enough.'

'Good thing.' Gerlach smiled. 'Pretty ladies shouldn't discuss politics. Anyway I'm looking forward to this movie. Grethe Weiser's a real piece of work.'

A piece of work. What did that mean?

He gave Rosa's drab, olive-green suit an appraising look. She had come straight from work, though she was wearing lipstick, and had stuck a pink carnation in her hat in honour of the occasion.

'Ever thought of letting your hair down?'

Rosa blushed. She was entirely unused to direct comments on her looks or being called a pretty lady or having a man rake his eyes over her with such merciless attention. She wasn't going to tell him that it had never occurred to her to wear her hair in anything but braids.

'Sometimes.'

'You should. Ditch the glasses too. It would suit you.'

He rattled the ice round in his glass, like a gambler rolling a dice.

'So you do that then? Think up stories?'

'Just fragments really. Impressions.'

'Clever girl.'

'I've always liked writing, you see. I used to want to be a writer, when I was younger, and I read somewhere that the place to start would be to record the details of what you see in everyday life. Even quite ordinary things. They don't have to be dramatic or important. It makes you notice more, you see, and it trains you to describe—'

'Because . . .' Gerlach interrupted, shaking his head slowly. 'It's beginning to make sense to me now. It was a story, wasn't it? Your tale about the lady on the *Wilhelm Gustloff.*'

'Not at all.'

His odd, sharp smile curled across his thin lips. 'Tell me. I can take a joke. You were just making up . . . what did you call it? . . . an impression, to impress me.'

Rosa felt the blood rush to her cheeks again, this time in agitation.

'I promise you. It definitely happened. I wouldn't lie. I wasn't trying to impress you. And I don't know why you keep asking about it.'

'Why wouldn't I? It's not every day a girl sees a murder.'

'I didn't say it was a murder.'

'Sounded that way to me. Have you changed your mind, then?'

'I know what I saw.'

'Told anyone else about it yet?'

Exasperated, her voice rose.

'Of course I haven't! I don't even want to remember it. I don't want to talk about it at all. Though I'm beginning to think I should.'

Reaching a hand across her roughly, he grabbed her, his fingernails making sharp scarlet crescents in her forearm.

'Now then, sweetheart. No need to get upset. People are listening. Don't make a scene.'

He looked about him, with an explanatory grin, then let her arm go and rubbed the bristles on his jaw.

'Forget I said anything. I shouldn't have mentioned it. How about a smoke before we go in?'

He felt in his pocket and freed a box of cigarettes, extracted one and clenched it between his lips and he felt in his other pocket for a light. And that was when Rosa froze. She had always had a good eye for detail, and the detail which caught her eye now, and made her heart race, was his matchbook. A little fold of white card with gold lettering on it.

Wilhelm Gustloff

She remembered the matchbooks that rested on the coffee tables on the ship. She had even thought of bringing one home as a memento, until circumstances had provided other, more horrible memories of her trip. But how would August Gerlach have come by those matches unless he had been on the *Wilhelm Gustloff* himself? And if he had been on the *Wilhelm Gustloff*, why was he pretending that he hadn't?

Rosa knew there might be an innocent explanation, but innocent explanations were increasingly difficult to come by. She focused her eyes on the table and took a deliberate sip of chocolate, hoping that he had not noticed anything amiss, but Gerlach had registered her alarm and was watching her, she knew it, the smoke of his cigarette pulsing like his own breath.

He leant towards her, bringing with him a pungent gust of lemon and vetiver aftershave. His eyes narrowed, as though he was squinting down the barrel of a gun.

'Anything wrong, sweetheart?'

'Nothing. I'll just pop into the ladies' before the film starts.'

'Don't be long.'

She left the café, but instead of turning left, down the steps leading to the Kino, she slipped through the foyer into a narrow tunnel and entered the Sportpalast itself. For a second she halted at the entrance and looked around at the sheer scale of it. She had been to the Sportpalast before, she and Susi had come skating here as girls, but in its deserted state the arena appeared impossibly vast.

It was silent and semi-dark like some great cathedral, with tiers of balconies rising up to the ceiling and thousands of chairs ranked expectantly before an empty dais. The walls were still decked from Hitler's speech a couple of days ago, festooned by banners reading *We follow our Führer*, garlanded with ivy wreaths and the obligatory giant eagle with outstretched wings poised above the lectern.

After a second's hesitation, she moved quickly. Even though it would be several minutes before Gerlach came to look for her, she threaded her way urgently along the stalls, making for the far end where, she guessed, there would be a side exit leading onto Pallasstrasse through which she could slip away. As she hurried she calculated what to do. She had no idea who August Gerlach was but she knew that he could find her – he *would* find her – if she didn't act fast. He might not know where she lived, but he had discovered where she worked – she was sure she had never told him – and he would seek her out. In her fright she felt curiously liberated. She realized that Gerlach had answered a question for her, a question she had not even asked herself.

Rosa hastened along Lützowstrasse, hugging the inside of the pavement, keeping close to the shade of the buildings. The street-lamps cast jagged shadows, inking in the side streets and glancing off the cobbles. A group of boys overtook her, laughing, a car blared past, and behind her she heard the rapid pacing of a man's footsteps growing closer. Seized with alarm, she looked around for somewhere to conceal herself and saw, down a side street, the entrance to a cinema.

The musty, velour-carpeted foyer was deserted. Judging by the music emerging from a curtained entrance, the programme had already begun and the ticket clerk had gone off duty. Nor was there anyone waiting behind the coat check counter, so she slipped inside the auditorium and stood at the back of the stalls in the glimmering light. The stalls were sparsely populated. Only a few people were dotted at random among the rows as the imperial blare of the Ufa Tonwoche newsreel announced another military manoeuvre. The footage showed German army cars entering the Sudetenland and the camera panned along the route, filling up the screen with smiling faces, flowers, and right-arm salutes. Children running alongside, town squares decorated with swastikas and smiling faces everywhere. The camera cut to a newsstand and the sight of it made Rosa think, yet again, of Rupert Allingham, in his office the other day, in his ash-flecked suit and tie at half mast, talking about Prague.

After she had read the report of the dead girl from her book of Observations, he had asked her why she wrote. Not presuming to confide her journalistic ambitions, she had said,

'People always want things to be neat, but I like to look at the underside of things, like . . .' she had searched for an appropriate image, 'like turning a carpet over and seeing the pattern beneath.'

Rupert's eyes had lit up, like a teacher with a good pupil.

'That's exactly what journalism is about. Untidying the things that people want tidied, looking at what other people have brushed under the carpet.'

'That's journalism?'

'Sure. A better description of journalism would be hard to find. Look at things as clearly as you can, and then write about them as clearly as you can. That's journalism. All the rest is entertainment.'

Emboldened by this discovery, she had asked,

'So what about the lady on the cruise ship? Might you be able to write about what happened to her?'

'Tell you what, you can help me write the story.'

She had stared at him, mesmerized, clutching the bag on her lap.

'Do you really mean that?'

'I do mean it, Fräulein Winter. You seem a most intelligent young woman and a punctilious writer. It's a shame you're so happily settled with the Führerin. I could do with an office assistant.'

Now, standing in the dim light of the cinema stalls, she made her decision. She would leave the Führerin's office straight away.

She would call the next morning and pretend that she was needed urgently at home, to help with her parents, and give no forwarding address. Then she would collect Hans-Otto from school with Brummer, and let him walk the dog, which was his favourite job in the world, and later she would visit the office of Herr Allingham and ask to be taken on as his assistant. In a new job, under the protection of an English journalist, she would be safe from any further attentions of Herr August Gerlach.

But before that, there was one last thing she needed to do.

In Derfflingerstrasse the offices of the Frauenschaft were deserted, but as the Führerin's assistant Rosa was allowed to keep a key on her ring for emergencies. Though she didn't dare turn on the main lights, it was easy to navigate the darkened corridor to her office and sit down at the desk, where a green-shaded lamp spilled a pool of light onto her new typewriter. Rosa sat for a moment, abstractedly chewing her nail. She had spent years in this office, at this desk, compiling figures, sorting the names and addresses of women into impersonal columns as though they were some vast mathematical exercise. Filing human beings, diligently, methodically, the way a bookkeeper files his figures or a scientist moves formulae around a board. Typing millions of bland, bureaucratic words in letters and directives and reports. And now, she realized, those bureaucratic words, those directives, that unthinking obedience to authority, were the only weapons anyone had.

Decisively she pulled the machine towards her, removed the cover, and from a wire basket beside her desk drew out a sheet of paper with the heavy Gothic letterhead of the Office of the Führerin of the Greater Reich and two sheets of carbon paper. She wound them all into the machine, and began to type.

To whom it may concern,

A medical examination has been carried out on Hans-Otto Kramer at these offices today. I am pleased to tell you that after exhaustive tests, the boy has been found to be normal in all respects and free from congenital disease. After professional consideration of the case of Hans-Otto Kramer it has been decided that no further action will be taken. Educational authorities are ordered to desist from enquiries forthwith.

An illegible squiggle.

She stamped the bottom of the paper with the official stamp of the Reichsmütterdienst Department of Infant Health, and a second, indigo stamp bearing the swastika and the eagle.

Then she typed beneath it, '*By order of Gertrud Scholtz-Klink, Reich Führerin.*'

Chapter Thirty-eight

It was past midnight by the time Clara got back to the apartment, but she was not in the least tired. The discovery that she had been shadowed by Himmler's men, and that Goebbels himself would be forestalling any further surveillance, exhilarated her, but the thoughts that were spinning round her head made it certain that there was no chance she would be able to sleep any time soon.

She sank down in her armchair with a cup of coffee. Rummaging in a pile of books for a packet of cigarettes, she encountered the album which had been left by Ada Freitag on the *Wilhelm Gustloff*. The events of the past few days had driven all thought of it from her mind.

She sat back and examined it slowly. It was a beautifully decorated album, about nine inches square, its heavy cardboard covers the same plush crimson and gilt as prestige cinema décor. Picked out in embossed, scrolly golden letters on the front was the title *Stars of the Ufa Screen* and underneath the line *Brought to you by Reetsma Cigarettes*. Inside was a page devoted to the Reetsma brand '*loved around the world for their rich sophistication*', followed by tinted photographs presented against a metallic gold background. Each page had a framed space for a single cigarette card, which was secured beneath plastic film, with a name and brief description underneath. Clara turned the pages slowly. All the faces were familiar to her, fixed in the studio's artificial glare, their smiles pearly and their skin shimmering under the lights. There was Hans Albers, Zarah Leander, Gustav Fröhlich, Emil Jannings and Kristina Söderbaum. It was like looking at a montage of her own life over the past five years, or the public side of it at least. Clara had worked with all of these actors, at some point, in a stream of mostly forgettable romantic comedies, spy capers and historical biopics, and she had enjoyed it too – the actors' talent was usually in inverse proportion to the quality of the scripts they were obliged to perform. Unconsciously she smiled as she flicked through. Everyone was there, even Ursula Schilling, pouting distantly, and on one of the last pages, a picture of Clara herself. The photograph had been taken to publicize her film the previous year with the air ace Ernst Udet, who was now head of the Luftwaffe's technical division. She examined it more closely. The picture looked both like and unlike her, dressed in a gingham dirndl, her hair braided, gazing rapt at the sky above. She marvelled at the silky shimmer of her skin. She looked for all the world a confident, happy woman, gazing expectantly into the distance, '*A flower of German womanhood*', as one of the reviews had called her. Though *Der Angriff*, more snidely, had reminded readers of her foreign blood by referring to her as an '*English rose*'.

As she looked at the card, something curious occurred to her. A spy, Leo had once told her, uses all their senses. Sight, touch, hearing, taste, and even smell. The smell of earth recently disturbed, of cooking on a man's clothes, of a gun that has been discharged, all were invisible clues that were hard to disguise. The smell she detected now was sweet and powdery, a complex mix of narcissus, violet and hyacinth which struck a chord in her memory. *Je Reviens*. The legendary perfume from the House of Worth.

Eva Braun's favourite perfume.

Peeling back the plastic and slipping the card out of its sleeve to examine it more closely, she turned it over and for an instant she was perplexed, then astonished. The back of the card was covered in fine rounded letters, minutely compressed, with a date at the top. She had seen that handwriting somewhere before.

July 5th. A red letter day. Hairdresser and seamstress. Tonight, after three weeks, I will finally see my man!

Even as she looked across to the desk it came to her. The same handwriting was on the perfume bottle that Eva Braun had given her.

She ran her fingers over the card for a while, like braille, as its implications sank in. She had in her hand the ultimate card trick. A diary hidden on cigarette cards.

That was what had distressed Eva Braun. That was what was obsessing her. It was not the fact that her infertility had been discovered, nor her fear of being abandoned by Hitler, which had provoked such suicidal despair, but the realization that the diary she had kept secretly had been stolen. Clara thought of Eva's words as she lay on the floor of her villa, sleeping pills scattered across the floor. '*It's not just that. It's something else. I can't tell you. Something awful. When I discovered, I realized I might as well be dead.*'

Eva had always kept a diary, until Bormann banned it, but diaries were a habit that was hard to get out of. Perhaps, like Goebbels, Eva's diary was a psychological necessity, a vital outlet for turbulent emotions that must otherwise be kept under wraps. And a way that everyone would know that she mattered, and that Hitler had promised to marry her.

She must have cast around for a way to keep it without being discovered, and resolved to hide it in plain sight. Everyone knew Eva was a film fan. They made jokes about it. Eva's cigarette card album went everywhere with her. The album was proof, if proof were needed, of the essential frivolity of her nature. Eva collected cigarette cards like a child, she was as star-struck as a teenager, so where better to keep her confessions until the time came to reveal them to the world? Yet Eva's diary ended up on a cruise ship in the middle of the Atlantic and the woman who stole it, Ada Freitag, was almost certainly killed for it.

That was Ada Freitag's ulterior motive. She needed to leave in a hurry not because she had any interest in poisoning the Führer, but because she had discovered Eva Braun's diary, and understood its implications. She would be planning to sell it, no doubt, only Heydrich's men had got there first. They had disposed of Ada Freitag without having any idea of the real weapon that she was carrying. It was not poison that was to damage Hitler; it was far more personal than that.

Quickly Clara went through the album, peeling back the plastic and systematically slipping out the cards. On the back of a picture of Hans Albers was an account of a day at the Berghof.

Our perfect day ended with a Western. Those cowboy films bore me stiff but Wolf loves them. He says the American conquest of the Red Indian lands is like the German search for Lebensraum.

She turned over Ursula Schilling's card.

He says the Poles are more like animals than human beings. Completely stupid and primitive, and their ruling class is degraded by lower races. They deserve extermination, not assimilation.

She skimmed quickly, the letters blurring beneath her eyes as she read through the gossip and heartache and female longing interspersed with fragments of military talk.

Wolf calls his plan the Plan Green. It starts with Czechoslovakia, and then Poland.

How many times have I heard him talk about after the war? It's always after the war. Now I don't think there will ever be an after the war. Once Himmler finds out that will be an end of me so I may as well take the initiative and end myself.

Another, on a photograph of Lída Baarová, dated July 1938.

Mimi Reiter came last night. She says she visited Wolf in his apartment and he had told her everything. She was telling me because he was too weak to tell me himself. I'm too young for him. He wants to end it. My God, I want to die.

Then Clara picked out the card with her own picture on it.

Last night Wolf said that after the war he would marry me. When is after the war, I asked? When Poland is subjugated, he explained. Very soon, Poland will cease to exist.

This more than anything was what the British government needed to see. *Poland will cease to exist.* It put the lie to any idea that Hitler would end with the Sudetenland. The people in London should know, as they cast around for an alternative to war, that the Führer's true ambition was not a small, disputed portion of southern Czechoslovakia but an entire country, and then another, in his quest for a greater Reich. Eva's diary, written so artlessly, and hidden so artfully, laid bare the mind of the Führer like nothing else.

Chapter Thirty-nine

In the corner of the Volkspark Friedrichshain, beyond the bunkers lying like open graves in the bleached grass, workers were raking dead leaves into a bonfire, as though burning the last of summer itself. The first heavy drops of rain, foreshadowing a storm, dappled the dusty pavements and the prospect of a Berlin autumn brought a chill to the bones.

As Clara walked she thought of Max and hoped that Steffi Schaeffer had managed to hide him. Berlin had become a city of the hidden. Of refugees, their jewels stitched against their skin in heavy, invisible seams, carrying their secrets close. Of U-boats, concealed in back rooms and attics, with forged papers and desperate plans, and of plotters hidden in safe houses, waiting for the moment to strike. Of food, secreted in bags, taken to those who were hiding, and of secrets concealed on cards, telling the truths that no one dared speak.

Clara, too, had attempted her own form of concealment.

That morning she had taken her copy of *Mein Kampf*, a smart edition bound in wine-red leather that had been a personal gift from the Führer to all cast members of *The Pilot's Bride* – a film he was said to have especially enjoyed. Turning to Chapter Five, *The World War*, she took a sharp knife and carved a rectangle down through the centre of the book block, then she collected the deck of cigarette cards which comprised Eva Braun's diary and placed them in the space she had created, before sticking the first page of Chapter Six down to the previous page. Looking around her apartment, wondering where to conceal the book, a moment of inspiration struck her and she slid the volume beneath the wobbly leg of her desk. A copy of *Mein Kampf* was part of the furniture in most German homes, so when one part of the furniture was being used to prop up another, what intruder would give it a second glance?

In her bag she carried a purse, identity documents and a packet of cigarettes, in one of which the tobacco had been replaced with a rolled cigarette paper bearing the next day's date. A veneer of tobacco had been reinserted at the tip. She also had her fallback, the ticket Alois Kassner had given her to his cabaret on Friedrichstrasse. As cover stories went, an invitation to the theatre from the great Kassner himself would surely dazzle the most suspicious of policemen.

Missing the meeting at the Siegessäule had been unavoidable, but the plan had always been that she could communicate through a message in the Dead Letter Box, which, Hamilton said, was checked regularly. With the Munich Agreement signed, and so many people believing war had been averted, it was more crucial than ever that the people back in London heard what Eva Braun had to say.

She slid her hand into her coat pocket, where a single card remained: the one with her own photograph on it.

Last night Wolf told me that after the war he would marry me. When is after the war, I asked. When Poland is subjugated, he explained. Very soon, Poland will cease to exist.

The Märchenbrunnen, the fairy-tale fountain, was a piece of baroque whimsy crafted for the children of Berlin in the days when family promenades on Sunday afternoons were routine and children considerably easier to enchant. Situated on the north-western end of the Volkspark and accessed through a pair of arches, it was flanked by two long stone benches and fenced off from the rest of the park by a parade of pillars. Marble versions of Rapunzel, Hansel and Gretel and others, interspersed by rabbits and stags, posed joylessly around the water as though some wintry magician had turned them to stone. The spouting tortoises, designed to issue jets of water into the air, were turned off and the tiered pools lay stagnant. Clara waited as an old lady, bundled up spherically against the chill, with an equally rotund poodle on a leash, made a leisurely progress around the fountain before turning out of the gate towards the Friedenstrasse. There was no one else in sight, apart from a leaf raker about a hundred yards away, focusing on the grass beneath a group of lime trees. Swiftly, Clara approached the bench on the left-hand side, closest to the pillar, and let one hand drop. There was the cavity, exactly as Guy Hamilton had described, a six-inch indentation large enough, she hoped, to conceal a packet of Reetsma cigarettes.

She sat for a moment. In the stillness of the park, the distant traffic was muted like the faint roar of the sea. Taking out her compact, she could see that there was no one behind her and the leaf raker, having completed his pile of leaves, was gradually moving away. She was about to extract the cigarette packet from her bag when she remembered something that Leo had taught her.

If time allows, perform a trial run.

Rising smartly she walked back through the stone arch and along a mossy gravelled path, fringed with evergreen shrubs. The vegetation was damp from the recent shower, with silver beads of rain trapped in the clefts of the leaves and a dank, loamy smell rising from the earth. She performed a loop of the park, walking at a measured pace right around a small lake, before returning along a different path and re-entering the arch. When she did, she discovered that the stone bench was now occupied by a man in a sage-green, Loden overcoat who stood up as she approached.

She had not seen him in five years, but he had barely changed.

Leo Quinn was tall and sinewy, leaner, perhaps, than ever, with the same high cheekbones and strong jaw, but a few more lines around his eyes. His face, though she had half-forgotten it, was instantly familiar; that demeanour, so valuable in a spy, that seemed to register expressions with only a flicker before they were suppressed. The delicate Irish colouring, fine red-gold stubble on his chin and the brush of hair resistant to pomade. The firm mouth, whose lines appeared to be compressing some intense emotion. The shock of seeing him knocked the breath out of her. The noise drained from the world and every lineament of her body quivered, like an instrument touched by a bow. After a few seconds she said,

'I might have guessed it would be you, after that message you sent.'

'I didn't send any message.'

'You must have done.'

'What was it?'

'Ovid? The man from London Films quoted a line of Ovid. I assumed it was a message from you.'

'It wasn't.'

Her heart plummeted within her.

'Shall we walk?' he said.

They headed out of the park and turned left in the direction of Alexanderplatz. He kept in step, the way she remembered, hands in pockets, eyes straight ahead, not looking at her. He must have seen her approach the DLB the first time and then waited – knowing she would make a trial run, because that was what he had taught her.

'What did it say? This line that wasn't a message?'

'*Good manners and a fine disposition are the best beauty treatments.*'

He smiled tightly.

'I see.'

'What do you see?' she said, almost stepping off the kerb into the path of a tram, and feeling his hand lightly restraining her.

'It's an exercise I set.'

'You set it? Are you a teacher now?'

'In a manner of speaking.'

'Oh. I didn't know.'

He fell silent again. There was so much Clara wanted to say, but she could see no way to breach this wall of awkwardness that had grown up between them, consigning them to an icy formality. All the times she had dreamt of being reunited with him and now this. His eyes avoided her. All the questions she yearned to ask him over the years hovered unspoken as chill courtesy imprisoned them. Was he married now? Engaged? Was Leo happy to see her, or did the terrible memory of their parting play through his head, the way it did through hers?

They walked without a route. Where were they heading? Leo kept his hands plunged deep in his pockets, his gaze fixed straight ahead, his steps keeping pace with her own in the way she remembered, as though they shared a purpose. As they progressed northwards, through the fringes of Friedrichshain towards Prenzlauer Berg, to her consternation she realized that their path was taking them down a street which would lead straight past the former SIS safe apartment – the yellow-painted, turn-of-the-century block, with white-scrolled detail above the entrance where, five years ago, he had asked her to marry him. Leo must have detected it too, because a wince went through him and without looking up at it he turned, sharply, to cross the road.

When they were safely past the block and had rounded the corner, he finally spoke.

'I should apologize. I'm here because of a last-minute change of circumstances. The man who should have been here was diverted. So please forgive me if it seems inappropriate.'

'It doesn't.'

'Good.' His mouth was still taut, as though he was holding everything back.

'I did go yesterday, to the Siegessäule. But I got waylaid,' she said. 'There was no way to warn you.'

'Of course. It doesn't matter. You found the DLB. I assume you were about to set up another meeting.'

'Yes. There are things I need to communicate. I need to talk to you, Leo.'

'By all means.'

'Not here.'

'Where?'

'My apartment.'

'And that is . . .?'

'Winterfeldtstrasse. Number 35. Apartment six.'

'I'll be there in an hour.'

He made an abrupt turn, rounded a corner and disappeared from sight.

By the time he knocked at her door, Clara was still in a daze. As she let him in Leo took a quick, hungry look around the room, as if he wanted to absorb everything in it at a single glance, because of what it might say about her. The photographs on the mantelpiece, the potted geranium on the kitchen table, the oil painting of a saxophone player in jagged greys and browns which he recognized as by the artist Bruno Weiss.

'You said you had something to show me.'

She went across the drawing room and his eyes followed, taking in the small, blue-covered copy of Rilke's poems on the desk, as she removed the leather-bound *Mein Kampf* from beneath its wobbly leg.

'I found these.' She prised the page open and took out the stack of cards. He frowned.

'Eva Braun was banned from keeping a diary by Martin Bormann. He said it was too dangerous because intimate details about the Führer could fall into enemy hands, but Eva couldn't stop herself. Her diary was important to her – it was the only place she could talk about her real feelings – so she found a way to hide it. Everyone knew she was a mad-keen film fan, and she collected cigarette cards of the actors, so it wouldn't seem strange to take her album around with her, and that's where she wrote it. All her fears about Hitler, everything he confided to her about his plans. All in her own handwriting. See.'

She turned over the cards and handed them to Leo, who shuffled through them with growing amazement.

'How did you get this?'

'The album was stolen from Eva Braun, and the woman who stole it disappeared on a cruise. It was my godson who found it . . .'

'Your godson?'

'Erich Schmidt. Remember?'

It was the first time she had referred to their shared past. He nodded, head bent, still scrutinizing the cards.

'There's this one too.'

She felt in her pocket and withdrew the card bearing the portrait of herself. Leo hesitated, squinted at the picture, then turned it over and read.

Last night Wolf told me that after the war he would marry me. When is after the war, I asked. When Poland is subjugated, he explained. Very soon, Poland will cease to exist.

'This is astonishing.'

'It's written proof, Leo. That's what they need. You must take these back to London. I'll give you other examples of her handwriting, to verify it. We can't let the politicians think it's all over; that Hitler's demands have been met and he's no threat any longer. I heard Richard Dimbleby on the wireless saying Chamberlain's achievement was a triumph. It's dangerous to assume that Hitler has no aggressive intentions. It terrifies me.'

'Don't be terrified, Clara. No one I know believes any such thing.'

It was the first time he had used her name and the first time she had heard a note of anything in his voice that was like concern. He stood there, in his coat, while his sea-green eyes, unreadable as ever, pulled her in like a tide. The stillness between them was almost tangible.

She said, 'Why did you not come to the Siegessäule?'

'I did. I was right there. You didn't see me. But then, you were with a man.'

'That was Max Brandt. He's one of ours. Codename Steinbrecher. I wasn't expecting him there at all. He surprised me.'

'You had your arm in his.'

'That was ... work.'

'It didn't look like work,' his voice was bureaucratically flat, 'when you kissed him.'

'I was saying goodbye. He's a good man, Leo, and he's in danger. He needed to leave Berlin and he wanted to see me before he did. If you were there, you should have come and spoken to me.'

'Should I?'

'Yes. You should. If you were that close, the least you could do was make contact.'

They stood, separated by only a narrow, trembling distance, and he was so quiet that she feared for a moment he was angry. When he did speak, his voice was low and level.

'Is that what you think, Clara? The *least* I could do? I watched the only woman I have ever loved arm in arm with another man. I watched you kiss him. And you think I should have made contact? It was all I could do to walk away.'

Five years stood between them. Five years in which the thought of her had been drumming through his head, the woman who made flesh all the beauty and mystery of women he had ever learned or written about, whose contours he had traced so often in his mind. He remembered the day, five years earlier, when she had come to him, her face wet and pearls of raindrops captured in her hair, and he had realized he would never love or want a woman more than her.

She was trying to frame a reply. The words took shape in her mouth, but they struggled on her lips as she tried to quiet her mental turbulence.

'Are you free?'

'I haven't been free since the day I met you.'

His eyes were gulping her in, then he reached out and she felt the tensions of her ordinary life fall from her like chains. She stepped towards him and ran her hand across his face, discovering the feel of it still inside her fingers, imprinted there. Her body fitted into his perfectly as though they had been designed for each other.

Leo wanted to talk, but knew that if he began to talk, he would not stop, so he kissed her, and then he found that he was shrugging off his coat and jacket, easing his braces, while their mouths met.

She pulled away.

'Wait.'

He tried not to stare at her too obviously as she undressed, unpeeling the layers of clothing and uncovering the body he remembered so well until she was entirely naked. She lifted her arms to free the clasp of her necklace and he recalled the same gesture when she had been standing before a mirror in a West End apartment, her slim forearms raised to comb her hair. The elegance of her shoulder blades, the wrist where blue veins ran like ore through a stone, and the dark river of her hair flecked with gold.

He took her pearl necklace, set it down, tenderly kissed her naked neck and encircled her trembling body with his own.

Much later, when the evening sun was a faint glow and a few stars already glimmered in the sky, she brought him coffee and toast and sat naked in bed beside him. He was smiling at her, as though he would never stop. He looked around the room and every item in it, from the desk, to the red armchair, to the pictures on the wall, filled him with indescribable tenderness, because they belonged to her. Clara's possessions seemed imbued with her, unlike the contents of his own soulless Bloomsbury flat, which had nothing of him in it, apart from a clock on the mantelpiece left by his late father, ticking away his life. He sensed a great iceberg of emotion that had lain submerged was melting and overflowing inside him.

Downstairs someone was banging away at a piano, and the dusky light filtering through the leaves of the tree outside cast the room with a greenish tint. Clara felt as though they were suspended in that aqueous green light, inviolate from everything around them, and she had the momentary bliss of satisfaction, as when a puzzle is completed and every piece has fallen into place.

'I thought about you all the time. I had no idea where you were.'

'I tried to forget you. I deliberately attempted to block Germany from my mind. I involved myself in other areas.'

'And other women?'

His only answer was a shrug, a gesture that dismissed every woman he had met in the past five years, and expressed the absolute irrelevance of her question.

'I tried different ways of thinking about us. All sorts of metaphors. I had an image of us as two planets, circling each other from afar but never actually leaving each other's orbit. Pulled by such gravitational attraction that our paths would always be joined.'

'Did you worry about me?'

'Of course.'

She laid her head on his chest, so his voice was a low rumble, reverberating through his flesh and entering hers.

'Why did you never contact me?'

'I wrote to you. I must have written a hundred letters. But I never sent them.'

'I often thought of telephoning. Just to hear your voice.'

He traced a curl of hair around her ear.

'You probably couldn't have found me if you'd tried. It's a

strange, transient place, the Intelligence Service. People disappear without trace and you don't know whether they've been sacked, or rumbled, or simply posted elsewhere. That happened to me, until I was approached by a man called Dansey . . .'

She sat up.

'Lieutenant Colonel Dansey?'

'You've heard of him?'

'Guy Hamilton told me about him. What's he like?'

Leo recalled the tall, lean figure with a clipped moustache and wire-rimmed spectacles who had taken him for lunch at the Savoy Grill.

'I think he's very astute. Hamilton probably told you Dansey has firm ideas about the security of our network in Europe. And he's working on alternatives. He's looking for people who will be able to move around Europe fairly easily, if circumstances arise. Who are fluent in several languages and so on. With a valid reason to travel.'

'People like me.'

'Yes. He mentioned you specifically.'

'Is that why you're here then? Because Dansey sent you?'

'It might be why he approached me, but it's not why I came. I came because war could break out at any time, and I wanted to know what you planned to do.'

'If that was all, you could have asked Rupert.'

His eyes gleamed. He caught her in his arms again and kissed her, burying his face in her flesh and inhaling the deep warm scent of her.

'I came, Clara, because every day away from you convinced me that I shouldn't live a second more of my life without you. When I insisted on you leaving Berlin if we were to be married, I was a fearful, anxious fool. All I could see was you being arrested, or suffering, and I wanted to save you from that. I thought the prospect of you risking your life was more than I could bear. But being without you entirely was far, far worse.'

'What did Dansey want of me?'

'His idea is to establish an outfit inside Germany who could play an important part when war comes. He's keen to recruit women because he thinks they have more patience. They pay closer attention to detail. They can read relationships and human motivations better than men, he believes. I suppose that's true. I was never good at judging you. He wants to know what you might do, if war comes. Whether you would agree to stay here.'

'I see.'

Suddenly she didn't want to think about the future, or not that part of it. She lay back in his arms, remembering the time they had first met, when he told her about his hobby, translating classical literature.

'Are you still doing your translations?'

'German at the moment. I'm working on Rilke's Sonnets to Orpheus right now. Rilke has a wonderful way of making the German language sound soft and fluid.'

'Who was Orpheus? I can't quite remember.'

'He was the man who crossed the boundary between life and death to fetch his wife from the underworld. He was a beautiful singer – his music transfixed the whole of nature. Animals would come and kneel before him when he sang. He could coax the rocks and stones to dance. Ovid wrote about him originally.'

That reminded her. 'What did you mean when you said you set that piece of Ovid as an exercise? A teaching exercise? You're not a schoolteacher, are you? I assumed you were working for the film company.'

'I am, some of the time.'

'So what are you teaching?'

'I'm teaching people how to use codes.'

'Codes?'

'Not something you know about right now, but anyone who works with us will need to understand codes, ciphers and all sorts of secret communication techniques. That's the area I'm working in. At the moment the outfit I work with is still pretty basic. You won't find us in the telephone directory.'

'So what exactly do you do?'

'I can't tell you, Clara, not until you need to know. But the fact is, we're going to need more secure methods of communication. And codes will be an essential part of that. It seemed important to me that agents had something that would be easily memorized, yet individual. Poems are a common device, but everyone chooses *Ozymandius*, or, I don't know, *The Charge of the Light Brigade* – poems that are easily recognized, even by foreigners. We wanted something entirely unpublished, that could never be found in a reference book, so I suggested my translations of Ovid.'

She made a wry face. 'Which have still not been published?'

He laughed. 'Perhaps someday. But they're serving a more important function right now.'

Leo ran a finger down her slender white neck and kissed the hollow at the base of her throat, breathing in the faint rose, violet and vanilla notes of her perfume, Bourjois' *Soir de Paris*. He had bought a bottle of it in London, and kept it in his sock drawer. It was an act of foolish weakness, and he had considered giving it away, but never quite got round to it. The scent of her had hung over his life for five long years.

Clara gazed at him, wondering how it was possible to feel so happy, with all the agony and anxiety that was going on in the city around. War might come soon, and what would that mean for Erich, who was so keen to fight for his country? And all the friends she had here in Berlin? Five years ago, Leo had wanted her to leave Germany and now, it seemed, he was asking her to stay. Perhaps she would not, after all, need to choose between love and duty.

'Your Orpheus. The one who fetched his wife. What happened to her?'

'She was allowed to leave the underworld, following him, unless he looked back.'

'What happened if he looked back?'

'She stayed there.'

He leant over and kissed her again, deep and lingering.

'It's a story, Clara.'

She looked out at the dusk. Beyond the window a swirl of migrating birds was massing, wheeling and turning in the darkening sky. A susurration of starlings, that's what it was called, a perfect aerial formation, tilting and diving through the early evening mist, changing direction abruptly like the whisk of a living cloak, narrowing to a twisting ribbon then bulging into a cloud. Gradually more and more birds joined the flock so that eventually a great throng speckled the sky like a single living thing, massing above the city rooftops, scattering and then rejoining, soaring up into the vault of clouds, preparing to journey to another latitude to seek shelter from the gathering winter storms.

Author's note

The Oster Conspiracy was a wide-ranging military plot to oust Hitler in September 1938. The planned coup involved senior German military and intelligence leaders, members of the Berlin police and many other individuals. The plan was to mount a raid on the Reich Chancellery but it failed at the eleventh hour, stymied by Chamberlain's decision to appease Hitler.

There has been great dispute about the whereabouts of Eva Braun's missing diary. While her diary up to 1935 is attested, after that her writing has gone missing, and one document, published in 1949 purporting to be her diary, has been widely dismissed as a fake.

In 1939, *Time* Magazine published an article about the relationship between Eva Braun and Hitler, saying that Hitler had 'at least partly supported' Eva for several years and that she had confided to intimates that she expected to marry him within a year. Her suicide attempts are well known. Many of the women associated with Hitler attempted or committed suicide and Eva Braun made her first attempt in 1931 and then another in 1935.

The cruise liner the *Wilhelm Gustloff* may have started out in the service of pleasure, but it became a byword for tragedy in maritime history. When war broke out the *Wilhelm Gustloff* was used by the military as a hospital ship and U–Boat training school until 30th January 1945, when the captain was ordered to evacuate German refugees and military fleeing from the Red Army from the East Prussian port of Gotenhafen. The ship was torpedoed by a Soviet submarine and more than nine thousand people died in the freezing Baltic waters, making it the worst shipping disaster in history. The sinking of the pride of the Strength Through Joy programme, exactly twelve years to the day since Hitler seized power, seemed to symbolize the destruction of the Thousand–Year Reich.

On 9th November 1938, at the goading of Goebbels, a wave of violence against Jews and Jewish property was unleashed throughout Germany in the worst pogrom since the Middle Ages. It gained the name Kristallnacht from the amount of broken glass that littered the streets the next morning. The violence shocked the world and convinced many who had previously been complacent of the Nazis' true intentions towards the Jews. It was said that Goebbels planned the violence in order to regain the Führer's favour after the disgrace of his affair.

Acknowledgements

In writing *A War of Flowers* I am indebted to many people. I would like to thank my agent, Caradoc King, as well as Linda Shaughnessy at AP Watt/United Agents for their cheering enthusiasm. At Simon & Schuster I am grateful to my editor Suzanne Baboneau for her wise advice and suggestions as well as to Ian Chapman, Clare Hey and Hannah Corbett. In Berlin, the staff of the Adlon Hotel were superlatively helpful. Above all, thanks to Philip, William, Charlie and Naomi for spending more time discussing the Third Reich than most people would choose.

London, 2014